NEVER WILL I EVER

CE RICCI

Editing: Shauna Stevenson of Ink Machine Editing
Proofreading: Amanda Mili of Amandanomaly
Epigraph Poetry: Hydrus
Alternate Cover Design: Cassie Chapman of Opulent Designs

Trail

To the ones with wars waging in their mind:

I know the noise is unbearable.

Don't forget your resilience is deafening.

The voice like venom, curls in me
Hissing hate, where love should be
It builds a cage, of whispered blame
A prison carved from poisoned shame.

What fear had bound, love sets free
All silence falls, the murmurs flee
No longer drowning, in buried guilt
My heart reborn, my soul rebuilt.

—_hydrus, *Spiraled*

THEME SONG:

In Loving Memory — First and Forever

PLAYLIST:

this is me trying — Taylor Swift
A Crooked Melody — Holding Absence
Kill the Mood — You Me At Six
Somebody — Memphis May Fire
My Consequences — Palisades
Dark Days (feat. Jeris Johnson) — Point North, Jeris Johnson
What It Cost — Bad Omens
Like A Villain — Bad Omens
I'm Not — Zero 9:36
The Only Ones — Caskets
Haven't Had Enough — Marianas Trench
I Don't Belong Here — I Prevail
WYDRN — You Me At Six
@ my worst — blackbear
Nowhere Left To Sink — Like Moths To Flames
Desperate Measures — Marianas Trench
Me Against Myself — Wage War
in the dark — guccihighwaters
Hurricane — Hands Like Houses
Enemy — The Plot In You
Blood Sport — Sleep Token
Take Me First — Bad Omens
Nightmare — From Ashes to New
Fade — Palisades
Lost — Dermot Kennedy
Out Of The Woods (Taylor's Version) — Taylor Swift
Break Free — Like A Storm
Ascensionism — Sleep Token
Epiphany — UNWELL
What Do You Gotta Lose? — Islander
Burning Down (with Joe Jonas) — Alex Warren, Joe Jonas
Top 10 staTues tHat CriEd bloOd — Bring Me The Horizon
Trapped — The Word Alive

Listen to the playlist on Spotify

AUTHOR'S NOTE

While this is technically a standalone and can be read separately from any of my other works, I highly recommend reading *Don't You Dare* first. Avery is portrayed as somewhat of an antagonist in *Don't You Dare*, and this is his "redemption" story. One plotline directly feeds the other in cause and effect. The majority of the events within *Don't You Dare* happen prior to the beginning of *Never Will I Ever*, and that includes the shifted state of Kaleb and Avery's relationship from friends/teammates to enemies.

This book contains content circling around internalized homophobia and may be triggering to some readers. Please proceed with caution.

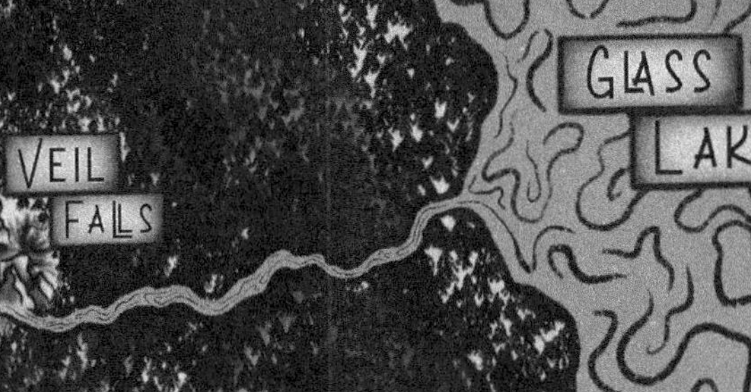

GLASS
LAKE
VEIL
FALLS

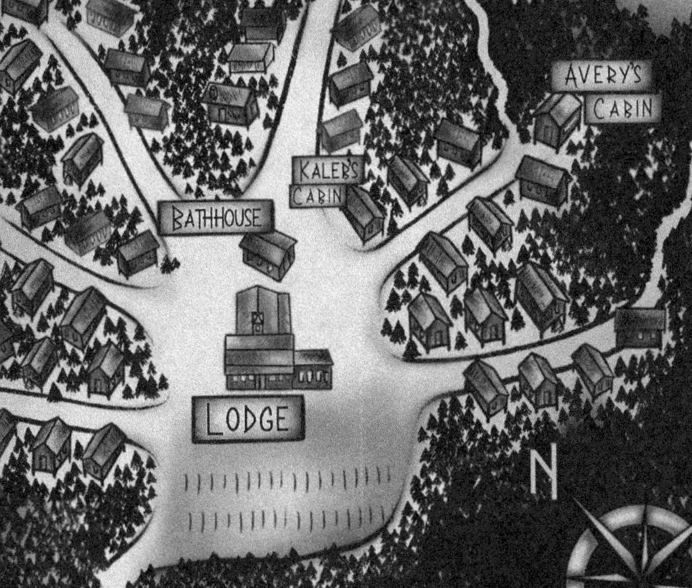

LOVER'S LEAP
THE CLEARING
AVERY'S
CABIN
KALEB'S
CABIN
BATHHOUSE
LODGE
ALPINE
RIDGE
N
E
W
S

PROLOGUE

Avery

"I take it you know why you're here, Avery?"

My gaze lifts from my lap, where it was trained on my interlocked fingers to keep from fidgeting. Too bad all it's actually achieved is making my hands clammy with a cold sweat while I've been sitting here, silently waiting under the penetrating scrutiny of Foltyn College's dean.

Dean Ian Marshall.

Also known as one of the few people in the world who's capable of scaring me as shitless as I am right now.

"The photo, sir," I manage past the baseball-sized knot lodged in my throat.

"It's more than just the photo," Dean Marshall says, the deep timbre of his voice leaving little room for debate. "It's your intentions behind your actions that are the issue. Something I think you're all too aware of."

More cold sweat seeps through my clothes as his words slice through me, and it's only now I realize the true gravity of what I've done. By adding the photo of Keene and Aspen kissing to Keene's slideshow—the one shown on the scoreboard for Family Night—I might as well have signed my own death warrant. Or at least the death warrant of my baseball career.

My silence is drawn out too long, and it must make him impatient, because the frown lines creasing his forehead deepen. "Don't you have anything to say for yourself? Any reasoning behind your actions?"

Plenty.

But coming out with them now, especially to the dean, will only look like a last-ditch effort to keep from being punished.

Self-preservation calls for me to lie instead. To tell him I didn't do anything with malicious intent, and do my best to salvage what I can from the wreckage I've caused. Too bad for me, the truth is plain as day: I publicly outed my teammate and his best friend, and lying about it now would only dig an even deeper grave than the one I've already begun to bury myself in.

What I can offer Dean Marshall is the truth. Or as much of it as I'm willing to share.

"I regret my actions, sir," I start, doing my best to keep my voice steady. "Ones released out of anger and spite during a moment of blind rage. It wasn't premeditated, and looking back now, I see just how wrong I was to act on those impulses."

"Only looking back on it? Not when you were in the middle of digging through your teammate's phone or sending a personal photo to knowingly be broadcast to thousands of people?"

I already knew this meeting had a very high likelihood of ending poorly—no doubt with my baseball career being a thing of the past. But the bite in his tone creates a sinking feeling in my gut I can't shake.

This is so much worse than just losing baseball.

My jaw tics, and I clear my throat. "As I said, sir, I was blinded by rage. I didn't think about the repercussions my actions would have on anyone involved."

"No, you didn't. Because if you had, I'd certainly hope some form of common sense would have led you to pause and think about what you were doing. The way it would not only reflect on you, but the damage it would cause your teammate." His eyes take on the same hardness his tone already possesses. "And then, thanks to cell phones and technology, videos were taken and the whole thing went viral on the internet within hours."

I wince, already more than aware of the fallout my actions have had on my teammate, Keene. Aspen, too, though I don't really give a damn about that dickhead. Keene is who I care about. Or *cared*, I guess. Even if I had a funny way of showing it by outing his and Aspen's relationship.

It's not one of my proudest moments, and God knows I'd take it back now if I had the chance. But that's the thing about hindsight, right? It's always twenty-twenty.

Not waiting for a reply or more excuses, Dean Marshall continues laying into me.

"Of course, on top of the havoc you've wreaked in Mr. Kohl's and Mr. Waters's personal lives, there's also the reputation of the baseball program, and even this university, to think about."

My heart crawls up into my throat, becoming nearly impossible to breathe around. I choke on it as I cough out the word. "Sir?"

"I've had parents calling and emailing since the incident. Hundreds of them, especially those with students in the LGBTQ+ community here at Foltyn. They're all demanding action be taken."

My brain snags on his last sentence as more fear and regret crashes over me in waves. They pull me under, lock and chain themselves around my ankles until I might as well be drowning in them. At this rate, letting them take me forever might be preferable.

Wetting my lips, I murmur, "I can't begin to apologize for what my actions have caused, sir. It was foolish, tasteless, and uncalled for, and had I thought ahead to the way it would make others in the LGBTQ+ community feel, things never would have escalated this far. I can assure you."

Dean Marshall studies me, surely looking for a crack in my sincerity where I know he'll find none. Because, on top of hurting both Keene and Aspen, and possibly screwing myself out of a future here at Foltyn, I've become the one thing I never dreamed of.

My father.

To the point where I don't even recognize myself anymore. All I see is him and his bias. The distaste he has for anyone who isn't straight has rubbed off on me, turning me against them.

Turning me against…myself.

After another moment of silence, the dean leans back in his chair, keeping his intense, penetrating stare on me. "We take this kind of thing very seriously here at Foltyn. Diversity and acceptance are two pillars this university was built upon, and providing our students with a safe space where they can be themselves is of the utmost importance to me and the rest of the administration."

"I understand, sir. And I'm more than happy to apologize or do whatever is necessary to prove I will never be the cause of something like this again. I was already planning to reach out to Keene as it is. Just tell me what you need me to do, and I'll do it."

His fingers tap on the wooden desk absently, every light thud ratcheting my heart rate higher and higher. "I wish it were enough, Mr. Reynolds, but intolerance isn't something we can have here. Which is why we're going to cut to the chase rather than drag out a done deal even further than we already have."

I open my mouth to ask what he means by a "done deal," but no words come out. They're stuck in the back of my throat, terrified to escape and be faced with whatever comes next. All I know is it can't be good.

And it's not, when Dean Marshall answers my unspoken question with a cold, harsh finality.

"After much consideration, the admissions office and I have decided to expel you from Foltyn College. Effective immediately."

ONE

Avery

Three Weeks Later — June

The blaring sound of my alarm jars me from sleep and causes me to bolt straight up in my bed. I quickly grab for my phone, bleary-eyed and frantic, to silence it and check the time.

Seven o'clock.

Fuck my life.

There's not been one summer of my life where I've woken up this early for anything other than baseball. But as the fog of sleep slowly starts to lift from my brain, the realization of why I'm actually awake sinks in all over again.

I was supposed to spend the summer relaxing, hanging out with some of the guys who live in the area all year, or taking regular trips to the coast to escape the heat that tends to descend on the Portland-Vancouver area during the later parts of the summer. Instead, I'll be spending the next eight weeks of my life corralling crotch goblins at a goddamn summer camp in the Oregon wilderness.

But then again, nothing about my life has been going the way I thought, though I'm smart enough to realize it's of my own doing.

Groaning, I force myself from the warmth of my bed and start getting ready to meet my doom. My feet drag all the way through my morning routine, as if taking a ten-minute shower instead of five is going to delay the inevitable.

I finished packing last night, so all there's left to do is put my toiletries together, haul the two duffels downstairs, and load them into my G Class parked in the garage, which I do a half-hour later.

Dad's Escalade is still parked beside it, letting me know he hasn't left for work yet, and when I walk back into the house, I find him standing in the kitchen with his back to me as he pops a pod into the Keurig. His hair—the same medium-blond color as mine—is combed and styled with gel, and he's fitted in one of his custom three-piece suits.

"I thought you had a meeting this morning."

He turns and leans against the counter. "Got pushed to the afternoon. But that just means I can see you off."

Of course he'd want to. He's the one who thought up this slightly hair-brained plot about to be set into motion.

As it turns out, Alpine Ridge is the same camp Dean Marshall's brother, Colin, owns and runs. Dad is the one who does the books for the camp, and thanks to his friendship with Colin, it was easy enough for me to be hired as the camp's newest summer counselor.

Yay me.

"You didn't need to stick around," I tell him, moving through the kitchen to grab a banana from the counter for a quick road snack. "I'm about to hit the road anyway."

His coffee finishes brewing, making me think I can quickly sneak out while he fixes it to go. But he might as well have eyes in the back of his head, because even with his attention locked on pouring it into the thermos, he stops me from escaping.

"You really need to make a good impression, Avery. Don't forget that."

"Yeah, Dad. I got it," I tell him, a little more snap to my tone than is probably merited. But I know what's on the line here. I know better than anyone.

Dad's theory of me working at the camp goes like this: By me getting into the dean's brother's good graces, I will, in turn, get back into the dean's as well. And maybe once he's seen the growth and progress I've made while working at the camp, I might be allowed back into Foltyn this fall.

It's a long shot, maybe even downright insane, but it's becoming more and more apparent that this might be my only chance to complete my degree on schedule. It's too late to get into another school, even a community college. And even if I could, it would set me back almost an entire year, because not all my credits would transfer with me.

Getting back into Foltyn for my senior year is the only option.

So, while I have little to no faith it will work, I'm tossing all my eggs in this basket anyway. And praying for a goddamn miracle.

His gaze lifts, eyes narrowing on me. "Cut the attitude. You're the one who got yourself into a mess so big, no amount of money I've thrown at the school in the past makes a difference now. Offering them more only makes it look like bribery to get you back in."

I almost laugh because it was all rubbing elbows from the beginning anyway. The entire reason I got into Foltyn in the first place is due to it being his alma mater. That, and the sizable donation he made to the college, was more than enough to secure my position on the baseball team—because heaven forbid he say I'm talented enough to earn the spot on my own.

Then again, all he's ever done is throw money at his problems and expect them to go away. And this is one circumstance where it just won't happen.

"I'll put my best foot forward. I promise."

"You need to do more than that, Avery," he says sharply. "You need to do everything in your power to win over Colin."

"I know, Dad," I say, this time a little more forcefully. "You saying it over and over again isn't going to do anything but stress me out more when I feel like I'm already being thrown to the wolves."

I expect him to continue pushing the subject. That's who Dad is, after all. Driving his point home until I can hear him, word for word, while I fucking sleep. All he ever does is talk, meanwhile anything I have to say goes in one ear and out the other. So when he actually listens to me, dropping the subject, I finally feel a moment of relief.

But only for a moment.

"Look," he says, voice finally taking a softer tone—something entirely different from him. "I hope you know I'm only hard on you because I want to see you succeed. I just hate knowing you possibly won't get the chance because of one mistake."

More like a series of mistakes.

A bit of emotion sticks in the back of my throat, so I just nod instead.

He does too before clapping me on the shoulder. "I hope you know I get it. The kind of…*lifestyle* your teammate has doesn't sit well with me either. But no matter how disgusted we might be by the things they do together, the kind of crap you pulled can't happen in the twenty-first century."

All the blood rushing through my veins quickly turns to ice as his words register.

I bet he didn't even notice the tone of his voice or the implication of what he's said; the homophobia and bias laced in a statement that spilled from his lips without a second thought. Not when it came out as easily as it did.

Every time it happens, a set of claws digs into my brain and a venomous whisper fills my head like smoke. This time is no different.

Disgusting, like he said. Absolutely despicable.

Clearing my throat does nothing to help the way my heart is lodged in my throat, but I still manage to choke out my response past it.

"Yeah, Dad. I know."

It's something I've always known.

Just like I know the parts of myself I've refused to give voice to can never come to light. Because there's no way in hell he's ever going to accept the *real* me as his only son.

It's a quick hour-and-a-half drive from our house in Vancouver to where Alpine Ridge Summer Camp is nestled in the forest near the base of Mount Hood. Much too quick for my liking, seeing as I've yet to work out how I'll wriggle my way into the good graces of the camp director. Especially if he already knows about my history at Foltyn.

I'd be a fool to think he doesn't—what happened made a lot of news channels around here—but part of me remains optimistic anyway. I have to, otherwise there's no way I'll be able to stick this out.

Something I doubt I'll accomplish as it is. Because, while I might be an athlete, I'm the furthest thing from an outdoorsman.

Once I'm parked in the lot, staring at the massive lodge, the feeling of dread inside me only grows. But instead of wallowing in it, I shove it down before grabbing my bags from the trunk and heading toward the building I can only assume houses the camp director's office.

An assumption that must be correct when a man who looks so similar to the dean, he has to be his brother, exits the lodge. His eyes lock on me while he waits at the top of the stairs leading to an expansive deck, and the authority radiating from him has my stomach revolting.

"You might as well be the spitting image of your father, Avery. Glad to see you made it," he says, extending his hand to me as I reach him.

I accept it before giving it a firm shake, praying to God my hands aren't as clammy as I think they are.

"Director Marshall," I say, keeping my tone as even and professional as I can manage. "It's a pleasure to meet you."

His lips twitch a moment with a hint of amusement before he releases my hand. "The pleasure's all mine. Let's get you in my office and go over a couple things before we get you settled in."

Not one to argue with my new boss, I follow him through the doors to the lodge and down a hall to the immediate left, not stopping until we reach the final door labeled "Director Marshall." He pushes it open before motioning for me to enter, calling through a walkie talkie as he does to ask for a grounds escort to meet us at the lodge in ten minutes.

"Take a load off," he says, nodding to the chair across from his desk. "We can chat for a bit while we wait for the rest of your welcoming committee."

I do as he says, sliding into the chair as the door falls closed with a soft *snick*. When he takes a seat opposite me, I'm immediately taken back to the moment I was sitting across the desk from another Mr. Marshall. When my entire future unraveled before my eyes.

It only serves to remind me how important being here is.

"Thank you for making time for me this morning," I start, doing my best to feel him out. See what he knows or what he's heard—if anything. "I know camp is set to kick off tomorrow, and I was hoping you could give me a better feel for things before I'm—"

"Thrown to the wolves?" he supplies with a wry grin on his face, and when I wince at the idiom I used verbatim this morning, he lets out a deep laugh. "I've spoken to your father at length, and believe me, you've got nothing to worry about when it comes to working here. The kids are great—the counselors too. I have no doubt you'll ease into the job just fine."

I'm left staring at him, taken aback by the comfort radiating from him. Like a warm hug or something. He still has the air of authority—enough to have me on my best behavior—but it's giving the exact opposite impression I made of Dean Marshall.

Which is…unexpected.

"Thank you, sir," I manage, after finding my voice again. "It certainly makes me feel a bit better about spending the summer here."

There's a moment of silence while he studies me before he gives a quick nod. "I have to say, I was surprised when your father contacted me about getting you the job. Especially with how last minute it was."

"Trust me, it was last minute for me too, sir."

He waves before leaning back in his chair. "Call me Colin. There's no need to stand on formality here, and I certainly don't require any kind of power trip." Another smile forms on his lips, this one a little more knowing. "If there's one thing you'll learn in your time here at Alpine Ridge, Avery, it's that I'm not my brother."

His mention of Dean Marshall sets my nerves on edge all over again, constricting my lungs and causing my heart rate to ratchet up a notch. "I'd never begin to presume you and Dean Marshall are the same person. Brothers or not."

One salt-and-pepper brow arches dubiously. "Really? So then you aren't just here for the summer in hopes I'll put a good word in for you to be reinstated at Foltyn come fall?"

Once again, I'm left speechless. Mouth hanging open, ready to defend myself, the words just won't come out. They can't. Whether it be from pure shock or unwillingness to lie to my boss in the first five minutes, I'm not sure. Either way, Colin doesn't wait for me to give any sort of answer before continuing.

"I've known your father for a long time, Avery, and Jason Reynolds isn't one to beat around the bush. Quite frankly, neither am I. So when I asked him why in the world you wanted to come work at a summer camp, he laid it all out for me."

Well, fuck a motherfucking duck.

A wave of nausea hits me, and it's like I can see my entire future blow to smithereens all over again. Because if *all* entails every piece of this plan Dad cooked up, then I'm screwed before we even begin.

"Colin, I—"

He holds his hand up. "I know it's not your idea to be here. Even without your father telling me, it was obvious from the moment I saw you walk up those steps. You've never spent a day of your life at a summer camp. But that doesn't matter to me."

"It doesn't?" I ask slowly, to which he shakes his head.

"What *does* is—while you're here—you'll not only give these kids your all, but you'll also make the most of it for yourself."

The tiniest bout of relief hits me, and maybe I'm not as screwed as I thought.

"Absolutely," I tell him, my tone earnest. "My intention is to make the most of my summer here. You could tell me right now that you're estranged from your brother or something, and I'd still make the decision to stay."

A deep chuckle comes from him. "We're far from estranged, though I don't know how much help I'll be in your quest to be reinstated as a student at Foltyn. If I know anything about Ian, it's that he isn't one to change his mind or give second chances lightly. And if he does, the number of times it's happened can be counted on one hand."

My heart, which had just started to soar with hope, is immediately shot down, falling into the pit of my stomach as it's weighed down by the realization that this all might be in vain from the start.

Is it too late to take back what I said about staying no matter what?

He must take my silence as defeat, and he leans back in his chair. "I'm not trying to burst any bubbles for you, kid. But just like you've chosen to be up front with me, I'm choosing to be up front with you. I think there's always hope, and that's why I plan to give you the best shot I can by assigning you to Elijah's group."

Confusion is evident in my tone as I murmur, "Elijah?"

His lips lift in a smirk before he spins a picture frame sitting on his desk around to face me. Inside it is a photograph that can't be more than a couple years old from Colin's features alone. In the image, he's standing beneath the Alpine Ridge sign hung over the entrance to the camp with a dark-haired kid who's probably eight or nine.

"Elijah is my nephew. Who is also your dean's son."

All the wheels and gears in my brain come screeching to a halt at one tiny piece of information neither my father or I were aware of.

The dean has a son…and he attends camp here.

"I'm sorry…" I mutter, trying to wrap my brain around what is happening here. "After knowing everything—my mistakes at Foltyn, my father's not-so-subtle scheming—you're going to trust me with Dean Marshall's son? *Your* nephew?"

There's a gleam to Colin's eyes when he nods. "That's exactly *why* I'm doing it."

Yeah, brain is still not computing.

And from the way Colin laughs, my expression must make it extremely apparent.

"The only place Eli hates more than being home with his father is here," Colin states before he gives me a *what can you do?* shrug. "He's been coming for a few years now, but he doesn't have fun. Usually spends most of the time alone or attached to my hip, rather than making friends with his peers. This is the summer I want to change that."

I wet my lips, following his train of thought. But I'm not all that fond of the station it stops at. "So naturally, you're blackmailing me into…what? Being his friend?"

Another deep chuckle bursts from him as he shakes his head. "Not at all. But I'd like to think of it as us doing each other a favor. A win-win, if you will. You keeping an eye on Eli for me and making sure he has a bit of fun this summer gives me one less thing to worry about while I'm running this place. In exchange, I'm more than happy to put in a good word for you with his father. And who knows," he says, a slight twinkle in his eyes, "maybe you'll make enough of an impact on the kid and he'll do the same thing."

Yeah, I highly doubt that. Kids have never been much of my thing, and I swear to God, they know it the second I walk in the room.

"I'll do my best," is all I manage. Because, honestly, what other option do I have at this point? I've been backed into a corner by my father, and now Colin is only trying to help me make the most of it.

Yet something about this whole situation doesn't make sense to me.

My brows crash together in the center, and no matter how I try to work it out, I'm still left with one burning question unanswered.

"I don't mean to sound ungrateful, but why would you help me? Knowing what I did, realizing my father plotted this whole thing to get me back into school… Why aren't you just showing me the door?"

Colin's head cants to the side as his dark eyes travel over my face, studying and analyzing it in the same way his brother did a few weeks ago. It's the only time since I've met the man where I've truly *felt* a similar vibe from him.

And, for whatever reason, he must see something in me his brother didn't.

"I'm a firm believer of second chances, Avery. Doing a bad thing doesn't automatically make you a bad person. But I do want to be sure there won't be any issues here this summer. With campers or counselors who might…" He trails off, clearly making an effort to word his thoughts correctly. "Lead a different life than you agree with."

"Never," I reply, my head shaking vehemently. "That part of me is in the past, and I never intend to make the same mistake again."

His face softens, and for the first time, I feel truly at ease with the circumstances I've found myself in. Or as comfortable as possible, considering I still know jack shit about kids, summer camp, outdoorsing, or the job I'm meant to do for the next eight weeks.

But hey, this is a start.

"Great, then just know I've set you up with a good group of kids," he tells me, attention shifting to the file folder on his desk he's already begun flipping through. "And you'll be paired with Kal for the duration of the program. He's one of the best counselors we have on staff and knows this place like the back of his hand. Hopefully, with him by your side, you won't feel like a fish out of water."

I nod. "Thank you, si— Colin."

His lips quirk at my catch. "Very good. Now, during the month of

June, we like to—"

Wherever the rest of his thought was heading is cut off by his office door opening without warning, revealing a brown-haired young man with an all-too-familiar face on the opposite side of the threshold.

Kaleb LaMothe.

My now ex-teammate from Foltyn, who also happens to be the last person I'd ever want to see here. Or ever again, if I had a say in it.

After all, he's the reason Coach—and in turn, the dean—found out about what I did with that stupid slideshow photo. If he'd never turned me in, I'd still be on the team and in school. Which means I wouldn't have to spend most of my summer here when I'd much rather be…well, anywhere else.

And to make matters worse, he's wearing a forest green shirt with the camp's logo on the corner, making it a safe bet he works here too.

His eyes—damn near the same color as said shirt—lock with mine for a brief moment before I shift my attention back to Colin.

"Ah, perfect timing as always, Kal," he says, motioning for him to enter.

Bile works its way into my mouth as my eyes sink closed, and I send up a silent prayer to any God who might listen that all these pieces snapping together are only a nightmare. But even without opening my eyes, I know it's my reality.

Kal…as in *Kaleb*.

The same guy who I'll be spending the entire summer working with.

Fuck.

TWO

Kaleb

The pulse hammering in my throat hasn't lessened since the moment I walked into Colin's office, ready to show the new summer counselor around the grounds, only to find Avery Reynolds sitting in the chair across from him.

Not while I ask Colin what the hell is going on. Not while I listen to him explain that Avery is the new counselor on staff this season. Not when he explains how Avery is going to be assigned to the same group of kids as me for the summer so I can show him the ropes.

Even as I slip out of Colin's office with Avery on my tail, I can still feel the thrum of blood rushing beneath my skin. It floods me with a scalding heat that rivals the sun's. Hot enough, even the cool mountain breeze can't seem to temper it.

Awkward silence creates a toxic fog between us, and despite being in the open air on this gorgeous June day, it's stifling. And though I wouldn't have thought it possible, it only gets worse the second Avery tries to break the ice as we head down the deck steps.

"So…it's a small world."

It is, and his presence here is making it smaller and smaller by the second. Which is why I have no intention of engaging in any bullshit small talk with him. Or any kind of talking, for that matter. Around the kids and for my job's sake? Sure, I'll play nice. But I'm planning to make sure any and all encounters besides those required of us are kept to a minimum.

It's the only way this will work.

"Let's not."

He doesn't take the hint.

"Kaleb. I—"

"The grounds are set up in something of a half circle," I start, cutting in before he has a chance to finish his thought. I don't wanna hear anything he has to say.

We pass by the bathhouse, which is situated near the center of camp, and I continue explaining the layout. "You've already seen the lodge. Offices and housing for administration, bathrooms, laundry facilities, and the cafeteria are all in or near it. And then all the cabins for both campers and counselors run down six paths that radiate in an arc from the center of the complex."

Rather than try explaining it again if he's confused, I stop at the activities board near the bottom of the steps and rip one of the maps off. I press it into his chest—the heat in my veins shifting to straight-up boiling levels when I feel the hardness of his pecs beneath my palm— before turning away.

"At least there's indoor plumbing," he says while folding the map and tucking it into the pocket of his jeans.

I don't answer, instead leading Avery down the third path from the left—where all the cabins for the eleven-year-olds are located—that winds between the firs and hemlocks. Silent prayers for peace and tranquility are sent into the universe, and all I can do now is hope they're answered. Or maybe being immersed in nature can bring those things to me. Otherwise, I very well might lose my shit on this guy.

"Counselors have their own cabins for our age group. It's set up so there's one on either end of the path. I'll be on the end closest to the center of the complex and you'll be set up on the far end."

"So I'm the first one eaten by bears," he deadpans from behind me.

"We can only hope," I mutter under my breath.

The cabin layouts might be the only fortunate part of this entire situation. The small amount of added distance between his sleeping location and mine should make it easy enough to avoid him during my downtime at the very least.

I chance a glance at him to find dread and discomfort written all over his chiseled face. It's got nothing on the anxiety etched into those piercing blue eyes that are the same color as the sky on a clear day, or the way his six-two frame seems to shrink with anxiety.

Even out of his element, Avery's still able to hold on to that conventionally attractive rich-boy swagger he has. Much to my displeasure. I'm sure he smooth-talked his way right into Colin's good graces too. He's just got that air about him. Always saying the right thing at the right time, oozing charm and charisma at every turn.

I'd be lying if I said I hadn't fallen victim to it my first couple years at Foltyn too, back when I was still doing my best to find new friends and fit into the team. We built a friendship over the first few years at school, fraught with laughter and memories that now serve no purpose but to haunt me. But after what he did to Keene and Aspen, I feel like I barely know him. Like everything we shared was just his persona, and in reality, we're nothing more than acquaintances.

And now, I have no problem keeping it that way.

Silence once again lingers between us as we reach the end of the path that dead-ends at the steps leading up to Avery's cabin. I take them two at a time, reaching the top in two strides, and begin unlocking the door.

"You and I will each have a master key that unlocks your cabin as well as all the other cabins on this path."

"Including your cabin?"

The question gives me enough pause to stop what I'm doing. Because I sure as hell hadn't thought about that.

Fucking wonderful.

"I said *all the cabins*, didn't I?" I manage to grind out before flicking the lock out of place and shoving the door open for him.

A double bed, lounge chair, and nightstand between the two take up the majority of the cabin's footprint. There's a small built-in coat rack behind the door, as well as a few cubbies to store clothes, shoes, and toiletries.

It's as simple and understated on the inside as it is on the outside—though it's actually one of the nicer cabins on the property. It's one of the ones built after last summer, when we got the funding to expand the program, allowing us to almost double the number of kids able to attend this season.

I drop his key on the tiny hook beside the door and lean against the doorjamb, watching Avery like a hawk as he quietly glances around the space.

"This is it?" he asks while setting his bags on the bed.

Something between incredulity and disgust leaks from his tone, and it instantly grates on my nerves. I shouldn't be surprised this style of living wouldn't be up to his standards. When he heard the word *cabin,* no doubt he thought of some fancy ski chalet in Vail or Park City, not the tiny one-room style those of us without butt-loads of money think of.

The fact that he has to walk a few hundred yards to the bathroom or won't be able to send all his clothes out to be laundered will be a rude awakening for him.

"Home sweet home for the next eight weeks."

A low groan comes from him as he runs his fingers through his golden locks. "If I survive that long."

More irritation courses through me, and I've just about had it with his bullshit.

"What the hell are you doing here, Avery?"

The frankness of my question must take him off guard because he freezes instantly, those sky blues locking with mine. And for the briefest moment, I think I see something alluding to uncertainty in their depths.

"Look, I wasn't aware you—"

"Save it," I seethe, cutting him off. "I asked what the hell you're doing here. That's all I wanna know."

Biting his head off must snap him out of whatever stupor he briefly fell into, because on a dime, the fighter in him comes out with a vengeance.

"Why're you coming at me like this?" he snarls. "If one of us should be pissed at the other, it's me. Because *you* were the one who got me kicked out of Foltyn, not the other way around."

I arch a brow. "Last time I checked, you got yourself kicked out."

Something between a snort and a laugh comes from him; a clear attempt to make little of my accusation. Too bad for him, all it does is light a fire under my ass.

"Try and brush it off. Blame me if you want, but what you did was wrong," I snap, arms crossing over my chest. "It's not my fault you can't own it or take responsibility for your actions."

A sneer takes over his face, one I can only describe as vicious and feral. Anger and even a little hatred swimming in his glare as he crosses the room to me, getting up in my face like his proximity does anything to intimidate me.

"In case you didn't realize, I've done everything in my power to make it right. Apologized and—"

"An apology is supposed to magically make the fact that you outed not just one person, but two people, better?" I scoff and shake my head, knowing full well it doesn't. "Why'd you do it, anyway?"

The sneer on his face deepens, and he steps in closer, making his inch of height he has on me feel more like a foot. Close enough for me to catch a whiff of his cologne or body spray or whatever the hell he wears. It smells like ocean salt and some sort of citrus, and it makes my stomach flip unexpectedly before a buzzing feeling sets in. It feels eerily like… butterflies. Even in the midst of whatever kind of showdown we're having.

Then the asshole goes and opens his mouth again, effectively breaking the moment and reminding me exactly why I can't stand him.

"The time for asking questions was the second you saw me looking through Keene's phone. Not now, after the damage is done."

"Damage *you* caused," I point out.

"And it all would have been avoided if you'd spoken up."

His statement gives me pause, because even without him saying it, I've wondered if it's true. Plenty of times over the past few weeks, I've thought about how things could have played out differently. Because, while I'm perfectly aware that Avery made his own choices, I made mine too. And I chose to not say anything to him at that moment, instead quietly observing rather than making my presence known.

Maybe I could have talked to him. Distracted him enough to stop him from finding the picture—which ended up being exactly the kind of ammunition Avery was looking for. Or at the very least, stopping him from sending the damn thing.

But the more I dwell on those what-ifs, the more miserable I get.

Avery shakes his head, still spitting mad from the looks of it, but he also takes a step back, giving us both some much-needed space. "This is pointless. You're never gonna agree with my actions, just like I sure as fuck won't agree with yours."

"Finally. Something we can agree on." I'm practically seething when I circle back to my original thought. "So, are you gonna tell me why the hell you're here?"

His blue eyes turn to ice as he glares at me. "Nah, I'm gonna just let you fill in all the blanks. Feel free to go to Colin with your theories, though. You know, 'cause you've already had the practice."

My jaw tics hard enough my molars might crack from the pressure, and I'm damn sure steam is shooting straight out of my ears.

This fucking douchewaffle.

"Forget it, Reynolds." Shoving off the doorjamb, I head down the stairs and call over my shoulder, "Campers arrive tomorrow morning, seven o'clock. Do us both a favor and stay out of my way until then."

THREE

Kaleb

Week One

Cars begin arriving at seven on the dot the next morning, and Avery is nowhere to be found. Which checks out, honestly. I know there's no way he's taking this seriously, and that's exactly the reason I asked why he was here. Because, while this might be all fun and games to him, working here is something I take very seriously.

And as much as I enjoy being right, it also pisses me off to no end.

Half of the campers in our age group have arrived, unloaded, and checked in by the time Avery comes skidding to a stop beside me.

Not bothering to glance up from the clipboard in my hands, I mutter, "You're late."

"Only by fifteen minutes," he says in a huff.

Four words out of his arrogant mouth already have my irritation spiking, but I do my best to remain composed. "Fifteen minutes, one minute, or an hour. The amount of time you're late by doesn't change the fact that you're still late."

A sharp scoff comes from him. "You're really getting off on this shit, y'know that? You have some sort of superiority complex I don't know about?"

I finally lift my gaze to find his blue eyes aimed at me in a glare. "If being on time and responsible is a superiority complex, then yeah, I guess I do."

He blinks, frustration written all over his face.

Well, he can join the club. Because I'm sure as hell annoyed to no end by his inability to be on time for the kids' arrivals. Or his presence here in general.

I'm about to tell him this too, when out of nowhere, his fingers wrap around my wrist, causing a small zing of electricity to shoot straight through my chest. And that's the best way to describe it. Electric. Not the same white-hot heat that ripples through my extremities when I get angry, nor the jolt of adrenaline when fear kicks in. It's a sensation I've never really felt before, apart from yesterday in his cabin, and I don't really know what to do with it.

Avery uses his grip to haul me toward the side of the lodge, and it snaps me out of the momentary stupor I fell into at his touch.

"Reynolds, I'm a little busy—"

He stops us dead in our tracks, turning on me and cutting me off before I have the chance to finish my thought. "This isn't going to work."

I yank my arm free from his hold and snarl, "You pulling me away from what I was doing? Yeah, it sure as hell isn't."

"I meant this" —he motions between our chests— "isn't going to work. This bickering and snarkiness. If it keeps up, one of us is bound to snap. From the way things have gone the past twenty-four hours, it might even get nuclear. And that can't happen in front of all these kids."

He happens to be right. Unfortunately.

And him being right only pisses me off more. Still, I keep my temper reined in as best I can. The last thing we need right now is me losing my shit on him.

"For once, I'll agree with you. So let's make it easy on both of us." My eyes narrow on those sky blues. "Tell Colin you're no longer interested in working here. I'm sure there were plenty of applicants for the position who would gladly take your place, even this last minute. If not, we have counselors-in-training who can help me. Then all our problems are solved."

A frown creases his forehead. "What? No. I'm not going anywhere."

I shouldn't be surprised by his unwillingness to listen. I've known him long enough to understand he's stubborn as a mule and not one to back down from any sort of confrontation.

Taking the time to look at him—I mean really fucking look at the guy—I do my best to figure out, once again, what the hell his game is here. Because none of it makes any sense to me.

This isn't a place he'd be caught dead of his own volition. He knows it, I know it, and most importantly, it's written all over him. In the way his hair and clothes are a disheveled mess, like he just threw himself together after rolling out of bed. In the whites of his eyes, bloodshot to hell, no doubt from lack of sleep.

Which brings me to ask him the same damn question as yesterday.

"Why?"

"Because I need to be here." His tone is insistent, but not as much as the look in those bloodshot eyes. "I just do, okay? So would you just accept it so we can move on and try to get along?"

My mind catches on one, single word.

Need.

Jonesing it outdoors wouldn't be Avery's scene unless it was on some rooftop bar for brunch with his richie-rich friends back in Vancouver. Not roughing it in the wilderness, even if we do have running water.

He's here out of some sort of necessity, and it's backed him into a corner.

Which is why, rather than fighting with him more—possibly bringing out the raging bull living deep inside him—I let it slide. I'll just wait for him to crack instead. Which he will, eventually.

"Look, I don't know how you got this job or why you think you need it in the first place. I don't really care either," I tell him, my tone low and serious. "But this camp is *my* safe space. *My* haven away from real life. I *want* to be here, and I'll be damned to hell before I let you ruin it for me or for any of these kids who feel the same way."

His voice is earnest as he utters, "I won't. I swear."

A promise from him means next to nothing, but I don't really have another option than to take it right now.

"Fine." I slip a sheet of paper out from the clipboard and hand it to him while trying to keep the irritation from showing in my tone. "These are the bunking assignments for the kids. Three per cabin. They're all unlocked already, no thanks to you, so you'll just need to take the kids to get settled in as they arrive. The CITs can help you. I'll take care of checking them in and all the goodbyes."

I don't bother waiting for a response, instead turning on my heel to head back to the safety of the parking lot.

It's five to eight by the time my father's truck rolls into the camp's parking lot.

He's barely thrown the vehicle into park when my twin brothers bolt out the back doors, making a beeline straight past me to their friend, Liam, who's waiting for Avery to come back and take him to his cabin.

Colton practically tackles Liam, Dayton not far behind. The three of them instantly start chattering animatedly at each other, surely filling in the blanks they've missed in each other's lives since they saw each other skiing at Mount Bachelor this past winter.

"Nice to see you too, guys!" I shout to the twins, holding my arms out to the side. "What am I? Chopped liver?"

Dayton's nose wrinkles in disgust at the same time Colton yells back, "We saw you yesterday!"

"Doesn't mean you can't at least say hi," I mutter to myself as I check the two of them off the list and head over to Dad's truck to grab their bags.

"Your mom barely got a goodbye out of them this morning," Dad says by way of greeting as he pulls their duffels from the bed of the truck. "They're just excited. I wouldn't take it personally."

He hands me Cole's bag, and I roll my eyes before hauling it over my shoulder. "Eight weeks without their parents. Of course they're excited."

"Especially when they think their big brother will let them get away with everything."

A snort mixed with a laugh leaves me. "They won't be getting away with a damn thing if I have anything to say about it."

His deep, warm chuckle floats over me like warm honey, and a tiny twinge of homesickness courses through me. I don't see my parents nearly enough since heading to college in Portland, leaving them back in Bend, and it's not until I'm in their presence again that I realize how much I miss them.

"I'm certain they'll be testing you on that." His expression sobers slightly as we approach the edge of the parking lot where the twins are. "I know you don't have a lot of time, but how're you doing? I'm sure not a lot has changed in the past twenty-four hours, but…"

My eyes search Dad's face momentarily, debating if I should tell him the truth or not. But needing to talk to *someone* about it wins out, and a long sigh leaves me.

"Avery's here," I tell him quietly.

"Avery?"

"From school. The one who was on my team who…" I give him a silent, imploring look. Begging him to understand what I'm saying without spelling it out where other parents, counselors, or kids could hear, even if they're all too busy with their own conversations to eavesdrop.

I know of a few older kids who've been attending camp here regularly for years who are out and open about their sexual orientation. Not only to their families but publicly as well. They don't need to find out about the shit one of their counselors pulled not even a month ago, outing someone in their own community.

My own community.

Thankfully, my father just nods in understanding before his gaze tracks Dayton and Colton instead. "If you don't feel safe, you have the right to say something."

I shake my head. "It's not my safety I'm worried about. There's no way he's going to find out about me while we're here."

"Then what's the issue?"

I explain my line of thinking with the queer campers, then add, "Plus, I don't want his bigoted, biased bullshit to rub off on anyone. Look at Day and Cole; they just want to fit in with their friends and be cool. Kids their age are impressionable, and I'm concerned he might do or say something that'll hurt one of them with some off-hand comment. Or worse, guide some of them down the path he followed."

"Valid concerns." He gives me a thoughtful look before asking, "So what are you gonna do about it?"

Another sigh leaves me as I scratch the back of my neck. "I don't know yet. But if you've taught me anything, it's that hatred and bias aren't ingrained in us from birth. It's a line of thinking that's taught or learned. And it's a chance the camp is taking by letting him be here."

A grin appears on his face and he nods. "I stand by teaching you that, and again, I see your concerns. But I think you're looking at this from the wrong perspective."

I blink, frowning. "Meaning?"

"Maybe instead of worrying about what he might accidentally teach them, you can make this summer about what you know you can teach *him*."

"You think I can reverse his bigotry?" I ask, dumbfounded.

Dad simply shrugs. "It might be harder than getting him fired, but I don't think it would hurt to try."

Yeah, except that would mean spending more time with the dick than I already have to. Something not very high on my to-do list.

Doubt must be written all over my face, because Dad lets out another low chuckle. "No need to look like I ruined your summer before it's begun. I'm just offering some food for thought."

"As if I needed more on my plate," I mumble, my voice laced with sarcasm as I grab Dayton's bag from him too. "But thanks."

A smile tilts the corner of his lips and he claps me on the shoulder. "I'll let you get back to it. But your mom and I are proud of you. And we'll keep being proud of you no matter what you decide to do."

"Thanks, Dad."

I'm pulled in for a quick hug before he releases me and heads back toward his truck.

"Wait, aren't you gonna say bye to the twins?" I call after him.

He waves me off, a grin on his face. "Not a chance, kid. They're too preoccupied, and I've gotta get back home anyway. Make sure those two don't kill each other."

"I'll do my best."

Dad's truck has barely disappeared from sight when I turn around to find Avery standing with Liam, Colton, and Dayton. His eyes are locked on the bunking assignments, probably searching for all their names, when Colton all but yanks the paper from his grasp.

"Cole!" I shout, immediately moving toward them, and by the time I've reached the group of them, he's already put the paper back in Avery's waiting hands.

"Sorry," Cole says, and at least he has the decency to look a bit sheepish.

I arch a brow. "Not to me."

His nose wrinkles a little before he looks up at Avery instead. "Sorry. I was rude."

"It's all good," he tells Colton. He pauses for a second, glancing from Cole back to me with his brows furrowed slightly. "I take it you know them?"

"Only their entire lives," I mutter, pointing at their names on the bunking assignments. "Dayton and Colton *LaMothe*. My brothers."

His brows shoot up as he, once again, looks between the twins and me. Only this time, to try and place the resemblance.

There's no mistaking the two of them; they're identical. Down to the scraggly bodies, mops of light brown hair, and hazel eyes. But I don't share many of their features. Which makes sense, seeing as their dad isn't mine. At least, not biologically, though that doesn't mean shit to me. He's still the only dad I've ever known.

"I don't see it," Avery confirms after a minute.

"Usually how it goes," Dayton confirms with a lilt of laughter. "We don't like to claim him most of the time anyway."

I roll my eyes, already regretting my request to be assigned to their group this year. "Hilarious, Day."

My attention shifts to Avery again to find him already staring at me, and the instant our gazes collide, the buzzing feeling from earlier is back. Resurfaces with a roar, ripping through me and impossible to ignore.

Clearing my throat, I nod toward the twins. "All our kids are here, so I'll take my brothers to their cabin if you'll take Liam."

He nods before breaking eye contact to glance at Liam. "Let's get a move on, kid. Your friends are waiting."

Liam's giddy, excited energy radiates off him as he says bye to the twins before heading off with Avery for the cabins. The tingly electric feeling fades the farther the two of them walk away, disappearing entirely when they also disappear from sight.

When I finally allow my gaze to shift back to the twins, they're both already watching me with curiosity.

"Who was that guy?" Colton asks, arms crossed over his chest like he's some kind of badass, not my twerp of a brother I could snap like a twig with one hand.

"Yeah, he's never been a counselor here before," Day chimes in. "Do you know him?"

Cole's brows furrow as he shifts his attention to Dayton, cocking his head. "Didn't you feel that tension between them? Of course they know each other." He looks at me again. "So who is he?"

Ah, yes. How I've missed this—classic Day and Cole. Always bouncing off each other, reading each other's minds, and never letting another person get a word in edgewise.

"Are we playing Twenty Questions and I didn't realize it?"

Dayton shrugs before grabbing his bag from me. "If we are, we've still got like seventeen to go. Technically eighteen, since Cole asked the same question twice."

"Smartass," I murmur before handing Colton his bag too. "Yes, I know him. That's Avery. I played baseball with him at Foltyn."

Dayton's eyes widen and he smacks Colton in the chest. "Oh my God. *That* Avery?"

I let out a long sigh before nodding.

The nice thing about being out to my family is not only the freedom to be myself with all of them, but it also gives the chance for Mom, Dad, and me to teach the twins about the queer community. And it allows me to share things about my life—things like what happened this spring at Foltyn with Avery and Keene—so the twins can learn from them.

Teaching them to be loving and accepting toward those who are different from them. Not a couple little assholes who can't handle some diversity or people being their most authentic selves.

Colton's the first to ask the question we all want the answer to. "Why is he here?"

I roll my lips inward before answering honestly. "I don't know. Haven't managed to figure it out yet."

Both their noses wrinkle up, speaking more about their feelings than words ever could. And if I had any worries about my brothers being influenced by Avery this summer, they're completely gone with that single look.

But this is supposed to be the fun time of year, and I'm not about to let it start off with heavy shit. So I change the subject.

"C'mon, let's get you to your cabin," I say before ushering them deeper into the camp. "I'm sure you're both excited. Seemed like it when you couldn't even say hi earlier."

They both nod, the same giddy energy they had when they first got here, back with a vengeance. But then Dayton lets out a little disgruntled noise before whining, "But why'd you have to pair us with Elijah for a bunkmate?"

"Dayton Matthew," I hiss in warning, glancing around to make sure no one—especially Elijah—is around to overhear my dickhead little brother's callow remark..

"Kaleb Jackson," he retorts back, all attitude and sass.

Oh, the joys of fighting with a preteen. And lucky me, I get to spend the camp season doing it with not just the twins but eighteen others too. Then add in the one guy on the planet I'd rather never see again being my co-counselor, and this is bound to be one interesting summer.

What the hell have I gotten myself into?

FOUR

Kaleb

It's quarter after midnight when I step into the bathhouse, both expecting and hoping for it to be deserted this time of night. Most of the camp is usually dead asleep by now, doing their best to recharge for a jam-packed day sure to come tomorrow.

Tonight, though, it seems someone had the same idea as me since one of the three showers is already in use, causing steam to fill the room.

I glance at the vanity to find a small leather toiletry bag—the letters AJR embossed on the side—and my mood instantly takes a plummet off Mount Hood. While I might not know what the J stands for, the A and R are clearly Avery Reynolds.

"Fucking great," I mutter under my breath before dropping my own things on the sink to unpack my shampoo and body wash.

I've worked at the camp for the past three summers, and it's always grueling. Long, sometimes very hot, days outdoors. Constantly handling a bunch of kids who need this, that, or the other thing. Activities packed in our schedule from dawn to dusk to make sure they're all so exhausted when it's lights out, there's no shenanigans after—something a few returning campers are notorious for causing.

So when it comes to the end of the day, I need these thirty minutes of alone time to take the hottest shower imaginable. It's my time to wash away not only the dirt and grime from the day, but also all the stress and frustration I have to keep bottled up while I'm around the kids.

Stress *Avery* now adds to.

He's fucking everywhere.

Spending all this time with him is starting to really wear on me, and it's only been a few days. And most of it is thanks to the intense buzzing feeling I get whenever we're within a few feet of each other.

I felt it when we were in his cabin the day he got here, then when he grabbed me and pulled me to the side the following morning. A few more times in the days since then too, like when we took the boys on the lake and I was forced to witness Avery in nothing but a pair of swim trunks for hours at a time.

It's taken me a few days to place the feeling. And after today, I know exactly what it is…no matter how much I wish I didn't.

It's attraction. Desire.

Fucking lust.

All things I'd never want to feel for him.

I thought I'd left this stupid crush in the past, all the way back in freshman year. Tucked it in the *Never Gonna Happen* box and buried it in the recesses of my mind. Add in everything he's done recently, and I was certain that box would never see the light of day again.

A mistaken notion on my part, it seems, since the head in my shorts is severely at odds with the one on my shoulders. Which is just fucking wonderful.

I do my best to shove thoughts of him aside, even if he's within a couple feet of me at the moment, and slip into the empty stall beside him. Blowing out a long breath, I flip the nozzle on the shower to let it heat and then I undress, all the while perfectly aware of that damn feeling growing inside me.

Avery hasn't made a peep while I've been in here, so he's either ignoring me, or he must not have heard me over the running water in his own stall. Either way, I can only be thankful and then hope he's in and out before I'm done…or vice versa.

No run-ins. No interactions.

Last thing I need after my epiphany earlier is to run into him half naked in a towel. Or just plain naked. Or just run into him in general.

Complete avoidance would be preferable, really.

I start on my hair, lathering shampoo in my palm before sticking my head beneath the spray to rinse. Ignoring the electric feeling from being this close to him is nearly impossible, and I even go as far as turning the dial on the shower down to cold. But the frigid water does nothing to temper the roaring desire at knowing he's only a couple feet away from me.

Naked and wet and—

A soft moan comes from the stall beside me, and I almost drop my bottle of body wash on the floor.

What the—?

Another groan, this one deeper and more drawn out, echoes through the bathhouse. Loud enough that there's no way he knows I'm in here.

He'd only be doing what I think he's doing if he assumed he was still alone.

Oh my God.

As a few more seconds pass, I do my best to keep perfectly silent…

and listen for any other tell-tale sounds to confirm my suspicions. Because maybe it's not what I think. Hell, part of me is praying to whatever god might exist that Avery *isn't* currently jacking off in the stall beside me.

But God must hate me, because after another soft moan fades, I can hear the distinct sound of skin moving over more skin.

"Fucking hell," comes a lust-thickened voice, barely more than a rough whisper, over the water pelting down on the tile floor.

I'm hot all over, the cold water dousing my skin doing nothing to calm the fire burning inside me. And it only gets worse as more of his groans reverberate through the bathroom like they're in surround sound. So it's not surprising when the erotic noises are enough to stir my cock to life.

Fucking hell is right.

Flipping the shower cold enough to become hypothermic, I douse my entire body in the spray before gripping my cock around the base and squeezing. Hard. Because I can't…I just can't—

"Oh, shit," Avery groans. Then a loud *smack* of his hand against the tiled wall sends another bolt of lust straight to my dick.

Ah, screw it.

If I'm gonna get hard listening to the asshole getting off, I might as well use it to my benefit. At least, that's the logic my dick has thought up as I flip the water over to scalding, adding some soap to my palm before wrapping my fist around my cock.

Stroking at a slow, leisurely pace, my eyes fall closed and my head drops back. I allow the pleasure to build within me, despite knowing this is a terrible idea with him only feet away.

But I had to spend all day helping him lift those canoes, seeing the sun shining down on his naked, tanned torso the whole time. And it was torture. I had to look away at one point, because having him catch me jaw-dropped and ogling would only add fuel to the fire between us.

Now, though? There's no reason for me to keep it from shifting back to the forefront of my brain.

Visions of wet, smooth skin and carved muscle race through my thoughts as Avery's soft, low pants continue raining down on me like the shower I'm standing beneath. The combination immediately invades my senses, making my blood boil with the need for release.

My teeth sink into my lower lip hard enough for the familiar tang of copper to coat my tongue. But it's better than the alternative: letting moans or expletives slip free.

The steam and temperature of the shower added to the white-hot lust running through my veins like lava starts overwhelming me, and I press my forehead to the cool tile wall to keep from overheating. But I don't stop my hand from moving, nor the images from flooding my brain.

Of Avery in the exact same position as me, only this wall separating us.

His fist around what I'm sure is a thick and veiny cock. The muscles of his forearm and neck becoming corded and strained with effort as he brings himself closer and closer to ecstasy. To the infinite bliss that is—

Avery lets out a sharp hiss before a long, slow sigh of pleasure is mixed in with the, "Oh, fuck, yes," he mutters.

—release.

His curse draws my own balls up, and I swear, I'm right behind him. I move my palm over my length while also thrusting into my fist, fucking it with reckless abandon and rolling the head with every upstroke. The pressure and pace I'm keeping primes me to launch sky-high into the stratosphere, and I'm craving the euphoria that comes with it.

So much so, I don't even care about the plummet back to Earth after.

A soft moan manages to slip past my lips, and I sink my teeth into the inside of my cheek to keep it from happening again.

God, I'm close. I'm so fucking close, I can feel my release barreling down my spine as my hand glides over my length faster and faster. Desperation takes over, and a low moan disguised as a sigh slips free from my mouth right as—

The shower curtain on my stall is yanked to the side without warning, revealing Avery on the other side. A towel sits low on his hips, and it's the only thing giving him a barrier of decency. But me, on the other hand? I'm bare-ass naked, harder than I've ever been, and seconds away from coming.

All of which is mortifying when realization sets in.

"What the actual fuck?" I snap, grabbing the shower curtain and wrestling it from his grip to hide my erection from view. But it's too little, too late. From the way he blinks up at me, nearly stunned to silence, he got more than an eyeful.

Fuck me running.

He just stands there, staring while the water pounds down over me. Which makes me uncomfortable as hell, but for all the wrong reasons. Because now that he's in sight—water still dripping from his hair and cascading down his chest—my cock has more concrete images to work with.

And that's *really* not what needs to happen right now.

I aim my best death glare at him, hoping it hides the straight-up lust I'm trying my best to rein in. "Do you mind? A little privacy while I shower would be nice."

Avery still looks stunned as he mutters out an explanation I didn't ask for. "The place was empty when I came in here. But I heard the shower still running when I turned mine off."

"That's generally what happens when another person is in a different shower stall."

"I didn't realize someone else would be in here at this time." He shakes his head, still a little stunned. "I thought it just…turned on."

I arch a brow and scoff. "So, naturally, that possessed you to barge into the stall and check? Rather than, I don't know, asking if someone was in here? Or run the opposite way, in case the place was haunted?"

The barrage of questions paired with my taunting quickly lights his very short fuse, snapping him into true asshole-Avery form. And while it isn't something I enjoy, at least it tamps my libido down enough so I'm no longer saluting him at the waist.

"I don't know what I was thinking, Kaleb. It's been a long-as-shit week, and it's not even over yet. I might as well be an extra on *The Walking Dead* right now, and I sure as hell didn't think someone else would've come in here at fucking midnight!"

"And my stuff sitting out there on the counter wasn't a dead giveaway?" I muse.

"Oh, my God," he says, shaking his head while stepping back. "Did you not hear a word I just said? I'm minutes away from hallucinations, for Christ's sake. You think I really *saw* it?"

He's got a point, even if I'll never admit it aloud. I remember my first week of camp as a counselor, and it's like he said—zombified.

"Okay, fine," I concede before noting the water slowly starting to cool as it hits my skin. "But are we done here? I kind of want to finish my shower."

I go to pull the curtain back into place without waiting for his answer, but he grabs the fabric again and holds it open. So once again, I'm forced to grab it back and cover myself.

Jesus Christ.

"Oh, hell no. We're not even close to being done. You wanna sit and question me? Well, let's talk about what the hell *you're* doing in here," he growls before jutting his chin toward me. "Because it looks an awful lot like you're perving in a boy's camp."

I open my mouth, ready to call him out for doing the exact same thing minutes earlier…only to realize I can't. If he knew I was getting off to the sounds he was making, it would only make worse implications.

And the last thing I want is to give him more opportunities for uncovering my sexuality.

So, on the fly, I come up with a cover plausible enough to deny perving of *any* kind.

"Oh, fuck off, Reynolds. Don't act like you've never gotten a little hard from cleaning your dick."

"Really? Cleaning it? That's what we're calling it these days?"

A dubious look appears on his face, brows arched in challenge when he crosses his arms over his broad chest, smattered with a fine dusting of blond hair.

Abort, abort, abort.

"Fine, you got me, okay? I was jerking it. You really gonna tell me you're prepared to go eight whole weeks without getting off?" I pause and shake my head. "But it's not like I was…*perving* on them. They were nowhere in my thoughts."

Just the idea makes me wanna gag.

Perving on *him*, on the other hand…that just makes me horny. Unfortunately.

There's still a slight amount of judgment in his tone when he asks, "And you knowingly did that with someone else in the stall next to you?"

He's got me there, and I do the only thing I can in this situation.

I lie.

"You're not the only one exhausted enough to think you were the only one in here."

A slight blush tints his cheeks, and I'm not sure if it's from the steam in the bathhouse or the insinuation I made. Either way, it's enough to throw him a little off balance, and he clears his throat before he plays it off as best he can.

"Yeah, well…make sure you're actually alone next time." He coughs before clearing his throat again. "But I, uh, I guess you can…get back to it."

The buzzing feeling hasn't gone away while we've been in this little showdown so much as it's faded into the background with the conversation. But now that it's over, and he's still standing here in only a damn towel… well, shit. Let's just say I'm happy my dick is currently hidden from view.

"Thanks," I murmur sarcastically, painfully aware of the thickness suddenly present in my voice. I try to keep my eyes locked on his face instead of his insane body while he steps back toward the counter, but nope. The second he turns his back toward me to comb through his hair, I'm ensnared by those muscles instead of his abs and pecs.

"You can shut the curtain now, LaMothe," he says while meeting my gaze through the mirror above the sink. "Unless you're planning to give me a show."

My stomach rolls, a mix of fear and anticipation rushing through me as I yank the fabric shut, effectively closing me off from him. And it's only when he's out of sight that I feel as if I can finally breathe again.

I need to get this baseless attraction under control.

I guess it's not entirely baseless; Avery's an obviously good-looking guy, from an objective standpoint. It's something I noticed early on when I met him; it was just super easy to lock down because, one, he's fucking straight. And two, we were friends, and I wasn't gonna ruin that.

Thankfully, after seeing him become a grade-A asshole, the attraction began fading on its own. Though, apparently not as much as I thought, if the state of my cock has anything to say about the matter.

I squeeze around the base again, trying to ease some of the pressure building, but it's no use. Release is the only thing that'll bring me relief at this point.

And, God, I hate myself for how much I wanna be listening to his voice while it happens.

"I shower every night at this time, just so you know," I call out from behind the curtain, slowly stroking my length some more as I wait for him to respond. When he remains silent, I add, "Wouldn't want to have this kind of run-in again."

Still nothing.

From the lack of response, I don't even know if he's still in here or if he's just screwing with me all over again. I'm not sure why it matters to me. I can get off just fine with or without him here.

And I certainly have no fucking clue if giving him that tidbit of information was meant to be a warning…or a hopeful invitation.

FIVE

Avery

Week Two

I fucking hate this place.

Loathe it with the passion of a thousand burning suns, and I have no idea how I'm supposed to survive the next two months out here in the middle of nowhere. We're only a week in, and I've already regretted every second I've been living in a tiny log cabin tucked deep within the bug-infested wilderness.

Even with every activity over the past few days being on the lake just outside of camp—all thanks to the unseasonably hot temperature for June—I'm still miserable. Don't get me wrong, I love being out on the water, but I'd much rather it be on a sailboat. Or anything that's a lot harder to tip over than a kayak or paddleboard.

And believe me, I did tip over. On multiple occasions.

Needless to say, I'm entirely out of my element here. To the point where I might as well be Matt Damon in *The Martian*, stuck on a foreign planet and having to find a way to survive.

But today, we're finally doing something that should be easy, even for me. Hiking.

After all, hiking is just walking in the woods, right? Maybe add in some hills, rocks, and tree roots as obstacles, but it's still walking. And it's not like we'll be going all that fast when there's twenty-ish kids with way shorter legs who need to keep the pace too.

At least, that's the small amount of hope I'm holding on to as I check all the boys' packs for the things they might need on our excursion. Water bottles, sunscreen, trail maps, first aid kits. EpiPens for any of the boys who have allergies to things found in the woods.

The crunching of footsteps comes up behind me as I'm about to zip up the final pack, and when I rise, I find none other than Kaleb staring at me. Not just the typical kind of staring, but the kind that breeds the transparent feeling in those awful dreams where you show up at school in only your underwear.

And with *that* thought, I'm instantly brought back to the other night in the showers. Which makes me feel hot in very *different* ways. Ways I really would rather not think about.

"Can I help you?" I ask after his staring reaches the point of discomfort.

Kaleb's brow arches, a dubious look etched into his features as his eyes scrape their way up and down my body. "What the hell are you wearing?"

What?

I glance down, taking in my forest green camp tee and khaki shorts before looking back up at him with a frown. "The exact same thing as you."

He taps the toe of his dirt-covered hiking boots to the toe of my boat shoes. The same ones I'd wear when Dad and I'd go out sailing on the Columbia River or any typical day visiting the coast.

My frown turns into something of a scowl. "You have a problem with my shoes now?"

"For hiking? Yeah. Going up and down five miles of trails wearing those is a sure way to end up with feet covered in cuts. Or worse, blisters."

"Because you're the expert, right?"

He blinks those stupidly green eyes at me. "Yeah. I kinda am."

This fucking guy. So sure of himself and what he's saying.

Granted, he was right earlier this week when we took the kids out in the kayaks, telling me I'd end up as red as a lobster because I didn't put enough sunscreen on for this high of altitude. Something the petty, stubborn side of me refused to listen to. And wouldn't you know, he was right, and I had a sunburn from hell that took three days to tan over.

Him calling that outcome has only made him more smug. I can read it all over his face right now as we have this little staredown.

"I'll take my chances."

Kaleb's perfect, white teeth sink into his bottom lip before he lets out a wry laugh. "Suit yourself, Reynolds. Not my feet that'll be two slabs of raw meat afterward."

"Whatever," I mutter, brushing past him. "You coming with me to get the kids or what?"

"Oh, they're on their way," he tells me while grabbing his pack. "I just came from telling them all to hit the bathrooms before meeting us here."

He's right; not more than five minutes later, we're handing out their packs and doing our headcount. And in true Kaleb fashion, he's taking every opportunity he can to roast me in front of the kids as they count off, all the while flashing me little looks to gauge my reaction.

Playing annoyed isn't hard, but ignoring the weird swirling flutter in my gut definitely is. Because while we still clearly bicker like children, there's now this strange undertone to it. Has been ever since the other night in the shower.

Maybe even since the day I got here.

I could be imagining it now, especially since I caught him jerking it after I'd just finished doing the same thing, all while having no idea he was in the stall right beside me. Or maybe because it was his sharp jaw, chiseled six-one frame, and forest green eyes running through my errant thoughts the entire time.

Do not go there. Not right now.

Kaleb calls for the kids to fall in line, and without any more preamble or digs, he sets off with a single-file line of eleven-year-olds behind him. I wait and fall into step at the back of the group as we head up the trail; one, to make sure there aren't any stragglers getting lost in the wilderness— hello, lawsuit waiting to happen—and two, because it's as far away from Kaleb as humanly possible.

The more distance between us at this point, the better.

"You two don't get along, do you?"

I glance up from where I've been carefully staring down at the trail to prevent myself from tripping or stubbing my toes on a root, only to find Elijah Marshall has fallen back in step beside me.

A little scoff leaves me. "That obvious, huh?"

The dark-haired pipsqueak looks up at me, his brown eyes peering through a set of dark-framed glasses. He's a tiny guy, easily half a head shorter than the rest of the boys in his age group, and is reserved and soft-spoken to match his stature.

"Just a bit. You're both good at pretending for the most part, though."

I smirk, already really liking this kid, along with his lack of filter.

We've spoken a couple times over the past week, but nothing more than him asking for help getting his kayak to push off from the dock or grabbing the hammock carabiners from the top shelf since he couldn't reach. All in all, not a whole lot to go off, and definitely not enough to be fulfilling this so-called favor with his uncle.

"How do you spend all this time with someone you don't like?" he asks suddenly, cutting through my thoughts.

"Now, hang on," I muse, slowing my pace to walk beside him. "Who said I don't like him?"

Elijah gives me one of those *give me a break* looks, eyebrows basically pulled up into his hairline. Which is hilarious with those glasses on. "You asked if it was obvious. And it is."

I let out a sharp laugh as I glance up ahead. Kaleb's still at the front—easily spotted by the National Park snapback sitting backward on his head that rises well over everyone else—leading the pack toward our destination.

"I don't *not* like him. We just…" My sentence falls off at the end, not entirely sure how I feel about him. I just know my dick and my brain aren't in agreement, and I'm almost positive all this mountain air is fucking with my sanity.

"You just don't get along all the time," he supplies.

His way of circling back makes me crack a grin. "Exactly. We have to work together, so we need to be civil despite our history."

"History?" he asks, and I don't miss the way he perks up with curiosity.

My teeth scrape over my bottom lip and I debate how much of this story to divulge. But if I'm really going to take Colin's advice to heart and build some sort of relationship with the kid, I've gotta start somewhere. Might as well be with what landed me in his life to begin with.

"We played baseball together in college until he got me kicked out about a month ago."

I glance over at him just in time to catch his eyes widen into saucers.

"He got you kicked out, and you can still stand to look at him every day?"

"Well…it's more like I did something to get myself kicked out. But if he hadn't said anything about what I'd done, I probably wouldn't have been."

"So he's a snitch."

That gets a chuckle out of me. "At first, that's kinda how I felt. But what I did was wrong, so I can't blame him for snitching."

His nose scrunches up as looks at me. "If you know it was wrong, then why'd you do it?"

The question is one I've been asked plenty of times before now, seeing as it's so obvious, but this is the first time I find myself actually willing to answer it. "Because I was hurt and angry, so I wanted to hurt that person back. But it turns out hurting them back didn't even make me feel better. Instead, it made everything worse."

He nods, his brows still knit together as he processes. But one of the gears in his brain must hit a snag, and his head snaps up again.

"You didn't like…commit murder or anything, did you?"

I burst out laughing before deciding I really like this kid. I don't think getting to know him over the next couple months will be much of a hardship. "Nothing illegal, I promise."

A sharp, dramatic breath leaves him. "That's good."

The subject changes after that, and I'm quick to realize he's a quirky, curious, and extremely observant kid. With a major emphasis on observant, because right around mile two, he notices the gap between us and the next kid has more than tripled in size.

"What's wrong?" Elijah asks before looking down at my feet. Then he stops mid-step and starts giggling uncontrollably. "Kal was right. You really do look more ready to go on a yacht than you do to go hiking."

The jab only sends a slight twinge of annoyance through me, but I'm willing to chalk it up to the searing pain shooting through my heels and pinky toes with every step.

"Yeah, yeah. Everyone's a critic today," I mutter, still giving him a faint smile through the burning around my toes and heels. "C'mon, kid. Pick up the pace. The last thing we want is to be left behind."

SIX

Avery

It's just before dinner time, and I haven't even had a chance to put on a shirt after changing from our hike—let alone take stock of the injuries on my feet—when the door to my cabin bursts open and Kaleb comes barreling in.

My brows furrow as I snap the button of my shorts closed. "Ever heard of knocking? I could've been indecent."

"Yeah, well, then we'd be even," he says absently while glancing around the cabin in an almost frantic sort of search. In fact, his eyes haven't so much as landed on me once.

"You lose something?"

The question causes his gaze to collide with mine, worry and fear running rampant in those forest depths as he says a single word.

"Elijah."

My brows shoot up. "You lost a kid?"

A grimace appears on his face. "Can we go with misplaced?"

"How do you misplace an entire human being?" I ask, equally amused and concerned. "A shoe or a key or something, sure. But a person would—"

"Yeah, I got it," he snaps, still panicked and on edge. Probably more so thanks to my jeering.

"And you've checked the cafeteria? They were supposed to go there right from the hike for dinner."

Kaleb shakes his head. "He's not there."

Well, shit.

"What about the bathhouse? Colin's office? His cabin? You checked there too?" I ask, listing any of the places I can think the kid might be.

"Yes, obviously." He starts raking his fingers through the thicker brown hair on the top, creating a haphazard mess. "No one's seen him since the hike. I have no idea where he is, and I figured with how you two were talking earlier, he might be here or have said something to you."

"Not at all." The small amount of worry in my gut grows as I grab a clean camp tee and slide it over my head. "But we can go look for him."

"And what about the other kids?"

I arch a brow. "They're eleven, Kaleb, and there are other counselors in the dining hall. We can leave them to eat dinner without us while we look for him."

"Goddamnit," he mutters, glancing at me again. "Fine, but we should split up and cover more ground."

"Fine by me."

I toe into my shoes again, doing my best to ignore the painful blisters and scrapes covering my feet, and follow him down the steps of my cabin.

"How do you wanna do this?" I ask, falling into step with him as we rush down the path toward the lodge.

"I'll keep looking around the center of the complex. Maybe he's just moving while I am, so I'm always missing him. You check the paths to the other cabins. And maybe some other areas of the grounds. Over by Glass Lake, the clearing. I doubt he'd wander off that far, but at least we're covering all our bases."

He stops once we reach the outside of the lodge and hands me one of the walkie-talkies we've been using on hikes and other excursions. "Radio in if you find him. If you don't, meet me back here in an hour and we can…"

The way he trails off tells me he's clearly thinking the worst. Hell, I wouldn't be lying if I wasn't too. This is probably every camp counselor's nightmare, especially deep into the wilderness like this, the nearest town almost ten miles away. The only way to make it worse would be if it was dark…which it will be in a couple hours.

Without thinking, I place my hand on his arm and give a comforting squeeze, not taking into account the way it would amplify the electricity crackling in the air between us. It's something that's almost constant now when we're around each other.

"We'll find him. Don't worry."

His Adam's apple bobs as he swallows harshly, and he nods. "We'll find him."

After a couple seconds, the burn of his skin beneath my palm becomes impossible to ignore—as does the hissing sound in my head, slowly turning into a snarl—and I pull my hand away. Yet our gazes stay locked together, harnessed by gravity or whatever else is responsible for the way we keep being pulled together like this.

"Please try not to alert anyone that we've lost a kid," he says softly, and I see the same bit of fear from when he burst into my cabin swimming in his eyes again. "Especially Colin. You know, until we're certain."

A smirk I don't entirely feel lifts the corner of my mouth. "We? Last I checked, he was lost on your watch and not mine."

The jab earns me an eye roll, effectively breaking the moment. "See you in a bit."

We part ways at the lodge, and I head up through all the rows of cabins—thinking maybe he went off and found another one of the groups—only to come up empty.

I don't have any luck up near the hiking path, and he's not in the field off the far end of the lake either. But just as I'm about to leave the field and head back in, I finally spot him.

Across the lake.

Sitting at the edge of the dock, legs dangling in the water.

Alone.

It's not until I see him that I realize how truly anxious I've been about him being missing. Relief floods through me, washing through every cell of my body. It's probably also why I take off in a dead sprint until I reach the trail leading to the dock. Swear to God, I've never run faster in my life, even with the plethora of blisters I earned today.

The second he comes into view again at the end of the path, I can finally breathe.

From this distance, he appears unharmed. And even though he's maybe fifty yards away, the slump of his back and downward droop of his head make it obvious he's upset about something.

Or like he's a child version of Atlas, the weight of the world resting on his shoulders.

Slowly, I close the distance to Elijah, and when I reach his side, I choose not to speak. Instead, I slide out of my shoes before taking a seat beside him, ready to submerge my feet in the cool lake water.

"You probably shouldn't do that," Elijah mutters without so much as looking at me. "Your blisters could get infected."

He makes a valid point, but…

"I'll take my chances," I reply, plunging my feet through the surface.

Silence lingers between us, allowing the sounds of nature to fill the void. Birds chirp off in the distance, and the wind creates small waves in the lake that lap against the edge of the dock.

It's peaceful. Calming.

Elijah might as well be an ice sculpture, giving off every *I don't want to talk* vibe possible. But as more time and silence stretches, I can almost feel him melting beside me.

And then, without any prompting, he speaks.

"I hate coming here."

I shift my attention to him, treading carefully with my response. "To the lake?"

"Alpine Ridge," he corrects, kicking his feet in the water. "It sucks here."

I've got to give Colin credit; he's spot-on about Elijah not enjoying his time here. But that didn't seem to be the case earlier today on the hike, and I wonder what's changed since then.

"You're telling me you didn't have fun today?"

His brow raises, but he still doesn't look at me. "You think climbing mountains is fun? It's literally walking uphill to nowhere before turning around and going back down."

My lips quirk, because, yeah. Hiking is kind of insane when you put it in that perspective.

"And you didn't have a good time out here earlier this week?" I ask, arching a brow. "All the kayaking and stuff?"

This time, all I get is a headshake.

"Then why do you keep coming? I mean, I know your uncle runs the place, but…" I trail off, purposely leaving the sentence open-ended so he can fill it as he pleases. Hopefully he does, giving me more than a couple short words as an answer.

When those two saucers for eyes finally move away from the water and look up at me, I can see the breakthrough we're about to make.

"I don't really have a choice. Dad wants me to come. Make friends, be outside, *experience the world*," he says, a bit of mocking sarcasm laced in his tone on the last one. There's a shrug of indifference before he adds, "So I just do it, even if none of those things actually happen."

"You have friends, though," I point out. I've seen him laugh and joke around with some of the other boys at lunch or during the activities. In fact, never once during this past week would I have thought he was the same kid Colin described to me on the first day.

Not until this moment.

A soft snort comes from him. "Maybe we get along, but those guys aren't my friends."

I bite my lip before hedging, "Dayton and Colton seem nice. They're your bunkmates, right? And from what I understand, they've been coming here just as long as you have."

This time I get another shrug. "I always feel like a third wheel because of their whole…twin bond thing."

"What about Liam or Jordan or Bradley?" I ask, listing off a bunch of kids in our group. "I've seen you laughing and joking with them a few times."

"They're too sporty and outdoorsy."

I know I shouldn't laugh, but I can't help the slight chuckle falling from my lips. "You're at a wilderness summer camp, kid. Isn't that the entire point?"

"That is the point," he says. "But that's not me. I'd rather spend my summer in my room—"

"If you say playing video games, I'm going to scream," I cut in. To drive the point home, I open my mouth and suck in a deep breath, ready to let it rip.

He clamps his hand over my mouth, and for the first time since I've sat down beside him, a smile creeps into his expression. "Don't tell me you're one of those adults who hates video games."

I laugh beneath his palm before pushing it from my face. "First of all, I'm *not* an adult. I might be old enough to be considered one, but I promise, I'm just as much of a kid as you are. And second, I love video games. But those are for the rainy winter days, not the insanely nice weather we get during the summer."

"Unless you're someone who hates going outside," he points out. "Then video games are great *every* day."

"Fair enough. But have you tried finding something out here that you do enjoy? Archery or the ropes course or scavenger hunts? Anything at all?"

"They're okay, but I don't really like any of it." His shoulders lift in another damn shrug before his voice comes out more lost and alone than I've ever heard it. "It makes me feel like I don't belong here."

I didn't think it was possible for my heart to break for someone else, but here I am, feeling it all the same. And I hate it for him.

Maybe because I understand what he's saying more than I care to admit.

"You're not alone in that feeling," I muse more to myself than to him. "But you know what we gotta do in the moments where we don't think we fit in?"

"I have a feeling *go home* isn't the right answer," he says, a brow arched.

"Nice try." I grin before bumping my shoulder against his. "Nah, kid. We just fake it 'til we make it."

He takes a second to mull it over before he taps his foot against mine.

"And how's that working for you? Wearing boating shoes for hiking?" he says, his tone teasing. "I mean, c'mon. Who does that?"

I chuckle, shaking my head. "I never said I was good at faking it, okay? It's a work in progress. But it's getting easier every day, just like it will for you."

Even with his nod of agreement, I can tell he's not completely sold on the idea. We've got to start somewhere, though.

"Maybe you're right."

Our conversation fades, the sounds of nature taking the place of words instead. I'm not sure how long we stay wrapped in this tranquil bubble while looking out over the alpine lake. But I do know it's the most at peace I've felt since arriving here.

The feeling doesn't last much longer, though, because when I absently glance behind us, I spot Kaleb.

He's walking down the path toward us, a mixture of relief and irritation written in his expression that's visible even from this distance. The crease in his brow and slight frown etched at the corner of his lips makes it all too apparent he's not happy to find Elijah and me here together.

Probably because I didn't do the one thing I was supposed to: call back on the walkie-talkie if I found him.

"Elijah, you're supposed to be up at the lodge for dinner right now," he says as he reaches us, eyes locked on the kid beside me.

"I don't want to eat up there," Eli mutters beside me, kicking at the water absently. "I don't want to be here at all."

Intuition hits me, and I think I understand what problem he might be having.

"Let's go up and I'll sit with you," I find myself saying before I can think better of it.

Elijah's head snaps over to me, giving me doe eyes like I just hung the moon or some shit. "Really?"

Bingo.

I shrug. "I mean, why not? There's no rules against it." *At least, I don't think there is.* But just to be sure, I glance over at Kaleb, who nods.

"There's no problem with it," Kaleb confirms. "But you do need to eat. We've had a long day, and tomorrow will be just as long. You need the energy."

Eli lets out a long, dramatic sigh. "Great. Another long, draining day in the wilderness planned for tomorrow. Just what I wanted."

The mouth on this kid. I have to roll my lips inward to keep from laughing.

"C'mon," I say before bumping his shoulder with mine. "Let's get back to the rest of the guys before we get in even more trouble."

Between hiking earlier today and running around looking for Elijah afterward, my feet are indeed two slabs of raw meat by the time dinner is over. A fact that becomes even more apparent when I take a seat back on the dock and remove my shoes to find patches of inflamed skin that sting when the cool air hits them.

"Fucking hell," I mutter under my breath, taking in the carnage.

I flick open the first aid kit I grabbed from the lodge and start on cleaning the blisters when I hear the crunching of twigs and footsteps, alerting me I'm no longer alone on the dock. And though the voice is obvious once he speaks, I could've guessed it was Kaleb without turning around.

"Thought I might find you here," he says as he drops to the wood beside me.

Lifting my gaze to collide with his reveals those green irises dancing with delight. A true *I told you so* expression sits on his smug face, and as much as I hate admitting it, I deserve it.

He was right by telling me hiking in damn boat shoes was a bad idea.

"I take it you've come to gloat?"

The corner of his mouth lifts a bit more before he juts his chin toward my feet. "Nah, I think the state of your feet does that rather disgusting job for me."

My attention shifts back to my feet, and I realize, yeah, they sure do. But at least none of them are on the bottom of my foot, which would make it entirely worse.

"Here, let me," he says, grabbing the roll of gauze before starting to wrap my left heel. He glances up at me for a moment when I don't fight him on it. "Unless you'd rather me not. But I've had enough first aid training to do this in my sleep."

All I can do is nod for him to continue, because I'm left speechless, truly unable to say a single word. Though maybe it's because my subconscious knows it's better for him to take care of it correctly rather than, once again, making a fool of myself.

Or it's due to the zaps of energy coursing through me where his skin lingers on mine that I'm desperately trying to ignore.

He keeps tending to my wounds in silence for a while, simultaneously taking in the carnage as he goes. But when he moves to my other foot, he lets out a low whistle.

"Damn, you did a number on yourself," he muses before wrapping the heel. "I have an extra pair of hiking boots, you know. So do plenty of the other counselors. All you had to do was ask around to borrow a pair in your size."

"And here I thought you said there wouldn't be any gloating," I say dryly.

"I wouldn't call it gloating so much as informing you so this doesn't happen again." He moves, wrapping a rather tender spot, and we both wince when the gauze makes contact with my skin.

"Motherfuck," I mutter. "Might be better to chop 'em off at this rate."

His mouth twitches into something of a smile. "Still might have to after you decided to stick them into the lake water earlier. You did wash them out after, right?"

I roll my eyes. "I might be inept when it comes to packing for a couple months in the wilderness, but I know basic first aid protocol."

There's another quiver of his lips, and I can tell he's fighting back another comment. Or more laughter. Hell, probably both, if I had to bet on it, and it has me flashing back to the days at the beginning of college, where we'd often toss banter back and forth. But that's all in the past now, and I doubt that'll change anytime soon.

Thankfully, he doesn't make a peep while he continues wrapping gauze around my foot, which might be the only good thing to happen today—apart from my conversations with Elijah this evening.

His willingness to talk with me about what's bothering him is the first time I've actually felt useful since arriving here. Honestly, it was probably the first time in a while I've felt understood by someone else.

And it was talking to a freaking preteen.

But that's because I get it; I've been on the side of not fitting in. Of not feeling comfortable being myself or showing who I really am to the people around me. Of trying to be the person my father wants me to be. And look what it's done. I've become jaded and guarded, cutting off any and every type of relationship at the knees. It's isolating, living like this, and it's something I can see in Elijah too.

The last thing I want is to see the kid go down the same road I did. So even if it might not be my place, here I am, inserting myself anyway.

"I need to ask you for a favor," I hedge, my hand swishing in the water while Kaleb continues to work.

He glances up from his task, a hint of a smile on his lips. "Asking for boots now isn't gonna help the situation. But yeah, you can use mine next time."

"Very funny," I mutter, laying the sarcasm on thick, because that's not where I was going with this—though I will definitely put a pin in his offer for later. No way in hell I want to deal with the pain and embarrassment of him playing nurse to my stupidity all over again.

Kaleb is sure getting amusement out of it, though. Which grates on my damn nerves as always, but I'm still thankful for him helping me right now. He doesn't owe me anything, especially when we've been butting heads since the moment I arrived.

"What is it you really wanted to ask?"

I tap my fingers against the worn wood of the dock and wet my lips. "Do you think your brothers would bring Elijah into their circle a bit? Is that something you can make happen?"

A weird expression crosses his face at my request, his lips parting slightly, and those forest-green eyes widening a bit. It's some mixture of bewilderment and…maybe awe? All I know is he's looking at me like he doesn't even recognize me. Or like I've been body snatched by someone who actually gives a shit about anyone other than myself.

Then again, this very well might be the first time it's ever happened, so I can't really blame him.

His attention flicks away from me to the water as his mouth snaps closed. Even when he clears his throat, his voice still comes out a little graveled. "I'll see what I can do. Or Colin can."

The last thing that kid wants is his uncle coming to his rescue, trying to make friends for him. It sure as hell wouldn't do a whole lot to help him feel included or less alone.

And the entire point of me being placed with Eli's group was so Colin *didn't* have to worry about him this summer.

"Don't involve Colin," I tell him with a shake of my head. "It'll only make the situation worse."

"And what is the situation, exactly?"

Divulging something Elijah has told me in confidence doesn't feel right, but neither does sitting on this information if there are any ideas Kaleb might have to help him. After all, he's known the kid far longer than I have.

I blow out a long breath and shake my head. "He hates it here. Thinks of himself as an outsider. Feels like he doesn't belong."

Understanding crosses Kaleb's face, but he doesn't look all that surprised as he nods.

"I wish I could say I wasn't expecting that answer, but he's been that way since his first year here. Very closed off and fearful of rejection," he says as he finishes dressing my wounds. "But not with you. You've gotten through to him more in the past week than I've managed to in three years. Something I'd be annoyed by if I wasn't grateful he's at least opening up to someone."

I sigh and roll my shoulders, like it would be enough to get rid of the anxiety, stress, and worry knotted in them. "It doesn't feel like enough."

When I lift my gaze to meet his again, he's wearing that same expression from earlier. The one reading like he's never seen me until right now, and it brings back the awful feeling of being paper thin. Transparent as glass.

"Why do you keep looking at me like that?" I snap, my discomfort coming out as irritation.

He looks away quickly and shakes his head, but a smile hints at the corner of his lips. "I don't know. You're just really good with him. It's different than I expected."

Yeah, well, I can't say I expected it either. But being fucked up by the expectations of a parent has a way of bonding people, no matter how different they might seem at the surface. Doesn't mean I want Kaleb to see that part of me, though. If he does, it's terrifying to think he might see even more things he's not supposed to.

"Gotta mix it up sometimes," I deadpan, attention fixated on checking my palms for invisible slivers to keep from looking at him. "Being an asshole all the time would just make me predictable. Better to keep everyone on their toes."

"Yeah, that's gotta be it," he murmurs, and when I hear the amusement in his voice, I'm forced to look up after all.

A full-on grin sits on his lips now, and I think it's the first time I've ever seen him smile at me. A real smile, not one of those patronizing or smug ones I've been getting since I arrived here. This is just pure…I don't know.

Happiness seems like the wrong word. It's almost like he's seeing something I'm not, and it makes me more unsettled; the same swirling feeling in my gut returning to accompany the electric buzz between us.

"It is."

He lets out something between a laugh and a scoff. "Couldn't possibly be that you actually give a shit about the kid, right?"

My lips form into a thin line and I shake my head. "Nope. Just doing my job."

And when Elijah goes home to tell his dad about his awesome counselor who helped him get through the summer at a camp he hates going to, there's no way in hell I won't get back into Foltyn.

He's a means to an end. The win-win Colin offered me. That's it.

At least, that's what I'm trying to tell myself.

SEVEN

Kaleb

A few more days pass without incident, and the end of the week means a nighttime group activity. Tonight is campfires and s'mores, and even at almost twenty-one years old, it's gotta be my favorite pastime of coming to summer camp at Alpine Ridge. Even if it's something that isn't a guarantee here, thanks to fire bans usually coming into effect by the beginning of July. But we had a wet spring this year and plan to take advantage of the opportunity for roasting marshmallows on the fire until the forest dries up and we can't anymore.

Of course, wrangling a group of eleven-year-olds to sit still—even for snacks and treats—is a lot harder than it seems. I don't know if it's because I'm young enough for them to see me as cool but not old enough for them to truly respect me when I tell them to do something. I just know it's frustrating as hell, especially when they want to try testing my patience.

Liam and Jordan in particular have been doing it constantly this year. Of course, knowing I'm Day and Cole's older brother is the most likely reason they think pushing the limits won't get them in trouble in the first place.

"Do you think your parents are gonna let you come back here if one of you loses an eye from running around play-fighting with sticks?" I ask the two of them when they're busy swinging their marshmallow-tipped sticks at each other like they're swords. But my point does little to sway them into behaving, because they straight up ignore me.

"If you two don't sit down and listen, I'll walk you back to your cabin right now," Avery says, not even looking up from where he's shoving marshmallows on Elijah's and Max's sticks. And while I expect them to ignore him just like they did me, I'm shocked to find they actually do as he says without any complaint.

Well, I'll be damned.

After everyone has their s'more and no one is asking for seconds, I lean over toward Avery and murmur, "How'd you do that?"

Avery's eyes flick up to meet my gaze. "What do you mean?"

Doing my best to keep my voice low and not disturb the moment of peace and quiet, I elaborate. "Get them to calm down so fast."

A frown furrows his brow together and he shrugs. "I don't know. I just told them what I wouldn't wanna hear at their age."

"I do the same thing and it only works half the time."

"Maybe it's because they know you're a pushover," he says nonchalantly.

My jaw drops open, and before I think better of it, I give him a playful shove on the shoulder. "The hell I am."

"Keep telling yourself that, LaMothe," he taunts before moving toward the empty spot on the opposite side of the fire.

I watch him, wondering how the hell the person I'm seeing in front of me is the same guy who used that photo to out one of our teammates. It's like I'm staring at the version of him I thought I knew freshman year, and it doesn't compute properly in my brain as I take the final vacant seat between two of the kids.

All of us settle in, the crackling from the fire and the soft whistle of the wind floating through the trees creating a calming effect over the group. It's one of my favorite things about being out here every summer. Being one with nature. Feeling so small and insignificant inside a much larger whole.

It puts my soul at ease.

But not as much as it normally would, and I know the reason is sitting directly across from me.

The light from the flames illuminates his entire face, casting a warm glow over the sharp lines and planes of his nose and cheekbones. A bit of stubble has grown in on his jaw and cheeks, adding a more rugged look to him than I'm used to seeing. Aging him a bit too, so he looks more mid-to-late-twenties rather than only a few months older than me.

And I hate how much more attractive it makes him.

I know if I keep looking at him that way, he's bound to catch on. Or worse, catch me in the act, and that's going to cause more issues, which is the last thing—

"We should play a game," Jordan says, breaking through my thoughts.

I'm all for a game, especially if it means escaping being put on the spot to tell ghost stories like last year on fire nights. I'm not much of a storyteller in general, and games are the perfect way to save me from a repeat embarrassment.

I lean forward, elbows resting on my knees. "What kind of game were you thinking?"

Jordan glances at Colton, then to Liam. "That TikTok game might work, right?"

"TikTok game?" I ask.

"The 'put a finger down' one," my brother supplies as he looks at me. "You know the one."

I can't help the laugh that comes bursting out. "You're talking about Never Have I Ever."

"No, it's called Put a Finger Down," Liam insists.

"Yeah, but it's based on Never Have I Ever." I look between all the boys, each of whom are staring at me like I've lost my damn mind. "You just say 'never have I ever' and then finish the sentence with something you've never done. And anyone who has done it has to put a finger down. Last person with at least one finger up is the winner."

"Why would you say a bunch of things you've never done?" Jordan asks, face all scrunched up in confusion.

"Sounds kinda lame," Liam surmises, looking around the fire for confirmation from his friends and peers. Which he gets from a good majority of them.

Fucking kids these days.

And yes, I understand how much even thinking that sentence makes me sound like my grandparents.

"It's more fun this way, I promise." My gaze instantly shifts to Avery across the fire, and I give him a pleading look for some kind of backup here. Lord knows he's played this at least once in his life.

Of course, in a shocking turn of events, there's no backup to be found.

"Don't look at me." He crosses his arms over his chest. "I'm not involved in this."

That's what he might think. "Oh, yes you are. You'll be playing too."

A deep frown draws down the corners of his lips. "For real?"

"Absolutely. Participation in camp activities is mandatory." I arch a brow at him. "I take it you've got some skeletons in the closet you're reluctant to share?"

Avery's scowl deepens, and with the fire casting an eerie glow across his face, he looks more like a murderous psychopath ready to run rampant through the camp with a chainsaw than a regular ole college student.

Or *ex* college student, rather.

But he doesn't complain or make another peep as the boys take their turns going around the campfire. They're listing off things so ridiculous—never have I ever been to the moon or seen an alien, being two of them—and no one has put a single finger down by the time it gets over to Avery on the opposite side of the fire.

"I don't think you're understanding how the game works," he mutters, looking at one of my brothers who is seated beside him. Not that I can blame him, because Dayton just said "never have I ever died."

Then again, Colton is the twin who got most of the brains while they shared a womb.

"Never have I ever attended summer camp," Avery says, and I watch as every single boy puts a finger down. Myself included.

"You need to put a finger down too," Dayton grouses when he notices Avery still has all five fingers up.

"I work here. I've never *attended* one. There's a difference."

A lot of eyes roll at his technicality, and they keep going right around the circle.

Now that the boys understand the goal better, they get a little more competitive and ruthless. Some of them purposely start going for each other, trying to get their friends out. Some of them try coming for Avery and me too, saying they've never graduated high school or played college baseball before.

Elijah, who has been very quiet and keeping to himself since his little runaway incident, even gets in on the fun. He stares Avery dead in the eye as he says, "Never have I ever worn boat shoes to go hiking."

"You're dead to me," Avery says as he puts down his third finger, and I can't help but chuckle at the entire exchange.

Meanwhile, I'm still sitting here with only one more finger to go, and at this rate, I'll be the first one out. And while it's just all fun and games with a bunch of kids, my competitive side just can't help it.

So when I see both of my brothers sitting there with two fingers left, I go in to even the score a bit.

"Never have I ever had a twin."

The death glare Dayton and Colton give me as they each go down to a single finger could melt ice. But the kids, my brothers included, seem to be having a good time with it, and that's what matters most. Of course, there are still a few off-the-wall statements just to be funny as we circle around again for the second time, but I'll chalk it up to kids being kids.

It moves to Liam next, who honestly looks ready to jump out of his seat with excitement for his turn; he's practically overflowing with anticipation. And I'll take that any day over the lot of them being bored.

"Never have I ever…" Liam says, eyes flicking around the campfire deviously. "Kissed another boy."

The instant his words register, a cold sweat breaks out over my skin.

I'm comfortable in my sexuality, having learned a long time ago that being gay is nothing to be ashamed of. It's one of many reasons I'm out to my entire family: brothers, aunts, grandparents and all. Even some of my friends back at Foltyn, like my roommate Daniel, are aware of it. It's nothing I'm trying to hide from the world, even if I'm not out screaming it from the rooftops.

It's simply part of who I am.

Broadcasting it in front of Avery is something entirely different, though. There's no telling how he'll react, but if past circumstances are anything to go on, I know it won't be good.

Which is why I have every intention of lying in front of all these kids, if only to save my own ass.

Except, I catch the way Colton and Dayton glance over at me, waiting expectantly for me to put a finger down. Because they're smart enough to know I should be.

Fucking shit.

Slowly, I lower my last remaining finger to my palm, effectively knocking me out of the game. But doing it as discreetly as possible does nothing to stop the few gasps echoing around the campfire.

"Wait, you've kissed a *boy*?" Liam says, his nose a little scrunched up. "You're not supposed to."

I quickly gather myself, answering to get ahead of any negative connotations that the boys might associate with the queer community. "Who says you're not supposed to?"

"Like, everyone."

I shake my head. "See, that's where you're wrong. You can kiss whoever you want, as long as you have their permission."

"But doesn't kissing another boy make you gay?" asks Max.

My lips roll inward on instinct, and *fuck,* I don't really want to go here right now. Especially when I can feel the heat from Avery's attention locked on me. But to hell if I'm going to let any of these kids think there's something wrong with having a sexuality other than straight.

"Why do you say it like it's a bad thing?" When Max or none of the other boys answer, I continue. "But no. There is such a thing as an innocent kiss between two people who happen to be the same gender. It doesn't automatically make you gay. Plus, there's bisexual, for one, which is when you like boys and girls." I pause, debating about diving deeper into things like pan or ace, but then decide better of it. It's a topic for another time, probably when they're a bit older.

"So which one are you?" This comes from Jordan.

My teeth sink into the fleshy part of my cheek before I say the words I told myself I'd never be ashamed of.

"I do happen to be gay."

From the silence that descends over the fire and furrowed brows all around, it's clear they're processing. Hell, I'm doing my best too, but it's almost impossible when I feel Avery staring at me.

I don't have to look at him to confirm it; the heat from the roaring fire has nothing on the scorching blaze his eyes locked on my face are creating. It burns holes right through me until I'm seared to a crisp.

And when I do finally garner the balls to meet his gaze from across the fire, I swear I might burst into fucking flames.

I'm a goddamn glass house, and my brothers just threw rocks at all the windows and walls, breaking and shattering them pane by pane. It was an accident, nothing malicious behind their expectations to out myself. Because, to them, it wouldn't be *outing* myself; they were simply waiting for me to tell the truth.

Too bad the truth is going to have massive repercussions.

EIGHT

Avery

Kaleb and I get all the kids into their cabins without argument, despite us making the poor decision to hop them up on sugar an hour before we're expecting them to climb into bed. Even Bradley, who has been notorious the past week for bouncing around between bunks in his, Liam, and Max's cabin, doesn't fight us on it.

Guess that's what happens after a long day in the sun followed by staying up late around the campfire. No sugar rush can fight that level of exhaustion.

After I'm done checking the cabins to the left of the trail, I turn to find Kaleb. I can make out his silhouette heading toward me as he finishes checking on the cabins to the right.

"All good?" he asks, shoving his hands into the pockets of his bomber jacket.

He's looked good all night—plaid flannel and camp tee beneath the caramel colored fabric. A pair of dark washed jeans hug his legs in a way that makes it seem like they were made for him, and after almost two weeks out here, his stubble has grown out into something of a short beard.

All things still noticeable in the moonlight cutting through the trees.

All things I hate myself for noticing.

"Yeah," I say a little too stiffly, trying to ignore my rolling stomach. "We're all good."

"Great." He pauses, awkwardly rubbing the back of his neck. "I'm gonna go double check the fire, but you can head off to bed."

My brows crash together in confusion. "We flooded it with enough water to drown a fish before taking the kids to their cabins," I remind him.

He blinks a couple times and shakes his head. "Well, I still gotta clean up around it. Get the food back in the lodge so we don't attract any animals to the grounds."

Not bothering to wait for a response, he starts back toward the pit. And that's when I realize he's looking for any excuse to get away from me. For whatever reason, I can't let it happen, though. Can't stand the thought of him walking away and…fuck, I don't know.

After the shit just aired during that stupid game, I don't know fucking anything.

Which is why I close the distance between us before falling in step beside him. "I can help you. I don't mind."

"You really don't have to."

"Okay," I say slowly. "But isn't it kind of my job?"

He doesn't answer, just keeps walking. If possible, at an even quicker pace. But he can't outrun me, similar to how I can't outrun all the thoughts and questions racing through my brain, thanks to his candor with the kids.

And it's those thoughts that cause me to break through the stagnant silence floating between us.

"You did good with them tonight." When he glances up at me, I add,

"With the kids, I mean."

I catch the faint tic of his jaw. "I certainly hope so. It's kind of my job."

The clear echoing of my statement from a moment ago isn't lost on me, and while his poking fun like that would normally set my blood to boil, this time it forces an awkward laugh out of me.

"No, I just mean…like how you handled everything."

There's no hint of understanding on his face before he turns away again, and it frustrates me to hell. I don't know if he's pretending to be dense or if I'm really not being clear about what I'm trying to say.

Hell, I'm not even sure I know what I'm trying to get at. Or where I'm hoping this conversation will go. I just know there are so many things I want to ask and know, and I have no idea how to verbalize them without sounding like a complete idiot.

"You know, with the whole…being gay thing."

God, could I be any more of a fucking imbecile?

The look on his face tells me he's thinking the exact same thing. It also tells me this is not a conversation he wants to be having right now, especially if the way his lips curve down is anything to go off.

"Yeah," is all he says, a rough gravel to his tone now, before he looks over at me. "Is it going to be a problem?"

I wish I fucking knew.

There was a roar of disgust inside my head when the truth slipped out earlier, but in the moments since, it's sunk back into the recesses of my mind. With it gone, I feel like I'm staring at the same infuriating guy I've known for three years.

At least, I thought I knew him. Now, I'm not so sure.

"I just…I thought you were straight."

A sharp scoff comes from him, and he shakes his head before glaring at me. "Why? Because straight is the default?"

The question takes me aback, mostly because I've never thought about it in that way. But now since he's said it, I realize I really have seen it as the standard for everyone I meet. I assume they're straight.

Same way everyone assumes I am.

"I'm sorry, I didn't—"

He tosses a hand out, waving me off. "Save it. You wouldn't be the first, and I doubt you'll be the last."

We reach the fire pit then, and we both start gathering the remaining boxes of graham crackers, chocolate, and marshmallows before heading into the lodge's kitchen to put them away. And since I'm not sure what to say after his dismissal, awkward silence stifles us the entire time.

But the silence gives me time to think, and right now, thinking is the last thing I should be doing. All my mind can seem to focus on is the fact that Kaleb is gay, and I'm—

Repulsive. Absolutely disgusting!

The voice—the one fraught with shame and outrage that I can never manage to block out—is snarling in my head now, digging its claws in as I watch him lock the back door again. Which is exactly what I should do with these feelings that've been rapidly increasing since he walked into Colin's office my first day here. Lock them up. Immediately. Shove them in a box at the back of my mind and throw away the fucking key.

There's no other option.

Still, I'm itching to say something—to break this overwhelming silence—as we make our way back toward the cabins. But I can't think of anything at this point.

Hell, what do you say to someone who was all but outed by his brothers in front of twenty-plus people—and one of them was the guy who did the exact same thing to one of your friends, but on a much larger scale?

Realization smacks me square in the face at the thought, and it's enough to stop me dead in my tracks. My sudden halt must take Kaleb off guard, because he stops too, annoyance and a tiny amount of concern mixed together in his expression as I blink at him.

"Wait, is this why you're pissed at me? Why you went to Coach about the photo?" I ask. "Because you're gay too?"

His brows crash together even more, and if that weren't enough to alert me of my mistake, then the sharp tone of his voice sure as hell does the job.

"Not that it matters to you, but Keene is *bi*, not gay. And though you don't actually give two shits, no, they aren't the same thing either. Like I pointed out to the kids."

I open my mouth, but he cuts me off before I get a word in edgewise.

"And for the record," he snarls, closing the space between us and pressing a finger into my chest. "I turned you in because what you did was a piece of shit thing to do. My sexuality has nothing to do with it."

I'd almost be convinced if it weren't for the small amount of apprehension lingering in those eyes. It'd be damn near impossible to hide when we're this close. Even earlier tonight at the fire, as his secret was shared, I caught a glimpse of something similar.

And the alarm, no matter how slight, tells me one thing.

He's lying.

"Your mouth is saying one thing, but your eyes are saying another, LaMothe."

The tension between us is laced with something a little more potent than it normally is. It's become this overwhelming urge to just throw him against the nearest hard surface and kiss him until neither of us can breathe, crashing into me with lust-filled waves.

And it only gets worse when he steps in closer, nostrils flared with anger.

"Fuck off, Reynolds. You don't know shit about me."

The desire coursing through me spikes with a mixture of anger, bringing my blood to a boiling point. He must realize it too, because the finger against my chest flattens into a palm before he pushes me away. Not enough to cause a stumble, just to garner a bit of space.

But it sets me right the fuck off.

Just not in the way I'd ever expect.

Because, instead of throwing a fist in his face or spewing some hateful words the way my mind is craving to, I wrap my hand around the back of his neck and slam my mouth to his.

A soft yelp comes from him, probably out of shock, and it gives me the opportunity to slip my tongue past his lips. The first brush it makes against his sends a bolt of lust all the way to my cock, and as they tangle together, a deep groan rumbles from within his chest. One I swallow down with hunger, greedy for more.

Because this is it. What I've been searching for. What I've been dying to have.

What's been missing all these years because I've been too much of a coward to allow myself to have it.

But at this moment, none of that matters. Nothing does except the sweeping press of my lips on his. And, after a few moments of hesitation on his part...the way it feels for him to kiss me back.

My hand at the back of his neck snakes up, curling into the hair at the back of his head to anchor him in place. The other grabs his hip as I back him toward the closest tree, and the second his back collides with it, I press my entire body weight against him. I continue devouring him like my life depends on it in what is sure to be the greatest kiss of my life.

Which is…fucking insane. But it's the truth.

Even while this—touching another man—is something I've been taught is unnatural and disgusting my whole life, something that feels this good can't be wrong. No matter how many times I've been told differently or how foreign the concept might be.

It is *wrong! You vile, worthless scum!*

But the snarling in my head is quickly drowned out by the feel and taste of him, allowing me to lose myself in the moment and let instinct take over.

I roll my hips into his, eliciting another groan, this time from both of us. And God, if it isn't fucking amazing. Everything about this is.

The scratch and scrape of his facial hair against my skin.

The firmness of his body, even through his clothes.

The thick ridge of his cock rubbing mine through our jeans.

The way his fingers dig into my hips beneath my hoodie as he truly gives in, kissing me back with the same passionate fury.

His teeth sink into my bottom lip—the bite of pain causing my dick to throb painfully behind my zipper—and when he releases it, the faint taste of blood hits my tongue. It spurs me on and makes me kiss him harder.

We grapple for control over one another, dueling with our tongues and hands while our hips keep bumping and rocking together. I think he's about to wrap his fists in my hoodie and pull me closer when his palms move up to my pecs. Or maybe spin me around and pin me against the tree instead, pressing against me to the point where there's not a single air molecule between our bodies.

But he does none of those things, and instead, he flattens them against my chest to push me away for the second time tonight. Enough to not only break our connection but send me stumbling blindly backward.

His chest is heaving like he's just run a marathon as he glares at me with a mixture of rage and lust. "What the fucking hell, Reynolds?" he seethes.

Shit.

I'm sure he wants an answer, but I'm too busy staring at him in the dim moonlight while I wait for the world to shift back onto its axis. Only it doesn't. It stays tilted, and the whole thing has me off balance.

I must be out of my goddamn mind. The fresh mountain air, the sun beating down on us from dawn to dusk, and spending every waking moment in the forest must really be fucking with my sanity. It can be the only explanation for what is happening to me. Why I can't seem to fight the lust running rampant through my system.

"Reynolds?" he says again, and it's clear from his tone he wants an answer.

Too bad for both of us, I don't have one.

I lick my lips, and I swear I can still taste his on them. Feel where they just were, their sudden disappearance creating a cooling effect on mine. There's a burning rawness to them from where his stubble was scraping against my skin too—something I didn't know I'd enjoy.

Replaying every second of that kiss like it's my life force isn't what needs to happen right now, yet it's all my brain seems capable of. But then I feel it. The voice, crawling its way to the front of my mind. Sinking its talons deep enough, I actually wince when it speaks to me.

You wretched monstrosity. What have you done?

The words echo in my mind, bouncing off the inside of my skull in rapid succession, and soon enough, I'll be buried by it. Lost beneath piles of self-loathing and regret.

I need to be far, *far* away from Kaleb when it happens.

So I do the only logical thing.

I turn and flee, disappearing down the path to my cabin at a speed Usain Bolt would be jealous of. I don't stop until I'm locked safely inside, my back slamming against the wooden door before sliding down it.

And then the shame spiral consumes me.

NINE

Kaleb

I'm left leaning against the tree I was just mauled against—alone and painfully hard—fixated on the moonlit path Avery just disappeared down.

The immediate urge to run after him and demand answers hits me, but I fight it tooth and nail. Knowing I'd probably come up empty handed anyway helps me garner enough self-control not to give in, and God only knows the state I'd find him in if I listened to my instincts. So instead, I rush inside my cabin, grab a change of clothes and my toiletries, and head off to the shower.

The hope is that some time alone to process this, rather than rashly following him, might give me some insight into why in the ever-loving fuck Avery—one of the biggest homophobes I've ever met—would pin me to a tree and kiss me like I was the air he breathes.

No matter how many times I work through it, any attempt to understand is in vain.

The cornerstone for all the theories I come up with can't possibly be true.

Because that would mean…

I shove my thoughts to the side and do my best to focus on the task at hand. But every move I make as I shower is on autopilot, and my mind is pulled back to one single idea. The only one that makes sense.

He's got the same secret I do.

Did.

The semantics of it all doesn't change the mere idea from being enough to drive me crazy.

Not more than twenty minutes later, I'm dressed in a pair of plaid cotton pants and a Foltyn baseball hoodie and heading back to my cabin for the night. My time in the shower didn't do much to wash away the taste and feel of him. They're both permanently embedded in the forefront of my brain now, and there's no sign of forgetting anytime soon. These errant and frustrating thoughts continue racing long after I turn out the lights, and no amount of tossing and turning on my mattress has any effect on calming them down. The quiet only makes it worse, the frustrating thoughts from earlier creeping back in with a vengeance.

And I realize if I've got any hope of sleeping tonight, I need answers.

Unfortunately, there's only one way I'm gonna be getting them.

Not bothering to talk myself out of it, I rip the covers off and slip into a pair of shoes before I barrel down the steps to set out deeper down the wooded path. It's shrouded in quiet darkness, nothing more than the moonlight slicing through the thick conifers to light the way. When I reach Avery's cabin, I find it in a similar state.

Dark.

There's no soft glow of a lamp coming through the window. No sound coming from inside either. Neither fact is enough to stop me from storming up the steps and slamming my fist on the door.

"Avery. We need to talk," I say through the door, still pounding on the wood.

There's no answer for a minute, but then the door is ripped open hard enough to come right off the hinges.

I can't see much more than Avery's silhouette through the blackness, but it's enough to know he's there. No doubt glaring at me for waking him in the midst of his beauty sleep.

"What are you doing?" he hisses, though his voice is still riddled with gravel and shards of glass. "You're gonna wake the kids, beating your damn fist on the door like you're a deranged maniac."

"Oh, now I'm the insane one?" I snap, stepping through the doorway and letting the door fall closed behind me. Because I don't give a shit about anything other than answers right now. If any of the kids wake up—and I doubt they will—we'll deal with it later.

The second I'm closed in the darkness with him, confined in such close proximity, I realize my mistake.

Because even after the short amount of time we've been here, this cabin smells like him. Overwhelmingly so. Ocean salt and citrus invade my nostrils, and when I attempt to focus on something else, I realize I can hear every little breath each of us takes.

The darkness has heightened all my senses, and I don't know how I can feel him without his touch, but I can. His presence in the room is layered over me like a second skin. Enough to set my every nerve on edge, but the lack of physical connection keeps what remains of my sanity intact.

Yeah, I really didn't think this through.

Silence lingers between us as I drown in wonder and in him. Then I'm breaking through the quiet like I'm bursting through the sea in search of oxygen.

"What are you doing here?" I murmur into the void.

No sound comes from wherever he is, then I hear the faint click of the lamp, and I'm temporarily blinded as light floods the room. After blinking a few times, I find him leaning against the opposite wall.

Shirtless, with only a pair of gray sweats hanging low on his hips that showcase a spectacular V tapering into the waistband.

Yeah, this really wasn't a good idea.

Avery crosses his arms over his chest, his muscles moving and flexing beneath his tanned skin. "You're asking me? You're the one who just barged in here after midnight like you own the damn place."

"I meant *here*. At Alpine Ridge."

Because the real reason can't be to kiss me and drive me fucking mad with lust that makes absolutely no sense for me to have.

"You're back on this shit? Seriously?" His fingers sift through his golden hair, frustration evident in his voice. "Couldn't it have just waited 'til morning?"

My teeth scrape over my bottom lip and I shake my head. "I need answers."

To more than one thing.

The look on his face is one of exhaustion. Physical, but also mental. Like he too has reached his breaking point. Maybe that's why, for the first time in over a week, I get a real answer from him.

"I'm trying to get back into Foltyn."

I blink, registering an answer I wasn't expecting. "And somehow you think spending the summer with a bunch of kids in the woods is going to make the dean, and the entire admissions office, rethink their decision to kick you out?"

He opens his mouth, clearly about to pop off at me, but I'm taken off guard when he closes it again without saying a single word. Then his lips form into a tight line, two tiny dimples popping at the corners of his mouth when he does it, like he's trying to keep from saying something he might regret. Which is…very unlike the Avery I've come to know.

His blue gaze flicks around the cabin, clearly in search of a way out of this conversation. But he must not find a single escape route, because he sighs and mutters, "It was my dad's idea."

"Your dad's idea," I repeat dryly.

"It sounds insane even to my own ears, but yeah." The exhaustion on his face gives way to a hint of misery when his attention lands on me. "He thinks if I can get Colin to like me, he might talk to Dean Marshall on my behalf."

For what might be the twentieth time today, he surprises me. Not only by the honesty in his answer, but how easily he offered it up.

My immediate reaction to this information is to go into protective mode. Specifically for Elijah, who is sure to be nothing more than another pawn in this whole scheme. God only knows the impact this knowledge would have on the kid if he learned the counselor who's taken him under his wing is only doing so because of some messed-up, self-serving ulterior motive.

He'd be crushed.

"That's…"

"Ridiculous?" Avery supplies.

"Disgusting," I say instead, my nose wrinkled up to echo my statement. "It's disgusting that you'd stoop to this level. And I'm sure now, you're using a kid to get to his father?"

A sharp scoff comes from him. "Like I said, it wasn't my idea to start with, but I'm not really left with much of a choice. If I want a degree by the end of next school year, Foltyn is the place I need to get it."

"And Elijah's just collateral."

He winces. "That's not true, and you know it."

"Do I?" I counter, taking a single step toward him. "Because you sure as hell were quick to deny it the other day. And that boy, for whatever reason, looks up to you. He thinks you care about him. All you're going to do is break his damn heart when he finds out it was all a lie."

The eyes staring back at me harden into ice as his tongue toys with the inside of his cheek. And again, I can see him gaining as much control as he can over his emotions.

"Think what you want, Kaleb," he finally says, tone flat and empty. "Because I know you just want to keep on living with this image you have of me in your head, not willing to alter it even when I've proven to be more than you see me as."

Wetting my lips, I shake my head. "I guess we're at an impasse, then, because I don't think you've proven a thing. A few soft moments in the forest while you're away from the real world doesn't erase all the bullshit from earlier this year."

That gets to him, causing the line of his jaw to tic and pulse as he clenches his teeth. "Fine. If that's the case, we're done here." When I make no move to leave, he continues. "You can go now. I'd like to go back to sleep."

But I still don't go. Don't fucking move from the spot my feet are anchored to like a lifeline. I can't leave until the question—the entire reason I came here in the first place—is answered. Until the burning in my mind is finally put to rest.

"Why did you kiss me?"

And how the fuck are you so good at pretending it didn't happen at all?

Just like that, I watch as he shutters off. Instantly shifting back into the guarded, hostile asshole I've known him to be.

"Call it a momentary lapse in judgment."

Liar.

My arms cross over my chest, and I shake my head. He's not getting out of this that easily. Not if I have anything to say about it.

"Try again. With the real answer this time."

His face takes on the appearance of chiseled stone, but it's nothing more than a mask. Hard and unyielding, perfectly smooth and showing no way to slip beneath it.

He closes the space between us until he's directly in front of me, once again trying to use the inch of height he has on me to his advantage. Daggers form in his eyes as they glare into my soul, and he cocks his head to the side.

"What do you want me to say, Kaleb? Tell me what you wanna hear, and I'll fucking say it."

Frustration sets in as I realize the only thing this conversation is gonna get me is a trip to the nuthouse. And maybe Avery a trip to the morgue. I'm about ready to send him six feet under if these games he's playing don't end soon.

"I really don't like you," I tell him suddenly, as if that weren't completely obvious. "You're a preppy, rich asshole who thinks only of yourself because you're under this delusion that you're better than everyone else around you. And I can't stand it."

I'd be doing myself a favor by remembering that.

He doesn't miss a beat, snarling out his own comeback. "And you're a smug, overly-confident dickhead who loves nothing more than saying *I told you so*. And as if that weren't bad enough, you're a goddamn narc to boot. So needless to say, I don't like you either."

I can feel the anger radiating off him, hitting me in wave after wave. But the tension lining his voice is off. After all, I've seen him pissed at plenty of people over the past couple years, and I'm observant enough to realize this is different.

Like it's not really *me* he's pissed at.

And I still feel something else. Something besides the anger.

A current of energy snapping back and forth, cycling in the negative space between us as it creates an electric charge powerful enough to blow the entire grounds to smithereens. It's the same feeling I got as he pinned me against the tree earlier and kissed the daylights outta me.

"Then why'd you kiss me, Avery?" I ask again, but the edge my tone possessed before is nowhere to be found this time.

And as I watch him—studying every line and feature of his face—a crack forms in that stone mask of his. Torment seeps from the fracture. More and more of it oozes to the surface until he finally lets it fall to the floor.

"I…don't know." He pauses, clears his throat. "I don't know what came over me, because I'm not…"

He doesn't continue the sentence, and honestly, I don't have it in me to force the conversation anymore either. I'm too busy fighting off the electric buzzing I felt earlier as it crashes over us like a tidal wave. But try as I might, it's no use. I'm still drowning in it, sinking under wave after intoxicating wave.

What the hell is happening right now?

I shake my head, knowing here and now is the time to lock up this unfounded attraction for good so it doesn't see the light of day again.

It's the only way I'll survive the rest of the summer here with him.

My voice comes out raw, like it was shredded with a thousand razor blades. "Well, there's not going to be a repeat. So remember that before you try coming back, begging for more."

The certainty and finality in my statement has an effect on him. More than he'd like, I'm sure. But he can't hide it now; no mask can repair itself that quickly. It takes time to piece it back together after being broken and dismantled to this degree.

He sure as hell tries, though, as his words leave him with a bite of venom.

"Never will I ever."

TEN

Kaleb

I didn't sleep a wink after storming out of Avery's cabin last night, and it's showing as I drop onto the bench between my brothers for breakfast. Meanwhile, the two of them are bright-eyed and bushy-tailed, ready to take on the day packed full of activities.

And apparently, ready to irritate me to no end at the drop of a hat.

"You look like crap," Colton pipes up the second I reach for my fork.

I glare down at him, in no mood to deal with his shit this morning. "Just because you're not at home doesn't mean you're allowed to use that word, Cole. You know that."

My brother cocks his head. "Would you rather I say you look like a steaming pile of poo?"

Jesus take the fucking wheel.

"I'd rather you not be a pain in my ass at seven in the morning," I mutter before stabbing my eggs and shoving them into my mouth.

"So you can say ass, but he can't say crap?" Dayton asks, brows furrowed.

Cole nods before aiming a smug little smile at me. "Seems pretty hypocritical if you ask me."

My fork clatters to the table, my cool nowhere to be found this morning.

"I'm an adult, and the both of you are far from one."

"So what you're saying is we can be hypocrites when we're adults," Day concludes, a smarmy little smile on his lips.

Colton smirks back. "I think that's exactly what he's saying."

Do not kill your brothers. Do not *kill your brothers.*

I begin counting backward from ten, begging for the control I normally have over my emotions to make a reappearance, if only so I don't commit fratricide. Unfortunately, I don't even make it to five when Avery enters the cafeteria looking as worse for wear as I do. His hair is done and he's freshly showered, giving off that typical put-together appearance he always has, but his face tells another story. Even from here, I can see the heaviness in his features and dark circles formed under his blue eyes as they find me.

He holds my gaze only for a brief moment before turning toward the breakfast line, but the rush of heat coursing through my body happens regardless.

And I fucking hate it.

"You aren't the only one who looks like a pile of poo," Dayton says, and when I shift my gaze to my brothers, I find them both looking at Avery.

While I know Dayton's comment was only meant to be funny, there's something in Colton's expression that lets me know he's seeing more than he might let on. He's been eleven going on twenty-one ever since he started middle school, and he notices everything.

A fact proven when the next question leaves his mouth.

"Did you two get in a fight because of what happened last night?"

I stop chewing mid-bite, the food instantly turning to ash in my mouth before I force it down my throat. The line I'm treading here is a very fine one, and while I will never make a habit out of lying to my brothers, there's no part of me that wants to tell them the gory details of Avery pinning me to a tree and mauling me with his mouth.

So I settle for the most watered-down version of the truth.

"We talked about it, but it wasn't a fight."

I can feel Colton studying me from my left, while Dayton remains blissfully ignorant to my right. It's an uncomfortable feeling—like I'm beneath a microscope—and the heat scalding the back of my head where I know Avery has his gaze locked on me isn't helping matters.

But rather than giving in—turning to find those baby blue eyes—I hold strong and shove another forkful of food in my mouth.

Colton, on the other hand, doesn't give a damn and twists his upper body to not-so-discreetly look behind us.

"Colton, turn around and eat," I force out between gritted teeth.

My brother lets out a huff of annoyance before doing as I say. His hazel gaze lifts to mine, and he gives me another one of his devilish smirks. "Something's definitely up, 'cause he's staring at you."

"Maybe he wants to kill him," Day chimes in.

"Would the two of you just give it a rest already?" I snap, my temper flaring far quicker than it normally would. Probably due to lack of sleep and the plethora of emotions still congealing inside my chest and stomach from that kiss.

It's evident in the way Colton's brows shoot up in surprise, and how Dayton all but drops his fork to his plate, that neither of them expected me to snap at them over some playful ribbing.

"Sorry, K."

"Yeah, sorry," Dayton murmurs, picking up his fork again.

Setting my fork on the wooden table, I pinch the bridge of my nose and let out a groan. The twins have always been nosy, as most kids their age can be, and under normal circumstances, I'd dish shit right back at them. But despite these being far from normal circumstances, and I'm more than deserving of setting boundaries with them, the last thing I want is to ruin their mood going into the day.

"Look, I'm sorry too, okay? Like I said, I'm tired, and it's made me cranky, but it's not fair for me to take it out on you." I pause, hedging back toward the topic of Avery. "But there is something Avery and I talked about yesterday, and it involves the two of you."

Glancing between the two of them, I see equal parts curiosity and anxiousness written on their faces.

Dayton is the first to speak, asking the same question I'm sure he'd ask if he were being called to the principal's office. "Are we in trouble?"

I keep my smile under lock and key and shake my head. "No, you're not. But I need the two of you to start being more inclusive with Elijah."

Dayton lets out a low groan before starting back in on his breakfast, but it's Colton who looks downright pissed I even suggested it. He looks ready to argue, but I aim a glare his way, stopping him in his tracks.

"Don't start that crap with me. You, Dayton, and Elijah were close your first summer here. There's no reason you can't be like that again."

"Again, you get to swear but we don't?" Dayton pipes up between his mouthfuls of food, entirely uninterested in the conversation.

"We were *kinda* friends when we were *eight*," Colton cuts in, his tone still slightly dejected. "But that was, like, three years ago. We're friends with Liam and Tyler now."

I arch a brow. "You do know you can be friends with *all* of them, right? There's no rule against it."

The way both their noses scrunch up, almost in disgust, tells me the idea is not at all appealing.

"Yeah, but Elijah's too quiet," Dayton says with a shrug. "He doesn't really try to make other friends, and it makes him seem kinda…weird."

He stops and looks at Colton, and my brothers share one of their infamous twin looks—the kind where anyone in the same room as them can tell they're having their own little silent conversation—before Cole speaks up.

"Tell you what. You find a way to make up with Avery and be friends, then we'll consider it."

Dayton nods, a little smirk on his lips before he glances behind us toward Avery. "Oh, and he's still watching us. Hell yeah, that's got my vote."

I gape at them, both awed and offended by their audacity. "This isn't a democracy, and we aren't bartering with blackmail about this. You'll start acting the way Mom and Dad raised you—which is to be nice and to include people—or I'll call them to come get you."

Colton rolls his eyes, entirely unfazed by the threat. In addition to being more vigilant, he's always been the ballsier one too. "Maybe you need to take your own advice."

"Good thing it's not up for discussion."

The two of them slump forward against the table, pouting at the same time a large form stops in front of us.

"Kal. Got a minute?"

I glance up to find Colin in front of me, looking down as if fully aware he just stumbled upon a little familial squabble. A fact further proved by the way my brothers both straighten up and immediately start shoveling food into their mouths.

"Yeah, sure."

He gives me a nod before motioning toward the hallway leading to his office with his head, a sure signal to follow when he starts in that direction.

"Someone's in trouble," Dayton murmurs under his breath.

"Yeah, he is," Cole confirms, then shovels more food in his mouth before adding, "No one wants to be called to the principal's office first thing in the morning."

I jab Colton in the ribs before standing. "Stop talking with your mouth full."

Colton sticks his tongue, covered in half-chewed eggs, out at me at the same time Dayton chimes in with a "Don't get fired!"

My brothers, ever supportive.

Rolling my eyes, I ignore the two heathens and head down the hall Colin disappeared down. There's only a few reasons he could be calling me to his office, but almost all of them are of little to no consequence. Probably just a change in the activity schedules for this week or a random check-in on how the group is doing, neither of which is anywhere in the realm of what my brothers are suggesting.

The door to Colin's office is open when I reach it, and I find him already seated behind his desk, shuffling through the schedules.

Rapping my knuckles against the wood, I step into the office and say, "Hey, you wanted to see me?"

Colin glances up, smiling when he motions for me to take a seat across from him. I'm not even in the chair fully when he pulls the rug out from under me with a single sentence.

"I just wanted to talk to you about Avery."

All the blood rushes from my face, my stomach dropping as I realize my brothers might've been on the right track after all, and this isn't just a normal chat with my boss. I've worked here long enough to know there are cameras scattered around the grounds—something I didn't think much of last night when Avery and I—

Fuck, fuck, fuck.

"What about him?" I ask, managing to keep my tone far more collected than I feel.

"Well, how's he doing with the kids?"

A sense of relief floods me. Of course he wants to talk about work. Not the fact that two of his counselors were making out and dry humping against a tree twelve hours ago.

Shrugging, I offer the most nonchalant response I can. "Fine, I guess."

Colin arches a brow before saying, "Fine, you guess. Really, Kal? I figured you'd have plenty more to say than just three words."

My thoughts are flooded with the events of the past few weeks—from the moment I stepped into this very office to find Avery inside it, all the way to fifteen minutes ago when our gazes collided in the cafeteria.

And while there have been moments where Avery's proven himself to be more than some homophobic asshole, I'm having a hard time letting go of that version of him. Which has me debating if telling Colin how I'm really feeling is the right move or not.

The only thing I *am* sure of is that I don't think I'll survive the entire summer with him here. Especially after what happened last night.

So without thinking too hard about the consequences…I spill my fucking guts.

"If I'm being perfectly honest, I don't want him here." I pause to gauge Colin's reaction, only for his expression to remain impassive and unreadable. "I don't want to work with him, and while he's doing the best he can, it's more than obvious this isn't the place for him. He's cocky, conceited, and arrogant, and I think that's a dangerous thing to have around such impressionable kids. And that's not even mentioning the whole…" I trail off, letting the thought linger between us like a toxic cloud.

Colin hikes a brow up when I leave the sentence hanging, prompting, "The whole…"

I sigh, squeezing my eyes shut and pinching the bridge of my nose. "I'm sure you know about what happened back at school. With him outing one of our teammates and getting expelled."

My words are acidic at best as they leave my lips, while fully knowing I more than likely just signed his death warrant. And once again, I don't know how I feel about it.

Colin still gives nothing away in his features as he simply states, "I'm aware of what happened at Foltyn last spring, yes."

The floor drops out from under me for the third time since sitting down across from this man, and I'm almost positive my eyes are bugging out of my skull like in one of those old cartoons.

"Then why did you hire him?" I exclaim, unable to hide the mixture of surprise and dismay in my tone. "Do you really think someone who'd do that should be here working with all these kids?"

Colin leans back in his chair, resting his elbows on the armrests and steepling his fingers together. It's a position I've seen Coach—as well as plenty of other authority figures—in many times over the last few years. And paired with his stoic expression and hard eyes, I know he's about to lay down the law.

"Look, Kal. I'm going to tell you the same thing I told Avery the day he got here: I believe in second chances. And one mistake, failure, or decision shouldn't have the power to define you as a bad person."

"*One* mistake?" I echo before barking out a laugh. "Just last night, he all but told me about this little plan to use you and Elijah to get back into

Foltyn this fall."

He leans back in his chair, resting his elbows on the arm rests before steepling his fingers. "You've seen the two of them interact together more than anyone else since camp started. You really think that's the case?" Colin aims a knowing look my way. "This is the first year I've seen Elijah act remotely himself. The kid wants to do this kind of stuff as much as he'd want to never eat sugar again, but I can already see a change in him."

"So you don't care that he's getting close to Elijah just to garner favor with your brother?"

For the first time in this entire conversation, I see a flicker of irritation in Colin's expression. "Avery's connecting with him, and that's all I could ask for. While it might be a bit unorthodox, I think they both have things to teach each other this summer, regardless of how their relationship initially started. Wouldn't you agree?"

I offer a nod in concession of his point, but it doesn't stop me from carefully forming a rebuttal. "I see where you're coming from, but—"

"That's all I need to hear."

"Colin—" I start to protest, but he's already cutting me off at the knees before I get out anything except his name.

"If the only issue you truly have is because of what happened this past spring, then I'm going to encourage you to use it as an opportunity to mend fences." Colin's eyes soften around the edges, and he takes on a softer tone. One he hasn't used with me since I was a kid attending this camp myself. "You and I both know you can handle this, Kal. You've risen above far greater things in your short life. Spending the summer working beside Avery won't even register as a blip in the grand scheme of your life."

Shit.

My teeth sink into my tongue, and I'm half tempted to tell him about the little stunt Elijah pulled with going MIA on us, which would surely put an entirely different view of Avery in Colin's head. But unfortunately, I'm just as responsible for Elijah as Avery is—all bringing it up to Colin would accomplish is making *both* of us look incompetent.

So rather than chancing it, I accept defeat with a curt nod and rise from my seat. "If that's all, I better get back to the kids before they start a food fight in the dining hall."

Colin's lip twitches, and I can't tell if he's amused with my statement or my feeble attempt to hide my irritation with his decision. "Enjoy your overnighter up on the mountain."

Shit, I'd completely forgotten about that. And after last night, followed by this conversation, it's not fucking likely.

I manage to keep the comment to myself, though, and simply nod.

I'm through the open threshold of the office seconds later, ready to get the kids started on today's adventure, only to turn straight into Avery. My hand grabs the wall to steady myself, and when my gaze lifts to his face, I find a hardened glare and jaw lined with tension.

Shit.

It's obvious from his expression alone he overheard enough of my conversation with Colin to piss him off. And now I'm surely going to pay the price for it.

"For someone who's all about being on time, you're the only one making us late today," he snaps, disdain dripping from his tone as he crosses his arms. "The kids are already outside, ready to hit the trail, if you're done trying to get me fired."

Double shit.

It's at that moment when I catch something in his gaze that doesn't quite match the fury he's aiming my way. Something that looks eerily like...hurt.

And though it makes no sense, the realization is a blade right through my gut.

I don't even have a chance to respond before he's storming back toward the dining hall without another word.

ELEVEN

Avery

Pissed off doesn't begin to cover how I'm feeling about Kaleb's little attempt to get me booted from camp, but I do my best to shove down the frustration and hurt it causes by focusing on the task at hand: getting twenty-something kids up a mountain safely.

Of course, it's a little difficult to rein in the irritation when we'll be forced in each other's proximity for the next twenty-four hours, no referee or mediator in sight.

Then again, we'll be on a mountain with no one around to stop me from pushing him off the nearest cliff.

Despite the appealing thought of murder in the morning, I manage to keep my frustrations in check while we hike up the mountain. Unfortunately, however, I think most of the kids can tell the two of us are in some sort of stalemate; Elijah more than any of the others.

"Do you want to talk about why you're so pissed, or would you rather keep taking it out on every rock we pass?" Elijah finally asks.

His big, brown eyes glance up at me from behind his glasses, and while my instinct wants me to lie or play it off, I can't. Not with this kid.

Jaw tight, I nod up the trail toward Kaleb.

"He doesn't want me here."

"Kaleb?" he asks, his brows crashing together in confusion. "Okay, but you already knew that. Why is it suddenly making you all angry?"

Leave it to an eleven-year-old to deduce it like that.

Scraping my teeth over my lip, I debate on what to say. Being honest with the kid is one thing, but airing all the dirty laundry between us is another. After all, I'm the one supposed to connect with *him*. On *his* level. The shared history between Kaleb and me is on a level that Elijah shouldn't be worrying about for a few more years, minimum.

Careful not to divulge too much, I go with, "I didn't think he'd take his dislike to these lengths." *To where it's impossible to breathe the same air as him and not wanna throat-punch him or mentally plot his murder.*

"That's all?"

I nod. "Yep, that's all."

If Elijah wants more details than that, he doesn't let on.

He does frown, though, two vertical lines forming above the bridge of his glasses. Then he does a little shrug that lifts his backpack before offering, "You could try pulling your weight around camp. Maybe that will help make it up to him."

I nearly trip on a root because I'm too busy gawking at him.

"I pull my weight," I say, albeit a little defensively.

In reality, I do my best around camp, and it's gotten a little easier since the first day, but I'm more than aware that this whole "outdoors" thing is my downfall. Just like I know Kaleb has had to pick up a fair amount of slack because of it.

"My dad always says actions speak louder than words," Elijah pipes up as we continue trekking up the mountain. "Maybe you can offer to set up the tent. Or start the fire or cook us dinner."

If only it were that simple…

I know he's only trying his best to be helpful. He doesn't know the depth and details of the chasm dividing Kaleb and me, so I can't fault the kid for thinking putting together a stupid tent or doing any of that other stuff is gonna do anything to bridge the gap.

There's not a chance in hell I'll be breaking that news to him, though.

My lips pull up in a tight smile. "I guess I can give that a try. Under one condition."

His head whips toward me. "Condition?"

"Yep," I confirm, unable to stop the teasing smirk from forming. "You need to start making nice with the twins."

His nose wrinkles up like he's just smelled something horrible.

"What's that look for?"

"Because I don't want to be nice to the kids who don't like me," he mutters, shooting me an indignant look.

Yeah, me neither, kid. But that's life.

"You told me the three of you were kinda friends at one point. There's no reason you can't be again. So why don't you extend the olive branch and see what happens?"

His face is still drawn up in a tight grimace, which tells me all I need to know about his thoughts on the idea. Yet, to my surprise, he lets out a relenting sigh and mutters, "I guess I can try."

A little bolt of pride zings through me, and I feel a smile pull at my lips.

Never would I ever have thought I'd get anything from this experience, especially when my father laid out his hair-brained plan. But I feel like I'm making a tiny difference with Elijah, and that's pretty much the only thing keeping me sane.

It's not lost on me that the same advice could very well be applied to my situation with Kaleb, but that's something I'm choosing to think about later. My issues aren't something that can be solved as easily, but Elijah's? His will be a lot simpler.

Everything is when you're that young.

After another half an hour of hiking at the back of the pack with Elijah—all the while listening to him animatedly talk about the video game he's dying to play once he goes home—we reach the area where we're meant to set up camp for the night.

The second Kaleb catches sight of us bringing up the end of the pack, relief crosses his face, only to be quickly replaced by an impassive mask. The two of us did fall a little behind, taking our time on the way up, and it's likely he thought we got lost along the way. Maybe even thought he'd have to come find us.

Though, at this rate, I'd be willing to bet my inheritance that he'd sooner leave me on this mountain to die of starvation than be the one to round up a search party.

"Set up camp, lunch, then group activities, right?" I ask, confirming the schedule I already memorized this morning. Honestly, I just want to see if he'll acknowledge me, or better yet, maybe explain what his issue is.

But all I get is an emotionless *yep* in response before he walks right past me. Almost like I'm not even there. Little does he realize, it'll be nearly impossible to pretend I don't exist when we're sleeping a foot apart in the same tent tonight.

Because, of course we are.

Because God fucking hates me.

A quick glance around reveals most of the groups, if not all, seem to have their tents handled, already working with each other to put the poles together and run them through the fabric. Even Elijah's keeping his word, pulling out tent pieces and handing them off to Dayton. Or maybe that one is Colton?

Regardless, I have to admit, the kid is taking my challenge for him in stride, and it's got me thinking…maybe I ought to do the same.

Attention flicking from each set of kids at various steps in the process, I determine it looks easy enough. If anything, I'll give it the good ol' college try and hope it somehow earns me brownie points with my infuriating co-counselor.

I can't believe I'm about to take the advice of a freaking tweenager.

Shoving down any lingering self-doubt, I head to where Kaleb's hiking pack is resting near the east side of our campsite. He usually packs the tents down at the bottom of the packs, so it takes me a minute of rummaging around some of the food and other supplies we'd brought up for the night before I find it.

That's when Kaleb turns, catching me red-handed with my hands in his backpack.

Eyes widening slightly, he closes the few yards between us and snatches his bag out of my hand. "What are you doing?"

"I was gonna set up the tent," I tell him matter-of-factly. Rising to my full height, I look him dead in the eye and force my tone to remain calm and even when I ask, "Is that all right?"

"Considering you've probably never put a tent together in your life and I can do it in my sleep, I think I'll pass."

He moves to walk away, backpack and tent in tow, but my hand wraps around his wrist before he's out of arm's reach. I ignore the way his skin seems to crackle with electricity beneath my touch, instead focusing on the blazing green eyes currently pinning me with a death glare.

"Let go of me," he says in a deadly whisper.

I don't let go. Because fuck him if he thinks I'm gonna take this shit lying down.

"Do you really have to be this much of a dick?" I snap.

A sharp scoff fills the already charged air between us. "I'm the one being a dick? You clearly didn't look in the mirror this morning if you honestly think that's the case."

"I haven't done anything to you, LaMothe, and you damn well know that. But you, on the other hand? You've had it out for me since the moment you saw me sitting in Colin's office the very first day."

He rolls his eyes. "That's not—"

"Really? So you weren't trying to get me fired just this morning?"

Kaleb goes as still as a statue with a complexion to match; stone cold and marble white. A poker face if I've ever seen one. But it's his eyes that give him away—the slightest flicker of worry in them—confirming I've hit the nail on the head.

"That's what I thought." Grinding my teeth together, I release his wrist before I do something stupid. God knows touching him has led to some pretty stupid choices recently. I do step in closer, though, lowering my voice enough so any of the kids nearby won't hear. "I can't show you that I belong here if you won't let me. And after this morning, I'd say you owe me this chance."

He holds my gaze for what feels like a lifetime, nostrils flared in opposition. But rather than fighting me on it, he relents and holds the backpack out to me.

It's not quite a white flag, but I have a feeling it's the closest I'll be getting.

I grab the strap and haul it over my shoulder, praying to heaven and hell that I don't manage to screw this up. There's no doubt he'd use it as even more ammunition against me.

He's still staring at me like he wants to say something else but is holding his tongue, and it only creates another wave of frustration.

"What? What's the problem now?"

"Just…make sure it's staked into the ground," he mutters before glancing away. "The last thing we need is to be blown off a mountain in the middle of the night."

Oh, if he only fucking knew…

***

Despite me setting up the tent impeccably—and with no help—Kaleb doesn't say more than a word or two to me afterward. Even once everyone has a quick sandwich for lunch and we split them into groups for the afternoon activities, he barely acknowledges me. Or the stellar job I did on our abode for the evening.

Kaleb's group of boys are the ones who want to go on an additional hike higher up the mountain, leaving anyone who'd rather stay behind with me to fish at the stream nearby.

Let the record state, despite my love for being out on the water, I'm a sailor, not a fisherman. I don't bait hooks with worms, I don't gut a fresh catch, and the only fish I'm remotely interested in eating comes wrapped in rice and seaweed.

But…this was the better option than possibly getting lost on a mountain top.

The group that stays with me doesn't require much instruction or help, so it's a relatively easy job. Pretty sure the only real danger is one of them scraping a knee by falling in the stream. Or maybe catching something other than fish on their hooks.

Thankfully, it's rather uneventful on our side of things until Kaleb's group returns from their hiking excursion, ready to cook up dinner.

"Everything went fine down here?"

"Yes," I say curtly. "I'm not as helpless or incompetent as you make me out to be."

There's movement out of my peripheral, and I turn just enough to catch him nodding. If he has anything else to say or ask, he chooses to keep it to himself and calls for the kids to come grab the food instead.

Then he's off again, adding physical distance to the already gaping chasm metaphorically between us. Though I have to admit, the less I'm within five feet of the guy, the better. Anything less than that, and I catch the scent of his musky body wash or accidentally brush a shoulder with him, bringing me right back to us against that tree.

The taste of his lips, the feel of his body.

And I hate myself for longing for it all over again.

I knew this would happen. That all the self-loathing and disgust I managed to ignore while my lips were locked with his would roar to the surface with a vengeance. That the demons would slither through my thoughts like a viper, poisoning anything in its path.

The only time it wavers is when I can focus my mind elsewhere; usually on the kids.

I never thought I'd say it, but they make a great buffer, keeping both of us occupied enough in separate capacities. Allows us to be busy and distracted from the tension between us—and keeping the vicious thoughts in my head at bay—not to mention giving us an excuse to not interact with each other the way we'd have to if we were alone.

As the evening comes to a close, long after dinner and spooky stories are shared around the campfire, the kids start readying themselves to pack it in for the night. Kaleb and I split the evening duties—his idea to spend less time around me, no doubt—making one of us order them to their tents, the other handling the cleanup and extinguishing the fire. And to no surprise, he puts me on lights-out duty.

I can just hear his reasoning too.

I was worried Avery was incapable of putting the fire out and would burn the forest down. Or worse, tying the food up too close to camp and attracting a bear.

Like it's my fault I didn't grow up with a father who took me to do this kinda outdoorsy bullshit.

At least the kids make it easy for me to get them in for the night, allowing me to slip inside the tent and get ready for bed before Kaleb is done cleaning up. Dread fills my stomach while I wait for him to turn in, though, wondering if the suffocating silence between us will kill me in my sleep tonight or if it'll be him smothering me with a pillow instead.

Rustling outside the tent alerts me of his presence less than ten minutes later, followed by a long sigh as he crawls through the opening. My pulse thrums with anxiety when he zips us in a far-too-small bubble for the evening, and I swear, it only takes two seconds for the walls to start closing in around us.

You can do this. It's one night. Just go to sleep.

I know the feat will likely be impossible, though.

With every movement he makes, his musky scent overwhelms me. Grows stronger as he slides into his sleeping bag beside mine, the space between us now miniscule. My body vibrates and crackles with tension from his proximity, snapping across the space like an electric current. And apart from the occasional sound of swishing fabric, he drowns me with silence.

Until…he finally breaks it.

"How much did you hear? This morning, with Colin?"

A baseball-sized knot lodges itself in my trachea at the question, the unfortunate incident from this morning slicing through my brain until it's front and center. The comments Kaleb made have been trying to make it there all day, but they're impossible to shove away now.

"Do you really think someone who'd do that should be here working with all these kids?"

My eyes stay locked on the top of the tent while more bits of their conversation come back to mind. I can't be sure what was missed before I halted outside the door at the sound of them talking. All I know is that what I did hear I didn't fucking like, and if there was a prelude, I'd rather not know what was included.

"More than enough," I finally respond in a gruff whisper.

If I'm being honest with myself, it's not him trying to get me fired that's shredded me to the bone. It was the disgust and resentment in his voice. It was hearing just how low he thinks of me—of this person I've become.

It was realizing that, no matter how hard I try to make things right, the damage will never be erased.

A soft sigh breaks through the silence, followed by the sound of him turning.

"Look, I know it might seem like I have this…vendetta against you."

"Seem?" I echo with a scoff. "I'm not fucking obtuse, LaMothe. I know what hatred looks like."

Lord knows I've felt it about myself for long enough to recognize it.

Another wave of self-contempt slams into me, rising like the sea as it threatens to pull me under.

"Just answer me this." I rasp with more gravel than I'd like. "Is it because you think I don't belong here, that I can't do the job that I'm supposed to be doing? Or is it because of what I did last night?"

"What are—"

"Don't," I cut in, my voice straining to hold composure. "Don't act like you don't know exactly what I'm talking about."

Because up until I kissed him last night, I thought things may have been turning around. Sure, we probably wouldn't be best friends or texting each other to hang out after the sentencing to this hell-hole is over, but maybe we'd at least be cordial.

Civil.

I wait in silence for him to answer, not entirely sure which I'd prefer to leave his lips. Maybe because, with how hard I've been trying to make the best of the situation, I know the answer will cut like a knife through warm butter either way.

The fact that I care at all is problematic enough.

"I honestly don't know."

His soft voice slices through the silence of the forest, along with every plate of armor I've donned in protection.

My eyes sink closed, and I shake my head.

I have no idea how shit got so fucked-up between us, and at this point, I don't think there's much I can do to fix it. It might not even be worth trying.

Kaleb shifts beside me, and I can feel the heat of his stare on my cheek, even through the darkness. It burns, searing into me like a white-hot brand, and it takes all my willpower not to turn my head his way. Try to find his gaze in the darkness, only to wonder at the thoughts hidden behind his green eyes when they collide with mine.

"Look, Avery—"

"Forget it, it's done. Let's just…go to sleep," I mutter, rolling so my back is to him.

I can still feel his eyes on me, staring at the back of my head. My own sink closed, and I send an internal plea to anyone who might listen that he'll let it rest. No part of me wants to have it out with him on a mountain top with sleeping kids only a few yards away.

I'd rather him leave me to lick my wounds in peace.

After a few moments where the only noise is the wind whipping through the trees, the sensation of his gaze on me disappears. A low sigh sounds from behind me, followed by the rustling of his sleeping bag against the thin pad between him and the ground while he tries to get comfortable.

It's only after he stops moving that I swear I hear the faintest whisper.

"I'm sorry."

I doubt it, though.

It was probably just a trick of the wind.

TWELVE

Kaleb

Week Three

I can't keep doing this.

It's been five days since the overnighter up on the mountain, and after the extremely uncomfortable conversation we shared in the tent, things between us may be even worse.

We've just kicked off week three now, and the constant tension presses down on me like a boulder whenever we're forced to interact, even if it's in silence. It's suffocating, and if this is how the rest of the summer is gonna be, there's no way I'll last without losing my goddamn mind.

Though, from the stupid amount of attraction flooding my brain, I fear I already may have.

Even as I stare at him, his biceps flexing beneath his green counselor shirt while he pushes Elijah and Liam's canoe out from the dock, I feel it. This humming desire beneath my skin, and it makes me want to burn down this entire camp—which was once my place of refuge—if only to escape it.

It's fucking infuriating.

If I could wish for anything, it would be to rid myself of the attraction for him that's decided to rise to the surface. I'd much rather attach it to an anchor and drop it in the middle of the lake. Watch it sink to the muck at the bottom, never to see the light of day again.

But I can't.

I don't think I've ever been more frustrated by another person. By the enigma he's becoming simply by spending more time in his presence. It's almost like he's donning a mask; one that remains impenetrable ninety percent of the time, and it's those moments like right now, where it slips, that confound me.

Then there's his stubbornness. His stupid pride and ego.

God, that's really what sends me over the edge.

Shoving the thoughts away, I focus on loading the twins into their canoe before sending them out onto the lake. Of course, the task is mindless at best, seeing as they've done this plenty of times over the years they've attended camp, and it allows my brain to circle right back to Avery.

To the two of us lying in that tent on the mountain. To the moment *he* shut me down when I tried to apologize and explain myself for what happened with Colin. To how he's shifted from a raging asshole to nothing more than a kicked puppy over the past few days.

All I feel is guilty because of it.

I chance a glance in his direction to find him doing a damn good job at getting his half of the kids onto the lake without incident, and the feeling only intensifies.

When it comes to the job we're both here for, he's doing his best, and that's all anyone can ask of him, myself included. Going to Colin the way I did was fucked-up, and despite not wanting to admit it—even just to myself—it has more to do with me than it does Avery.

Jared and Max are the last two kids for me to get launched onto the lake, and once they're all out there, paddling around to their hearts' content, I finally look back at Avery.

Avery, who is frowning at his canoe like it personally offended him.

That's when I realize…it's the only one left.

Shit.

Now understanding Avery's less-than-thrilled demeanor, I steel myself for what is sure to go down as the most painful afternoon of my life. After all, it's not like we can pretend to be asleep to avoid talking to each other when we're trapped in a canoe together.

I motion toward the water craft. "Get in and let's get going."

Despite looking like he'd rather drown on the spot, he silently climbs in, grabs ahold of the paddles, and waits for me to join him. He won't even turn to look at me when I drop onto the bench behind him, even to hand me my paddle after pushing us off from the dock.

God, this is so fucking awkward.

We work together to paddle toward the center of Glass Lake, where we can keep an eye on the kids and provide any assistance, should they need it. It starts out relatively smoothly, by some miracle, but when we're about three-quarters across the lake, the canoe starts turning to the left.

The only reason for that to happen would be if someone wasn't paddling, and that someone certainly isn't me.

Doing my best to keep my annoyance under wraps, I mutter, "Unless you're looking to spin in circles, I need you to paddle too."

"I was. I just…" He pauses before cursing softly under his breath. "Shit."

That draws my attention from where I'd been watching the kids, and

I find his gaze locked on the water. Right at the spot where the arm of his paddle passes through the water.

"What?"

"It's—" He shakes the paddle rather violently, his biceps flexing in effort, only for it to move barely an inch. His jaw locks, remaining taut until he finally stops trying to free it from whatever managed to snag it below the water's surface.

"The blade is caught on something."

My mind automatically goes into problem solving mode, and I motion for him to swap places with me.

"Come back here to keep us balanced, and I'll move up there to get it."

He shakes his head, still focused on the water and shaking the paddle. "No, I got it handled."

Let the record state, he very clearly does *not* have it handled. His hold on the situation is non-existent, actually, and despite my better judgment, I reach toward him anyway to offer my assistance again.

"Shaking it like that isn't gonna do anything," I calmly reply while he continues to struggle. It's painful to watch. "Avery, let me just—"

"I got it, Kaleb!" he snaps, turning to glare at me. His nostrils flare with frustration before he snarls out, "I don't need your fucking help."

And there he is. The same Avery I saw all last year.

The one who blows up at the drop of a hat. Whose rage, I now realize, is fueled by insecurity and fear more than hatred. Who would rather make more of a fool of himself than dare accept my critique or assistance.

"Would you stop letting your pride get in the way and let me help?"

"No!" He shoots me a glare. "In case you weren't aware, you're really not as smart as you think you are. Not that you'd ever be willing to hear it."

Fuck it.

Carefully leaning forward and crouching in the bottom of the canoe, I reach out and make a grab for the paddle, only for him to shoulder my arm out of the way.

"I got it, LaMothe," he growls again.

"Give me the paddle," I hiss, this time managing to get my hand on the handle.

He makes an attempt to bat me away again, and snaps, "I'm not some damsel in distress, needing you to save the day."

"No, you're just an arrogant dick who won't admit when you're wrong."

All talking ceases then, both of us focused on our struggle to win the paddle in this childish game of tug-of-war; a feat proving to be rather difficult, considering it's still stuck on some unknown object beneath the surface. I'm also acutely aware of just how off-balance we are, the canoe swaying and shaking below us while I do my best to wrangle the paddle from his grip.

"Avery, just give it to me before we—"

The sentence dies on my lips the second he gives the handle a firm yank, pulling it free from the water's clutches. Unfortunately, the sudden movement causes our already off-balance canoe to finally capsize, sending us crashing into the lake.

My blood is boiling when I resurface, finding the canoe flipped over and the kids all staring. Some are attempting to cover their laughter, while others are too stunned to do anything other than gawk.

Avery's head pops up a few feet away, and it takes every ounce of my willpower to not shove his head back under and hold him there. From the fury written on his face, there's a damn good chance he's reining himself in from doing something similar.

Huffing out a sharp breath, I turn my attention back to the capsized canoe.

Glass Lake isn't all that large or cold, so while I could use this as an opportunity to teach the kids how to right a tipped canoe and clamber back in, I'm too pissed off to try. So instead, I grab the edge of the water craft and start hauling it to shore, all the while ignoring the building rage inside me.

I've spent years kayaking or canoeing the waters around camp, and not once have I fallen in. Then Avery shows up this summer and I end up looking like a drowned rat, fully clothed, in the middle of the fucking lake.

Un-fucking-believable.

The sound of water sloshing behind me draws my attention back to the shore to find Avery's sopping wet form finally back on dry land. His clothing clings to his toned body in a way that makes my own take notice, and though I didn't think it was possible, I become even more enraged.

Because why the *fuck* do I have to want this…this—

"Why can't you fucking listen to me for once?" I shout, the crack in my composure turning into a chasm.

If Avery's surprised by my outburst, it doesn't show, because he's immediately stomping toward me with flared nostrils and brows drawn down in fury.

"I'm not one of these kids, Kaleb. You're not in charge of me out here; I'm your *equal!*"

"Really? *Really?* Then why are all the kids still dry and in their canoes while we're soaking wet after tipping into the lake?" I scoff and peel my shirt over my head to wring out the excess water. "If you wanna be an equal, start acting like one."

When I glance back at him, I find his gaze tracing over my body before his glare collides with mine. And in that moment, I swear I can see right into his brain.

Or maybe those are just my own screaming thoughts.

"Like I said up on that mountain: I would if you'd actually fucking let me."

I wasn't aware of just *how* close he'd gotten to me in the midst of our shouting match, but I realize now, as I see the flecks of indigo is his otherwise sky-blue irises, we're far closer together than we should be. Only inches separate our chests, our faces…our lips.

The power of his proximity paired with my unfortunate desire engulfs me in heat, roaring through my veins like a wildfire, and if I don't garner some distance, there's no telling what I'll do. My sanity is hanging on by a thread, ready to snap at any given moment.

Right now, it could end with one of two things: kissing him or decking him.

Neither option feels preferable to the other, and so I do the only thing I can. I focus on the rage instead. On the frustration and resentment that's fueled every interaction we've had over the past few weeks before whispering in a low, deadly voice.

"I swear to God, Avery. You need to get out of my fucking face."

The warning doesn't work. If anything, Avery inches in closer, his nose nearly brushing mine now.

"Or what, golden boy? We both know you won't do a goddamn thing besides run back to Colin." His lip pulls back in a hateful snarl. "After all, tattling is what you do be—"

"That's enough," an authoritative voice booms from farther inland, cutting Avery's blow off at the knees.

My attention immediately snaps toward it, finding Colin with his arms crossed over his chest, glaring at the two of us.

I take a measured step away from Avery, my teeth gritting with irritation and rage.

"Can either of you account for the kids right now?"

My immediate reaction is to motion out to the lake, where the kids are…*fuck*. They could all be drowning at this point, and neither of us would have any clue. We've been too busy screaming at each other.

Shit.

"Sir—" I start in a feeble attempt at an explanation.

He holds a hand up before I have the chance to get more than a single word out, though, and I know better than to press further. Instead, I just watch as he grabs the walkie-talkie from his hip and lifts it to his mouth to speak.

"Christian. I need you to come watch the kids on the lake while I take care of something," he says stiffly.

Then, to just me and Avery, he utters five words that have my blood freezing to ice in my veins.

"My office. Both of you."

Colin's lecture is…rough.

I wasn't expecting it to go well, considering the scene we caused, and in front of the campers, no less. But I also wasn't prepared for the disappointment in Colin's eyes while he reprimanded the two of us.

"You two need to get over whatever is going on between you. I don't care about what happened back at Foltyn, and I don't give a damn about what happens after you leave here. But the time you spend here at this camp? *That* I care about." His attention flicks between us, pinning each of us with a hard stare. "Call a ceasefire. You can go back to hating each other once you're no longer on these premises." With that decided, he motions toward the door. "Now, go get yourselves cleaned up and back to your group."

Neither of us speaks to the other when we exit the office, and that doesn't change as we go through the rest of our day and into the evening. We painfully exist in the same sphere, trying our best not to rock the boat any further. Proverbially and literally, it seems.

To no surprise, the blowout by the lake resulted in the twins crawling even further up my ass when it comes to Avery. Asking questions about why we were fighting, of course, but also digging for more information. Colton especially, almost as if he can tell whatever tension that exists between Avery and me has become more potent. More volatile.

But then, after dinner, something changes.

There are brief periods of time when I can feel Avery's eyes on me. At first, I thought I was imagining it, but then there's a time or two when I catch his gaze before he quickly averts it, telling me it's not all in my head after all.

But still, neither of us says a damn thing to the other.

It's not until we're around the bonfire with the kids, letting them bullshit and yammer on without any real input from us, that we exchange a single word.

Avery walks up to me as I hand out roasting sticks to the kids, eyes cast downward at the clipboard in his hands. His jaw is taut, signaling there's still plenty of frustration lingering in him from earlier, but when his gaze lifts to mine, I'm surprised to find…something else in them.

Stress, maybe?

"Tomorrow's schedule," is all he says before holding the clipboard out for me.

My gaze stays locked with his as I take it from him and watch as he walks back to where he was sitting with Elijah.

I was the one who wrote up our list of activities, per usual, so I'm not sure why he's giving it to me. It's only when I finally pull my attention away from his face to glance at the clipboard that I see it.

On top of tomorrow's itinerary is a torn piece of paper, slipped beneath the clip.

A note.

I'm willing to bury the hatchet if you are.

My gaze rakes over the words written in his messy scrawl, the slightest knot forming in my throat at the olive branch he's extending. One, I'm well aware, I need to grab on to for dear life.

Colin made his stance clear: Despite everything that's happened—both before camp and during—we still have to find a way to work together.

If not…there's no telling what will transpire over the next month and a half. Or if either of us will even last that long.

Before I can think better of it, I grab the pen tucked behind the clip, scribble out a note on the back of his own, and walk over to where he's seated.

"Colin let me know about a change, actually," I say as I press the clipboard into his hands. "You should probably look it over."

He frowns up at me, questions and worry swirling in his blue eyes, before his gaze drops to where I scribbled out my response.

Midnight. The dock.
If you're late, I'll bury you instead.

THIRTEEN

Kaleb

I hear Avery well before I see him, and when I glance down at the Garmin on my wrist to catch the time, I can't help the little smirk that lifts my lips.

11:58 PM.

Well, would you look at that…

Lifting my gaze, I stare out over the dark water of the lake. It's a cloudy, starless night, the only light coming from the single lamp post above the end of the dock, casting an eerie glow over the seemingly endless pool of darkness.

Avery's weight on the boards causes the wood to creak beneath his feet as he approaches, only stopping when his shadow falls over me.

"Glad to see you actually can be on time," I say, keeping my attention trained on the water. "Saves me a lot of digging when I'm already fucking exhausted from swimming across the lake earlier."

I make sure it comes out in a joking manner—a way to ease some of the tension already present between us—and I'm hoping he'll throw shade or toss a jab right back. But all I get is a soft "yeah" as he drops down beside me and sets his flashlight in the foot of space between our bodies. I glance over to catch him slipping out of his damn boat shoes before sliding his feet through the water's smooth surface, causing it to ripple around his ankles.

Awkwardness stifles the air, almost clouding around us in a fog of poison that no amount of brisk mountain air can cleanse.

"So where's this hatchet you're so intent on burying?" I ask, another feeble attempt at breaking the ice between us. Or at least putting a crack in it.

Thankfully, this one seems to work, and a soft laugh fills the cool night air between us. It's a sound I've heard from him plenty of times before, but something about this one is different. Almost like it was earned, and that makes it feel a lot more…intimate.

"You know that's just an expression, right?" he finally asks.

"Obviously. Just figured you might actually bring one in symbolism or something."

"Symbolism? Seriously?" When I shrug, he lets out another low, throaty chuckle. "You're kind of a nerd, LaMothe."

"And if you're looking to bury this metaphorical hatchet, insulting me is the last way to do it," I point out.

His face falls ever so slightly, and he shakes his head. "Shit, yeah."

Well, this is going as well as I figured it would.

Silence sits between us again, allowing the sounds of the forest at night to come to life. The wind in the trees, rustling the leaves. The soft chirps of crickets, and the water gently lapping against the lakeshore.

And it would be so peaceful, if it weren't for the fucking vise wrapped around my chest.

I have no idea how to start this conversation, nor where he's wanting it to go, which is why I simply keep my mouth closed and wait. Even if it's hard not to push for answers. Even if it kills me to be this close to him, feeling the heat of his body radiating toward mine.

He blows out a long breath before whispering three words.

"I'm gay, Kaleb."

My mouth goes drier than Death Valley on a summer day as the statement registers in my brain. A statement that I wasn't prepared to hear from his lips, thinking this was him calling a ceasefire, like Colin demanded.

The last place I expected this to go was him…coming out to me.

"Is that the first time you've said it out loud?" I finally manage, pulling my gaze to him.

His throat works to swallow, Adam's apple bobbing with the effort. "Yeah, it is."

Thought so.

There's a part of me that had an inkling he might be gay. If not from the way he practically mauled me against that tree, rutting his hard length against me like an animal in heat, then from the small things I've picked up on. Not just here, either, but over the past year at school, with the shit he would say to Keene.

It's different hearing him confirm it, though.

"And how does it feel?"

He's quiet for a moment, lost in his thoughts as his teeth skate back and forth over his bottom lip. It's like he's got the weight of the world on his shoulders, when admitting a truth like that should lift it instead.

"Wrong," he finally supplies, a bit of gravel laced in his voice. "It feels wrong…because I don't want to be."

"Why?" I ask instantly, brows crashing together.

"What?"

"Why don't you want to be?"

Avery's lips form a grimace, distorting his features. "There's this…I dunno. A voice, I guess, in my head sometimes. Shame screaming at me, telling me how disgusting it is for me to want the things I do. Not wanting them in the first place would make it a helluva lot easier to manage."

Just like that, pieces start falling into place.

When it comes to sexuality, I've realized sometimes the ones who scream the loudest against us are the ones harboring the very same secret.

Internal homophobia isn't something I've ever struggled with, and I thank my lucky stars for that every single day. Having a family who is loving and accepting of me is all anyone asks for, but especially when you're a kid growing up in any aspect that "deviates from the norm."

Only having met Avery's father a handful of times over the past few years, it doesn't take a genius to realize he grew up with the exact opposite.

But what *doesn't* make sense is…

"Why did you wait until *now* to tell me? Why not years ago, when we were still friends?"

But even as I ask, I realize the answer. It's written in misery, right there on his face.

"I couldn't even admit it to myself, let alone another person." His head hangs in defeat as he stares at his hands, picking at his nails like they're the most interesting thing in the world. "I still…don't think I'm ready to say it to anyone else."

Rather than being angry or frustrated, I find myself nodding in understanding. His timeline is his own, and there's nothing wrong with waiting until he's ready. One person at a time, or the entire world at once. It's his choice to make.

Ironic, considering it was a choice he'd taken away from others.

His brows form a tight knot in the glow of the lamplight as he leans back on his palms, and it's almost like he was reading my mind when he mutters, "Keene ghosted me last year."

Once again, it takes me a second to process his statement, but something in it doesn't quite add up in my head. "What are you talking about?"

A hint of surprise flashes in his eyes, but his brows remain drawn. "He didn't tell you?"

Tell me what?!

But rather than screaming it for the world to hear, I shake my head silently.

Avery's gaze flicks to me briefly before shifting to the lake again. Despite the somewhat relaxed pose, tension still lines his face, clearly attempting to coax the words out of himself. But I don't press him. I wait.

I wait for him to be ready. However long that takes.

"Earlier during last school year, we started talking. Texting and whatever. A lot." He pauses and swallows before his gaze drops down to where his feet swish through the water. "We talked about…questioning things and accepting who we are and shit. As it turns out, we both were pretty fucked-up with our sexuality. It was for different reasons, sure, but it was the most I'd felt seen or understood in a long time. It was almost like I had someone going through it with me." He draws in a long, deep breath. "Except, he didn't know it was me he was talking to."

If I thought I was confused before, it's got nothing on how I'm feeling now, staring at him like he's grown two extra heads or started speaking in tongues.

"How is that possible?"

His teeth run over his lower lip before sinking them into the flesh momentarily. "Because all the conversations were happening on Toppr."

I can't help the way my brows shoot up at his mention of the gay hookup app, where anonymity is easily achieved, seeing as most people don't show their face. Just whatever body part they deemed hot enough to post as a profile photo.

After matching with someone, it's up to the user if they want to share more than that.

I've used it a time or two for hookups, but it wasn't really my style. But I had no clue Keene was even on it, let alone Avery.

"Okay, so you obviously never met in person under your usernames while this was all happening." All he does is shake his head in answer, so I move to my next question. "Then how did you know it was Keene?"

He rolls his tongue along the inside of his cheek. "His freckles on his stomach. I'd seen them countless times in the locker room, and so when his profile photo showed the same ones, I had suspicions. And then a few times we'd both be online within a very small vicinity, and that only confirmed my theory."

Well, damn. So much for anonymity.

My mind starts running with scenarios when I ask, "Did you confront him about it?"

That would explain a lot of the tension between the two of them last season. The blowout in the locker room, the jabs and taunts Avery would toss out at any given moment. If one of them was feeling something that the other wasn't, or if Avery decided he wasn't ready to confront his sexuality the way Keene was—

"No, he cut things off with me before I could ever work up the nerve to say something," he replies, fracturing all my internal theories. "At first, I thought it was because he figured out it was me. But then I realized it was because of Aspen, and it made me so fucking angry. How could he share all these private and personal things with me, only to just…" He trails off, letting the sentence hang in the air between us.

"You were constantly spewing hatred at him," I quickly point out, unable to leave the judgment out of my tone. "At every turn, it was another slur or threat or asshole remark. Things no human wants to hear, but especially when they're going through such a massive self-discovery. And you knew he was going through that, which only made it worse. Even if he did know it was you—"

"Trust me, I'm well aware of just how convoluted this whole thing is." Frustration laces the statement, and he shakes his head. "I can't even choose *myself* because of how fucking disgusting I feel by even wanting… what I want. But it's still how I feel."

The idea of Avery wanting Keene, or even moreso, the thought of them together, leaves a sour taste in my mouth. It feels wrong on so many levels, and I don't think it's just because of how protective I feel over Keene either. But that's something I can unpack another time. Alone, preferably.

Right now, I'd rather garner some understanding on the clusterfuck that got us to this moment.

Avery's head falls back between his shoulder blades, his eyes locked on the stars overhead when he speaks again.

"You don't know what it's like…constantly being at war with yourself. Actively fighting a battle in your mind about the things you want. Trying to convince yourself that it's okay, that this is who you are, but you're still revolted by it all the same. Still have this shame screaming at you every time the thought even occurs."

He's right; I have no clue the struggle that's been plaguing his mind.

And I sure as fuck have never felt as alone as he has. Probably for his entire life.

"I'm not saying the things I did or how I acted were logical," he continues, still talking to the sky with words meant for me. "It was all emotion-fueled, and I regretted sending in that photo the second I saw their faces that day on the field. But obviously it was too late. Pettiness and anger and jealousy had already gotten the best of me, and they paid the price for it." A soft scoff fills the air, and a tiny woeful smirk curls his lips at the corner. "And now, I guess I am too."

Another wave of guilt hits me, taking me off guard. At no point did I consider Avery's side of what happened, only how his actions impacted Aspen and Keene. And while I don't exactly *regret* saying something, I realize everything is a lot more nuanced than I originally thought.

"I didn't think they'd go as far as kicking you out of school," I whisper, unable to shake the guilt still gnawing at me. "I hope you know the only reason I said something to Coach was because it was the right thing to do. I'd have done the same thing if it were anyone else."

His head turns, and he meets my gaze. "Neither did I. But I made this bed, and now I need to lie in it. It was a fool's mission to try placing the blame on you."

"Maybe then, but it isn't now." I pause and blow out a long breath. "I'm sorry. About me going to Colin, I mean."

There's a beat of silence as he continues to study me, his expression remaining impassive before he murmurs, "We've both done things we aren't proud of. I think it's time we just let bygones be bygones."

"I think we're finally in agreement on something."

"About time," he says with a smirk.

I shrug. "It was bound to happen eventually, right?"

He lets out a soft laugh, and the sound draws out a smile from me too. But then his attention falls to my lips, and all the oxygen in the atmosphere disappears. We're frozen in the moment, locked in a memory, and I don't need to be a mind reader to know we're sharing the same thought.

The kiss.

The one that continues burning inside my head like a white-hot brand, despite my efforts to box it up and shove it aside, never to be touched again. In fact, it seems the more I attempt to ignore how it felt to have his body pressed against me, his lips on mine, the more my mind fixates on it instead.

My windpipe constricts as the memory plagues me, drying my mouth out and forcing me to wet my lips. A movement that Avery watches, ever the captive audience, and I realize…I want him to do it again.

Right here, right now.

Shit.

Avery clears his throat, breaking the moment, before his attention returns to the lake.

"There's a lot I need to work through while I'm here, I think. A lot of… accepting about who I am that I need to do. And who knows, maybe this"— he motions between us with his hand—"is the first step in that direction."

For some goddamn reason, my stomach does a little somersault while I whisper, "If you need someone to talk about it with, you know where to find me."

He nods a couple times before returning his focus to me and offering the smallest hint of a smile. And just like that, it turns out the most shocking revelation of the evening isn't Avery coming out to me or the whole sordid tale of him, Keene, and that stupid baseball game.

No.

It's knowing the offer I just made…is one I hope he takes.

FOURTEEN

Avery

Things with Kaleb are far less tense the following morning.

I'm not sure what I was expecting to happen. I knew going into it, he's not exactly the type to make a bunch of flyers and staple them to every available surface about what I'd told him. After what I did last year—and after how he turned me in for it—outing me would be the last way he'd retaliate.

But bare minimum, part of me still expected a fair amount of animosity between us. Maybe some awkwardness lingering in the midst of the dissipating tension.

Yet instead, when I gather my half of the kids from the bathhouse and drag them to the lodge for breakfast, I'm greeted with a sight I could've never imagined: Kaleb offering a slight nod and a smile from where he's seated between his brothers at one of the dining tables.

And my stomach starts doing gymnastics because of it.

Loading my plate and heading toward an empty table, I make every attempt to keep my gaze away from his side of the table. One little heart-to-heart doesn't make all the bullshit from the past automatically disappear. Like I said last night, at the very least, it's a step in the right direction.

"You seem to be in a good mood this morning."

Glancing up, I find Elijah sliding onto the bench beside me, his tray loaded with two bowls of…oatmeal, of all things.

I shrug while taking a sip of my orange juice. "Just another day."

"Nope," he says, shaking his head. "Something's different."

Realistically, I know there's zero chance Elijah can just *tell* I'm gay. Admitting it aloud to one person, even if it's for the first time, doesn't automatically put a flashing neon sign over my head that reads *homosexual crossing* for everyone to see.

But even that sound bit of logic doesn't stop my stomach from swirling in panic while I slowly set my glass back on the table.

"Uh, I'm not sure—"

"You didn't shave."

I glance at the kid, cocking my head. He's right, I didn't shave this morning. But I'm not quite sure how he made the leap from not shaving to me being in a good mood.

"Uh. No, I didn't."

He nods while chewing the bite of oatmeal he just shoved in his mouth, waiting until he swallows to speak. "Makes sense. I'd be happy if I didn't have to take a razor to my face every day too."

My lips twitch into a grin.

God, this kid.

There's something to be said about how unabashed he is, at least around me. While he might have a shyness about him when it comes to the kids his age, that seems to disappear when the two of us talk. He says the first thing on his mind without a second thought.

It's refreshing.

Fuck, maybe there's a lesson for me to learn from him too.

A sudden burning on the side of my face has my attention shifting from Elijah, subconsciously moving toward the source. Sure enough, Kaleb's eyes are already locked on me, and when our gazes collide, the slightest smirk pulls at his lips again. Not the devious kind that would make me wonder what sort of evil plan he's concocting in his head. It's the kind that two people share when they know something no one else does. Like an inside joke.

Or in my case, the secret I've been harboring since puberty.

And while it's terrifying to have this kind of trust in someone else, I can't keep myself from returning his grin.

Because I was wrong about Kaleb LaMothe; that much has become blatantly obvious.

He didn't owe me the time of day, let alone becoming the person I'd bare my inner shame and resentment to, but he took it on anyway. Then he offered to bear the weight of more of it, should the need arise.

More than anything, I wanna thank him for listening to what I had to say.

An idea begins taking form while Elijah does his best to interrogate me about the activities for the day. There's a small break in our schedule—an extra hour between lunch and our afternoon playing a game of kickball with our kids—and it may be the perfect opportunity to put this plan into motion.

Everything falls into place after our morning hike to the viewpoint over the lake, and once the kids are situated in the dining hall for lunch, I seize the moment and sneak away.

It's a quick ten-minute drive to the gas station down the road, and I'm in and out with a six pack of beer, a few random odds and ends, and a full tank of gas less than five minutes later. Probably not a smart move on my part to leave without telling anyone, but hey, how does the saying go? Better to ask for forgiveness than permission?

Once I'm back at camp, I slip from the car and make my way to Kaleb's cabin. Knowing my luck, he's probably in there, taking the little bit of extra time we've been given to relax. Yet when I peek in the window, I find it's dark and empty inside.

Bingo.

I quickly pull the note I'd penned before heading off to the store and tuck it in with one of the bottles, the glass holding it in place.

Thanks for hearing me out.
Cheers to starting over.
— A

My original idea was to just leave it at his door for him to find, but since it's broad daylight, there's a good chance one of the kids will see it. I'm not looking to blow up this newfound truce with Kaleb by bringing illicit substances on the premises, and kids finding the alcohol and ratting him out to Colin would be a surefire way to do just that. Or worse, they could decide to claim it as theirs, and we'd have a whole different set of issues on our hands.

Erring on the side of caution, I pull out my master key and shove it into the lock. Trespassing is a better option at this point, and all I can do is hope the sentiment outweighs the crime.

I quickly slip inside and leave the six pack and note on the chair in the corner of his cabin—which is somehow appallingly clean—then sneak out again before anyone notices my presence.

Maybe he'll be upset with me for breaking the rules, or maybe he won't care in the slightest. It's a toss up with him. But at the very least, it's a white flag. A symbol of peace.

I just hope it's enough.

We're out on the make-shift kickball field an hour later, and truthfully, this might be the first time I'm somewhat in my element since arriving at camp three weeks ago. Something about a set of bases and a pitcher's mound immediately puts me at ease, and even though it stings knowing I'll never set foot on one competitively again, I'm still looking forward to it.

Plus, if it gives me a chance to be better at something than Kaleb for a change, then I'm all for it.

Kaleb and I each chose a captain to pick teams, and to my surprise, he calls Tyler to be his. I'd have assumed he would choose one of the twins, who look rather irritated by their brother picking someone else over them.

Then, likely shocking no one, I chose Elijah for mine.

Well, maybe Elijah was a little stunned by it, because the kid is frowning at me from behind his glasses as he walks over to me.

"Why did you do that? I'm always picked last for this kind of stuff."

I had a feeling that may be the case, since he's one of the least athletic of the group. But I wasn't prepared for the words to leave his mouth, nor the way they'd hit me like a suckerpunch to the gut.

Resting my hand on his shoulder, I lean down to eye level with him and offer an encouraging smile. "Because I think you might make a better leader than a follower."

"What makes you say that?"

"Just a feeling." I shrug before letting my grin turn a little devious.

"And wouldn't it be nice to be the one who picked the kids on the winning team?"

His eyes light up and he nods, a matching grin spreading over his face.

When I rise back to my full height, I immediately feel Kaleb watching me. He's wearing a curious expression as our gazes lock, and I may as well be a piece of glass beneath his analytical stare.

He silently holds me there, almost in a magnetic field I can't break out of, before I shake it off to glance at Elijah, who's taking turns calling out names of the kids he wants on our team. And while I can't read his mind, I know he's never felt this important before. I can hear the pride and confidence in his voice with every name he calls.

Like a natural-born leader.

The corner of Kaleb's lips lifts in the slightest smirk as his attention returns to me, and he nods ever so slightly. His approval sends warmth flooding through my extremities, and a smile tugs my own lips up.

The teams are finalized a few minutes later, and with our separate teams, Kaleb and I assign a kicking order and field positions.

The entire group, regardless of which team they're on, is buzzing with excitement as we head into the first inning. The kids really seem to be enjoying the change of pace from all the hiking, fishing, and kayaking.

Or maybe that's just my own bias talking.

To keep things fair, Kaleb and I take on the role of pitching for our respective teams, and with my team in the field first, I take my place on the pitcher's plate.

It's bittersweet, feeling the rubber beneath my feet again, knowing this is likely the only capacity I'll be in this position again. A sense of longing curls in my stomach at the thought, but as Colton comes up to the plate as the first kicker, I push it aside and do what I do best.

Well, I take it easy on them, of course. After all, they're just kids.

A couple even get a decent kick off me before my team manages to round up three outs, and we're swapping positions for our chance to kick. On my way in, Kaleb holds out the clipboard we're keeping score on in exchange for the ball.

"Feel free to double check my math," he teases over his shoulder while heading onto the field.

I frown and glance down at the paper.

His team didn't score at all, so I'm not sure what math he could possibly—

My eyes land on a note scribbled near the top of the page in what I've come to recognize as Kaleb's handwriting.

> *Apparently, pitching skills in baseball translates to kickball.*
> *Who would've thought?*

I smirk, glancing up to find him already grinning at me while bouncing the ball at the pitcher's plate—almost like he's preparing for a game of dodgeball instead.

Chuckling to myself at his antics, I return my attention to his note and scribble out a response while my kids take their turn kicking.

> That sounds an awful lot like a compliment. You feeling okay?
> Not having heat stroke or something? I'd hate to win by forfeit.

I keep my expression stoic as I hand off the clipboard to him between the next half-inning, making sure to underline *and* bold the three runs my team scored this at-kick.

It's childish to pass notes to each other like this, I know that. But the amount of time we have without a billion sets of preteen ears around is limited, so if I want any sort of private conversation with Kaleb—even one tossing playful jabs—then this is how it's gotta happen.

And once we hit three outs and I'm handed the clipboard again, I find myself giddy to see what he's written next.

The only way you'll beat me in kickball is in your dreams.

I snort as I read the message, shaking my head before calling out that Liam, Jared, and Max are the next three up to kick.

The inning is so quick, all three of the boys getting out one after another, I don't even have a chance to write out a reply before passing off the clipboard to Kaleb. Though, from the smug grin on his face, part of me wants to whack him upside the head with it instead.

A few more innings pass without much excitement, both with regard to the game and the little taunting notes from Kaleb. It's not until the top of the fifth inning that I notice him scribbling on the paper, a small smirk on his lips.

Call me crazy, but something tells me it's not the score he's grinning at, despite his team coming from behind to tie the game during this at-kick.

When I head back in for our turn to kick and Kaleb hands me the clipboard, I have to force myself not to check what it says the second it's in my hands.

My willpower lasts all of three seconds.

Found something interesting in my cabin after lunch.

My stomach twists in a knot of anxiety as I reread his message a couple times, noting that the butterflies may as well be a swarm of hornets at this point.

Clearing my throat, I call out the kicking order for my team while scribbling out a flippant response.

Oh, don't tell me. A spider? No, maybe a raccoon?

My mind races through the possible reactions I'll get from my olive branch, creating a swirling whirlpool of nerves in the pit of my stomach. They don't dissipate in the time we're on offense either. They might actually grow in all the time it takes for Kaleb's team to round up three outs, but not before my team earns two runs.

With the score at 5-3—my team in the lead—we head back onto the field for the last full inning. My team is jacked up with excitement, feeling the high of a potential win, and as much as I'd love to share their enthusiasm, I'm trying to keep my lunch from making a reappearance when I offer the clipboard to Kaleb.

His eyes sparkle with mischief as he takes it, and unlike me, he reads the note on the spot before I can even walk away. His expression turns impish as he shakes his head, muttering a playfully sarcastic, "You're hilarious," just loud enough for me to hear.

The smallest amount of relief sinks down to my bones.

He's not mad about my tiny stint of trespassing, which was my main concern.

But with those extinguished by his banter, I'm able to focus on leading my team to another shut-out half-inning. It's a close call at one point, but with Elijah and Max working together to get Colton out in one helluva double play, we manage to maintain our two-run lead.

"I don't know if I should be annoyed or impressed," Kaleb muses during our hand-off.

Laughing, I offer him a quick, "Why not both?" before heading in, reading his note on the way.

You planning to make me drink alone?

There's those stupid butterflies again, which are equally as annoying as the stupid grin pulling at my lips, no matter how hard I try to keep it from forming. But what really has me struggling to keep my composure are the vibrations running through my body strong enough to register on the damn Richter scale.

What the fuck is wrong with me?

"What are you smiling about?"

Startled by the question, I glance over to find Elijah trying to sneak a peek at what I'm looking at.

Shit.

Despite my recent efforts to quell the shaming voice inside me, the instincts shaped by it are still very much alive. Which is why I end up tucking the clipboard beneath my arm to hide the exchanges…and let the lie fall from my lips with ease.

"That we're winning, obviously." I motion toward the field with my chin. "Any chance I have to beat Kaleb at something is gonna make me happier than a kid on Christmas morning."

Apparently, so does flirting with him.

Disgusting.

I wince and put up every mental block I can as the word bounces through my mind like a pinball, and instead, focus on the grin Elijah's now wearing.

"Thanks for making me captain."

I chuckle. "You don't have to thank me. The way you're playing proves I was right; you're a natural leader."

He shakes his head. "I don't ever play like this when I'm not captain."

"Because you've never been this confident." When his brows crinkle in confusion, I elaborate. "Being picked last blows, right? You don't feel very good about yourself when that happens, so why would you feel like you're going to play well? But when you feel important and valued, like as a captain, you'll play like you belong. It becomes a self-fulfilling prophecy either way."

Elijah studies me for a moment, mulling my point over in his mind.

"Confidence," he echoes, the word clearly tasting funny on his tongue from his expression.

"Believe in yourself, kid. You belong here."

There's a beat of silence before he floors me by whispering, "So do you, you know."

I'm caught off-guard by the simple earnestness of the statement, and it has my heart squeezing behind my ribs.

Unfortunately, I don't have the chance to thank him, because cheering breaks out on the field and draws my attention back up. Kaleb's team is rushing toward home plate, clearly having just found their last out for the inning, and I haven't even written back to Kaleb.

Quickly updating the score, I write the first thing I can think of before tucking the pen beneath the metal clip.

Is that supposed to be an offer?

Kaleb eyes me with piqued curiosity when I hand it to him, and I do my best not to look every bit as nervous as I feel. Because, now that I have the chance to actually *think* about the message I just wrote, I realize just how flirty it sounds.

Fucking hell. There really should be a rule book for this kinda thing. *Flirting With The Frienemy 101*, sure to be an instant bestseller.

Tamping down my worry, I focus on getting three more outs, and more importantly, securing a victory for Elijah's first time as a captain. Luck is on my side, it seems, because it only takes three kickers to get three outs, and the game ends with my team still on the field.

Despite winning, there are a few gripes from the kids who miss out on another chance to kick—Max being the loudest, as always—but the boys are all in good spirits. Winning and losing teams alike, they congratulate each other with high fives and handshakes, and Colton even asks if we can have a game once a week.

"We'll see," Kaleb says with a laugh before motioning toward the field. "But for now, I need a few of you to gather the bases. The rest of you, head back and clean up for dinner."

The kids break off, nearly ten of them heading back onto the field while the rest make their way back into camp. I'm about to follow the latter group, if only to make sure they don't get into any mischief unsupervised, when Kaleb calls out after me.

"Reynolds! Can you read these instructions about the activity list for tomorrow while I wait on these guys?"

I frown as he tosses me the clipboard, wondering why the hell he's wanting me to look at the activity list when tomorrow is our day off. It's on the tip of my tongue to ask, but the words die on my lips when, right there at the top, in his neat, all-caps handwriting, is a message.

Use that key again tonight, and you'll find out.

I'm not sure when he had the chance to read or respond to it, but it's right there, staring me in the face. Reading over the note two more times, I do my best to analyze the subtext of the nine words written there.

Is he…flirting back? Or is this just him accepting my offer to bury the hatchet and being friendly?

When I glance up, I find he's already turned to let the kids stack the bases in his arms. He laughs animatedly at whatever the group of them are yammering on about, completely oblivious to me watching.

Another wave of vibrations hits me, spreading warmth from my chest all the way to my toes, and reviving the swarm in my stomach along the way.

Regardless of his intent, my body's reaction is clear about one important thing: I'm in way over my fucking head.

And there's a part of me—no matter how small—that's enjoying every minute of it.

FIFTEEN

Avery

My anxiety spikes to an all-time high as I climb the steps to Kaleb's cabin just past eleven.

The kids have been in bed for a while now, and I took my time decompressing and showering off the dirt and grime from the day's activities. But all that time to myself has put me more in my head than I was earlier.

I've never been much of an overthinker, but something about Kaleb—about this unwarranted *attraction* to him—is turning me upside down and inside out all at once.

Take right now, for example.

Did he actually mean it when he said I could use the key and just come in? Or was that his way of asking me to come over and drink the beers I'd left in his cabin *using that key?*

Indecision wars within me for a solid minute as I stand at his door like an imbecile, hands shaking and palms damp with sweat. I'm barely able to make out his form lounging on the bed through the cracks in his blinds, but that brings up a whole new layer of indecision.

If I do use the key, should I at least knock to alert him of my presence—make sure he's decent?

As if I haven't seen him in various states of undress while sharing a locker room the past two years?

"Oh, for fuck's sake. Get a grip, Reynolds," I mutter under my breath before raising my fist to the door and rapping on the wood. The ten-second wait for him to open the damn thing might as well be a millenia, my nerves are that shot.

"I told you you could've just come in," he says in way of greeting before stepping back, allowing me to enter.

Painfully aware of just how quickly my heart is beating, I take a single step into the cabin and close the door behind me.

"I didn't know if you were…decent."

Kaleb arches a brow as he drops back down on his mattress. "You ripped open my shower curtain while I was bare-ass naked like a week ago. There's little left to the imagination at this point."

I cough, attempting to cover the sound of me nearly choking on my own spit from the surprise of him bringing up the night of the shower.

"Fair enough," I manage.

Shit, how could I have forgotten that?

Just the memory of Kaleb's angry glare and water cascading over his smooth, tanned skin has my cock stirring behind my sweats—which is the last thing I want it to do when I'm about to sit in a confined space with the object of my unfortunate desire.

Two forest-green eyes meet mine, and I swear he knows exactly where my thoughts are lingering. His penetrating stare always seems to see right through me.

"You planning to just stand awkwardly in the doorway the whole night, or are you gonna come in?"

Fuck. Right.

Crossing the room, I take a seat on the edge of his bed. Maybe not the best option, all things considered, but it seemed like a better option than the chair all the way in the other corner.

He's already reaching over to the small cooler beside his bed, grabbing the six-pack I'd left him and setting it on the mattress between us. Pulling one from the sleeve, he cracks it open and hands it to me before snagging one for himself.

"Did you know this was my favorite, or was it just a lucky guess?" he asks, lifting the bottle in question.

It's the same beer I'd seen him drink on occasion last season. A few times we'd gone out with some of our teammates to Stagger, for one, but at a few parties on campus too. I wasn't exactly thinking about those moments when I selected it at the store, but something tells me it wasn't a totally subconscious choice.

"Uh, I just grabbed the first thing I saw."

There's no telling if he buys the half-truth, but he doesn't say anything. Just lets out a soft hum as he takes a drink, his throat working to swallow the liquid.

Averting my gaze, I take a swig of my own beer, then another.

I've never been one to down drinks quickly, but being in a confined space with Kaleb smelling like the forest after it rains has me in desperate need to take the edge off. Adding the fact that we're both sitting on his bed, barely three feet apart, and I need all the help I can get to relax.

Fortunately, the tension lining my shoulders and neck leave right around the time I finish off my first beer.

Alcohol is a beautiful thing sometimes.

Kaleb also takes some of the pressure off by putting old episodes of *Criminal Minds* on his laptop as background noise. A fact which is surprising, not because of the choice of show, but that he has the passwords for the Wi-Fi.

Would've been nice to know about for the past few weeks.

The two of us settle in with our backs against the cabin wall, the laptop on the edge of his desk and the six-pack positioned in the few feet of space between our legs. Silence blankets us while we watch, and despite it being a comfortable quietness, I can't fully relax. My senses are heightened from his proximity; his addictive scent and the heat of his body setting me on edge.

So I drink, if only to dull the pull I feel toward him.

My second beer is nearly gone when Kaleb's voice snags my attention from his laptop screen. "Slow your roll, dude, or you're gonna be drunk in no time."

It doesn't come out judgmental, like I've come to expect. Instead, it's more of a warning, which has me arching a brow at him.

"You can't be serious." When he hitches a brow up in return and shrugs, I scoff. "There's no chance in hell we're getting lit off three beers apiece, let alone off one or two."

"There you go again, underestimating the power of elevation change." A little smirk plays at his lips as he lifts his own beer to hide it. "Need I remind you of that God-awful sunburn you got that first week when you didn't listen to me?"

I remember it all too well, but there's not a chance I'll be admitting it to him. If anything, the need to double-down in opposition flares inside me before I mutter, "And there you go, being a fucking know-it-all again."

And with that, I finish off the beer in my hand before slipping the empty bottle back in the carton, only to grab another in replacement.

A low, smooth chuckle that slides over me like satin comes from Kaleb, and when I glance over again, he's shaking his head.

"Suit yourself, Reynolds. But don't come crying to me when you're hungover tomorrow."

"It's three beers," I remind him. Cracking the drink open, I toss the cap at his head, but he's quick to bat it away before it hits its mark. "I'm more likely to be mauled beyond recognition by a mountain lion on my way back to my cabin later than be hungover in the morning."

He arches a brow, tossing back in a playful lilt, "Is that your way of trying to score an invite to stay the night here? To keep your pretty face safe from the wildlife?"

While the comment was surely a meaningless joke from his tone alone, it instantly has the few feet of space between us feeling like nothing more than centimeters. Because…fuck, there's part of me that wants to feign fear of the things that go bump in the wilderness if it means staying the night here with him.

How repulsive to think such a thing!

I shake my head—to dislodge the ugly claws sinking into my mind—while my cheeks heat. "You'd probably be the one luring it here in the first place. Setting me up for cougar bait would be an easy way to rid yourself of me."

His soft laugh floats through the air between us. "You're proving yourself rather impossible to be rid of, Reynolds. At this point, I'm done trying."

Having no idea how to respond, I take another pull from my bottle and refocus my attention on the show.

A few minutes pass without us saying a word, the only sound coming from Kaleb's laptop and the occasional sloshing of beer as we continue drinking. Again, it's not entirely uncomfortable, but tension still lines my back and shoulders regardless.

My every atom is attuned to him, lying in wait for his next move or breath or—

"This is…"

Swallowing, I glance at him and wait for him to finish the thought. Surely the word *weird* or *awkward* is about to spill from his lips, and after all that's happened, I can't say I'd blame him for it either.

But then his gaze meets mine, and he offers a shrug.

"I don't know. It's…nice, I guess."

Well, I'll be fucking damned.

My lips twitch up, hinting at a smile, as I take another sip from my drink. "You say that like we didn't used to spend time together before now."

"Maybe," he murmurs, his eyes locked on mine. "But we both know a lot has changed since we first met freshman year."

Understatement of the century.

There's a lot of history between us, and as of late, it hasn't been good. But since our conversation on the dock, it feels like we've begun mending fences. Maybe even rebuilding a friendship. One I hadn't realized I'd been missing until now.

Then again, how deep of a friendship was it to begin with if we've both hidden such integral parts of who we are?

"You didn't have to keep it a secret, you know," I find myself saying. When his brows furrow, clearly confused about my statement, I tack on, "That you were gay."

His expression relaxes and he lets out a soft snort. "For a second you were making it sound like I was keeping a murder spree or drug addiction from you, not my sexuality."

"Who's to say you still aren't?" I volley back, arching a brow. "I don't know what you do in your free time."

He lets out an amused laugh, and it causes my stomach to do cartwheels and backflips like a goddamn gymnast. "You caught me. I'm lucky those kids didn't bring homicide or habitual drug use into the mix during Never Have I Ever, or I'd really be outed for all my secrets."

The statement comes out so blunt and dry, I can't help but smile. Something about his phrasing catches in my brain, though, like a fish on a hook. And while I have no room to be asking for details like this from him, the question spills free anyway.

"Are you, though? Out?"

Kaleb shakes his head back and forth, but more in a way of weighing his words than a flat out no. "It's not something I broadcast to the world, but it's not really a secret either. My family knows, and yeah, I had that awkward 'coming out' moment with my parents in high school. Some people at Foltyn know—"

"But I didn't," I cut in immediately.

A statement, not a question.

As I hold his gaze, I realize…fuck, it might even be an accusation.

Kaleb's expression shutters slightly, almost as if he's donning a suit of armor before walking into a duel. "I don't let my sexuality define me, which is exactly why I make no efforts to hide or confirm it. With anyone."

The words are the truth, no doubt, but his clipped tone gives off more than that. Almost like a bit he's been rehearsing for whenever I finally decided to bring it up.

Just another layer of protection.

"Except me." I eye him with equal parts suspicion and curiosity. "You hid it from me, LaMothe. It was written all over your face at the campfire that night. Don't try denying it now."

There's no sign of backing down in his gaze when he utters, "It wasn't until you started harassing Keene and Aspen that I realized I had something to hide from you in the first place." He pauses, his gaze holding mine, almost searching before he speaks again. "You remember that night last year when we were all out at Stagger? The one where you were basically harassing Aspen?"

I'm brought back to that night instantly, remembering the taunts and insults I'd thrown at my teammate's best friend. The memory has shame—an entirely different kind than I'm used to—churning my stomach, and I nod.

Kaleb waits a beat before divulging a truth I never saw coming.

"I was there *with* a guy that night."

Shaking my head, I try to make sense of what he's telling me. Because there's no way in hell I could've missed a detail like that.

"We were out with some of the guys on the team," I reason.

"In the beginning, yeah. But then the guy I'd been seeing for a few weeks showed up, even if the rest of you didn't make the connection for yourselves. I sure as hell wasn't gonna do it for you at that point." He takes another drink from his bottle before wiping his mouth with the back of his hand. "Before then, though? Before I saw how fucking mean you could be to someone different than you? I never once tried hiding it from you."

The statement may as well be a blow from his fist, hitting me in the chest hard enough to cause my heart to stumble behind my ribs.

Shame and guilt aren't new feelings to me. I've long since grown used to being buried by them, suffocating silently beneath their weight. But never like this.

Never for something I had control over.

"You're right, okay?" I mutter, still a little breathless from his revelation. "I know I was a dick, and you had every reason to keep it from me once you saw that side of me. But, Kaleb…we were friends three years before that ever happened."

His jaw tightens ever so slightly before his gaze finally falls away from mine.

It's the first time he's backed down, and I'm not prepared for it. I certainly don't relish in it. Not now, after we've managed to make some headway in repairing all this fucked-up brokeness between us.

Fuck me.

Kaleb's attention stays locked on the beer, and he looks like there's something he wants to say. I can see him willing the thoughts to remain inside, fighting tooth and nail to pull them back from the tip of his tongue before they dare spill free.

In the end, his battle of wills is a losing one.

"Because I was afraid of you looking at me differently."

For as much as I was craving his answer, part of me wishes I never heard it. Because, the truth is, I *would have* looked at him differently. There's a damn good chance I would've treated him exactly how I did Aspen and Keene last year.

Maybe even worse.

He was right to keep it from me back then. Hell, he was right to keep it from me until his brothers all but forced the information out of him, leaving him with no other option.

But admitting this? It *is* his choice. His decision to take a risk in shedding a piece of his armor. Even if it's just one, it's enough to expose him. Make him as vulnerable to me as I was with him on the dock.

"I'm sorry."

The words leave my lips before I realize it, and they instantly have

Kaleb's gaze lifting to mine. He studies me, a pensive expression on his face, and for what might be the first time since I arrived at camp, I catch his eyes softening around the edges.

"I don't…" He lets out a breathy laugh, shaking his head. "Never have I ever heard those words leave your mouth."

His statement immediately has me holding up a palm. "Oh, no. We're not playing that game again."

He chuckles. "Why not? Afraid of some skeletons to come creeping outta your closet this time?"

From the playful lilt in his voice and grin tugging at his lips, he's perfectly aware of his word choice. Probably did it intentionally, if I had to bet money on it.

But despite the light, jesting tone, a darker side of the joke slices me straight to the bone.

"There's nothing in my closet left to hide," I mumble, focused on my now-empty beer. "I'm fucking sick of hiding it as it is."

He doesn't miss a beat before asking, "Is that why you kissed me? So you couldn't hide anymore?"

I release a long sigh, which turns into a bit of a groan.

I've been both waiting for and dreading this question. Probably because the answer is just as convoluted as my feelings about my sexuality; a tangled web of fear, loathing, and desire I can't even make sense of, let alone explain to someone else.

"I don't know," I whisper slowly, measuring my words. "Until that night with the whole campfire game, you being anything other than straight never crossed my mind. Even if it had, I'd never allowed myself to even think of *any* guy like that. Not when it felt so unattainable." I lift my gaze back to his and shrug. "But then the truth came out, and you were right there, and I just…couldn't stop myself."

His lips lift in the ghost of a smile. "Sounds like we've gotta work on your self-control."

"Yeah, well, I wasn't exactly planning to lust after the one guy I can't fucking stand."

Whoa, where the fuck did that come from?

Apparently the alcohol, while not enough to get me drunk, has loosened my lips enough to let my inside thoughts slip out. Because that most definitely was *not* something sober me would have said.

Or maybe Kaleb is right, and the elevation is making it hit me harder than expected.

Kaleb seems to take it in stride, though, because he smirks, and he raises his bottle toward me in mock cheers. "Can't stand, huh? And here I thought we were on our way to friends again."

Despite his playful tone, I'm hit with a wave of unease and start picking at the paper wrapping around the beer bottle, and mutter out a gruff, "Only just."

And with the way my mouth is going, we're sure to head right back to enemy territory.

Continuing my task, I peel the paper off until it's bare glass, and shove the remnants of the label through the neck. Only once I've finished the task do I lift my gaze, landing first on the bow of his lips, framed by his dark scruff, before reaching his eyes.

"Attraction is a strange thing," he whispers, all low and husky. "I'd be a fucking liar if I said I wasn't attracted to you."

The words hang in the air between us, leaving me speechless.

I'd have to be blind and stupid not to realize the tension between the two of us has changed ever since I kissed him. Granted, it caused a lot of animosity to kick up a notch for a hot minute. But since making an effort to truly mend fences, a lot of the tension has shifted in nature, becoming a strange sort of simmering that feels eerily similar to…butterflies.

They rip though my stomach in a flurry whenever our eyes lock. Or when we're close enough that I can feel the heat of his body radiating toward mine, they turn into a swarm so violent, sometimes I think I might take flight myself.

Kaleb swallows roughly before glancing away, effectively breaking the moment.

I'm surprised to find myself…disappointed by it, but I know he probably did us both a favor. We're currently skating on thin ice as it is. One wrong move, and we both risk it cracking beneath our feet. Or worse, falling beneath the surface with no way out.

Self-preservation tells me I should flee for solid ground, for safety and security, rather than diving headfirst into whatever Kaleb has begun stirring up inside me.

Because, his acceptance and forgiveness aside, I'm still conflicted.

About how I feel. Who I am.

And…who I want.

It's revolting!

Shame's voice scratches against the inside of my skull, and my eyes sink closed. As if removing the object of my desire from view is enough to stop it from screaming at me.

Kaleb clears his throat. "If that was too much—"

Eyes still closed, I shake my head, the back of it rolling against the wooden cabin wall.

"Don't apologize. Not when you were right," I mutter.

The second part wasn't meant to be said aloud, and definitely not for his ears, but it's too late to take it back now. Especially when he softly asks, "About what?"

Steeling myself, I blink my eyes open and find his gaze fixed on me. His attention has my mouth feeling drier than the Sahara, and I wet my lips subconsciously.

"That I'd be back, begging for more. And I hate that you were right."

The words leave my lips in a harsh whisper, tasting acidic on my tongue. More vile insults are hurled through my mind, serving as a reminder that my desire for him, or any other guy, will likely never be truly set free.

Not when I'm defenseless against the claws ripping me apart inside my mind.

After a revelation like the one I just let slip, there's not much else to say on my end. Kaleb makes no effort to break the silence lingering between us either, and truthfully, I'm not expecting him to. Just like I'm not expecting him to return the senti—

"I was only half right," he murmurs, breaking through my thoughts.

My brows crash together. "How?"

"Because I also told you there wouldn't be a repeat."

His eyes are as dark as the evergreens surrounding the camp now as they bore into mine, and with the glow of the lamplight reflecting off their glassy surface, it looks like a forest on fire.

Or maybe it's the heat in his stare as it darts down to my lips that is scorching.

I wet them again on instinct, and his eyes tracking the movement sends another ripple of lust barreling down my spine.

My mind races, torn between ripping myself free from this moment and letting myself sink into it, even if it can only be that—a moment.

"So we're both going back on our word, huh?"

"Looks like it," he rasps, his voice all gravel and shattered glass. And then he closes the gap between our lips entirely.

SIXTEEN

Avery

Every atom of my body is on fire the second Kaleb's lips land on mine, and it's almost as if time comes to a complete halt while I bask in the flames. Relishing the burn, finding pleasure in it.

Just like the kiss against the tree, the hate-filled thoughts plaguing me fall silent, and I can finally listen to my body instead. Allow it to take charge for a change and just feel.

Exist the way I was meant to.

The empty beer bottles clatter to the floor, long since forgotten, as Kaleb's deft fingers work their way under my shirt. He shoves it up my body, only to break our kiss to whip it over my head and toss it aside. My heart pounds in my chest as I do the same to him, peeling the fabric off to reveal miles of smooth skin and toned muscle.

My eyes map his chest and stomach greedily, both devouring and memorizing him.

Kaleb doesn't allow me much time to ogle, though, before he grabs my chin and covers my mouth with his own in another searing kiss. He shifts while he claims my lips, pressing me back into the mattress in a way that has my cock aching behind my sweats. His mouth continues to devour mine as he brackets his arms on either side of my head in a way…fuck. It shouldn't be as hot as it is.

And now that he has me where he wants me, he fucking consumes me.

He grinds his pelvis down, and I almost come on the damn spot when I feel his hard length rubbing against mine, even through the fabric of our clothing.

Something between a groan and a curse leaves me, and he chuckles lightly against my skin.

"You good?"

I nod, rolling my hips up into his. I've never been better in my life.

Kaleb's returning grin is sinfully wicked. "Good. Just tell me if I'm going too fast."

My body's immediate reaction is that it's not fast enough; it wants more. Craves it, like an addict in withdrawal. But it's not the physical he's talking about, and that's what my mind catches on, if only for a moment.

For the briefest second, the darkness in my mind sneaks through the cracks and reminds me of how…wrong this is. How shameful what we're doing is, and how disgusted I should be with myself for allowing it to happen.

But if this is wrong, then why does it feel so fucking perfect?

My brain is unable to formulate an answer, though, because Kaleb chooses that second to press his hips against me again.

A moan works its way from my throat, but he's quick to swallow it down as his hips continue rutting into mine at a slow, seductive pace.

"God, being the one pulling those sounds from you is so much hotter than just hearing them," he rasps, snagging my bottom lip between his teeth. "It's fun seeing you like this. Turned on and panting beneath me."

My cock throbs from his words and his touch but still aches for more friction.

He captures my lips again as his hand moves to my waistband, his fingers skating against my skin beneath the edge of the fabric in a way that steals all the oxygen from my lungs.

Emotions swirl within me like a tornado, each fighting for the spotlight, but the one I wasn't expecting feels suspiciously like…relief. That even after all the shit I've pulled, despite all the reasons I've given him to hate me, he wants me the same way I want him.

Kaleb breaks the kiss and pulls back just enough to meet my gaze. His cheeks are flushed with desire, and those dark-green eyes appear damn near black, dilated with lust and need.

Two fingers dip into my waistband ever so slightly, curling around the fabric.

"Can I…" He lets the unfinished question linger between us, eyes remaining locked with mine while we both take a second to catch our breath.

I want him to touch me, and while the thought terrifies me, it's thrilling at the same time.

So I nod.

Another seductive grin spreads over his lips, and he wastes no time closing the distance between us again. His mouth is more insistent now, molding to mine before coaxing it open so his tongue can slip inside.

My stomach tightens when his hand slowly drags my sweats down past my ass, taking my briefs along with them. Cool air hits my heated, sensitive skin, causing my bare cock to twitch between us.

Then his palm wraps around me, and I damn near die on the spot.

"Fucking perfect," Kaleb whispers as he begins stroking my length.

His hand moves up and down my shaft at a slow, leisurely pace that quickly becomes far too much like torture. Pair it with the way his lips caress my throat, and there's nothing to prevent me from becoming a panting, leaking mess beneath him; pinned down and at his mercy.

And he doesn't make any signs of stopping until that's exactly what happens.

"If you like this…" A low, seductive laugh leaves him as he kisses my throat. "Fuck, let's just say we haven't even started making you feel good, baby."

Some mixture of a moan and a whimper leaves me at his filthy promise—one more feral animal than human—and I'd be mortified by it if I wasn't so fucking turned on. From the way Kaleb hums in approval, he's rather enjoying it.

Goddamn sadist.

"Are you ready for more?" he goads.

His smile is audible through his teasing tone, and when I witness the sight in all its glory after he leans back, my stomach flip-flops like a goddamn fish. He must realize what he's doing to me, the smug asshole, because he takes it a step further by scraping his teeth over his lower lip.

Christ, have mercy.

I nod and let out a soft hum, not sure I can manage words at the moment—even one as simple as *yes* or *please.*

Thankfully, Kaleb doesn't force them from me, instead pushing himself up onto his knees. I greedily drink in the sight as his toned muscles and tanned skin make their appearance, mapping every inch of him with my gaze before falling to the thick ridge bulging against his sweats.

His gaze stays trained on my face while he slowly hooks a thumb into his waistband and pushes it down until his cock springs free. He's long and veiny, with a bead of pre-cum gathered on the mushroom tip, and if my heart rate wasn't already kicked up a notch from the desire licking through my bloodstream, it certainly would be now.

Especially when the first instinct that hits me is to lean forward and taste it.

Absolutely deplorable!

I'm not sure if the alcohol is muddling my thoughts or if the lust flooding my system is too potent to fight, but either way, Shame's voice is instantly drowned out. Gone before the venom could spread, swept away by the aching want sinking its fangs into me deeper than my shame ever could.

Kaleb's palm wraps around his length, his attention still locked on my face as he begins stroking himself. With his free hand, he slowly pulls open the desk drawer beside his bed and retrieves a bottle.

Lube.

He pops the cap open, and all the air in my lungs disappears when he pours the liquid over my length, covering me with it. My fingers grip the comforter beneath me, the cool sensation sending another sinful zap of electricity through my body.

Jesus Christ, how the fuck am I this turned on?

He's barely touching me, and I'm already set to detonate.

"I need you to tell me when to stop," he whispers, drawing my attention back to his face. "Can you do that for me?"

"Yeah," I manage to choke out with a nod. "I can do that."

As if that's all he needed, Kaleb releases his cock and lowers himself back down, covering me with his body. He captures my lips again, but in a kiss slower than the last. Less frenzied and more controlled as he grinds and rolls his hips against mine.

I'm on fire at every point where our skin meets, but the feeling of his bare cock bumping and sliding along mine might be my undoing. Well, that's until he shifts his weight to one elbow, reaches between us, and wraps his palm around both our lengths.

"Oh shit," I groan into his mouth before sealing my lips back to his.

The feel of his warm skin against mine is everything my fantasies have been made of. For years now, even if his face wasn't the one attached to it until recently.

And for *him* to be the one giving this to me? After everything? It's bringing out so many feelings, I couldn't possibly unpack them all while his fist is wrapped around us.

Breaking the kiss, Kaleb's mouth carves a path along my jaw before dipping to my throat. I'm on fire everywhere he touches me, lost in the pleasure and relishing the burn created by his skin on mine.

And, damn, I want more.

I wanna be consumed in flames.

My hands are everywhere after that; sliding up his back, gripping his shoulders, snaking into his hair. Anywhere I can touch him, I do, exploring and mapping his body while he takes us closer to the edge.

"You feel fucking amazing," Kaleb utters, his breath hot against my skin before he pulls back. I can tell his control is slipping from the way his eyes have taken on an animalistic gleam, and that's before his gaze falls to where he grips us. "God, and see how good we look together?"

He gives us another firm stroke, and I glance down in time to watch him smear the pre-cum leaking from our tips down the length of our shafts.

The sight is sinfully erotic.

Just not as much as the filthy grin on his lips.

"Fuck," I mutter, my balls getting heavy with the need for release. "I'm close."

Slamming my eyes closed, I do my best to get lost in the delicious friction of his cock against mine. His mouth brushes mine, and he takes his time licking and nipping at my lips before sealing his own against them. Fuses them down to the atom while our tongues flick and tangle together.

A sharp zing of impending release hits me in the stomach, and I gasp against his lips. He must take it as a negative sound, though, because he quickly pulls back to look at me.

"Should I stop?"

"Only if you wanna fucking die," I pant, arching into his touch. "Because if you stop before I come, there's nothing stopping me from burying you right alongside that stupid hatchet."

A soft laugh leaves him, but he continues jacking us, squeezing a little when he circles around the heads. "Then by all means. Come for me."

Kaleb's lips trail over my jaw, peppering kiss after kiss to my skin as they move back toward my ear. The heat of his breath has my stomach tightening, desire slamming into me like tidal waves in an unrelenting storm.

He's lost all rhythm now, his palm sliding over us in quick, rapid movements. My fingers dig into his hip, the other hand wrapping around the back of his neck, and I drag his mouth back to mine in a searing kiss.

It's messy, brutal, and wholly fucking addictive.

I hiss in pleasure, my teeth sinking into his lower lip as release barrels down my spine at a break-neck speed. Unable to hold on any longer, I'm shot into the stratosphere while cum spills from my cock, landing on my stomach and chest in a sticky mess.

I gasp, trying to catch my breath while Kaleb continues chasing his own orgasm at a frenzied pace, jacking us from root to tip. He's all rolling hips and breathless pants, and it's a sight unlike anything I've ever seen before.

"That's perfect," he groans while spreading the cum leaked over his fingers down our shafts. "I'm right there too."

My dick is hyper-sensitive now, with every nerve ending feeling like it's been hit by a cattle prod, but I don't dare ask him to stop or release me. Not when he's this close, teetering on the edge and about to fall into peaceful oblivion.

I feel his cock pulse against mine before another round of cum lands on my torso, mixing with my own release. He works himself through his orgasm, letting out a guttural moan loud enough to wake the dead as his forehead drops to mine.

"Ohholyfuckingshit," he moans in a single breath, lips mere inches away from mine.

Inches that feel like miles until he closes the distance with a hard, searing kiss.

His movements cease and his hand releases us, but our kiss carries on until he collapses on top of me. He shifts, keeping the majority of his weight on his elbows, and I find myself wishing he wouldn't. I wanna be pinned down and smothered by him; crushed until I'm nothing more than finely ground powder beneath his body.

Anything to keep me in the moment, to keep the self-loathing from snaking its way in. I can already feel Shame clawing its way out of the darkest recesses of my mind, waiting in the shadows like a viper ready to strike.

I focus on Kaleb's steady heartbeat against my chest instead, racing the rhythm of my own as we come down from our high in peaceful silence.

Out of nowhere, I'm smacked in the face with something he let slip in the heat of the moment. I'd almost missed it—I think I did when he actually said it—but now…

"You heard me in the shower."

Kaleb's body tenses infinitesimally before he pulls back. Two green eyes search my face for a brief second, seemingly gauging what my reaction might be, before he murmurs, "It's possible, yes."

I wasn't expecting him to admit it. Kinda makes me wonder what else I can get him to fess up to. So, with a soft hum, I press further. "And is it also possible that the state I caught you in was because of what you were hearing?"

A sheepish grin pulls at his lips, but what floors me is the way his cheeks and ears tint pink at my statement. I don't think there's ever been a moment where I've seen Kaleb LaMothe embarrassed, even when he was stark naked and hard in front of me.

Though, apparently, bringing it up is enough to do the trick.

"Like I said. I'd be a liar if I said I wasn't attracted to you."

A smile threatens to spread over my lips, but I manage to hold it back.

"Technically still are one, Mr. Don't Come Looking For A Repeat." I tap my fingers against his side in thought. "Are we still sticking by that threat, by the way?"

After an orgasm like the one I just had, I certainly hope that statement no longer rings true. I don't think I've felt a high like that in my life, and I know I'd love to feel it again.

Disgu—

Kaleb's laughter cuts through the poisonous thoughts, and he rolls over to his side. My attention shifts along with him, and I find him smirking down at me knowingly.

Smugly, like always. Yet, for the first time, I don't exactly hate it.

"We'll see how you feel in the morning, hmm?"

Considering the claws already piercing my mind, I think that's probably a good idea.

SEVENTEEN

Kaleb

Week Four

As the rest of the week passes, thankfully, so does most of the awkwardness and strife with my co-counselor. There are moments of lingering discord when I slip back into my habit of acting as the "sole leader" of this group, and Avery's stubbornness still has its way of sneaking into the equation, but overall, things have become relatively peaceful between us.

And thank God for that.

We actually managed to survive the rest of the week without incident, bringing us to another blissful, kid-free Sunday. Well, after getting the heathens to breakfast, then we have all the freedom in the world.

My brothers are bouncing off the walls this morning, acting a fool and pelting one another with pine cones while I attempt to herd them, Elijah, and my remaining half of kids to the dining hall.

I'm all for getting the rambunctious energy out now, especially if it means their listening ears are firmly in place once I hand them off to the other counselors in charge of wrangling them for the day. But the second I get nailed in the back of the head with a pine cone, all the fun and games are over.

"You might be my brothers, but I'm not above making the two of you sit in Colin's office all day if you don't cut it out," I threaten, turning to them and arching a brow. "And seeing as I know what they've got planned for you today, you really don't want that to happen."

The twins share an *oh shit* look before promptly dropping the projectiles and pretending like they've been angels this entire time.

"What are you gonna do today?" Day asks while he fiddles with the baseball cap on his head.

Colton snorts. "Probably spend it up on the mountain, like the weirdo he is."

Dayton nods before tacking on, "Or getting far away from Avery."

I actually hadn't given much thought to how I'd spend my day off. Normally, I'd only take a half day to do my laundry or maybe go into town for lunch if I was feeling something different, especially if the kids had been trying the day before.

But the mention of Avery has my thoughts shifting to unexpected places. Ones that *include* him, rather than entertain ways to put as much distance between us as I possibly can.

"I don't know why you guys don't like Avery."

This comes from Elijah, and I glance over my shoulder to find the kid trailing just behind the twins.

Colton scoffs. "Maybe because he's a complete d—"

"You better quit while you're ahead, Colton," I cut him off, aiming my harshest *don't fuck with me* glare his way. Lord knows he wouldn't get away with that language with Mom or Dad around.

"Okay, but if the boat shoes fit…" Dayton says with one of those *what can you do?* shrugs.

"He's actually really nice," Elijah pipes up, and when I glance over at the kid, I find him staring at his hands like they're the most interesting things in the world before he speaks again. "You guys just don't really give him much of a chance to be."

Colton and Dayton share a look—one that speaks louder than actual words of disbelief actually could—and shrug it off.

In Elijah's eyes, he and Avery are friends. He might even look up to the guy in somewhat of an older brother fashion, and there's no part of me that wants to soil that image of Avery for him. As it is, I'm starting to find myself agreeing with the kid.

The Avery that's slowly creeping to the surface—managing to shine through some of the assholery I've seen over the past year—is the same one I met freshman year. The one I wanted to be friends with. The one that, as much as I didn't want to admit it, had my stomach in knots whenever I'd hear him laugh or catch him grinning at me after a good play on the field.

And as I've started getting more and more glimpses of that version of him, all those feelings are rushing back in. Especially after what happened last week.

"Elijah's right," I finally confirm, eyeing the kid before shooting him a knowing smirk. "There's more to him than meets the eye."

When my attention moves to my brothers, I find them both staring at me like I've grown two extra heads.

Dayton is the first to speak, cocking his head to the side in confusion. "Who are you, and what have you done with our brother?"

"Yeah," Cole says slowly. "Did you hit your head and suddenly forget that he—"

"No." I cut him off before he can bring up what happened back at Foltyn. The last thing I need is one of the other kids catching wind and repeating it to another counselor, or worse, their parents.

Ironic, considering it wasn't that long ago I was looking to get him kicked out myself.

Cole narrows his eyes ever so slightly. "And now you're defending him."

Shit. Am I?

"We've put the past in the past" is the response I settle on, my attention flicking between my brothers. "Sometimes in life, people make mistakes. And sometimes they deserve the benefit of the doubt that they won't make those same ones again."

They don't look very convinced, if the vacant expressions are anything to go by, but thankfully, they decide to drop it when we enter the lodge. At that point, they become these half-human, half-feral-animal creatures, rushing to the buffet line for breakfast.

All except for Elijah.

There's an innocent smile plastered to his face when I glance over at him, about to ask if he's planning on eating this morning. I don't get the chance before he speaks instead.

"I'm glad you and Avery are friends again."

Then he's off to join the rest of the campers in line, like he didn't just pin me in place with a simple statement.

Are we friends now?

It doesn't quite feel like the right word, but I do know there's a sense of calm surrounding us that didn't exist before. I'd fully expected things to return to their strained, slightly volatile nature after what happened in my cabin last weekend, but to my surprise, it's been…normal. Or what normal should be.

Sure, we haven't exactly talked about the way we devoured each other like animals in heat until we were covered in our own cum, but that's okay. If he wants to leave it as a one-time thing, or if it was too much too soon, then I'm not gonna push the subject. It's not worth disrupting the newfound peace we've established, and honestly, I'm not really looking to put it under a microscope. I'd much rather enjoy where we are now. Maybe even replace some of the bullshit between us with something better.

Hell, we could *actually* be friends.

An idea clicks in my head, and after making sure the kids are all accounted for, I slip down the hall leading toward Colin's office and snag a piece of scrap paper. Then, taking a page from Avery's playbook, I scribble out a quick note on it.

10:00am, north trailhead.
There's something I want to show you.
— K

I make a beeline for Avery's cabin after that. A stupid grin tugs at my lips, and I wonder how he's gonna feel about me returning the favor when I slip inside and leave the note on his bed.

If this goes as planned, I'm sure I'll find out soon enough.

"You're late."

I glance down at my Garmin, noting the time as 10:02, before lifting my gaze to Avery. While I may have just seen him in the dining hall at breakfast, the sight of him leaning against the trail marker, waiting for me, does something weird to my stomach.

Choosing to ignore the weird fluttering altogether, I shake my head and sigh. "Look, my brothers were a couple of menaces after breakfast. I couldn't exactly leave them in the hands of someone else when they're acting a fool."

"Guess you're lucky I didn't impose the same terms as you, otherwise you'd be six feet under right now."

I hate the stupid smile pulling at my lips when I recall the threat I'd given him, but I can't seem to stop it either.

God, was that really only last week?

With how smooth things have been going the past few days, it may as well have been a millenia ago.

"Consider me grateful that you're sparing me from meeting an untimely demise," I joke, reaching up and placing my palm over my heart. "I'll be forever in your debt."

Rolling his eyes, he pushes off the sign and motions toward the trail. "You gonna tell me where the hell we're going?"

"Nope. It's a surprise."

And with that, I make my way past him and start up the trail.

He lets out a long, resounding sigh, and I glance over just in time to catch him glaring at me. "Of course not. Because why would you ever make anything easy or simple or enjoyable for me?"

The snort that slips out can't be helped. Leave it to Avery to complain about a surprise.

"You've met my brothers, and should know dramatics aren't gonna work on me." I flash him a grin—which earns me the finger this time—before adding, "Now, let's get your ass in gear. We only have so many hours of daylight, and I'm planning to use every one of them."

To his credit, he does start moving. But not without another smartass comment.

"I thought I was getting the day off, Drill Sergeant."

So fucking dramatic.

I don't dignify his comment with a response, and instead, keep up my pace. The trail to the base of Veil Falls is steep yet relatively short, and I know it won't be long before the sound of rushing water greets our ears.

Of course, by the time that actually happens, Avery is breathing heavily and glaring at me like we just hiked five miles straight uphill.

"Sometimes I really wonder if you're trying to kill me out here."

"Oh, relax," I chide, barely giving him a second glance. "You're a college athlete. We've had practices harder than this."

"Did you forget I'm a pitcher?" he asks between pants while locking his hands behind his head. "Coach didn't make us do half the shit that the rest of you were forced into."

Damn, he has a point there.

"Well, on the bright side, it's all downhill from here." Literally.

"Fucking hilarious, LaMothe," he gripes before dropping onto a nearby rock and making a big show of gulping down water. "You know, you really—"

The rest of his sentence dies on the spot when he finally quits his antics long enough to take in his surroundings, including the massive waterfall looming a few hundred feet from where we've stopped on the trail.

Avery pushes off from his make-shift seat, theatrics forgotten and a bit more pep in his step now. Almost as if the sound of rushing water was the song of a siren, luring him to the source. And because I seem to be a moth to his flame, I follow.

"Goddamn," he whispers on a breath nearly drowned out by the noise.

Thought so.

I paint an innocent smirk on my face when he looks back at me. "Well? Worth it, Mr. Complains-A-Lot?"

"You're so fucking smug sometimes," Avery mutters, but his eyes are dancing with child-like excitement before he looks back at the pool of aqua-colored water gathered at the base of the falls. "Are we allowed to swim in it?"

My forehead creases as I glance between him and the water. "It's glacial runoff, so it's cold as shit. But, yeah, I have once or twice."

It seems to be all the confirmation he needs, because without a second thought, he strips out of his clothes, leaving him in a pair of light-gray boxer briefs that mold to his muscular thighs and ass.

Damn, is it a sight to behold.

I watch, completely enraptured by the way his muscles move and flex, as he walks toward some rocks off the edge of the water; a perfect jumping spot if the water wasn't colder than Antarctica.

A wicked grin crosses his face, creating a complete juxtaposition to the halo of blond hair shining in the sunlight. "You coming?"

I shake my head. Vehemently. "You're insane."

"You're the one who hikes for fun, and you're calling *me* insane?" he counters, brow arched in opposition.

Brushing off his little dig, I motion toward the water pooling below the falls. "Then by all means, if you're looking to freeze your dick off, go ahead. I may have said you're dramatic earlier, but at least the theatrics will be merited once you're a human popsicle."

"Then you give it a nice lick to warm it up again."

The dirty comment lingers in the air between us, and I'm not sure who's more shocked by it coming outta his mouth. It honestly might be him, going off the blush creeping over his cheeks.

"I'll…keep that in mind," I manage through my surprise.

It's the first mention of anything remotely sexual since our night in my cabin, and my mind instantly pulls the memory front and center. His skin beneath my touch, his body arching into mine while I took us sky high, they play out in my mind like a movie.

That night was fun. More than fun, honestly. It was sinful and addictive. Down right intoxicating in a way that had nothing to do with the beer we'd been drinking. It was each other.

From the blush still lingering on Avery's skin, paired with the heat in his gaze as he looks at me, I have a sneaking suspicion his mind has gone to a similar place.

Clearing his throat, he breaks our connection and looks back at the frigid water.

"Are you really—"

I don't have the chance to finish the rest of my question, but I don't really need to when Avery's actions answer for me. He takes two steps back from the ledge and then takes a running leap into the air. His body crashes through the water seconds later before disappearing from sight, leaving bubbles and ripples in his wake.

"Like I said. Insane," I mumble under my breath.

I watch the spot where his body vanished below the surface, waiting for him to reappear dripping wet and freezing, if only so I can gloat about being right. But as nearly a minute passes without any sign of him, I start to worry that the frigid water sent his system into shock and he drowned on my watch.

Ah, shit.

Instincts start kicking in, and I strip my shirt over my head and set to work on my boot laces. I've just toed them both off when I catch a blur moving in the water swimming back toward the surface.

"Holy shit," Avery gasps, his damp hair and skin glistening in the sun. His eyes are comically wide when he turns toward me, and with all my panic now dissipating into the ether, I burst out laughing.

The look on his face is one I've experienced myself, because, as it turns out, I had the same bright idea Avery just acted on my first summer as a counselor. And much like him, I also quickly realized after jumping in just how much of a mistake it was.

"Shit. The first hit takes your breath away," he says, but there's a smile on his lips…even if they're turning the slightest bit blue already.

"Full of regrets, huh?" I call out, unable to keep the smugness from my tone. It's his own fault for not listening to me, yet again. Sometimes I think he does it just to spite me. "I've got my *I told you so* on hand whenever you're ready to hear it."

"As if I'd ever give you the satisfaction."

Snorting, I shake my head. "No truer words have been spoken."

Avery swims toward me until he's lingering below the rocks he'd jumped off. The aqua hue of the water reflects off his eyes, making them appear even bluer than normal as he stares up at me.

"You decide to come in after all?"

What?

"Uh, no?"

"Then why" —he lifts his hand and motions to my chest— "are you half-dressed?"

I frown and glance down, only to remember my state of undress.

Oh, right.

"You took a minute to come back up. I was just preparing to play lifeguard and save your ass."

He bursts out laughing and shakes his head, the water flicking off the ends of his hair from the movement. "Careful, LaMothe. Willing to freeze your ass off to save me? I might think you actually care about me or something."

"More like I didn't want to get fired for letting you die," I toss back dryly.

That only makes him laugh harder, and the sound does something weird to my stomach. I don't think I've heard him sound this carefree since…fuck, maybe sophomore year? The days we'd spend screwing around in the batting cages instantly come to mind, and I let myself linger in those moments as I slip back into my boots.

"Why'd you bring me here if you weren't planning to take a little dip?"

Because it's beautiful and I wanted to share it with you.

The thought hits me like a freight train, causing me to momentarily falter before responding with something a little safer than the unfiltered truth.

"Because I was looking for some fun today, and thought you might like to join. I didn't take into account that you'd see a body of water and would automatically want to jump in it."

His scoff floats on the breeze. "That's like bringing a kid to a candy store and saying he's only allowed to look."

"Like I said. You're insane."

"It's not even that cold once you get used to it."

And I'm the king of England.

I throw my head back and chuckle. "Yeah, sure. Okay."

"It's not," he insists. Then he uses the back of his hand to splash the freezing cold water up at me, the droplets landing on my bare chest. "See? Not bad at all."

Wiping the icy drops from my skin, I shoot him a glare. "Dick."

Smirking, he does it again, but I manage to step back enough that only a few drops meet their mark.

"If you don't come in, I'm just gonna keep splashing you."

"You wouldn't."

"Try me. I dare you," he taunts, arching a brow and positioning his hands for another attack.

Yeah, I don't think so. I've seen Avery's stubbornness firsthand, and there's not a chance in hell I'm betting against it. Which is why, with an annoyed grumble, I toe my boots back off and strip the rest of the way to my briefs.

My bare skin heats beneath the afternoon sun, but it's scorching where I can feel Avery's gaze watching me.

"Not getting any younger, LaMothe!" he chides before swimming away from the edge.

Fucking relentless asshole.

But rather than tossing more snide remarks with him, I take a long, slow inhale.

And then I jump.

EIGHTEEN

Kaleb

I'll never admit it aloud, but Avery is right: After the initial shock from breaking through the cool surface, my body acclimates to the temperature rather quickly. Though, from the shit-eating grin on his face, he's well aware of it.

Guess I'm not the only smug bastard between the two of us.

Knowing we can't stay in here forever unless we want to risk hypothermia, I move away from the ledge we jumped from, swimming closer to the falls. Avery's right behind me when I glance over my shoulder, his gaze fixated on where the water pours over the looming cliff.

"It looks like we can go behind it," he finally shouts over the roaring water.

My eyes narrow in laser-like focus on one section of the falls that's a bit more translucent before determining he might be right. It'd make sense too, seeing as it was named Veil Falls.

Gesturing toward the falls, I duck below the surface and swim beneath the pouring water, only to pop out inside a cave on the other side. Avery's head pops up a few feet away from me, and he lets out a soft laugh while he takes in our surroundings.

"Did you know this was back here?" he yells, motioning around the cave we've found ourselves in.

Shaking my head, I glance around the hidden grotto cut into the earth, a sense of awe and wonder filling me. Had I known, I would've gladly braved the freezing water to do some exploring over the past few summers. It's things like this that stem my deep love for nature. Finding hidden gems, completely untouched by humans.

Earth at its purest.

We venture farther back into the cave, still close enough to the entrance for light to shine through the opening of the falls but deep enough for the sound of rushing water to start fading into the background. The water is more shallow back here, barely hitting our chests now, with the ground sloping up toward rocky ledges carved along the grotto walls.

"Feel free to offer your apology at any time," Avery says, a hint of smugness in his tone that would've grated on my nerves a few days ago.

Now, it just makes me wanna toss playful jabs right back at him.

"And what would I be apologizing for, exactly?"

"Oh, I don't know. For calling me dramatic and insane, to start."

I laugh. "Why would I apologize for telling the truth?"

His hand swipes at the water, sending a playful splash of it right at my face. "You dick. Take it back."

Laughter bubbles up from my chest at the indignation in his voice, and I barely have the chance to wipe my face before two more splashes land, blurring my vision. Instinct kicks in, and I swipe my arm across the surface, sending a wall of water flying in his direction.

It's once I catch sight of his playful glare that I realize my mistake. But it's too late, because—

"Oh, it's fucking on."

He lunges at me seconds later, and I don't have time to do anything before two hands grip my hips and drag me beneath the surface. I do my best to wrestle myself free from his hold and swim for the edge of the cave, but Avery's arms lock around me like a vise until I can't do anything but writhe against him.

We break through the surface a few moments later, both of us gasping for air, but he makes no move to release me. Water drips from his hair and cascades down his face, carving a path that my eyes greedily follow.

Fuck me, he's…beautiful.

"I'm still waiting on that apology."

I lick a stray drop of water from my lips and shake my head. "Not happening."

He lets out a sharp scoff and grumbles, "Of course not."

A small smile pulls at his lips, though, and my stomach rolls the same way it did earlier. With a feeling I now recognize as anticipation. But for what, I have no clue.

"Planning to force it out of me instead?" I ask, still a little breathless.

His gaze drifts down to my lips, locking there for a minute while his Adam's apple bobs. The heat and desire in his eyes speak louder than any words ever could, and from the tension lining his jaw, he has no intention of letting them spill from his lips at all.

He doesn't need to, though.

He wants to kiss me again. Or for me to be the one to drag his mouth to mine.

I've caught the same look a few times since getting each other off in my cabin, but he's never done anything about it. There's been a little bit of flirting and plenty of banter, which only adds to the sexual tension crackling between us, yeah. Physically, though? We haven't crossed that line again.

Until now.

Letting desire guide me, my hand curls around the back of his neck and I pull his mouth to mine.

He's frozen for a moment, just long enough for the thought of *oh, I fucked up* to run through my head. But then he melts into the kiss, matching my fervor with his own. My tongue slides against the seam of his lips, coaxing him to open for me so I can dive in for more. His soft moan sends a zap of lust straight to my cock before he parts them, and I swallow it down like a man dying of thirst.

Though he was the one locking me in place moments ago, I quickly take control and slide my hands over the globes of his ass, loving the way they feel beneath my palms, before cupping the back of his thighs. I lift him in my arms, allowing his legs to wrap around my waist while his hands find purchase on my shoulders. Our cocks are aligned now, bumping against each other while I shift us until he's pressed backed into the cave wall.

The hard lines of his body, drenched in icy water, mold perfectly to mine like a pair of matching puzzle pieces. And now that I have him right where I want him, I lose all sense of control.

"You feel so good pressed up against me like this," I murmur between kisses and nips. "Makes me want to take my time and tease you until you're begging me for more."

God, just the thought nearly has me coming undone.

Sliding my hands up a little, I knead the globes of his ass, palming each one while I roll my hips into his. The moan that leaves him could put a porn star to shame, and it stokes the fire raging inside me more.

My lips leave his and skate over his jaw, carving a path along the ridge of it before pressing a kiss to his throat, just below his ear. He trembles ever so slightly as my lips continue exploring his damp skin, working their way down his neck and over his collarbone.

His breathing is quick and shallow, even a bit shaky, and I'm not sure if it's from the cold, nerves, or pending excitement.

Hell, maybe it's a bit of all three.

The tips of my fingers inch closer to his crease, still over the soaking wet fabric clinging to his sculpted ass. His grip on my shoulders tightens when I gently slide them up and down his crack while allowing my mouth to explore his neck. His breathing kicks up a notch too, and at first I think it's the desire causing him to hold on for dear life. But when the cords in his neck tense beneath my lips too, I recognize it as another emotion entirely.

Fear.

Freezing my ministrations instantly, I lift my gaze to collide with his once I manage to drag my mouth away from his icy skin.

"You good?" I pant, giving him a quick once-over.

I feel his cock twitch, and while his dick may have an obvious answer to my question, it's clear from the tension now lining his body, his mind may disagree.

"Why would you think I'm not?"

Because your body feels like a rubber band ready to snap, for one.

"Just making sure," I reply, holding his gaze. "Have you ever—"

"What? Had sex?" Avery bites out, taking my thought and running in his own direction with it. "Because, yes, I have. Obviously."

I roll my lips inward in a piss-poor attempt to hide my amusement, particularly about the *obviously* part. It's quickly become apparent that nothing is as it seems when it comes to Avery Reynolds.

"I was gonna ask about anal play, but I'm glad to hear you've swiped your V-card. Congratulations, by the way."

I can't stop the smart-ass comment from slipping out, and honestly, teasing him might not be the best move right now. In fact, there's a huge likelihood for it to backfire, sending us straight back to where we were a couple weeks ago.

But if it can decrease his apparent anxiety by even a fraction, then I guess it's worth the risk.

"Oh." His cheeks take on a slight shade of pink as his teeth worry his lower lip. "No, I haven't. But I have a feeling you already knew that."

"Suspected," I murmur softly. "But it doesn't have to go any further than this, especially if we're just gonna end up in a weird place after."

His eyes snap back to mine, hardening to ice in an instant. "If you're just gonna assume I'll regret it, then maybe you're right; we shouldn't do this."

Wait, what?

While I'm busy trying to catch up with his line of thought, he attempts to get out of my hold. I don't let him go though, tightening my arms around him and keeping his body firmly pressed to mine.

This is what he does, I've come to realize.

He gets in his head and lashes out in the moments where he feels his control over a situation starting to slip. Like a caged animal terrified of being backed into a corner, he's willing to do what it takes to get free. Most of the time, that means fighting his way out.

But it's about time he stops reverting back to that instinct.

"Could you just chill for five seconds without taking everything I say to an extreme?" I challenge, pinning him with a hard stare. "I was asking because I don't want to push past a boundary you're not comfortable with. Not because I'm judging you for what you may or may not lack in experience."

The frustration in his stare starts to thaw, icy gaze becoming pools of the sky's reflection once again. It's fascinating, watching it melt away before my eyes. Feeling the tension lining his body slowly release as he relaxes in my hold.

"You're right."

I blink, unable to stop a smirk from forming. "I'm sorry, what was that? I didn't quite hear you."

"I'm not saying it again," he mutters, the definition of indignation.

A laugh bubbles up from me now that the tension has eased again.

Avery Reynolds, always having to be the most stubborn one in the room.

I don't let it deter me, though, and I slowly slide my fingers beneath his underwear until the pads brush over the top of his crease.

"Now that we've established that, I'm gonna ask you again. Are you good with this?"

There's a beat of silence where our gazes stay locked and I continue teasing his skin lightly with my fingertips before he whispers, "I'm okay with trying it."

That's all I needed to hear.

A sharp intake of breath leaves his lips when I press his back harder against the rocks, and my mouth is back on his in an instant, swallowing the sound down like nectar. I make quick work of his underwear, peeling the soaked fabric down his legs before tossing it on one of the nearby rocks.

The icy water is the last thing on my mind now. The cold doesn't even register anymore.

Every inch of my body has been lit on fire from touching Avery.

"I want my mouth on you while I do it," I rasp, then steal another kiss.

From the low moan that tries escaping between our fused lips, he's more than okay with the idea.

Shifting us, I press Avery's body up onto one of the rocky outcrops, leaving only his legs dangling in the water. His cock is at the perfect height for me now, the hardened length glistening with water droplets where it rests against his lower abdomen. The sight has my own dick throbbing with need.

Lust takes control as I take him in hand, giving him a gentle stroke.

A soft curse leaves him, and I glance up to find his heated gaze locked on me, a mixture of anxiety and desire.

"If you don't like something, tell me to stop, and I will. Okay?"

There's a beat of silence, and I almost think he's going to back out, before he releases a harsh exhale and nods.

Perfect.

Grinning, I lower my mouth to his skin and carve a path over his lower abdomen with my lips and tongue, lapping up stray droplets of water along my way. My hand jacks him in slow, even strokes as I do, twisting around the head of his cock each time until my mouth reaches him.

"I'm gonna make this so good for you, baby," I murmur before flicking my tongue over the crown. "Maybe even the best orgasm of your life."

He starts to laugh, but it quickly turns into a groan when my lips wrap around him, sucking just the tip into my mouth. My tongue pays special attention to the spot beneath the head, pressing and rolling against the sensitive nerve until his cock twitches between my lips.

His fingers immediately slide into my damp locks, holding me there as I tease his crown. I take my time with it, swirling my tongue around the head before licking his shaft down to the root and then coming back up again.

"Shit, Kaleb," he hisses, fingers tightening painfully in my hair.

Oh, baby. You haven't seen anything yet.

After a few more minutes of teasing him with my mouth, I pull off and lift one of his legs from the water, allowing the back of his knee to slide down my arm until it's draped over the crook of my elbow. His body naturally slips toward me from the movement, his lower back scraping over the rocky surface until his ass hangs over the edge.

He's spread open for me now; breathless and panting. Completely at my mercy.

And fuck, it's gotta be one of the sexiest, most erotic sights I've ever seen.

Raising my hand to his lips, I brush my fingers over the kiss-swollen flesh and smirk before whispering a soft command.

"Suck on them."

Heat flares in his gaze as he parts his lips and takes them in his mouth, obeying the order. His tongue swirls around the digits, sloppily coating them with his saliva while I hold his gaze and return to my own tormenting task.

But I want even more.

I want him writhing from my touch until he comes harder than he ever has in his life.

Pulling my fingers from his mouth, I slide the hand between his cheeks and swirl the pads against his hole. He tenses at the sensation, but with a few measured sucks of his crown, he relaxes against them again. It's only when he's losing himself in the pleasure of my lips around him, making tiny thrusts up into my mouth, that I finally press one finger past his rim.

"OhfuckingChrist," he moans, the words coming out in a single breath.

Humming around his length, I start working him open with slow, shallow pumps, taking my time with it, all the while teasing his cock with alternating deep sucks and teasing licks. I want him primed and ready to explode when I finally peg his prostate, sending him hurtling off a cliff into freefall.

It doesn't take long for Avery to start moving with me, rolling his hips up and sliding himself farther between my lips before sinking back on my finger. Using his hold on my head to take what he needs, focusing on the pleasure I'm giving him.

And my God, is it sinful to watch.

"This feels…so good," he pants in a whisper. "Your finger. Shit, Kaleb. It's—"

A low moan leaves him as I slowly work a second finger past his rim, cutting his thoughts off at the knees.

The desire in his gaze singes me while I lick and tease and fuck him from both sides, his eyes turning into balls of blue fire as he stares down at me. At my mouth while it lavishes his cock with attention, my fingers sinking inside him as I do.

"God, I love this view."

Same, baby. Fucking same.

Humming softly, I drop his gaze and start working him faster. Every lick and suck around his crown has him arching for more, only for my fingers to slide in deeper when his hips drop back down. Both of his hands are in my hair now, guiding my mouth over him at the speed he wants, and damn, is it arousing.

I'd all but forgotten about my own cock, both of my hands too occupied with Avery's body to bother worrying about it. It's aching now, though, begging to be touched, and it has me moaning around his shaft.

"Shit," he hisses, "Do that again, Kaleb. Fucking hell."

Another groan works its way up from my chest, vibrating against his dick, and his hands may as well be yanking my hair out at this point. He's thrusting his hips up into my waiting mouth in a way that tells me he's getting close. Barely hanging on by the thinnest thread imaginable.

Until that, too, finally snaps when I scrape my teeth along the underside of his cock.

"Oh, fucking mother of holy shit," he cries out, the long string of expletives falling from his lips, all while he's rocking between my mouth and hand. His cock pulses against my tongue, and I take him deeper still.

With a well-timed suck and firm press of my fingers against his prostate, he explodes in my mouth. The salty tang of cum hits my tastebuds, and I drink it down greedily, making no sign of stopping until he starts coming down from his high. Even then, I'm not quite ready to release him, enjoying each lick and suck as I clean him before he tightens his grip on my hair and forces me off him.

"I'm sensitive," he says with a breathy laugh.

I let out a soft hum and press a kiss to his stomach instead. "Fine, fine. Ruin my fun."

As slowly as I can manage, I pull my fingers from inside him and lower his leg again. He slides back into the water between me and the rocks, his hands finding purchase on my ribs for support while he comes down from his high.

My dick is still aching for release, but I shove the thoughts to the side and focus on Avery instead.

"Was that okay?"

Shit, that came out way more insecure than I meant it to.

I mean, I know what I'm doing in this department, so I'm not worried that it wasn't good for him—at least when it comes to physical pleasure. But there are a lot more layers to doing these kinds of things with Avery than just that. Namely, where his head is at afterward.

A harsh exhale leaves him, followed by a deep, carefree chuckle. "Are you kidding? I…" He trails off, shaking his head, then admits, "I've never felt something like that before."

Though it wasn't the context I'd been going for, I'm not ashamed to confess that I preen at the compliment. Like a damn peacock.

"Well, I told you it'd be the best orgasm of your life." I lean in and plant a kiss to his jaw, then his throat. "And I'll have you know, I've got a few more tricks up my sleeve that'll make a prostate massage feel like child's play."

The hands on my waist tighten fractionally. "Is that an offer?"

My lips pause against his skin, and I pull back. His gaze is hard to get a read on, and I realize I have a fifty-fifty shot at answering this wrong. There's no denying this attraction anymore, at least on my end. And God, do I love the sound of him coming undone from my touch.

Which means…

Shit, I think it was an offer.

I measure my words carefully before countering his question with one of my own. "Depends. Is it one you'd accept?"

He draws in a deep breath, blinking a couple times before he finally nods.

"If it stays between us, yeah."

Under normal circumstances, I'd be appalled by someone wanting to keep me as some dirty little secret. I'd probably tell them to go fuck themselves, actually, because there's not a person on this planet I'd be willing to go back in the closet for.

But this is Avery.

He's got a bus-load of baggage to unpack when it comes to his sexuality, and he's only just started. Who am I to judge the speed in which he does it? And honestly, despite our shared attraction and joint effort to move on from the past, there's no fucking way I want anyone to find out I'm fooling around with him either.

Which is why I find a smile tugging at my lips as I murmur, "Then yes. It was absolutely an offer."

NINETEEN

Avery

Week Five — July

In the days that have passed since our excursion to Veil Falls, Kaleb and I have found ourselves falling into a bit of a pattern. Spend the day wrangling the kids, stealing glances and secret smiles whenever they're all too busy to notice. And then every single night, long after the kids are tucked in for the evening, I find myself in Kaleb's cabin.

In his *bed*.

Sometimes, far later into the night than we should.

The amount of time we've spent learning each other's bodies has been well worth the lack of sleep. Though, in the moments where I have to tap into my outdoorsiness, sometimes I think I could use those extra hours of shut-eye.

Right now, as Kaleb and I set up today's weird geocache-style scavenger hunt for the kids, would be one of those moments. One, because we had to get up two hours early in order to finish placing all the items in time. And two, because I'm trying to navigate my way to the next location using only a fucking map and compass.

Kaleb's idea, not mine.

I let out a frustrated sigh and look over to where Kaleb is watching me with barely contained laughter.

God, he looks good with his stupid, grown-out beard and his stupid lumberjack flannel and that stupid hat sitting backward on his head. And let's not forget the stupid, mirthy smirk on his face.

"Need help?"

"Yes," I grumble, hating that I need his assistance. However, I've learned not to let my stubbornness get in the way of asking for help, and that has to count for something.

Kaleb steps closer and looks down at the map in my hand before checking the instruction sheet in his own. His brows draw down as he compares the two, only to look up and gather his bearings. The lightbulb flicks on almost instantly, and I watch in awe as he takes about thirty steps off the trail, pulls a small container that looks eerily like a rock from his backpack, and nestles it in with some other real rocks.

What the shit...

"Okay, next one," he calls as he makes his way back to the trail.

I glance back at the map and compass before looking back at him. "Tell me again why we're doing this?"

"We're double checking the instructions the kids will get when they start hunting. If we hide anything in the wrong place, they won't be able to find it."

"No, I meant with this shit," I say, holding up the tools I'm fucking useless with.

He chuckles and plucks them from my grasp. "It's meant to be a fun way for the kids to learn how to use them, along with landmark bearings, to navigate when they're hiking. There might come a time when they need the skill, so practicing is a good idea."

"Well, I'll make sure to tell Colin his little game isn't very *fun* for the ones who have to do the hiding."

"I'm the one who came up with the geo-hunt, actually."

I blink, not sure if I'm in awe of his brain power or if I loathe him for making me navigate *his* twisted perversion of a scavenger hunt.

Sorry, *geo*-hunt.

My face must give away my thoughts, because Kaleb shoots me a sheepish grin. "What? I was really into geocaching for a while. Creating the geo-hunt felt like a kid-friendly alternative for camp."

Of fucking course.

"And at some point while you were creating this tenth circle of Hell, did you somehow forget we live in the era of cell phones coming with GPS?"

Amusement has his green eyes gleaming like the forest in sunlight. "And if your phone died or you didn't have service? What would you do then?"

"Probably die," I deadpan.

"Exactly," he says, pointing at me with the hand holding the compass. "Call it an insurance policy."

And with that, he flips to the next set of instructions and sets out down the trail toward the location listed.

We continue hiding the containers, and I'll admit, the navigation part gets slightly easier for me after a while. Granted, Kaleb still has to help half the time, but at least I'm not completely incompetent by the time we're halfway done.

"How the hell did you get so good at all this?" I ask as we trek toward another set of hiding places along the eastern edge of Glass Lake. "I mean, besides spending your childhood summers living in the wilderness."

"My dad was the one who got me into the outdoors, if that's what you mean. It was something we did together when I was a kid, before I was old enough to come to camp."

"Maybe it's a genetics thing, then," I mutter.

Lord knows that would make sense, seeing as my father wouldn't be caught dead in the mountains unless he was in a ski chalet drinking some stupidly expensive bourbon with a business associate.

"Not quite possible, since he isn't my biological dad. Good theory, though."

He says it so casually, I almost miss the bomb he dropped.

Almost.

I blink at him a few times, the question coming out before I can stop it. "Are you adopted?"

He shakes his head before pausing, contemplating his words. "I mean, yes and no. My mom is my mother, he's my stepdad. Technically, he adopted me after they got married when I was five. But he's still the only father I've ever known, and he's never treated me like anything less than his own son, so I don't really think of it any differently."

"And he knows you're gay?"

He'd told me previously that his entire family knew about his sexual orientation, but I can't stop the question from coming anyway.

"He was the first person I told."

I blink, processing the information and wondering why he never told me these things before. More importantly, I wanna know why he feels comfortable enough to share them now.

As we continue hiking through the forest, hiding items for the hunt along the way, my mind continues reeling with these revelations.

His family is still blended, in a way, but from the outside, no one would ever know it. It's obvious from the way he and his brothers interact they were raised with laughter, love, and acceptance.

It fills me with a sense of longing.

I didn't want for much when it came to material things, but it's obvious that doesn't really matter in the grand scheme. I'd give up all the years of sailing or baseball camps or anything else to have a father who could accept me as I am. Who didn't ingrain hatred into the very marrow of my bones.

Hell, Kaleb's dad was able to accept that Kaleb is gay, and he isn't even related by blood. Why can't the one person biologically programmed to love me unconditionally do the same?

That one goddamn question swirls in my mind for far longer than I should allow it while Kaleb and I hide the remaining containers. It's still playing on a loop when we start heading back to the lodge, with twenty minutes to spare, and it's Kaleb's voice that finally pulls my thoughts free.

"Oh, by the way. I've got a surprise for you."

I glance over to where Kaleb is trekking down the path beside me, only to find him grinning at me deviously.

Arching a brow, I ask, "Is it a good one or a bad one?"

"Since when are surprises bad?"

My immediate thought is *always*, but that's because I personally don't like them. Blame it on the lack of surprise birthday parties as a kid.

"Under normal circumstances, it's rare." A returning grin pulls at my lips. "With you, on the other hand, it's a fifty-fifty shot."

He knocks me with his shoulder playfully, and the contact has electricity zinging through my entire body.

"I'm offended," Kaleb states, pressing a hand to his sternum. "Maybe I should tell Colin to forget it, then. That we couldn't use a two-day weekend after all."

My ears perk up immediately. As much as I've started enjoying myself while hanging around the kids, forty-eight hours without them really does have a nice ring to it.

"Two-day weekend?" I echo. When he nods in confirmation, I let out a little laugh before asking, "How the hell did you manage that?"

He shrugs, feigning indifference, but the little smirk he flashes makes it obvious that he's pleased with himself. "I guess having some seniority here has its perks."

It takes all my willpower not to roll my eyes.

"Last time I checked, I haven't even made it through one summer, so tell me again how this equates to seniority?"

His tongue presses into his cheek. "Okay, so maybe Colin was planning to give us one anyway."

Thought so.

"Sounds like this is more Colin's surprise than yours, LaMothe."

"Ah, see, but that's where you're wrong," he says, pointing at me. "My surprise is what we're gonna do over the two days we're blissfully tweenager-free."

"And let me guess, I won't be finding out beforehand what it is."

"See? You're finally starting to figure it out."

This time, I don't stop the eyeroll. "By any chance, is the place you're taking me somewhere back in civilization? Or are we taking another excursion up this godforsaken mountain?"

"Civilization? Not a chance in hell, city boy. But I think you'll like it regardless." A grin tugs at the corner of his mouth. "So, what do you say? You in?"

I pause dramatically, making a big show of pondering before I mutter, "Let me think about it."

Deep down, I think we both already know I'm in. It doesn't really matter where he takes me—the mountain, the city, the fucking moon—as long as he's there too.

I'm not quite sure what's happening between us now. Ever since Veil Falls, it's become nothing but light, flirty exchanges. Lots of laughter. And yeah, giving each other some pretty great orgasms.

It could be considered friends with benefits, I suppose.

But, while I can't speak for Kaleb, it feels like more than that for me.

Maybe because I have the freedom and safety to explore a part of me that…fuck, I'm still struggling to accept. Even with how much I've come to crave his body pressed against mine lately.

Those are the only moments, when I'm grounded by his touch, that I'm able to push the venomous attacks on my mind away. The heat of his skin, the pleasure in every kiss or caress, they act as an antidote to Shame's poison. But once I've retreated to my own bed, shrouded in the darkness of my own mind, there's nothing blocking out the cruel, vicious screams.

Repulsive. Abhorrent. Disgraceful.

Abomination.

They're not deafening when he's near, though.

And definitely not when he's smiling at me the way he is right now.

***

Later that afternoon, Kaleb and I break the kids into groups by their bunking arrangements and pairing them with another cabin. Each group of six is then assigned to me, Kaleb, or one of the counselors-in-training we stole for the afternoon, in case they need help. And also to make sure they don't get lost, though if we're relying only on compass and map skills, I don't know how much help I'd be in that particular scenario.

Shit, maybe I need a CIT to come with my group too.

After that, every group is given a different sheet of instructions to hunt for all six of their specific containers, and the only rule is that one kid is in charge of navigating per container, rotating so everyone gets a turn to test their skills with a map and compass. It also allows them to use their friends as help too, which makes the system all the more genius.

My group consists of Elijah, the twins, and the cabin containing Jordan, Tyler, and Jared. They're all bursting with excitement as we head up the trail, Jordan taking the first crack at navigating for us. The two groups with the other counselors head out to start their hunt, and once Kaleb wrangles his group of six as well, we set out with our kids toward the first location.

Despite every group searching for their own containers, every number is in the same general vicinity. The ones are all about a mile past the north trailhead, the twos are hidden down by the lake, and so on and so forth. Again, genius, not only to keep the groups together if we couldn't get CITs to come help us, but because it would've taken twice as long to hide these damn things otherwise. Especially with the bushwhacking—Kaleb's term for going off-trail—we did to actually get them in the right locations.

And even if I was annoyed by the efforts we went through this morning, I'll give it to him; he really did think of everything when he came up with this activity for the kids.

The two of us chat idly as we follow the lead of our navigators, keeping a steady pace up the trailhead until we reach a fork. Max is navigating for Kaleb's crew, and he's already turned off to the left and is climbing through the brush, the others in his group hot on his heels.

"Damn, they're quick," I mutter to him, watching as they search high and low around a tree for the first hidden container.

Kaleb smirks and is about to answer when the sound of shouting from my own group pulls his attention.

"Kaleb! Can you help us?"

We both glance over to where Colton just called from, finding they turned left at the fork and are now thirty yards away and heading down a gradual incline in efforts to find their own container. Well, Elijah and the twins are making their way; Jordan, Tyler, and Jared are still on the trail, looking warily in our direction.

Kaleb silently takes in the scene, and I watch the gears turn in his brain while he assesses the situation before calling back, "I've gotta check on my group, Cole, but I'm sure Avery can!"

I gape at him, not sure I heard him right. "You're joking."

"You're a quick learner, Aves. I'm sure you can handle it."

I don't miss the innuendo in his statement. After all, he knows just how fast of a learner I am. Last night was the perfect example of it, when I finally worked up enough nerve to try giving my first blowjob.

And boy, was he a fan.

Yet, what really has my stomach knotting on itself is the little nickname slipping free. I'm not sure he even realized what he said, but I do. After only ever being Avery or Reynolds to him, how could I not?

I shove it to the side, though, instead choosing to focus on Kaleb throwing me to the goddamn wolves.

"You live to torture me. You know that, right? Fucking sadist."

His grin only grows. "You say that like you don't know exactly where they're hidden."

Fair enough, though that doesn't negate the very real possibility that I'm about to make a fool of myself in front of these kids the way I did with Kaleb this morning.

Letting out a long sigh—and flipping Kaleb the bird behind my back—I head over to where my half a dozen heathens are waiting for some assistance.

"Okay, what's the issue here?" I ask once I reach them.

The twins and Elijah have climbed back up to the trail, and Dayton motions toward the map and instructions in Jordan's hands.

"Jordan followed the map, and the clue said it should be right down there"—he points at the spot they just climbed from—"but none of us are finding the container."

Six sets of eyes fall to me before Jordan holds out the map, compass, and instructions for me to take. And begrudgingly, I accept them.

Reading the instructions, I vaguely recall the location of where we hid this particular container. The problem is, the boys aren't anywhere near it. Okay, not entirely true. They just turned the wrong way at the fork and should be about sixty yards in the opposite direction.

"Uh, so I think you might've been holding the map wrong?" I point down at the spot where we actually are compared to where we should be. "This is where we really are, but you wanna go back to the fork and then go the same distance in the other direction."

Dayton looks up at me, dumbfounded, before he shoots a glare at Jordan. "Really? I thought you said you could use these."

"It was an honest mistake," I cut in, trying to sound as authoritative as I can manage.

With that bit of helpful information, the kids and I set off toward the actual location where the container is hidden. We approach Kaleb's group on the way, still in search of their first find, and I notice him studying me with a curious gaze when we pass by.

More than anything, I wish I knew what he was thinking. That I could crawl inside that mind of his and weave my way through his thoughts, dissecting them as I go. But that's unfortunately impossible, seeing as I'm not a sparkly vampire named Edward.

However, I do catch his subtle nod of approval before Elijah drags my attention away with his ever-inquisitive mind.

"When did you learn to read a map?"

This morning, and I'm only about sixty percent literate.

I shoot him a grin. "I've got some tricks up my sleeve, kid. Don't you worry."

Jordan stops suddenly, staring down at the map in his hands, and the rest of the group gathers around him while he checks our location with the compass.

"Okay, so it should be here, right?" Jordan asks before holding them out for me again.

Despite knowing this is, in fact, where we were supposed to be, I double check anyway. Using the map and compass, I align the two the way Kaleb showed me and then check my surroundings for landmarks.

"Yep," I confirm, then glance down at the instructions for the final clue. "Sounds to me like you'll be climbing into something hollow. Should be just down the hill a bit, but be careful when you—"

The six of them race off the trail, heading toward their destination: a large, hollowed-out tree stump big enough for one or two of them to climb inside.

With it being Jordan's find, Elijah and Colton link their hands together for leverage and a little boost off the ground. Then he climbs up the ten or so feet to the top of the stump before disappearing inside it.

"This is so cool!" I hear Jordan shout, and instantly, the others want their chance to get a look too, all climbing up the outside to peer down below.

A smile pulls at my lips while I watch them work together, and it only grows as they celebrate their success when Jordan emerges with the container in hand.

Elijah and Cole share a high five while Jordan holds out the container to Dayton so he can climb back out of the stump. Kaleb had hidden random things inside each find, and this one happens to have a tiny orange triceratops figure, which Jordan seems pretty pleased about when he pops it open.

The six of them clamber their way back to where I'm waiting on the trail, possibly more excited than they were when this adventure started—Elijah most of all.

"It's my turn next!" Elijah shouts with excitement before pressing his glasses back up the bridge of his nose.

I hand off the tools to him, doing my best not to laugh at his enthusiasm. After all, getting him to enjoy camp and connect with the other kids is half the reason I'm here, though that seems to be a fact I often forget.

Elijah is already reading the next set of instructions, the rest of the kids hanging on his every word, before he aligns the map and compass to get his bearings. When he looks up at me for approval, I motion toward the trail.

"Lead the way, kid."

They all set off, Elijah in the lead, and when I turn to follow, I find Kaleb's gaze on me again. His group is already heading off in the opposite direction under the leadership of their new navigator, disappearing down the trail with my own group hot on their heels. But Kaleb is still here. Watching. Waiting.

And when I get closer, I realize…he's fucking smiling.

"Not bad, rookie," he muses as we set out after the kids together. "We'll make a wilderness junkie out of you yet."

We continue like that, trailing after the kids and helping them as needed, for another couple hours, filling the time with easy jokes and conversation. And lots of passing glances too. I swear, every time I turn my back to chat with one of the kids or reorientate them, I can feel his gaze on me.

And when I finally refocus my attention on him, he doesn't look away. He just studies me for a second and grins, only to continue whatever conversation we were having before the interruption.

I think Elijah's even started to notice with how many times it's happened, because he asked why Kaleb keeps watching me. So when we're trekking with the kids to the sixth and final location, I take it as an opportunity to say something.

Discreetly.

"Since you're the one who made this whole game up, maybe you can help me with these last set of instructions," I murmur, holding them out for him to take.

His eyes narrow with equal parts suspicion and curiosity as he takes them from me, a smirk sitting on his lips when he glances down at the page. A smirk that grows into a full-blow smile when he reads the note I'd written near the top.

Stop looking at me like that. These kids notice everything.

My heart is racing, pulse thudding beneath my skin, and when his brow arches playfully after his attention returns to me, I can feel the idiotic smile crossing my face.

"Seems easy enough to follow."

But despite the warning, he still can't seem to look away.

And neither, it seems, can I.

TWENTY

Kaleb

After dinner the following evening, Avery and I start our journey to where I've planned our little overnight rendezvous for our two-day weekend. With each step we take up the trail, the late afternoon sun streaking through the tall pines, I become more aware of his presence behind me. Every atom of my body has become attuned to him lately, tingling with anticipation whenever we're alone in close proximity, the way we are now.

It's a sensation I've started to yearn for more than anything.

The crunching of our boots on the path serves as the soundtrack for our trek, along with the chirping of birds and the summer breeze rustling the trees. And, of course, there's Avery's bitching thrown in the mix too.

"Where in the ever-loving fuck are you leading me, LaMothe?" he muses, grinning as he takes in the forest on either side of the path. "Still looking for the best cliff to push me off so you're finally rid of me?"

"No need; I already know which one I'd pick," I bat right back before aiming a smirk over my shoulder.

His question is damn near perfectly timed too, because it's only a few more minutes of trekking up the path before we reach the spot in question. It's a flat section of rock leading out of the denser patch of trees, creating a small clearing near the edge of a cliff face.

I drop my pack to the ground in what looks to be a good spot for the tent, only to look up and find Avery taking in the view, precariously close to the edge.

Sidling up beside him, I muse, "You know, I was joking about shoving you off a cliff, but you're tempting fate by standing this close."

"Funny," he says dryly, gaze flicking to me for the briefest moment before traveling the length of the valley on the horizon. "What is this place?"

"We call it Lovers Leap."

He lets out some combination of a scoff and chuckle. "The perfect mixture of romantic and suicidal."

My lips quiver as I fight a smirk.

The more comfortable we've become with each other these past five weeks, the more I'm reminded why I used to enjoy knowing him. By taking him out of the context of school and baseball and all the bullshit, he's an entirely different person.

A person I actually…really like being around.

"Well, this is where we're camping for the night."

Avery's brow lifts as his eyes shift from me to the ledge and back. "Since you just admitted you have no intentions of murder, does that mean you're trying to seduce me?"

Considering the way my body craves him like a drug these days, there's a pretty good chance of it. But I'm not about to give him the satisfaction of admitting it, so I shoot him a teasing wink instead.

"Wouldn't you like to know?"

"Obviously, or I wouldn't have asked," he deadpans.

I roll my eyes. Sometimes his sarcasm makes it really hard to flirt with him. Not that I'm *flirting* flirting, per se; it's more like a playful teasing between friends. Friends who also happen to get each other off sometimes.

We make quick work of setting up camp, erecting the tent and building a fire with what's left of the dwindling daylight. And to Avery's credit, he has the fire lit without much of a struggle, leaving me with the chance to string up a hammock between two trees near the cliff's edge.

"Why'd you bring that?" he asks while I'm clipping the second carabiner to the straps, officially securing it in place.

"To have something for us to sit in?"

What else do you do with a hammock?

"You think we're both fitting in this thing?" he asks dubiously.

My brows furrow as I point to the label on the side. "It's built for two."

"Without breaking?"

"Seeing as we don't exceed the weight limit, I think we're pretty safe," I say with a laugh.

And with that, I slide into the opening and go into zero-gravity mode with my feet dangling out over the edge. I scoot a little to one side, making space for him to join me, but he still doesn't look convinced. In fact, he looks even more apprehensive as his teeth sink into his lower lip.

"What about—"

"Avery," I cut in, arching a brow. "Would you just trust me and get in the fucking hammock?"

Despite his apparent reservation, Avery turns and slowly sinks back into the fabric beside me. It dips under his weight and expands to make room for him.

"See. Told you it'd be fine."

He opens his mouth to argue—it's clear from the gleam in his eyes—but I'm quick to clamp my hand over his mouth, effectively smothering the thought before it dares to leave his lips.

"The only thing I wanna hear out of that mouth of yours is that I'm right," I tease.

The playfulness quickly dies, though, replaced with a building tension from the heat of his breath coasting over my skin. One glance at him tells me he's feeling it too, his eyes flaring with desire.

Slowly, I pull my hand away from his lips and drop it to my lap.

"My bad," I murmur, feeling a little sheepish and a whole lot embarrassed.

"All good," he whispers back, his voice a little hoarse before he clears his throat. "But you don't get to say *I told you so* until we're both out of this thing without it splitting at the seams."

"I'll have it ready and waiting, then."

A comfortable silence falls over while the sun sinks lower in the sky, hitting the horizon and casting shades of orange and pink against the clouds lingering overhead. The colors almost seem to dance against them, swaying and shifting with every passing minute.

I'm not sure how long we stay like that, simply existing while nature puts on a show for us. I just know it's a peace I haven't felt in a long time. Maybe ever.

I'm glad it's one I get to share with him.

"Thanks for bringing me up here," he says, almost as if he were reading my mind.

Glancing over, I find him looking at me with a crooked little grin. One I can't help matching.

"Thanks for joining me."

"As if I was going to pass up a two-day weekend," he mutters with an eye roll.

I laugh lightly. "Don't act like those kids aren't growing on you."

"Yeah, like this beard is growing on you?"

Now it's my turn to roll my eyes. "It's not that long. I've definitely had it grown out more than this."

"I like it," he murmurs. Lifting his hand, his fingers trace the line of my jaw where the stubble has grown into more of a scruff. "It's a different look than I'm used to seeing on you. It's…sexy."

The humming in my veins intensifies to an uncomfortable level at his compliment, and I don't know what to do with it. Just like I don't know what to do with whatever *this* is between us.

All I know is it's begun taking on a life of its own…and I don't exactly hate it.

A low laugh comes from me, and I turn away. "I'm probably looking like a lumberjack or some shit."

"Oh, with the flannel and bomber? Absolutely." He tilts my face back toward him, and I catch a glimmer of amusement in his eyes as he keeps playing with my facial hair. "But you make it work, somehow."

The tension crackling between us is more palpable than it was before, ebbing and flowing like an electric current I can't quite snap free from. Part of me doesn't want to bother trying.

"This is the only time of year I allow myself to go a little more rugged, but I still shave once or twice during camp. The kids don't care what I look like, so I really don't either, ya know?"

"Makes sense." He tilts his head to the side, studying me briefly before murmuring, "I think you look good either way, though."

My lips curve up in a hint of a smile. "Duly noted. Though, from the way you're still petting my face, I think this is clearly your preference."

His ministrations stop almost instantly, and he goes to pull his hand away when I catch his wrist. There's a question in his gaze when I pull his hand back to my face. "I wasn't saying that so you'd stop. It was just an observation."

His features take on a sheepish expression as his fingers resume scraping against my jawline. "Sorry."

"For what?" I whisper, not sure what he has to apologize for.

He's quiet for a beat before murmuring, "I don't know. It's just… I'm still learning how to do this." His eyes trace my face, pausing briefly on my lips, until they land on mine. "Shame still fights me when I openly want you, out where anyone could see."

"Good thing there's no one around for miles."

"Doesn't matter. It's there regardless."

A knot the size of a baseball lodges in my throat. I've seen firsthand how hard he's been working to push past what's been ingrained in him. There are times I feel it when I touch him, the way his body tenses before relaxing into me, and I hate it.

More than that, I hate his damn father for putting him in this position to begin with.

For creating the intricate web of lies and loathing inside his mind that he's been struggling to untangle. For feeding his shame's ruthless whispers until they're deafening.

Working to swallow down the sudden onslaught of emotion, I utter a strained, "Does it still feel wrong?"

He shakes his head, blue eyes glowing with the reflection of the sunset. And at this moment, I haven't seen another human look so fucking…beautiful.

"I guess I'm running into problems asking for it."

My throat catches again, and words fall off my lips before I can doubt the truth in them. "You don't have to ask."

Avery finally pulls his hand away when he leans back, his brows furrowing. "So I could lay one on you whenever I want? In front of anyone, and you'd be okay with that?"

"Would you even want to? If shame were taken out of the equation?"

He pauses for a moment, thinking the question over, which is one helluva surprise to me. Even when I thought he was straight, I never pegged him for the PDA type. But then again, I've been wrong about pretty much—

"I think so," he whispers, cutting off my thoughts. "In theory, I like the idea. But in reality…"

My lips twitch with amusement. "Well, in reality, this is still our workplace. And even though it's just summer camp, I'd still prefer to keep a bit of professionalism."

"Ever a stickler for the rules, aren't you, LaMothe?" he mutters with an eye roll.

"They're there for a reason, you know."

"Yeah. To be broken."

"Ah, yes. Your favorite pastime." When his brows draw down, I quickly tick off my points with my fingers. "The beers, for one. And sneaking into my cabin for another."

A light scoff leaves him. "Believe me, I had a fucking existential crisis over that decision."

"About breaking the rules? You?" I tease lightly.

He smirks, but his expression quickly sobers before he shakes his head. Emotions swirl in his eyes, vulnerability peeking through their depths that

I've never seen from him until now.

"More about how you'd react to me breaking them." His attention drops, unable to hold my gaze any longer while he continues. "I was terrified I'd mess everything up when we'd just wiped the slate clean. You know, after the kiss and the photo and everything else that happened before."

The vibe between us shifts at his admission, becoming thicker with emotion. I can feel it sticking to me like the air on a humid summer night, and it sends my mind into a tailspin over all the events of the past few weeks.

"Why me?" I ask softly, the question coming out before I can reel it in.

It's one that's been in my head since we spoke on the dock, where he gave me a secret he's shared with no one else. It keeps on tapping against the back of my skull, pleading for an answer, while we continue falling into whatever this is between us. I've just been able to ignore it until now.

He's silent for a moment, almost pondering the many meanings the question could have, but he doesn't ask me to elaborate. From the way his gaze drops to my lips again, he knows exactly what I mean.

"Because you feel safe. That's not something I've really felt before." His lips twitch at the corner, a wry smirk appearing. "Sure, I felt safe on Toppr, but that was just an illusion my anonymity created. It wasn't real, and I doubt I could've ever followed through with a meetup, had it even come to that."

"Not even with Keene?"

He shakes his head, now staring out at the sunset in front of us.

"The problem with being anonymous was that it was still hiding, and I'm so sick of hiding. I may have been testing the waters, so to speak, but I was still shoved so far inside the closet with no way out. And though Keene may have empathized with my struggles, he couldn't guide me out of it. He wasn't gonna challenge my ways of thinking or force me to stand in the mirror, look at myself, and see past all the shame and doubt and loathing. Not when he was still figuring it all out himself." His pensive expression has a daydream-like air to it now, and a small smile appears. "I guess he was just a stepping stone toward that, you know? Preparing me to be vulnerable enough to show all of that to the right person, whenever they came along."

My throat catches, not prepared for the insinuation that…

Shit.

"And that's me?"

His lips part, like he's about to say something, only for a soft laugh to come out instead.

"I mean, yeah. I guess so. You definitely challenge me. Whenever my instinct to fight comes out, you make me sit with it instead. Face it head on. And showing you those parts of me… I don't know, it just felt natural." His teeth scrape over his lower lip, worrying it while he stares at the fading sky. "Probably because I knew you couldn't hate me any more than you already did, right?"

My heart squeezes in my chest painfully as I slip my fingers under his chin, turn it toward me, and force him to meet my gaze. Because if there's ever been a moment where he needs to be certain about what I'm saying, it's this one.

"I don't hate you."

I never have.

I've been angry, frustrated, and irritated with him, just to name a few emotions. Never hate, though. Even when I wanted to, even when I saw the depths of his cruelty, it was impossible.

Maybe because, somewhere inside me, I knew what lay beneath the surface. I knew *this* version of him was waiting to be set free. And I swear, as I watch every bit of his lingering fear leave his eyes and disappear in the wind, I think it finally has.

"Until you, no one has managed to silence Shame's screams. Even momentarily."

All the oxygen leaves my lungs, and my ribs feel too fucking tight to breathe right as his gaze sweeps over my face.

This is the part that makes it so tricky between us.

Tossing jabs and banter, I can do all day. It's an easy rhythm we can fall into, keeping it light and playful between sessions where we strip each other to nothing. But whenever something pure or vulnerable leaves his mouth, it's like he takes a pocket knife and drives it into my chest.

Avery's thumb returns to my jaw, the pad scraping over my beard gently when he whispers, "Did you mean what you said before? About not needing to ask for permission?"

Fuck me.

I swallow harshly as my eyes flash down to his lips. Then I nod ever so slightly.

A small, shy smile appears before he slides his hand back to my hair. Reeling me in, his mouth finds mine and my stomach does that stupid flippy thing all over again.

His lips are soft and gentle, sweeping over mine in a sensual caress rather than one filled with unchecked passion, but it still charges every atom in my body. Lately, sharing even the faintest touch charges the air with enough electricity to power New York City for a damn decade, and this is the perfect example of that.

The reality is, I've never wanted someone the way I do Avery. Haven't craved the feeling of lips pressed to mine the way I do his, or the heat from his bare skin beneath my touch. And those things are only the beginning.

More times than I can count, my mind has fixated on the idea of getting him inside one of our cabins, pinning him to the bed, and fucking devouring him in whatever way he'll let me. In every way, preferably, leaving no inch of his body untouched or overlooked.

Yet, as tempting as it is, I can't bring myself to act on it.

I'm terrified of what it would do to the mess inside his head.

He's the first to break away, pulling back just enough to meet my gaze.

"That was…" I trail off, at a loss for words. Not just from the kiss, but the way he's looking at me. With more affection than I've ever seen him display.

Avery's thumb skates along my jaw again, tracing the line with his fingers still wrapped around the back of my neck. My pulse thrums beneath my skin when he presses his mouth to mine in another far-too-fleeting kiss, only to whisper three words that set my blood on fire.

"Yeah. That was."

And there's that fucking knife again.

It's not lost on me that the more his walls seem to come down, the higher I've tried to build my own. Stacking plates of armor and chainmail around my heart like a medieval soldier preparing for battle.

Self-preservation calls for it.

This—*us*—is fleeting at best. Finite and confined to a place of safety and refuge, where there's no chance of discovery or interference. But back in the real world—at Foltyn, should he get back in—this wouldn't be tenable. For more reasons than one.

Even if the two of us are willing to put the drama and the mistakes and the bullshit in the rearview, that doesn't mean everyone else is. I could sit here and list the people who'd likely rather me hook up with Satan himself instead of Avery.

That's a lot to overcome, and it's not even taking his own issues into account. Despite the progress he's made, Avery still has so much to work through. Shame and demons to overcome. Outside the little bubble we've found ourselves in, there's no telling how he'll handle it.

But instead of focusing on how it'll end or what could go wrong, I shove away the unknown.

I'm going to enjoy this for what it is…for as long as I have it.

TWENTY-ONE

Avery

We're quick to get settled in for the night, extinguishing the few embers still glowing from our fire earlier before slipping into our tent. My heart hammers against my ribs while Kaleb zips us in, a mixture of anticipation and nerves melding together to create knots in my stomach.

The only light comes from the lantern in the corner, which he's smart enough to keep on while we get ready for bed. It casts a warm glow over the inside of the tent, creating shadows that dance against the walls as the breeze hits them.

My eyes catch on Kaleb's body as he changes into a pair of sweats and a long-sleeve shirt for bed. The lean curves of his arms and shoulders appear even more golden in this lighting, and when his hip bones appear, popping against his waistband, something in my brain short circuits.

Oh, hell.

The way I crave him is disgusting, but not in the way I've been accustomed to feeling. It's almost…gluttonous. With a desperation that's downright embarrassing.

My only saving grace is catching him eyeing me with the same amount of desire.

Glancing away, I notice the liberties Kaleb took during setup tonight. Unlike the last time we'd shared this tent, he unzipped both of our sleeping bags and layered them on top of each other over the thin air pads, creating a makeshift bed for us instead. And I can't help my stupid smile as I slide between them.

I never thought I'd enjoy spending the night on the hard ground outside, but once Kaleb is tucked in beside me, I realize I'd be hard pressed to complain about sleeping in a prison cell. Having him here makes none of the details matter.

Rolling to my side, I drape an arm over his waist and nudge my forehead into the crook of his neck. He tightens an arm around me, his fingers lightly teasing the skin over my hip where my shirt has ridden up, and it's his light touch—barely a caress—that has my body reeling with desire all over again.

"Kaleb," I whisper.

"Yeah?"

Swallowing hard, I test the words on my tongue. "I want…"

Fuck.

Why is it so hard for me to say it? To push past this final fucking obstacle? To break free of the chains that have dragged me into the pits of self-loathing for far too long? To no longer be held captive by fear, imprisoned in a cage of my own making?

Just fucking *say it.*

I.

Want.

You.

Kaleb turns his head and presses a kiss to the top of my head. "What do you want, Aves?"

His voice is soft and gentle, floating over me like a summer breeze, and I ache for it to be whispered against my skin instead. For his breath to send shivers down my spine. For his touch to bring me to the brink of ecstasy and then shove me over the edge.

I want you.

Knowing how to say it better with my body, I turn into him more and press a kiss against his neck. I don't stop there, though, and I trace my lips up the column of his throat before nipping at the space below his ear. A shiver has his body vibrating beneath mine, and his fingers tighten on my waist.

"Jesus," he hisses, the words coming out all breathy.

Already feeling more confident, I grin against his skin before rocking my hips into him. My cock is already hard as granite, and when my hand strays toward his groin, I find his has also joined the action. I rub the heel of my palm over his length, stroking him over his sweats until he's arching for more friction.

"Kaleb."

His name leaves my lips in a whisper, but what comes next is nothing short of a plea.

"I want you."

He moans softly before rolling me to my back and sealing his lips to mine in a searing kiss; one we only break to strip each other down to nothing before coming back together again. His bare skin over mine sets me on fire, and it quickly becomes a raging inferno when he wraps his hand around me. The heat of his palm on my shaft has me arching into his touch instantly, both need and anticipation building inside me.

Kaleb strokes me a few times—long, slow pulls over my cock that are surely meant to torment me to no end—while I helplessly allow him to explore my mouth.

And that's what I am.

Helpless, and at the mercy of his every touch.

"You want me, hmm?" he whispers against my lips before taking the bottom one between his teeth.

Fuck, yes, my brain immediately screams. My mouth, on the other hand, can't seem to form the words, let alone speak them. So all I do is nod, my nose brushing his with the movement.

"How do you want me? Hand wrapped around you, stroking until you come? Or would you rather it be around both of us?" Lust and seduction drip from his words as his mouth moves from my lips to my jaw. He kisses and nips against my skin until he reaches my ear, his hot breath sending shivers rushing down my spine like an electric current as he continues, "Or maybe you want my mouth instead, licking and sucking until you spill down my throat."

Jesus Christ.

If there's one thing I can admit, it's that this version of Kaleb is my favorite. The confident aggressor in bed paired with the cool, reserved demeanor he normally carries is a juxtaposition equally intriguing as it is intoxicating. And I'll be damned if the vivid pictures this side of him paints in my brain aren't every kind of alluring.

I just don't know which one to choose. Or if I'd rather paint one of my own.

"What do you want, baby?" he asks again, voice raspy and demanding.

His palm gathers the pre-cum leaking from my tip and spreads it down my shaft in a way that feels so fucking good, I can't be responsible for the words that leave my lips next.

"I want you to fuck me."

Kaleb pauses, pulling back to look me in the eye. "What'd you just say?"

I didn't entirely mean to say it aloud—at least, not yet—but now that it's out in the open, the idea feels even more right than it did in my head.

This…*us*…feels…

Abhorrent!

Slamming the gate on Shame's voice, I replace it with my own.

Right.

This feels right.

"You heard me." I offer him a soft smile and curl my fingers around his neck. The butterflies in my stomach are a fluttering storm as his green irises stare straight through to my soul. "Don't make me say it again."

A pained expression etches his features, pulling back his lips in a grimace while he shakes his head. "If you can't even say it again, then I clearly shouldn't do it."

As if that's supposed to deter me?

"I wanna feel you inside me," I whisper immediately.

Shame screams inside my mind, curling its talons around the bars it's trapped behind, screeching for me to listen.

But I don't.

I lock it away instead, choosing to focus on right here. Right now.

On just how *right* this is.

"Aves…"

My fingers scrape against his scalp as I roll my hips up into his, allowing my still-aching dick to slide through his palm. "I wanna feel every inch of your perfect dick sliding in and out of me until I can't think straight."

I'm not above begging for it at this point.

Tension lines his jaw, but his nostrils flare with lust. "You don't know what you're asking."

"I'm asking for you to fuck me."

A strangled sound leaves him, and he lets out a sharp laugh. "I don't have lube, let alone condoms, so—"

Without waiting for him to finish, I roll to my side and reach for my bag, quickly producing the bottle of lube I'd snatched from his cabin this afternoon. Grabbing it was a whim more than anything, but just to be prepared on the off-chance things might progress to this.

And here we are.

Kaleb's face remains impassive as he takes the bottle I hold out for him, only to stare down at it like it's a gift from a foreign planet. His Adam's apple bobs when he swallows before setting it to the side, and it's only when he meets my gaze again that I see the wariness in his dark irises.

A knot forms in my throat, clogging my airway.

Shit, shit, shit.

"Did I do something wrong?" I manage to ask after an eternity of silence passes.

"I—" He lets out a soft, nervous laugh. "Are you sure?"

No, I'm not. Not entirely. But not for the reasons he's likely thinking.

I'm not afraid of having sex with a guy, or how I may feel about myself afterward. I'm long past the point where I can deny this is who I really am anymore. Hiding from this part of myself was never gonna be a tenable option anyway.

But what I'm fucking terrified of…is the way *Kaleb* is making me feel.

My teeth scrape over my bottom lip, and I nod. "Yeah. I'm sure."

"Condom?"

"I'm okay without one," I murmur, knowing I'd rather feel him without anything between us. "As long as you are too."

There's a beat of silence before more excuses start. "Have we done enough prepping, though? I mean, I don't want to—"

"I'm ready," I cut in.

He knows I'm ready too; he's been the one working me open with his fingers over the past few weeks, after all. But like me, he's scared.

The only difference is, I'm not willing to let the fear stop me anymore.

"You're the only thing stopping us," I whisper.

At this point, I fully expect him to shut it down. To say no, not yet, and give more reasons why we should wait. So when he picks up the bottle of lube again and pops the cap, my throat constricts around a ball of emotions.

His eyes stay locked on mine as he spreads lube over his fingers, coating them with the liquid.

"If it's too much at any point—"

"I'll tell you," I finish for him.

Tension radiates off him as he slips his hands between us, the lube-covered fingers finding my crease. He swirls them around and presses them against my rim, massaging the muscle before slowly sinking them inside. A low moan rips from my chest at the burn of them breaching me, but it's a feeling I've grown accustomed to. One I've started to crave, knowing how quickly it morphs into pleasure.

My heart hammers against my ribs, sending my pulse into overdrive as his deft fingers fuck me with long, tortured strokes. And like I knew it would, the pain subsides, and I start pressing back against his fingers. Seeking more pleasure until a needy frenzy takes over, leaving me panting and quaking beneath him.

"Kaleb, *please*. I'm ready."

I'm not above begging right now.

I'd do just about anything to have him inside me.

His nostrils flare as he pulls from my body and grabs the lube again. I watch, enraptured, as he douses his cock and spreads the cool liquid down his shaft in a few slow strokes. My desire kicks up another notch when he slowly lowers himself over me, resting his weight on one elbow to align himself. The head of his cock nudges against my hole, sending a bolt of lust and anticipation straight up my spine, but just when I think he's going to finally press inside, his entire body stills.

"What's wrong?"

A few silent seconds tick by before his forehead drops to mine, and I swear, I can feel him trembling against me; shaking as he struggles with whatever is happening inside his mind.

"Don't make me regret this," he utters, barely audible even in the stark silence.

My forehead rolls against his when I shake my head. "Never will I ever."

Taking the words at face value, his hand slides into my hair and he crashes my lips to his. They're soft as they move against mine, and I cup his jaw to run my fingers through the short beard I'm thoroughly obsessed with.

Then his hips move forward with a gentle thrust, the head of his cock sliding past my rim a few inches, finally giving me what I want. And if I was on fire before, I'm standing on the surface of the sun now. Burning alive, engulfed in heat and flames. The throbbing pain intensifies as he pulls back and presses in more, still barely penetrating me, and my hand moves to the back of his neck to hold on for dear life.

"Oh, fucking hell," I moan, eyes sinking closed.

From the tension I feel beneath my palm, he's doing his best to keep it together himself. But instead of thrusting in deeper, taking care for only his pleasure, he snakes a hand down and grips my cock. The lube still on his fingers makes it easy for his hand to glide up and down my shaft.

"Tell me what you need, baby," he murmurs, fist moving in long, slow pumps over my length. "I want you to feel good. As good as I do with my cock inside you."

My dick throbs in tandem with my ass, and it doesn't take long for his ministrations to shift my focus from pain to pleasure.

"Keep doing that," I pant, my head, falling back against the sleeping bag. "It helps."

He hums softly, his hand moving a bit faster now. His lips find my collarbone, raining down kisses against my skin until I start relaxing beneath him. It's only when I begin sighing and panting, the pain a distant memory, that he fully surrenders to his own desire.

Pulling back his hips, he gives another tentative thrust forward, allowing his cock to slide in deeper than before. Another wave of fire lights up my body as he slowly pumps his hips again and again, all the while murmuring praises against my skin.

You're doing great, baby.

We're halfway there.

Just relax and let me in.

Every bit of encouragement, paired with the way he strokes me while kissing my neck, dulls the sting while he slowly works himself deeper. To my surprise, any burn I was feeling is completely gone by the time his pelvis presses against my ass, seating himself fully inside me.

It's been replaced by a wanting ache. A bone-deep need that only he can fulfill.

"Holy shit," I exhale, tension coiling in my stomach.

My fingers find Kaleb's hair, sifting through the dark strands while he trails kisses along my jaw. The scratch of his beard over my heated flesh sends shivers down my spine, and he must notice, because he continues carving the path until he reaches the corner of my mouth.

"Okay?" he whispers, and I can feel his smile brushing against my lips.

I nod, groaning as he slides in again, burying himself to the hilt. "God, yes. Keep going."

A soft chuckle leaves him, but he follows my request and starts rolling his hips quicker before sealing his mouth to mine. His tongue seeks entry, which I happily provide, allowing it to flick and roll against my own in time with his thrusts.

I feel him everywhere, all my senses immersed in him.

Lost in pain, in pleasure, in the blissful freedom consuming me.

Breaking the kiss, my eyes squeezing shut as my head rolls back against the mattress. "Fuck, that feels…good."

Kaleb hums in agreement, his mouth on my throat again before nipping at the juncture of my neck and shoulder. The sharp bite of pain is quickly soothed by his tongue as his hips quicken his smooth, steady rhythm.

His hand picks up the pace too, jacking my length with hard, fast movements that I can't get enough of. I'm arching up into his touch for more, seeking more friction as his hips roll into my body. Every move I make inches me closer to where I wanna be, but it's still not enough.

I want more. I want fucking everything.

My hips move of their own accord, not just pumping my cock into his waiting palm but also sinking back on his length, impaling myself with it. I'm meeting him thrust for thrust now, chasing what I want just as much as taking what he's giving me.

"That's it. Take what you need," he rasps, "God, you feel fucking amazing. So tight wrapped around my cock."

Jesus Christ.

Every word that leaves his lips drives me a little more mad with want, the lust reaching an all-consuming level. Release builds at the base of my spine, curls and knots my stomach with tension that's sure to snap at a moment's notice. He must feel it too, because his rhythm starts to falter, becoming more rushed and irregular as he pistons his hips forward.

"Come for me, Aves," he pants. My eyes open, finding that his own have become two burning forests as he plunges his cock harder inside me. "Let me feel you clench around me."

Leaning back and straightening his spine, he becomes downright frenzied. The new position allows him to slide impossibly deeper with every thrust, but it also has the head of his cock hitting a new spot inside me. One that lights me up like the billboards in Times Square and tasting color when he drags a long, low moan from me.

A tingling sensation starts tapping on my nerve endings, spreading through my body like a wildfire with every swipe the head makes over my prostate, and I'm right there. I'm so fucking close, ready to plunge into ecstasy at any moment, that I don't know how I'm still hanging on.

"Kaleb," I moan, clawing at his arms in desperation. "God, please. I...I—"

The words die on my lips, pleasure sinking in so deep, I can't speak. Can't form a coherent thought that isn't *release.*

My gaze meets his, finding him staring down at me—into the darkest depths of my soul—and for the first time, I'm not afraid of what he sees lingering in the shadows. Not when he's the one who's shown me how to let in the light.

"I know, baby. I've got you."

That's all it takes for me to fall apart, Kaleb's name on my lips.

Release slams into me like a wrecking ball, dragging a groan from deep within my chest. Kaleb keeps pistoning inside me while he works me through my climax, stroking rapidly until I'm sticky and covered in my own cum. It's only when I'm empty and breathless, heart ready to burst from my chest, that he chases his own release.

I'm hyper-sensitive, every nerve ending inside me shot from pleasure, and pulsing around his length when he grabs my waist. Dragging me closer, he starts impaling me with his cock over and over. Fucking into me with reckless abandon. Using me for his pleasure.

The tendons in his neck tighten, his breathing coming in short staccato spurts when he mutters, "Where should I—"

"My chest," I answer immediately, still trying to catch my breath.

He pulls out of me in an instant, wrapping his palm around his shaft, and strokes himself over the edge. Soft curses fall from his lips as cum spills from him and lands on my skin, coating me with the liquid and mixing with my own release.

After he's worked himself dry, he sinks back on his heel, chest heaving with effort as he stares down at me. Neither of us say anything for a moment, a thousand unspoken words passing through our locked gazes.

He's the first to break away, grabbing the shirt he was wearing today before starting to clear away the evidence of our release from my stomach. I wrap my hand around his wrist, feeling more vulnerable by him doing this than I did with him inside me.

"I can—"

"I've got it," he whispers, meeting my gaze.

The simple reply instantly reminds of something he said earlier; a similar sentiment that now has my stomach fluttering.

I've got you.

My teeth sink into my lower lip and I release his wrist, allowing him to return to his task. He cleans the cum from my skin before gently wiping the lube from my crease, and the intimacy of this act has me in fucking knots.

Once he's done, he tosses it to the side and we both silently slip back into our underwear, then back between the sleeping bags for the night.

I'm not sure what the protocol is here. Despite all the evenings we've hooked up, we've never actually spent one *sleeping* together. The only time we've even slept in vicinity of each other was our one other tent experience, but after letting him fuck me for the first time, I really hope we won't be reliving that particular night.

Thankfully, Kaleb makes the decision for both of us when he drapes an arm over my waist and pulls me toward him, not stopping until my back is molded to his chest. I try not to notice how perfectly our bodies fit together like this, but it's impossible. It feels like I was made to be right here, wrapped in his embrace.

I was right about one thing I told him earlier: I've never felt safety like this.

Kaleb's nose nuzzles against the spot between my shoulder blades and then presses a kiss there before whispering against my skin, "Are you okay?"

"Never better," I murmur back, noting just how true it is.

For now, at least.

After what we just did—the line we just crossed—there's no chance I won't be dragged through the pits of hell by my subconscious. So I wait for the shame spiral to swirl inside my head, ripping apart the moment and casting it in an abhorrent light.

But as Kaleb's breathing evens out behind me, his soft breaths puffing against the back of my neck, I'm shocked to find…it doesn't.

It never comes.

TWENTY-TWO

Kaleb

Something's changed in Avery.

It wouldn't be noticeable to most people—hell, I barely realized it myself—but he has a sense of lightness about him now. Almost like he was Atlas being weighed down by the world inside his head, full of shame and loathing.

I don't know what I was expecting after we returned from our excursion to Lovers Leap, but it certainly wasn't him leaning deeper into this thing growing between us. He has, though. He's been back in my bed every night this week, allowing me to tease and explore his body until he was begging me to put him out of his misery.

To sink inside him and take us both straight to heaven.

And damn, has his confidence grown in the sex department. There's still moments of hesitation in his eyes, brief seconds where I can almost see those doubts dig their claws in, but it's never enough for him to truly falter. He pushes back against it and takes what he wants, only making him more attractive in my eyes—not that there was any issue in that area to begin with.

It's not just with me that his confidence has grown, either. The kids are really starting to take to him lately, and it's made him more relaxed when he's interacting with them. Max and Jared—who are usually at the front of the pack when we go on hikes—have been hanging back to hike with Avery and Elijah instead the past few days, and whenever we reach our destination, the group of them are laughing and joking around with each other. And yesterday, I was floored when Dayton decided to sit with him and Elijah at breakfast rather than me and Colton, only to talk our ears off about how cool he is when we had lunch together.

What's funny is, I have a sneaking suspicion Avery feels the same, or at the very least, the kids are starting to help him enjoy the day-to-day activities around camp too. Or maybe it's the goddamn prank war happening between Max's and Jordan's cabins that's done the trick, because I don't think I've seen him laugh as hard as he did earlier today when we finally had to step in.

"Okay, I get where you're coming from," he says later in the evening when we're alone in my cabin. "But aren't pranks part of this whole summer camp experience?"

I shoot a glare at him where he's lounging on my mattress in just a pair of sweats, while I attempt—and fail—to reconnect my laptop to the Wi-Fi. We were in the middle of an episode of *Criminal Minds* when the spinning circle of death appeared on the screen, and the damn thing has been buffering ever since.

"Putting a snake in someone's bed isn't a prank. It's *mean*."

"No one was hurt, the snake included, and it's not like we damaged any property."

I'll admit, he makes a fair point, but it's still—

"*We?*" I find myself asking, a bit shell-shocked. "You mean you *helped them?*"

He opens his mouth, realizing his slip up, before an impish grin appears. "I think this is a good time for me to plead the fifth."

I blink at him slowly, absolutely dumb-founded, before dryly uttering, "Please tell me you're joking."

From the way his grin grows, it's obvious he's not. "It's all in good fun, Kaleb. Lighten up."

I doubt the poor garden snake felt the same, but I choose to ignore that fact.

"At least tell me you weren't the instigator."

Waving me off with a laugh, he mutters, "Oh, God no. I just unlocked the cabin for them."

"I don't know if that makes it better or worse," I mumble under my breath with a shake of the head.

He hears it, though, because he immediately comes back with, "We've already established you've never done a rebellious thing in your life, so it's a toss up at this point."

Oh, hell no.

There's no way I'm gonna take his insults lying down. He wants to see rebellious? Fine. I can play that game, and it'll end with him panting and moaning for me to fuck him clear into next week.

With that thought alone, I abandon my mission with my laptop in favor of pinning him to the bed with my body.

"You really think I'm some Goody Two-shoes, huh?" I ask, trying to let my proximity do the work for me.

All I get is a shrug and a shit-eating smirk in response. Then he wraps an arm around my back and flips us; his go-to move when he's looking to change the subject to something a lot more…naked.

This fucker.

"I've gotten detention before, back in high school," I gripe, trying to keep my focus on the argument at hand. It's proving fairly difficult, though, when his lips skate over the pulse point below my jaw. I swear all my brain cells melt into a puddle of cerebral fluid when his lips are against my skin. Add in the low, seductive tone he speaks with, and I'm surprised I have any brain function at all.

"You're literally talking to someone who got expelled from college, there, LaMothe. You're gonna have to try harder than that."

There's no animosity as he says it, only humor dancing in his sky-blues when he pulls back. The sight of them aimed my way has my throat constricting, the way it's seemed to a lot lately whenever I catch him looking at me.

"Okay, well…sometimes I'll smoke a joint after the kids are in bed and break into the dining hall to get some snacks. Gotta curb the munchies somehow."

His brow arches, looking slightly impressed as he rests his forearms on either side of my head. "Didn't take you for a stoner."

"Stoner is the last word I'd use. It's really if I can't sleep," I protest, playfully shoving his shoulder.

"Hey, I'm not judging. I'm more appalled that you didn't think to share with me."

"Because I didn't bring any."

"Of course not, Mr. Goody Two-Shoes," he says with a laugh before pressing his lips to my jaw. "I'm just surprised you've brought drugs here before."

I wasn't the one who brought it. I'd actually confiscated the joints from one of the older campers after I'd caught him lighting up behind the bathhouse after lunch. And while I could choose to keep that little bit of information to myself, knowing it will only help prove his case rather than my own, I correct him anyway. Because I'm not gonna lie just to prove a point.

Damn my morals and shit.

"They were contraband, actually."

Avery's head drops to my shoulder, and his entire body vibrates against mine while he laughs. Not just a chuckle, but the real, genuine laughter that I've become highly addicted to in recent days.

"Why is that so funny?" I gripe with a smile.

His head lifts, amusement lingering on his features. "And Colin just let you keep it to enjoy yourself as a reward for snitching, did he?"

"Colin never found out, actually. I didn't turn the kid in."

From the way his brows arch imperceptibly, he's surprised by my admission. Which makes all the sense in the world considering what happened a couple months ago. Me…snitching on him.

I try not to focus too much on the term he used, but it still stings.

I don't regret doing the right thing by Aspen and Keene, but I'd be remiss to think that the entire situation isn't a lot more nuanced than I originally thought.

Part of me wishes I never would've turned him in, knowing him the way I do now. Knowing the loneliness and isolation he was experiencing. The fear of finally being vulnerable with someone, of saying the thing that's been hardest to admit, and worrying that those secrets aren't safe after all.

I can't excuse what he did. But damn if I don't hate knowing all of that now. Knowing that, if he'd shared those things with me when he needed someone to hear him the most, he wouldn't have felt all those things.

But the reality is, if everything didn't happen exactly as it did, he wouldn't have been expelled. He wouldn't have come to work here for the summer. We wouldn't be where we are right now, in my bed.

I never would've seen this side of him.

"Look at you, aiding and abetting underage stoners."

"Well, does that make me rebellious enough for you?" I ask jokingly, putting forth my best effort to shove down the guilty feeling welling inside of me. "If it helps, there were multiple joints, so it's not like it was a one-and-done thing."

"Definitely not," he replies, not missing a beat. "Plus, we both agreed that it's not really breaking in if you have a key."

A smile tugs at my lips, and when he meets my gaze, a matching one spreads across his face. There's something intimate about sharing the inside joke with him, even if no one else is around to be on the outside of it.

"Correct," I concede, still grinning. "But technically, I don't have a key. I just know where they keep the spare."

His eyes take on a devious glimmer, and it doesn't take a genius to know the request that's about to leave his lips.

"I think you should show me."

A sharp laugh leaves me, the words *not a chance* on the tip of my tongue, only for them to die there when Avery grinds his hips down into mine. The ridge of his erection against my own thickening cock quickly has me gasping instead, making it impossible to form a coherent thought, let alone argue with him.

Avery runs his lips over the column of my throat in a whisper of a kiss before trailing them along my jaw.

"If you want me to believe you're as much of a rebel as you make yourself out to be, you've gotta be willing to back it up," he murmurs in my ear. "Take a walk on the wild side with me."

I let out a low moan when he rolls his hips down into me.

"If you think I'm gonna do a damn thing right now other than pin you to the mattress below me, you've got another thing coming."

His low, seductive chuckle floats over my skin before he presses his lips to my thundering pulse. "I think you're in the wrong position to make those kinds of statements."

"Maybe, but I can change that in an instant."

To prove my point, I slide my hands to his hips. I plan to use the element of surprise to my advantage and flip us until his back lands against the mattress with a soft thud. But clearly I haven't learned to not underestimate Avery, because he's reversing our positions yet again and pinning my hands to my sides before I have the chance to so much as gloat.

Shit.

A triumphant smirk appears, matching the victorious glint in his eyes, when he peels his body away from mine to rise off the bed.

"What kind of game are you trying to play?" I rasp, glaring at him from the mattress.

"One called Put Up or Shut Up, LaMothe." He shrugs into his hoodie and motions toward the door. "Now, c'mon. Time to go."

Slightly annoyed and painfully turned on, I climb off the bed and adjust myself behind my zipper. I feel Avery watching me, and when I glance up, I find him aiming another self-satisfied smirk at me.

Oh, fuck that.

"You're gonna pay for this," I murmur, my voice low and deadly. "And mark my words, baby, it'll be heaven and hell all wrapped in one."

His smirk spreads into a full-blown grin, eyes twinkling from the filthy promise.

"Looking forward to it."

TWENTY-THREE

Kaleb

"You know, rule breaking looks good on you. Maybe you should do it more often."

Shifting my attention from where I've just rehidden the lodge's spare key, I find Avery watching me with a predatory gleam in his eyes. He grins and pushes off the deck railing he'd been leaning against, approaching with a panther-like prowl.

My throat bobs as I swallow, and I shove the back door to the lodge open.

"You really shouldn't be encouraging bad behavior in a place like this. Think of the children!"

Laughter bursts out of him, way louder than it should at this time of night, and I instantly slap my palm over his mouth. My reaction only has him laughing more, so I keep my hand firmly in place until his hysterics subside.

"That wasn't meant to be funny," I hiss when I finally release him.

"Oh, but it was."

"It wouldn't be if you got us caught."

Another soft chuckle leaves him, and he lets out a hum that's far more seductive than it should be. "Well, good thing there aren't any kids around to catch us."

With that, he steps past me and through the open doorway.

The idiot I am, I follow him into the darkened halls of the lodge until we reach the kitchen. It's only once we're inside, the door closed behind us, that I risk flipping on the light.

Avery doesn't wait, instantly taking off toward the cupboards in search of snacks, and I have to rein in my amusement.

"No, no. You're not gonna find anything out here."

He casts a dubious glance over his shoulder, but when I motion for him to leave the cabinets alone and join me across the room at another door, he follows.

Pulling the door open, I reveal the small walk-in pantry and usher him inside.

The pantry isn't all that large, barely big enough to fit three people with the door closed, with floor-to-ceiling shelves on one side and a countertop with cabinets on the other. The cabinets are where the kitchen staff stores most of the counter-top appliances and spare tin foil, plastic wrap, that kind of shit. Meanwhile, the shelves have tons of food lining them; everything from baking supplies to canned fruit and vegetables to what we actually came here for.

Junk food.

"So this is where you've been hiding all the good shit," he mutters, aiming a knowing glance in my direction. "I think I'm even more annoyed you kept *this* from me over the Wi-Fi password."

I snort, shaking my head. "You had to earn the spoils of war, Reynolds. I wasn't gonna just hand them over willy-nilly."

"You're such a fucking dick sometimes."

With that, he's back to focusing on the task at hand: snack raiding.

His hands immediately land on two single serving bags of salt and vinegar chips before looking in the basket of chocolates and candy. After a few moments of digging, he pulls out a handful of Tootsie Rolls and Rolos.

"Salty and sweet," I muse, eyeing the items he snatched from the shelves in approval. "Solid choices, I must admit."

"The superior combo."

Just like us.

The thought has my brain screeching to a halt, because what the fuck is my brain on right now? There's no *us* when it comes to me and Avery. It's just sex. Getting each other off and, hopefully, getting him past the backward way of thinking his stupid bigot of a father instilled in him. Anything more than that is off the table.

Shoving my rambling thoughts to the side, I pluck the snacks from his hands while he continues his search, and set them on the counter. "Grab me something too while you're still looking."

"Anything in particular?"

"Whatever works. I'm not picky."

I lean back against the cabinets and watch him fumble around the shelves some more. He's like a kid on Christmas morning right now, and it's kind of adorable. Adorable in a weird, I-wanna-bend-you-over-and-fuck-you-where-you-stand kinda way.

I try not to let my thoughts run away with that idea, but it's proving rather difficult when Avery's ass is staring me in the face while he continues scrounging up snacks. Adding a view like this to the teasing from earlier, and my dick is already rock solid and begging for attention.

A fact which Avery remains oblivious to until I can't fucking take it anymore.

I step forward, closing the already small amount of space between us, until my chest brushes against his back.

"Finding anything good?" I murmur before pressing a kiss to the side of his neck.

One hand lands on his hip and skims along his waistband, circling to the front before slowly dipping inside. His head falls back, landing on my shoulder when my nails scrape against the smattering of hair leading to his dick before retreating.

I repeat the process a few times, inching closer to his cock with every dip my hand makes into his pants but never quite getting there.

"Fuck," he whispers, already rocking his hips. "What are you doing?"

The question comes out thick with lust, alerting me that he knows exactly what I'm doing. But if he wants to play that game, fine by me. I'm more than happy to give him a taste of his own medicine.

"Oh, baby." I tsk, continuing my torment. "Did you already forget the promise I made you earlier? About making you pay for how fucking hard you made me, only to not do anything about it?"

He glances over his shoulder at me, blue eyes lit ablaze with desire. "Believe me, I didn't forget."

A filthy smirk tugs at my lips.

Good.

My mouth finds his throat, and I slowly lick a path up to his ear while hooking my thumb into his waistband. I take my time dragging the fabric down just past his perfect ass, enjoying his sharp intake of breath once he's exposed to me.

Reaching between us, I brush one finger over his crease, barely touching his skin while moving it from the base of his spine all the way down to the back of his upper thigh. It has the desired effect when he arches back for more, but each time he does, I quickly pull away.

The way he seeks my touch now is something of an addiction for me. Torturing him with feather-light caresses and the faintest brush of skin on skin sets my libido into hyperdrive, and I've even gone as far as turning it into a weapon.

Edging him to the brink of insanity before finally giving him what he wants.

Which should happen in just a few—

"Kaleb, please," he pants. "I need more."

Perfect.

My gaze flashes up into the pantry, taking stock of the items lining the shelves until I find something, literally anything, that might work as—

Gotcha.

With one hand, I reach above Avery's head and snatch the neck of the glass bottle labeled "olive oil" from the shelf. Using my thumb, I twist the cap off and let it fall to the floor before looking back at Avery.

"Ass out and forearms on the shelf, baby." Dragging my fingers down his spine until I reach his ass, I spread his cheeks apart and whisper, "And fair warning, this might get messy."

He glances over his shoulder like I've lost my goddamn mind, but damn if he doesn't follow my lead anyway, adjusting until he's in the position I've requested.

Bottle of olive oil still in my other hand, I slowly tip the opening toward his crease. The tinted liquid spills onto his skin seconds later, slipping between his cheeks.

"Shit," he mutters, his back and shoulders stiffening at the contact.

I chuckle, equally amused as turned on.

Part of me wants to drop to my knees and lick him clean, but the desperation to slide inside him has me shoving the thought to the side.

Using two fingers, I spread the oil up and down his crack, coating his rim with a thick layer before pressing one of them inside. His moan of pleasure could wake the dead, and it has my cock twitching in my pants.

"You're still gonna have to be quiet," I murmur before brushing my lips along the side of his throat. "We don't need the cameras in the hall to pick up on the sounds you make while I fuck you."

Adding a second finger, I work him open some more, scissoring the digits until he's panting and thrusting back for more.

"Need you," he whispers, his head dropping as he fucks himself faster on the digits.

"I know, baby," I muse, rather enjoying this brazen, unabashed side of him. Probably a bit more than I should, because I tack on, "And you can have me when I'm done paying you back for earlier."

Continuing my ministrations, I slide my fingers in and out of him teasingly. Pressing against his prostate and coaxing him closer to the edge, only to ease up the pressure all over again.

After a few minutes, Avery's head drops to the shelf in front of him and he curses under his breath.

"Kaleb, *please*," he hisses.

"You had enough?"

"Yes. Fuck. Yes," he pants, the words coming out in harsh, staccato breaths.

Thank God, because I don't know how much longer I could've lasted without caving myself, even with as much as I love teasing him.

Not wasting any more time, I shove my pants and underwear down just enough to free my aching length, and reach for the bottle of oil again. Pouring it over my shaft, I spread it, meanwhile focusing all my energy on not coming before I can sink inside him. With his teasing from earlier, not to mention all the sexual tension we built throughout the day, it's a wonder I haven't exploded already by just fingering his ass.

"Kaleb," he moans, and I don't think I've ever loved the sound of my name on his lips more.

A deep chuckle leaves me, and I kiss his shoulder. "Patience, baby."

He lets out a disgruntled noise that quickly turns into a groan when I rub the tip of my cock against his rim. The scent of olive oil invades my nostrils as I briefly tease his hole, swiping it over the tight bud before gently pressing my hips forward. His muscles give as I crown him, allowing the head of my cock to slide inside with little resistance. I had every intention of easing into it, but Avery has other plans apparently, pressing his hips back until I bottom out inside him.

"Oh my God," he moans, the words coming out on a harsh exhale.

Leaning closer, I press my chest to his back and whisper in his ear.

"I thought I told you to have patience," I tease, nipping at his earlobe. "Maybe I should pull out of you for that. Really teach you a lesson."

Despite my threat, there's no way in hell I can make good on it. My cock is already twitching inside him, the need to come built up like a skyscraper I'm desperate to jump from.

I glide in and out of his ass with ease thanks to the oil, pressing all the way to the hilt and holding myself there every few thrusts. And it feels so good. Too fucking good.

"I'm not gonna last," I pant.

He shakes his head, a low moan coming out before he manages a soft "me either" in response.

Good, then I'm making it quick and dirty.

Sweat beads along my hairline as I piston into him, every thrust getting harder and more hurried while I watch my cock disappear inside his body. I don't think I've ever been more mesmerized by a sight.

Fuck northern lights and star-filled skies and sunsets and mountain views.

There's nothing better than seeing my cock slide in and out of him while he grips the shelves in front of him for dear life.

"Your ass is…Goddamn, Aves. It's the thing dreams are made of. I wish you could see us like this. Watch as I slide in and out of you."

Shit, I may not have bottomed in years, but the thought of letting him have a view like this far outweighs my preferences on who gets to be inside the other. And besides, who says it has to be one way or the other with us.

Us.

My eyes sink closed briefly, that stupid word again, worming its way into my train of thought when it has no business being there. But I shove it away. Lock it up and throw away the key, and start driving into him with enough force to topple every damn shelf in this room.

Soon enough, he's slamming his hips back against me, impaling himself on my length with every thrust. We keep moving like that, bodies meeting with unrelenting force, as we drive each other further up the mountain, the peak damn near in sight now.

Avery's hand leaves the shelf, reaching between his legs to grab his dick, and starts jacking his length. Taking control of his pleasure.

And though he can't see it, a sinful smile pulls at my lips.

"That's right, baby. Fuck your fist," I command, my fingers tightening on his waist. "I want you with me. Squeezing and milking all the cum from my cock."

I snap my hips forward in quick succession with the command, damn near punishingly. Every press and grind of our bodies is more addicting than the last, loving the way it draws another moan or sigh from his perfect lips.

Our pace becomes frantic as the scent of sex and sweat fills the room, it's potency turning need into desperation. My lust reaches an all-time high, and I'm hyper-aware of the fire my body's been consumed in, each powerful thrust inside him stoking the flame.

And, fuck, I crave the burn.

"I'm getting—" He groans, forehead dropping to the shelf in front of him. "Shit, I'm close."

"Then come."

He's pushing back harder now, taking me to the hilt over and over again. Each thrust draws more harsh pants from him, and I realize I must be hitting that perfect spot inside him; the one that makes him fall apart, shattering into millions of pieces.

And shatter, he fucking does.

His ass clenches around my dick, clamping and squeezing as release slams into him. Cum spills from his cock, coating the floor between his feet, and the sight and sound of him coming undone sends me over the edge right after him.

I'm in free fall, the euphoric high taking over my extremities as I fill his ass, claiming him from the inside out.

"Fuck, fuck, fuck," I chant, using him to work through my orgasm.

My forehead falls to the space between his shoulder blades as I catch my breath, both my cock and his ass pulsing from release. I could stay right here forever, coming down from this high, but we've already risked too much by having sex behind a door that doesn't lock…that's also in a public building.

Cum begins dripping from him the second I pull from his body, and I press a quick kiss between his shoulder blades before stepping away.

"Hold on. Don't move."

Turning around, I flip open the cabinets until I find some paper towels to clean up with. After quickly righting myself, I tear off a few sheets at the perforated line and go back into the kitchen to wet them in the sink. To Avery's credit, he's still waiting there when I return, and I drop to a knee behind him and start cleaning him up.

Quickly but thoroughly, I wipe away the oil and cum coating his skin, mesmerized by my release slowly leaking past his rim. I fight the urge to push it back in, forcing him to keep it inside his ass, if only so he remembers just who it is that fucked him. Who he fucking belongs to. But those aren't the kinds of thoughts you have about the person you're just screwing for pleasure. It's the kind for…something a lot more complicated than that.

Something that's begun to look a lot more like what I actually want.

Shoving the thoughts aside, I finish my task before wiping the floor at his feet too. Once all proof of our sins has been erased, I pat his ass playfully, attempting to balance out the heavier feeling still resting on my chest.

"Good as new."

Rising, I step away and toss the used paper towels in the trash outside the door, giving him some room to straighten himself in peace. Or maybe it's to give myself a minute of reprieve from the emotions that've been tapping against my skull like a petulant child trying to get their mother's attention.

Avery steps out of the pantry a few moments later—the snacks I'd all but forgotten about in hand—and the only evidence of what we'd just done is the flush present on his cheeks and neck.

I'm just about to lead him out of the lodge and back to safety when he opens his mouth as if to speak, only for nothing to come out.

I frown. "What?"

He blinks a couple times before shaking his head, then lets out a disoriented little laugh. "Did you really just fuck me in the pantry using olive oil for lube?"

I chuckle and shoot him a mischievous wink, any and all heaviness gone thanks to the dazed expression on his face.

"Sure did, Aves. Rebellious enough for you?"

Moonlight streams in through the cabin's window, creating streaks of light against the wall over my bed that look like laser beams. I've been studying them silently for the better part of an hour, all while listening to the wind rustling the trees outside and the soft sound of Avery's gentle breathing.

He's peacefully asleep beside me, his forehead pressed against the side of my neck, and it stirs conflicted feelings in my chest.

I'm aware letting him spend the night is most likely a mistake. It's one I had no intention of making once we got back to the cabin—snacks in tow—to watch a few episodes of *Criminal Minds* before it was time for him to head to his own bed.

Something inside me held him there, though. Kept his body pressed against mine like it was my own personal source of gravity.

Of course, I told myself I just wanted five more minutes with him pressed against me, then I'd make him leave. But five turned to ten, then twenty, and before I realized it, Avery's breathing completely evened out, becoming a slow, steady rhythm against my ribcage.

After that, I didn't have it in me to wake him, so instead, I sunk into the heat of his body tucked against me. Pairing it with the orgasm from earlier, and it should have been enough to drag me into the peaceful oblivion that is sleep.

Should being the operative word.

Instead, my mind's been spinning like a top for hours now, no reprieve in sight, and it has everything to do with the agonizing man curled up beside me.

Shifting slightly, I glance down at his sleeping form illuminated by the light streaking in through the window.

He's softer when he's unconscious; the lines of his features are less sharp and severe than they are in the light of day. Or maybe it's that the mask he's been wearing has fallen to the side, and I'm seeing his true face.

The one—I'm beginning to realize—few people know exists.

Lifting the arm that he isn't tucked in, I slowly bring my hand to his face and gently caress his skin. My fingers trace his jaw from his ear to chin, then back again, committing the feel of it beneath my skin to memory. Despite having spent the better part of an hour touching and feeling every inch of him earlier, I can't seem to stop.

Can't seem to rein in the feelings causing my heart to stampede in my chest.

Can't seem to get enough of whatever this has become.

And that, right there, is the biggest fucking problem.

The emotions he's been stirring in me lately, but earlier tonight especially, are ones that complicate things. Severely.

Wanting to claim him? Own him? Make him mine?

That's not what this is supposed to be.

I've been convincing myself that this is just fun, casual sex for weeks. I've even gone as far as thinking of it like a community service, allowing Avery to safely explore his sexuality and overcome his demons with me rather than going out in the world and hurting other innocent people. But despite rationalizing the choice to my own mind, it wasn't able to stop what I'm feeling.

It goes deeper than lust and desire. And, yeah, it goes deeper than just friendship too.

I like him.

I fucking *want* him.

Not just his body, but *him*.

His mind, his flaws, his insecurities.

All the little pieces of who he is, no matter how deep Shame sank its claws into them. I wanna know each and every one, if only to show him that he doesn't need to be defined by those thoughts. That he's more than the trauma that brought him here.

Brought him to me.

Closing my eyes at the thought, I roll my head to the side, pull in a deep breath, and slowly release it.

This is so stupid.

My instincts are telling me to distance myself, because there's no way in fucking hell this can ever be anything more than what it is right now. And even with where we're at, there's little chance it'll end well.

After all, he's still the guy who was expelled for outing two innocent people.

And I'm still the guy who turned him in for it.

But despite it all, I still want him.

I don't know what the fuck I'm supposed to do with that.

TWENTY-FOUR

Avery

Week Six

With the second half of our time at camp in full swing now, apparently it's time for a staff review with Colin. According to Kaleb, he does this every year: pulls in all the counselors one by one, regardless of how long they've worked here, for a "check-in" before heading into the final three weeks.

"Check-in," I echo, staring at him from across the dining table.

Kaleb smirks. "Stop worrying, it's gonna go fine."

I glance to where his brothers are sitting, close enough to hear despite them conversing themselves, and lower my voice to a level only for Kaleb's ears.

"For you, maybe. You're the camp golden boy. Meanwhile, I'm the idiot who still can't manage to bait a hook without wanting to puke."

To his credit, Kaleb does his best not to laugh at my dramatics. He even manages to hold it in for a solid three seconds before he fails miserably, but I appreciate the effort regardless.

Of course, it does absolutely nothing to assuage my anxiety.

"You're no fucking help," I mutter under my breath.

"No swearing," Dayton, who is sitting directly beside Kaleb, chimes in between mouthfuls of eggs.

Ah, so they are *listening.*

Eyes still locked on me, Kaleb arches a brow. "I'm gonna say it again: You'll be fine."

"If that's true, why do I feel like I'm about to face the firing squad?" I ask as I rise from the bench. Then I raise my hand to my forehead and give him a mock salute.

Amusement gleams in his eyes while he watches me.

"Don't worry. If I'm wrong and you get fired, I'm sure you have a future on Broadway. Your theatrics would be put to good use there."

I roll my eyes. "Like I said. No fucking help."

I'm about to leave when Elijah appears out of nowhere and drops his tray on the table right where I'd been sitting.

"Avery! Where are you going?"

"Meeting with Colin," Kaleb answers for me.

Elijah frowns, glancing between the two of us. "Really? But we're playing Capture the Flag after breakfast."

I pat him on the shoulder a couple times. "I know, kid. But I gotta attend my own funeral first."

And with that, I leave them, allowing my feet to carry me toward my impending doom. All jokes aside, the nerves are overwhelming. Weak knees, sweaty palms, arms weighing a thousand pounds; the only thing stopping me from being Eminem is that I've managed to not puke on myself.

Yet.

My pulse thuds in my ears as I head down the hall to Colin's office, dulling my sense of hearing to the point where I can barely hear my fist knocking on the door, let alone his voice calling me into the room. Of course, once I'm inside, the door closed behind me, the deafening pounding may as well be a group of monkeys banging cymbals. I'm not even sure if Colin told me to take a seat when he motioned toward the chair across from him or if I took the gesture and ran with it.

Jesus Christ, get a grip.

But my PTSD from meeting with authority figures is real, and from the tension lining my back and shoulders while he silently closes the file on his desk—*my* file—it's not going away anytime soon.

"How's it going this morning, Avery?" Colin asks, gaze lifting to mine as he leans back in his chair.

"Um. It's…good," I stumble through the lie.

His eyes crinkle at the edges, and I know he sees right through it.

"Great, then let's hit the ground running with this," he starts, nodding toward the folder in front of him. "Normally, these reviews are a combination of my own assessments of your performance combined with any notes or comments from your co-counselor. We use them to outline your strengths and weaknesses, giving you a chance to hone the areas you've excelled in and also address your shortcomings during the remaining weeks before camp is over."

"Okay," I utter slowly.

There's no chance Kaleb has told him anything about our clandestine meetings every night. If I can be sure of anything, it's that.

But I'd be a fool if I wasn't a little worried about what his notes about me might say. Especially if they're from the first few weeks of camp when he was still treating me like Public Enemy Number One.

Either my face is giving my thoughts away, or Colin is a mindreader, because a sharp bark of laughter fills the office, and he shakes his head.

"You don't have anything to worry about, I promise."

Yeah, Kaleb said the same thing. But I'll only believe them when I still have a job to go back to after this little meeting.

Clearing my throat, I motion toward the tan file folder sitting on his desk, labeled with my name at the top. "What's the consensus?"

"In short? You're different than when you first arrived."

I arch a brow at the director. "I have a feeling you're not talking about my newfound skill at starting a campfire."

A smirk tugs at his lips before he shakes his head. "Not quite."

He looks back at the file in front of him for the briefest moment before flipping it closed entirely. Folding his hands together, he rests them atop it and meets my gaze again.

"From what I'm seeing, you've taken great strides. Not only with honing some outdoor skills for yourself, but with the kids, and also with your interpersonal relationships."

"Yeah, well, I wouldn't have gotten there without Kaleb's help."

The knowing gleam in his eyes is unmistakable, and while I expect him to make some sort of comment on the admission, he doesn't. Instead, he moves right along with the conversation.

"I have to admit, I had my reservations about having you at camp. Of course, those only grew when you and Kal couldn't seem to set aside your differences those first few weeks."

"I can't even begin to apologize for that, sir. We—"

"Colin, son," he cuts in, offering a gentle smile. "That being said, I'm glad to see how well the two of you have moved past it. And rocky start aside, Kal's had nothing but great things to say about you the past few weeks. Truly a complete one-eighty from where the two of you started, actually."

"What can I say? We took your reprimanding to heart."

"Now, unlike your co-counselor, Elijah's been singing your praises since the beginning. It's remarkable, really. He hasn't ever taken to a counselor the way he has with you. I was talking to him before breakfast, and if I had a nickel for every time your name came up in conversation, I could retire right now."

So that's where he disappeared to this morning.

"Regardless, I expect this plan of your father's should go off without a hitch, if you keep up the good work."

My gaze drops to my lap, fixating on my interlaced fingers. "I'd hardly call it *work*, s—Colin. Eli's a great kid. Just a lonely one."

"From where I'm sitting, lonely is the last word I'd use to describe him these days. I have you to thank for that." A warm smile appears on his face before he adds, "Turns out, all he really needed was someone who understood him."

He wasn't the only one. Without Elijah, I don't think I would've lasted those first few weeks out here. It makes me wonder how the hell he managed every summer without someone to talk to.

"Yeah, well…I see a lot of myself in him, I guess. Made it easy to connect."

"It's more than just Elijah, though. A lot of the other kids have been singing your praises too. And especially when it comes to you and Kaleb as a leadership team. Which is why, pending the next few weeks go well, I hope you consider coming back next summer."

I blink in shock. "Are you serious?"

He laughs one of those deep, feel-it-in-your-stomach laughs. "Of course. I wouldn't offer if I wasn't."

Truthfully, I haven't been thinking past tomorrow, let alone all the way into next summer, and the idea of coming back here for another summer sure as hell hadn't crossed my mind. But, damn, the thought of having another summer like this with Kaleb does have a lot of appeal.

"I'll definitely consider it. Thank you, Colin."

"It's my pleasure," he says with a nod. Leaning back in his chair, he steeples his fingers in front of him and studies me. "I can tell you're far more at peace than when you first got here, you know."

My lips twitch and I glance away, hating that I'm so easily read by the man sitting across from me. Because he's right.

Somehow, nothing's changed, and yet everything is different at the same time.

This place that felt so much like a prison when I first set foot in it has turned into a refuge. A place of enlightenment, providing me with a sense of freedom I'd never imagined. My father sending me here against my will ended up being the best thing that could've happened to me. To the struggles I'd been facing when it came to accepting myself.

The irony of it isn't lost on me either.

Returning my attention to Colin, I offer him a shrug. "I guess this place gave me something I didn't realize I needed."

Or rather some*one*.

"Would you like your *I told you so* now so you can lick your wounds, or would waiting 'til you're naked in my bed take some of the sting out of it?"

Glancing up from where I'm spearing marshmallows onto roasting sticks for the kids, I level Kaleb with an unamused stare.

The entire day passed without him inquiring about my meeting with Colin, even after I asked about how his went. I should've known he was lying in wait, ready to use it as ammunition when he saw the chance.

Apparently, now is that moment.

"You're so fucking smug," I reply, not dignifying his question with an answer.

Of course, he gets a kick out of that too, if the grin spreading across his lips is anything to go on.

"Oh, absolutely. Smug is my specialty that follows an appetizer of being right. Both pair well with stubbornness, or so I hear." He lifts the s'more in his hand in cheers toward me before adding, "And s'mores too."

I blink at him in equal parts awe and disbelief. Leave it to Kaleb to get a kick outta my PTSD when it comes to authority figures.

"I can't stand you."

He takes another bite of his dessert before murmuring, "Mmm, I've heard that before. Of course, I had you coming with my name on your lips right after, so…"

"For fuck's sake," I mutter under my breath while shooting him a glare. I don't know what the hell's gotten into him this evening, but if he's trying to turn me on by bringing back filthy memories of us in bed together, it's sure as shit starting to work.

All I get in return is another grin before he pops the rest of his s'more in his mouth. Part of the melted chocolate bar drips from the bite as he does it, landing on his lower lip.

"You've got chocolate…"

I reach up to wipe it away, only to remember we aren't alone. So I settle for pointing to the spot, allowing him to take care of it himself. Of course, doing it myself may have been the safer option, considering Kaleb wipes it with his thumb…only to stick it in his mouth and lick the chocolate off.

Oh, Jesus fucking Christ.

Kaleb's eyes take on a playful glimmer when he pulls the digit from between his lips, now completely clean. He's well aware of what he's doing, and pairing his lewd gesture with a hellish smile, I know I'm in deep shit. Especially when my cock starts stirring behind my zipper.

I clear my throat and glance away, doing my best to tamp down the lust threatening to take over. Consequences be damned.

"Problem there, Reynolds?" He asks it like he's the picture of innocence.

"Nope. All good."

Let the record state, I am not good. I'm barely holding it together, but there's no chance in hell I'm giving him the satisfaction of letting him know that. Especially when the dickhead has the audacity to continue acting like a saint, letting out a little hum and nodding toward the bag of marshmallows.

"Hand me some of those, will ya? I think I want another s'more."

Swallowing harshly, I grab the bag and hold it out to him, careful not to let my skin come into contact with his. Touching him is the last thing I need to do, and God knows if I don't put some space between us soon, I can't be held liable for what might follow.

"And just so you know, you'll be even better when it's your body I'm licking chocolate off of later tonight."

Yep. I'm gonna lose it. Right here, right now.

"You're playing with fire," I warn, nostrils flaring, but it only makes his grin wider.

"Counting on it, baby."

Gritting my teeth, I step away from him and head toward Elijah, who is chatting with Max and Dayton by the fire. Of course, the jackass may as well be beaming at this point at my attempts to use the kids as a shield from him stirring my libido any further.

Will there ever be a day he doesn't see right through me?

As I drop onto the log beside Elijah, I catch Colton watching me, a curiosity in his gaze when it locks with mine. Like his older brother's, it's a little unnerving, despite him being only eleven. Maybe because Kaleb and I have been doing our best to keep them, along with all our campers, in the dark about what's going on between us.

Something we've been doing a damn good job of, as far as I'm concerned.

Yet, from the discerning look on his younger brother's face as his eyes move from me to Kaleb, I have a feeling we've somehow blown that to smithereens.

TWENTY-FIVE

Kaleb

It's the time of day the kids hate but I've come to look forward to the most: lights out.

Cabin by cabin, I quickly take headcount by checking that everyone is ready for bed, and more importantly, actually *in* said bed. Which never seems to be the case when it comes to Bradley, and tonight is no different.

"Bed. Now," I tell him before pointing at his bunk, leaving no room for debate in my tone.

I could've been a bit gentler about it, but my anticipation has me on edge. My mind has been firmly fixated on thoughts of melted chocolate dripping all over Avery's sinful body, which has been playing on a loop for the past two hours.

And Bradley's antics are drawing out the time I have to turn my fantasy into reality.

Thankfully, the last stop I have for the night is the cabin Elijah and the twins are sharing, and they're always the easiest to wrangle into bed. A quick knock on the door before opening it reveals the three of them already on their respective bunks, chatting animatedly together.

Elijah included.

Well, I'll be damned.

My lips curl up, knowing Avery's attempts at breaking through to Elijah—and subsequently, breaking him out of his shell—seem to be working when we aren't around to see it too. A little tidbit of information I can't wait to share with him later. Preferably after we've both collapsed from exhaustion.

The conversation between the three boys dies down when they notice me standing in the doorway, and I quickly school my features before uttering, "Lights out, guys."

A couple grumbles echo through the cabin, and I let out a chuckle before flicking the lightswitch off.

I'm not foolish enough to think they'll go to bed immediately; I was a camper here at one time too. But they can talk in the dark until they fall asleep for all I care, because they're the only things standing between me and Avery in my bed.

"Goodnight," I call over my shoulder before pulling the door closed behind me.

A stupid smile crosses my face as I descend the cabin steps, thinking I'm finally in the clear. That's when I hear the door open and my name being called.

Turning, I find Colton standing there, barefooted and in his pajamas, illuminated by the light above the cabin door.

"You can keep talking with the lights off, Cole," I tell him with a smile. "Just make sure you get some sleep, okay?"

The inscrutable expression on his face tells me that wasn't the reason he followed me out here, which he confirms when he says, "Can I talk to you about something?"

Frowning, I nod. "Of course. You know you can talk to me about anything."

He crosses the small porch before taking a seat on the top step, and I follow suit by dropping to the wood beside him.

"What's going on with you?" he asks almost immediately.

I have to hand it to the kid, he doesn't beat around the bush, preferring to go in swinging a machete instead. Unfortunately, I'm not really sure which particular bush he's wanting to hack down right now.

"What are you talking about?"

He narrows his gaze on me. "Just because I'm only eleven doesn't mean I'm stupid, Kaleb."

Now I'm *really* confused.

A frown pulls at my brows as I turn toward him. "Why would you think I'd—"

"Because there's something going on with you and Avery." His stare doesn't falter when he adds, "I saw you two at the bonfire tonight."

It's an innocent statement, but the underlying judgment etched into its meaning tells me all I need to know. We slipped up. Weren't as careful as we should've been.

The reality is, it was only a matter of time before one of the kids noticed what was happening. I was just hoping it wouldn't be one of my brothers, if only to avoid the conversation we're evidently about to have.

I still make an attempt to play it off, though, and aim a smirk at Cole. "What, talking? That happens when you work with someone."

"Not you two," he comes back with a scoff. "A few weeks ago, you wanted him as far away from this place as possible."

This kid is way too fucking observant.

"We might've started off rocky, but you could've even called us friends at one point," I remind him while doing my best to keep the defensiveness from my voice.

"Friends don't look at each other like that."

"And how would you know that? You're a bit young to—"

"Don't try telling me I'm too young to be talking about this with you," he immediately cuts in, and the slightest amount of guilt gnaws at me.

Some of the conversations Cole and I have had over the past few months are ones I didn't expect to have with either of my brothers for another few years. About sexuality, human decency, and respecting others privacy, just to name a few. He's long since proven he's mature enough to talk about these kinds of topics.

When I don't respond right away, he crosses his arms and pushes further.

"After what he did, how can you even think…" He trails off, his nose wrinkling up. "I don't get it. You don't like him."

The problem is, I do. Very much. I like him a lot fucking more than I should.

"Well, things can change."

"He hasn't," he volleys back. "There's no chance he's any less of the asshole who caused all that shit back at your school."

"One, watch your language," I warn, leveling him with a hard look. "And two, you don't know that. You don't even know Avery."

"And sleeping with him means you do?"

How the hell?

There's no part of me that wants to answer this question, let alone discuss it with him. The issue is I can't very well lie to him. Not when he was just accusing me of it earlier.

In the end, I don't say anything at all. I can't bring myself to confirm or deny it.

Unfortunately, Cole seems to take my silence as confirmation enough.

"What happens when you leave here? He's still kicked out of school. Your friends still hate his guts."

Leave it to my brother to force the questions I'd been asking myself out in the open, only for me to realize I still don't have an answer. And I finally understand what Avery meant on the dock that night. What it truly means to struggle with the internal battle of wanting something but hating yourself for wanting it.

For fearing what it might mean if you actually let yourself have it.

"I don't know." My head sinks to my hands, and I rake my fingers haphazardly through my hair. "I wish I did, but…"

Fuck.

This has become more complicated than I could've ever anticipated, and no path before me seems like the one I should take. Ending things when we leave here, continuing to hide whatever this is like a dirty little secret, coming clean to everyone…they all feel like betrayal, in one way or another. If not to Keene or my morals, then to Avery.

To my heart.

"Well, you've always been yourself, and you've always stood up for the right thing," Cole says as he kicks a few stray pine needles off the step with his socked foot. "You know, that's one of the reasons you're my biggest role model."

His words hit me in the chest.

Sure, I've always felt a little closer to Cole despite our age difference, but I hadn't realized he would look up to me with such high esteem until…

Family Day.

He was there, sitting in the stands, when Keene and Aspen were outed. And it wasn't until later than night, after he pulled me to the side and told me he's afraid something like that will happen to him one day, that it hit me.

And it was Colton's fear that ultimately led me to Coach's office. Led me to turning Avery in.

Just the reminder has my throat constricting a bit when I choke out a soft, "I know, Cole."

He's quiet for a few heartbeats before he rises from his spot beside me and fires a bullet straight at my chest.

"What you're doing makes me think I shouldn't look up to you anymore."

I take in a sharp breath, disarmed by his evident disappointment as he walks toward the cabin door.

"Cole, I'm still the same person I was yesterday, last month, or a year ago," I call after him. "This doesn't change that."

So much for not lying to him.

The person I am right now is nothing like the Kaleb who stepped into Colin's office, only to find Avery sitting in the chair across from him. I'm nothing like the Kaleb who tried to get him kicked out simply because I couldn't handle the feelings he'd started pulling out of me the moment I saw him.

But at some point, I truly started to leave the past in the past. Started giving Avery the benefit of the doubt, allowing him to prove himself. And by pushing my own personal issues to the side…I finally got to see the person he really is. The one, deep down, I knew was there all along.

Though, from the look on my brother's face, that doesn't matter. If anything, he looks even more despondent as he pulls open the door and walks inside, only to turn and whisper one last parting thought.

"Like I said. You don't have to lie to me."

When the door clicks shut, I let out a long sigh and drag myself off the cabin porch.

I'm barely a hundred yards from the cabin, barely starting to process the conversation Colton and I had, when a familiar voice calls out from somewhere down the moonlit path.

"Hey, hey. There you are."

Turning, I find Avery closing the few yards between us. There's a devastating smile on his lips as he approaches, but his brows crash together, those sky blues taking on a hint of worry when he gets a better look at my face.

"Is everything okay?"

Not even close.

"Yeah, I'm good. Just got done getting the last of the kids into their beds for the night."

"Same," he murmurs with a nod. "Though I didn't think Jordan and Tyler would ever get in their bunks. I'd always thought the whole sugar-before-bed thing was a lie our parents would tell us so we didn't eat too many sweets, but I'm starting to think there's some truth behind it."

I offer the faintest smirk I can manage, but it feels wrong and foreign on my lips.

Avery must not notice, or the shadows of impending nightfall must hide my expression just enough, because he takes a few steps toward me. His hands land on my waist before sliding to my back, where his fingers link together just above my ass.

"You're still good with me sneaking over tonight, right? Watch some *Criminal Minds* before you let me do despicable things to you?"

There's a seductive glint in his eye when he asks, and the way his lips curl up gives me the urge to kiss that stupid, sinful smirk right off.

But my brother's words are too fresh, clawing at my mind like a trapped animal in dire need of escape.

"Actually, can I take a rain check?" I swallow hard and force the lies out. "I'm just beat from today. I don't think my body can handle anything more than crawling in bed and crashing."

He's able to mask his disappointment quickly, just not fast enough for me to miss it.

"Yeah, that's fine. There's always tomorrow."

All I can do is give him another tight smile and nod before stepping out of his hold.

We go through the rest of our nightly routine without talking much, and though he doesn't say anything, I can tell Avery feels my shift in demeanor. It's only when we're about to part ways, heading to our own cabins alone for the first time in weeks, that he breaks the silence.

"I'll see you in the morning, then?" he murmurs, brushing back the stray blond hairs the wind pushed over his forehead. I find myself wishing I could be the one to sweep them back instead.

But I keep my hands to myself and murmur, "Yeah. I'll see you at breakfast."

My cabin feels empty and dead inside when I reach it, and far too lonely without Avery. I hadn't realized just how accustomed I'd grown to having him in this space over the past few weeks, and it doesn't have anything to do with the sex.

Just him being around, existing in each other's presence.

Rebuilding a friendship.

And now that I'm here, alone with my thoughts, I realize this may be what lies in store after camp is over.

All the questions I'd been pushing down—the same ones my brother forced back to the surface—come barrelling back into my mind like a racehorse. No matter the way I twist and dissect the options, I can't seem to land on a solid plan of action. Nothing stands out as the obvious choice, and that same dejected feeling from my conversation with Cole starts to take hold.

Fuck.

The look on his face while we spoke said more than his words ever could. Rife with disappointment. Fraught with frustration.

I've never seen him so forlorn, and it's exactly what I was worried about. Why I didn't want anyone to find out Avery and I were sleeping together, let alone becoming friends again. I knew no one would understand. They wouldn't be able to see past all the shit that's happened, and they certainly wouldn't accept my willingness to push it to the side.

They'd only see it as a betrayal.

Of my friendship, of my community, of the respect of my loved ones.

Of my morals.

But isn't betraying my heart worse?

Ironically, that's the only question I'm able to answer without a second thought.

Yes. It's immeasurably worse.

And that's the only thing I'm holding on to as I slip out of my cabin and walk the moonlit path separating me from the person my heart is calling to.

TWENTY-SIX

Being in my cabin this early is strange to say the least. I've gotten so used to Kaleb taking up my evenings after the kids are in bed, I don't know what else to do other than lie here in the dark, staring at the wall, while the minutes slowly tick by.

Sleep evades me, despite my efforts to count sheep, and it's not difficult to unpack the reason why when I'm alone with my thoughts right now.

This thing between me and Kaleb has changed, and I'd be remiss to think either of us knows what it means. It may have started out as messing around and having some fun between the sheets, maybe even a safe space for me to truly accept and come into my sexuality, but something changed.

Even attempting to deduce it seems impossible.

I release a long, frustrated sigh, wishing my brain would focus on anything other than the guy likely fast asleep only a few hundred yards away.

He's always on my mind, though. Now more than ever.

Which is why I'm choosing to think of his raincheck tonight as a blessing in disguise, if only to temper the disappointment gnawing at my consciousness like a dog with a bone.

Despite my attempt at pushing them down, I'm still lost in my thoughts when the lock on my door flips open with a *snick* so soft, I almost miss it. The sound of the hinges creaking open grabs my attention, though, and I turn to lift my head just in time to see a dark silhouette closing the door.

Just the sight of him has my heart thundering against my ribs.

Kaleb.

He's silent as he crosses the tiny cabin to my bed, the only sound coming from his footfalls over the floorboards. The blankets and sheets are pulled back a few seconds later, cool air hitting the bare skin of my stomach before he crawls in the vacant space beside me.

He doesn't move, doesn't speak. I don't even think he breathes for a good minute while we lie beside each other, his body heat pressed against my back. My eyes sink closed as I relax into his touch, enjoying the light scrape of his fingers against my scalp that could very well be what I need to finally succumb to sleep.

Then his lips skate over my shoulders in a whisper; not quite a kiss, but more of a phantom caress, and my heart squeezes painfully.

Fuck.

Unable to stop myself, I shift, rolling to my other side to mirror his position. His ministrations immediately come to a halt with my movement, the pads of his fingers freezing against my scalp.

"I didn't mean to wake you," he murmurs after a beat of silence.

I shake my head. "You didn't."

My hand moves to his face, allowing my nails to scrape over the scruff running along his jaw. The feel of it, rough and scratchy beneath my fingers, feels so right when we're like this.

Locked together in the freedom of darkness.

Kaleb's breath coasts over my lips, the minty scent of his toothpaste and musk from his body wash invading my nostrils. It's a heady combination, I've come to realize, making him nearly impossible to resist.

Good thing I'm long past the point of trying.

Using my hold on his jaw, I pull him in, closing the inches between us. I press my lips to his in a gentle kiss. One that's only meant to be light and chaste.

Until the fingers laced through my hair tighten.

A bolt of desire zaps me in the stomach as Kaleb's tongue sweeps over my lower lip, and the hand still resting on my hip drags my body into his. He's rolling me to my back seconds later, sliding a knee between my thighs while he deepens the kiss.

The hand still on his jaw slides to the back of his head as our tongues tangle, flicking and teasing against the other in the way I've become addicted to. Slow and sensual, taking a leisurely pace that drives me mad with want in an instant. Same as it does him, from the way his erection presses sinfully against my hip.

He's the first to break the kiss, moving to my collarbone and slowly working his way up my throat.

"I thought you said you were too tired."

Teeth scrape over my earlobe, sending a shiver down my spine. "Not anymore."

It's all the permission I need to grab his jaw again and drag his mouth back to mine.

Never have I ever had a kiss shoot my senses into overdrive to the point of being hyperaware of every single place my body touches his. It creates a tingling sensation rippling through my extremities, and it only spreads with the scrape of his facial hair against my palm as I cup his face to drive my tongue past his lips.

He responds with the same passion and urgency, his hands tightening against my scalp while he continues grinding his hips down into mine until I'm a leaking mess behind my boxers.

"*Kaleb*," I pant.

His name comes out as a half-groan, half-sigh, and one hundred percent a plea.

He shifts his weight to his heels, sitting up to peel his clothes off at the sound of my desperation, and I'm quick to follow, shedding my boxers. The heat of his skin sinks deep into my bones when he layers his body over mine again, grounding me to this time and place and moment. Locking it in the marrow for safekeeping, where nothing and no one can touch it.

No doubt, no fear, no shame.

No mistakes or missteps.

All that exists is us.

This is who I am.

It's taken me more time than I'd like to admit, to accept it, but now that I have, I can't believe I thought I could live any differently.

"Please, touch me," I beg, arching into him.

I don't think I can handle the teasing tonight. I just need him inside me. Right fucking now. He must realize it too, and with a tight hold on my hips, he rolls us before dragging me on top of him.

"Want you to ride me," he growls in a harsh whisper. "Wanna feel you clench around me while my cock is buried inside you."

My dick twitches at the filthy image he's planted in my brain, and no more than three seconds later, I'm putting it into action.

Leaning over toward the desk beside the bed, I grab my nearly-empty bottle of lube and flick open the cap. After dousing my fingers with the cool liquid, I straddle his hips again and spread it over his length. He thrusts up into my palm with every gentle stroke I give him, gathering the pre-cum from his tip and spreading it back down his shaft to mix with the lube.

His hands land on my thighs with a tight grip as a tortured moan breaks past his lips.

"*Fucking* hell, Aves. I need to feel you, baby."

His plea is a drug with an intoxicating allure, coaxing the confidence I need to shift my weight backward until I'm positioned over him. My heart hammers against my ribs as the head of his cock presses against my rim, and when I drop my hips, the cool lube allows him to easily slide through the tight ring of muscle.

"Oh, Christ." His nails dig into my thighs as I sink farther onto his length, not stopping until he's fully seated inside me.

Inhaling sharply, I pause and allow myself to adjust to his intrusion. It doesn't burn anymore when he enters me, and after a few seconds, I start moving over his length. Pleasure immediately coils low in my stomach, building with every drop of my hips, and that's before his palm wraps around my cock.

"God," I whisper on a sigh.

Leaning forward, I close the space between our lips and kiss him like he's the air I breathe. His free hand slides back from my hip, gripping my waist while I sink down on his length again, impaling myself to the hilt. Filling myself with his cock until I might burst at the seams.

There's never been a better feeling than this. Him sheathed inside me, mouths and bodies joined together at the molecular level.

Two parts of a greater whole.

I move slowly over his length at first, dropping my hips in time with the leisurely strokes his palm makes over my shaft. Our tongues tangle while we move together, giving as much as we take. We fall into a sensual rhythm, with low moans and breathy pants filling the air around us, the mixture of them becoming something of a symphony I can't help but get lost in.

Then again, I think I've been lost in Kaleb far longer than I've realized.

"You feel so good," he mutters against my lips. "So right. So fucking mine."

Because I am yours.

The thought is in my head instantly, and I have to physically bite my lip to keep the words from spilling free. It's a sentiment that can't be taken back once it's spoken aloud, even in the heat of the moment. But it doesn't make it any less true.

I'm his.

I don't know how it happened, and I don't know why. All I know is that it did, and there was nothing I could've done to stop it. No way I could have shoved this down and made myself want him any less.

"Then don't stop," I pant out instead.

Then I kiss him with every ounce of passion and love coursing through my veins.

Because that's what this is, right? This pulse-racing, stomach-fluttering feeling I get when I'm near him? The way I can't stop smiling every time I catch him looking at me?

How he peers inside me, sees all the fucking damage and destruction that's created me, and doesn't look away?

What else is that, if not love?

And it fucking terrifies me.

Linking my fingers through the dark strands of his hair, I kiss him deeper still, letting my tongue flick and roll against his while I move over him in sharp, quick thrusts.

Like it's enough to erase the past, the mistakes, the pain.

Like it's the beginning of something new.

Like it can make him love me back.

He licks and nips at my mouth while I ride him, picking up speed and stroking me in quick, rapid succession. It feels like heaven and hell all at once while we drive each other mad with want, pushing each other closer to ecstasy, just not fast enough.

"Kaleb," I whisper, his name a plea falling from my lips.

For what, I don't know. I doubt he does either, but he takes action anyway, releasing my cock in favor of my hips for more control.

More speed.

More fucking everything.

"Stroke yourself, baby," he rasps, his lust-darkened gaze boring into mine. "Get there. Mark me. Come all over my chest."

His hips drive up into me, drawing low moans from my chest that he swallows down before they can ever leave my lips. My hand moves faster over my length, trying to keep up with his rapidly increasing rhythm that soon isn't a rhythm at all.

It's relentless and brutal and addictive in all the best ways.

I can feel my orgasm building higher, reaching a tipping point I'm desperate to fall over. All I need is one little push, and I'm there.

As if reading my mind, Kaleb pistons his hips faster, the pace becoming unreal. Like he's hell-bent on breaking me into a thousand tiny pieces every time he thrusts into my body. Like the only thing on his mind is me—

"Come for me, Aves," he commands, voice taut with tension. "Squeeze my cock until I follow you over the edge."

As if his words have a direct line to my dick, I shatter on demand, consumed by a wave of ecstasy unlike ever before. Stars form behind my eyes as he drives his hips up into me, his crown swiping over my prostate with every thrust while my thumb rubs the sensitive nerve under my tip. I don't let up as my cum coats his chest, not stopping until I'm a boneless heap on top of him.

"That's it, baby," he growls in my ear as his hands grip my waist harder.

He's lost all sense of control now, snapping his hips upward with absolutely no finesse. Sinking in deep, burying himself there while my ass clamps around him until he finally loses himself right behind me. I feel his cum filling me as his orgasm takes hold, claiming me from the inside out.

Marking me as his—which is the one thing I'm desperate to be.

He slows his movements before coming to a stop, his head rolling back as he stares up at me with an unreadable expression, chest heaving with effort. I let out a long, shaky breath and try to regain some control over my breathing as well, at a loss for words while we come down from our high.

He doesn't say anything either, instead sifting his fingers through my hair and dragging my lips to his in a kiss as passionate as it is tender.

One filled with emotion and desire.

Promises in the form of unspoken truths.

When he finally breaks away, I shift my weight to one side enough for his cock to slide free. I feel the loss of him instantly, an emptiness taking hold while his release slowly seeps past my rim, dripping over my ass and leg.

My heart hammers against my ribs as I curl into his side, sinking into the warmth of his skin against mine while his fingers dance over my back and shoulders.

"Kaleb," I whisper against his throat. Right where his pulse thrums beneath the surface, pounding to the rhythm of his rapidly beating heart.

And once again, I'm hit with the same thought.

Three simple words.

I love you.

But I can't say it.

Not because of any shame or guilt; we're long past the point of those things standing in the way of my feelings for him. It's fear that holds me back. Fear that he won't feel the same.

Or maybe it's the fear that he will.

Kaleb's fingers stop moving over my back, and his arm wraps around me, tightening until our bodies are pressed together at every point possible.

"I know," he murmurs, finally breaking the silence. "I know, baby."

My eyes sink closed, and I force myself to breathe evenly.

Despite his statement, there's no way he *actually* knows what I was thinking. Not really. But the thought that he could? That the musing swirling in his brain while he holds me could be the very same as my own? Well, it's enough to have my own rampant heart crawling into my throat.

Neither of us make any attempt to move, to peel ourselves apart and clean up, and I find myself grateful for it. I want to soak up as much of this moment as I can, knowing damn well how fleeting they can be.

Maybe that's why, after minutes or hours have passed, I find myself whispering three painfully vulnerable words.

Just not the ones I want to say.

"Please don't go."

Even as I ask, I know it's foolish. Apart from the night on the mountain and the one where I accidentally fell asleep, we haven't strayed from the status quo. Despite keeping each other up later and later into the night, we still sleep in our own cabins, all under the guise of not being caught by security cameras or by another person.

But I don't have it in me to give a fuck anymore.

We've been playing with fire for weeks, but at this point, I'm ready to set the whole goddamn forest ablaze if it means keeping him here.

His arms tighten around me before he presses his lips to the side of my head.

"I won't," he murmurs, his nose nuzzling my hair. "I'm not going anywhere."

TWENTY-SEVEN

Avery

I think the only thing better than falling asleep in Kaleb's arms is waking up in them, and that's been my reality the past couple days. Even if it means an alarm going off at the ass crack of dawn, forcing us to part ways so we don't get caught, I'll take it. I'll take every sleepy moan and half-conscious kiss I can get, and the knowledge that I'll spend the entire day with him takes some of the sting out of sneaking around.

It'd be kind of sickening to witness if I wasn't so goddamn happy.

Apparently my joy has become obvious to others too, but mostly Elijah, who never fails to comment on it…like right now.

"I'm just saying, you've been smiling a lot."

I can't help but laugh when I glance down at him while we walk down the trail to the lake, lagging behind the rest of the group as always.

"Last time I checked, smiling wasn't a bad thing, kid."

"It's just different."

"Yeah, well," I muse, ruffling his hair. "I don't think I'm the only one smiling a lot lately. From where I'm standing, you're actually having a pretty great time here this summer."

His little nose crinkles up and his cheeks turn a little red. "Yeah, I guess."

"You guess," I echo, arching a brow.

An indignant huff leaves him, and he rolls his eyes. "Fine, you win. I'm having fun."

"And?" He grumbles out something I can't quite make out, and I knock his shoulder with my arm. "Sorry, I didn't quite catch that."

"I said I liked camp too, okay? But I wouldn't if you weren't here."

A few deep chuckles break out from my chest as we reach the edge of the clearing. Kaleb's already over unlocking the shed, and I motion to where the other boys are all gathered, chatting and fucking around with each other.

"I'm sure you'd be just fine. Now, go hang out with your friends. I've gotta help Kaleb anyway."

After a lot of hiking over the past few days, we've decided to do something a little more relaxing post-lunch: spending the day out at Glass Lake. The kids are thrilled with the change of pace as we break out the paddleboards and kayaks, letting them choose whichever their preference is.

No canoes, though. Thank God, because I don't think I'd survive a repeat of that particular incident…even if I'd love nothing more than to get Kaleb dripping wet again. Especially when I know just how good those swim trunks look hanging low off his hips when they're saturated with water.

One by one, we get the kids fitted into life vests and launched off the dock in their watercraft of choice. Only the twins are left now, and I easily get Dayton situated on his paddleboard before giving him a proper send off into the water. However, when I turn around, it seems Kaleb is having slightly less success with Colton.

Colton's straddling the edge of his kayak, one foot in the watercraft while the other is still on the dock, and his legs are damn near shaking while he reaches for his paddle resting on the seat.

Kaleb's holding the edge of the kayak against the dock and notices his brother struggling. "Here, let me grab the paddle while you—"

"I can do it myself, Kaleb. I don't want your help," he snaps, glaring at his older brother.

The kid haphazardly climbs the rest of the way into the kayak, somehow managing not to fall in or tip it in the process.

Kaleb winces but releases the kayak once his brother is sitting safely in the seat and then rises to stand beside me.

Colton glances at me warily before moving his gaze to Kaleb. Distrust is written all over his face when he looks at his brother, lingering there before he inevitably paddles far away from shore.

While Colin may have insinuated that a ton of the kids love me during our meeting earlier this week, one thing remains evident: Colton LaMothe is not in that category. What's not so clear is why *Kaleb* seems to be on the receiving end of his brother's ire.

From what I've noticed since arriving at camp, Kaleb might be Colton's favorite person on this planet. All three of the brothers are close, don't get me wrong, but there's something different about Colton and Kaleb's relationship. So while it's not really any of my business, I can't stop the question from slipping out as we watch them all from the dock.

"What's been up with Cole the past couple days?"

Kaleb's gaze is fixated on his brother, who is currently using the kayak paddle as an extension of his arm to push Dayton off his paddle board. An attempt that becomes successful moments later, with the help of Max and Jordan, when Dayton goes crashing into the water.

I chuckle softly at the antics, but Kaleb doesn't so much as crack a smile. An unreadable emotion flashes in his eyes when he looks back at me, and I wouldn't have to read his mind to know *something* is up.

"Maybe he's just realizing that having his big brother around all summer isn't as great as he thought it would be."

It doesn't feel like the entire truth, but I don't press him on it. Instead, I slowly reach over and let my fingers graze his; a featherlight caress that has goose bumps popping up over his arms. It's meant to be more of a sweet gesture than anything, but the second my skin connects with his, an electric current sparks between us.

From the way his eyes flare when he looks at me, he feels it too.

"I guess his loss is my gain."

His brow arches imperceptibly before he murmurs a gruff, "Is it now?"

I nod, swallowing hard as our gazes stay locked together.

The urge to haul him against my chest and kiss the daylights out of him is damn near overwhelming, and I have to pull my hand away before I do just that. Kaleb's gaze breaks first, moving back to the kids for a brief second.

"We better get out there with them before someone drowns."

"They're wearing lifejackets," I remind him. "They'd have to try really hard for that to happen."

"Yeah, well, sometimes I wouldn't put it past Cole to hold Day underwater with his paddle."

The joke lightens the mood ever so slightly as we head over to the shed to grab our own paddle boards, but I can still feel a tinge of despondence in Kaleb. And I hate it. Hate that something has him feeling so sullen and dejected. Hate that I can't do something to change it.

Maybe that's why, before he can grab his board off the rack, I wrap my fingers around his wrist and drag him toward me. He crashes into my chest, his smooth, tanned skin pressed directly against mine, and I don't wait more than half a second before covering his mouth with mine.

Releasing his wrist, my fingers slide over his side and wrap around his lower back, holding him closer while my tongue flicks over his lower lip. Every inch of my body ignites, consumed in a fire of love and lust, and I relish in the burn.

"What are you doing?" he whispers after a moment, his hands gripping my waist.

"Kissing you. I would've thought that was obvious."

My lips cover his again, and this time, he's kissing me back with just as much fervor and passion. One hand slips up into his dark hair, loving the way it feels between my fingers, while the other moves up to his jaw to deepen the kiss. I back him against one of the racks while our tongues tangle together, every inch of our bodies so perfectly aligned, I could die on the spot.

The ridge of his rapidly thickening cock twitches against my hip, and I roll against him on instinct. A soft moan leaves him—or maybe it was me—and it only spurs me on. Releasing his hair, I slide a hand between us to palm him over his swim trunks, needing to touch him.

But that's what breaks the spell, and Kaleb's hand pushes against my chest to break the kiss.

"Okay, okay," he mutters, putting some distance between us. "We have to stop before we get carried away."

"So let's get carried away," I reply immediately.

His eyes may as well be on fire as he adjusts himself, hiding his erection as best he can. "Too much sunshine must be making you lose your damn mind."

Turning, he grabs a paddle board from the rack for me, then one for himself. Unfortunately for him, this leaves his delectable ass wide open, and I take the opportunity to give it a playful smack.

"Actually, it was definitely the way these trunks mold to your ass and sit low on your hips."

He shoots me a glare as he grabs his own board and pushes past me to exit the shed. "And you're gonna end up outing us to the entire camp if you can't keep your hands off me in broad daylight."

"There are worse things."

What the fuck did I just say?

I don't have time to process or unpack my Fruedian slip, though, because the second we step from the shed and turn the corner, I'm greeted with a sight that instantly sets my entire body on edge.

"Dad."

I damn near choke on the word as it falls from my lips, and my father's penetrating gaze shifts from the lake over to where Kaleb and I are standing.

"Avery. I've been wondering where the hell you were."

"We, uh…" I look helplessly at Kaleb for some sort of explanation, but he still has his gaze locked on my father. "We had to grab our boards before going out with the kids," I finally go with.

It's not exactly a lie, and it's certainly better than going with *we were too busy making out like horny teenagers* right outta the gate.

"What are you doing here?" I manage to ask, despite the baseball that's lodged itself in my throat.

My father glances down at his watch, and it's only then that I realize he's dressed impeccably, as always, in one of his tailored suits that cost more than all my paychecks from camp combined.

And he's certainly out of place standing at the edge of a lake in the mountains.

"I had a call scheduled with Colin to go over some quarterlies after balancing his books this week. Figured I might as well kill two birds with a trip here instead, seeing as I haven't heard from you since you left." He cants his head, eyes sliding over me with suspicion. "If it weren't for your name still on his payroll, I'd have thought you were eaten by a mountain lion out here or something."

My smile is tight and forced as my father wraps me in an awkward one-armed hug—one no doubt for Kaleb's benefit rather than my own.

"How're you fairing?"

"Uh, fine, I guess." I motion out toward the lake with the board under my arm. "Busy keeping all these kids in line."

"Easier said than done, I have no doubt."

The charm oozes off him like a toxic gas, infecting every air molecule around us until it's getting harder to breathe. Spending much more time in his presence is sure to suffocate me entirely.

Clearing my throat, I motion toward Kaleb beside me, who hasn't so much as moved since our path collided with my father's.

"Uh, Dad. You remember Kaleb, right? He's our left-fielder back at Foltyn."

I internally wince at the word *our*, the sting of no longer being on the team still very much present. But it's not until I look back at my father, noticing his eyes have hardened to stone, that I realize my mistake in making the introduction. He runs the payroll, so there's no way he'd miss Kaleb's full name on it, let alone fail to put together the pieces of how we know each other. A fact he confirms with as much venom as I've come to expect toward anyone on the bad side of Jason Reynolds.

"Yes, of course. You're the one who came forward about the…*incident* last spring, right?"

I feel Kaleb bristle beside me, and when I glance from my father to him, the tension lining his jaw is enough to make my own ache. Having spent as much time with him as I have this summer, it's obvious he's doing his best to not pop-off at the mouth—especially after all I've told him.

"That was me, yeah," he states after a beat, leaving it at that.

"But we've put it behind us," I quickly add, my attention shifting back to my father. "You know. Water under the bridge, as they say."

Disbelief lines my father's expression. "I clearly fail to see how it could possibly be under the bridge when his actions swept away your entire college career."

"Which would be a rightful repercussion after his actions," Kaleb snaps.

"Perhaps in the world you live in." My father studies him briefly, a knowing smile slowly creeping on his face. "But welcome to reality, where anything can be corrected with the right course of action."

My pulse thuds rapidly beneath my skin, and for whatever reason, I feel like he's not just talking about me getting kicked out of Foltyn. It almost feels like he's talking about *me* too. Like he's somehow figured out the secret I've been harboring and he plans on fixing it. Like he knows what Kaleb and I were just doing in that shed by simply looking at me.

Of course he knows. You reek of depravity.

Shame's venom seeps into my bloodstream like poison, spreading slowly through my body with every heartbeat.

Disgusting creature. An absolute disgrace.

I do my best to shove it back into the cage I've made inside my mind, but it's no use. I can't block it out. Not with my father standing right here in front of me. Shame feeds off him, growing in strength from his presence.

Kaleb's lips pull back slightly, but he doesn't say anything more. I feel like I'm drowning in tension between them, and I'm willing to do anything to find a liferaft to pull me above the surface.

Motioning toward the lake with my board, I mutter, "Uh, yeah. We actually have to get out there with the kids, so—"

"Colin's given you the rest of today off since I'm here," he cuts in, looking entirely disinterested in whatever I was going to say. "Now, why don't you go change and we can see what we can scrounge up for food around this place."

"Kitchen closed an hour ago," Kaleb says immediately, a demeaning smirk on his face. "And we just ate."

My father doesn't bat an eye at the information, instead smiling viciously as he switches gears. "We can go into town, then. I'm sure it would be a nice change of pace from…all *this*." Pausing, his attention finally shifts to me. "Besides, you and I have some things we need to discuss."

A sour taste hits my tongue, spreading into an ache at the back of my throat.

I don't want to go. Not in the fucking slightest. If anything, I want to go back in time to five minutes ago, when Kaleb and I were in that shed, and never come out.

But I also know nothing good can come of refusing him.

"I, uh…" I awkwardly adjust the board under my arm. "Let me just put this away first, and I can meet you at the lodge."

"Leave the board, I'll take care of it," Kaleb murmurs, drawing my attention over to him. There's a hint of worry in his gaze, his brows drawing down in the center slightly, and I wish I could do something to assuage it. I do my best with my own gaze, I swear I do, but it's all meaningless when his hand lands lightly on my shoulder and…I flinch.

I pull away from his touch—the press of his skin on mine that I've come to crave—before I can think better of it.

Shame cackles and shrieks with glee, its talons clanking against the cage that once contained it. A cage that's now been dismantled, piece by piece, by my father's presence.

I know it, and from the hurt in Kaleb's expression, he knows it too.

Shit, shit, shit.

"Kaleb, wait," I whisper.

His forest gaze collides with mine, speaking to me with it as he gives a subtle shake of his head.

Not now.

"I'll leave the two of you to…*catch up,*" he says instead, his focus flicking from my father, then back to me.

With that, he heads off to the shoreline and drops his board in the water.

And I watch after him, full of helpless anxiety, and knowing damn well that every step forward we've made was just taken out in a landslide.

TWENTY-EIGHT

Kaleb

I don't see Avery for the rest of the day, which is both a relief and unsettling at the same time. While I needed time to cool off from the encounter with his father, I would've thought the two of them wouldn't be more than an hour or so, and maybe he'd be back in time for dinner. Even with Colin giving him the day off to spend with his dad, I assumed he'd figure out some way to cut it short. But as evening bleeds into night with no sign of him, worry has long since slipped in.

After everything his father's done, and after all the work he's put in to overcome it…

My jaw tightens as I stare at my cabin door, and I force myself to reroute my line of thinking. Because my worry isn't just for Avery alone. It's also for me, for *this*.

I'm fucking terrified of *who* I'll be getting back after he spends the day around dear old dad. Especially after the way he recoiled from my touch earlier.

Thankfully, I don't have to wait much longer before the sound of footfalls on the cabin porch outside have my ears perking up. There's a soft knock before the door opens seconds later, revealing Avery.

He's still dressed in a pair of jeans and long-sleeved Henley he must've changed into before leaving camp for the day, and I have to admit, he's edible in it. Although, he'd look a helluva lot better with it on the floor.

Our eyes lock instantly before he whispers a soft, "Hey."

There's a smile on his face as he steps through the doorway before allowing it to fall closed behind him. It's the same one he's been giving me for weeks, and fuck if it isn't a sight for sore eyes. I hadn't realized just how anxious his absence was making me today until now.

Now, I feel like I can finally breathe again.

"Hi." The word comes out on a sigh, and it causes his grin to widen. "How was your day?"

"No, no. I wanna hear about yours," he says while dropping onto the bed beside me. "How much hell did you have to manage all on your own?"

"Eh, it went fine, I guess. The kids were menaces for the most part. Elijah wouldn't stop asking where you were, and I swear, Liam is gonna end up putting one of the other kids in the hospital with his fishing pole one of these days."

An airy laugh fills the cabin. "So, all in all, it went exactly as expected."

"Pretty much, yeah," I reply with a soft chuckle. Raking my fingers through his blond locks, I allow the warmth of his body and presence to let something deeper slip out. "Wasn't the same without you, though."

Avery shifts beside me, and when I glance down, I'm met with a devious glimmer in his blue eyes. "Dare I say it, but it sounds like you *missed* me, LaMothe."

"You can say it. Doesn't mean I'll admit it."

My denial only makes his grin spread wider, and he rolls until he's hovering over me.

"Mmm, I'll try not to let that go to my head."

"I honestly was beginning to think your dad kidnapped you," I say, my feeble attempt to make a joke. "Maybe he took one look at where you'd been staying and decided you'd faced enough punishment. Pitied you, told you to pack your shit and head back to the city."

Avery pulls back, and from the way his smile falters, I can tell there's something he hasn't said.

The light, playful teasing that charged the air with electricity is gone, replaced with the same gut-wrenching worry from earlier when I whisper, "What's wrong?"

"Actually, I do need to talk to you."

A sense of foreboding hits me, along with a wave of nausea. Any variation of "we need to talk" is anxiety inducing at best, and his face does little to assuage it from ramping up even higher.

"What did he say?"

Avery shakes his head as he drops down on the mattress beside me, his face contorted in a grimace.

"Um…in short? The plan may have already worked." His eyes lift to mine, the blue pools swirling with mixed emotions. "Elijah must've told his father about me when the kids got to do their calls home earlier this week, or maybe Colin said something after he did our check-ins. I'm not sure exactly, but the dean called my father and set a meeting for us to" —he lifts his hands and forms air quotes— "'see what we can do' about my expulsion."

Relief floods my bloodstream, and I smile. "Well, that's good news, right?"

After all, getting back into Foltyn is exactly what he wanted; the main reason Avery was here at camp in the first place. And while I hated the idea in the beginning—*loathed* being the more operative description—I'll be happy if this ends up working out in his favor.

Avery nods and murmurs, "Yeah, I guess. My dad is confident it's a done deal anyway."

His lack of enthusiasm, paired with the frown on his lips, causes me to take pause, but I do my best to lighten the mood. "Then what's the look for? We should be celebrating. Naked, preferably."

I know the reaction he'd normally have to that offer: his expression would perk up instantly, gaze heating to a low simmer as his mind shifts to filthy, delicious places. Instead, all I get is a deepening frown until a line creases his forehead, and two sullen, lifeless eyes staring back at me.

"He wants me to go home."

He drops the bomb so subtly, it takes a minute for me to register the damage it causes. But once I do, it's like the rug has been ripped out from under me at the same time a linebacker slams into my stomach.

Like all oxygen has left the atmosphere, and I'm flailing in freefall.

The look on my face must portray my every thought—all the fear and disappointment consuming me in waves—because Avery moves to take my hand in his.

I don't let him.

His jaw tightens, eyes shining with fury or sadness or maybe even both. "Kaleb…"

"He wants you to leave. Before camp is over?"

I don't bother to keep the incredulity from my tone, causing Avery to wince before he nods. Frustration slams into me the moment he does, and I shove off the bed to walk across the tiny room.

"Why?"

Shaking his head, he offers up the most bullshit explanation ever. "He doesn't think there's a reason for me to stay. I did what I came here to do, and now I should enjoy what's left of my summer back in the city before classes start up again."

Of fucking course.

I scoff, crossing my arms. "And you said yes."

It's a statement, not a question.

We wouldn't be having this conversation at all if it were a question.

A helpless expression paints his face, his gaze imploring me to understand when he murmurs, "He didn't really make it seem like I had much of a choice."

"Of course there's a choice!" I snap, tossing my arms out to the side. "You're an adult, Avery. You can do whatever the hell you want. He may be your father, but you aren't beholden to him or his commands."

"You know it's not that simple."

I can't help it; I laugh. One of those maniacal, sanity-hanging-by-a-thread laughs, because this has to be some sort of joke.

"Except it is that simple, Avery. You've spent this entire summer here, with me, taking back the parts of yourself that were mangled and ruined by shame. I've watched you struggle to push past all that damage, and now you're about to willingly walk right back into the lion's den and hand yourself over for slaughter."

He clenches his teeth, and I can see the anger slowly coming to a boil inside him while he grinds out, "Is that how little you think of me? That I'll roll over and submit all over again?"

"Isn't that exactly what you're doing right now?" I counter, standing my ground. "If you're this easy for him to control, what's stopping you from slipping right back into the same suit of armor you've been wearing your entire life?"

"Because I don't fucking *want* to!" he seethes, rising from the bed and crossing the room to me. "I don't want to go backward anymore, and I sure as hell don't want to hide. That's why I know I won't go backward."

"Then why did you flinch earlier?"

The question extinguishes all the fire in his eyes instantly. Gone is his anger, replaced with something I'd recognize as easily as my own reflection.

Shame.

"Kaleb…"

"I barely touched you, and you fucking flinched. So tell me again how you're not gonna go right back to the person you were before, when it took all of five seconds in your father's presence to have you recoiling from me."

An animalistic noise leaves me—some mix of a growl and a whimper—the memory of him pulling away slicing through me like a blade.

From the way he winces, I'm not the only one pained by it.

"It was an accident," he whispers, almost pleading.

"It was *instinct*," I correct, snarling out the word. "It was fight or flight, and you fucking fled."

His father is the only one who can pull that impulse from him. Ironic, since he's the one Avery needs to fight the most.

"He took me by surprise. I didn't have a clue he was gonna be there waiting for me! Give me some fucking credit."

"If you want credit, then earn it."

"I'm trying! *This* is me trying," he snaps, motioning between the two of us.

"Not from where I'm standing." My gaze drags over him, and I shake my head. "You're still doing what Daddy tells you. You're still taking the easy way out."

"That's not what this—"

"Of course that's what this is! God, Avery. How can't you see what's right in front of you? He's handed you poison instead of water every fucking moment of your life, and you keep drinking it!"

I'm shouting now, but I don't care. Let the entire camp hear us screaming at each other. Maybe if he has an audience to witness this, reality will sink into that thick skull of his.

His lips pull into a distorted grimace. "I didn't know any better. Not until I got here and you showed me another way."

"Yes, you did. Deep fucking inside you, you knew." My lips pull back in a sneer as I stare at him. "At a certain point, you're no longer a product of your environment. The responsibility eventually falls to you. To correct the way you *choose* to operate, rather than fall back into the comfort of what you've been taught."

Any and all arguments he has die on the spot, either too afraid of or too stunned by the guillotine of words hanging over us. I know it was harsh, but it needed to be said. Responsibility doesn't fall on him for his trauma, but healing it, reworking his way of thinking, and changing the things he can control, all do.

The worst part is, this whole time, I thought he was doing exactly that.

Clearly, I thought wrong.

"When?"

The single word comes out like it'd just been pulverised with a hammer. Avery's response doesn't fare much better.

"Tonight."

My eyes sink closed. *Of course.*

No doubt his father wanted him out of here as soon as possible.

Avery must read something in my expression, because I hear the floor creak under his weight, only to open my eyes and find him approaching slowly.

"It doesn't have to end like this."

A sharp laugh leaves me as I step away again. "Oh, really? Enlighten me, then. What happens when you go home? When you get back into Foltyn and classes start again?"

I throw every question in his face—all the ones I've been struggling with myself—to see what his answers might be. Because I know mine now; I've known them for a while, I think.

Don't betray your heart.

But what am I supposed to do when my heart betrays me instead?

A helpless look crosses Avery's features, eyes pleading as they lock with mine before glancing around the cabin. Searching, like the answer is written somewhere on the wood inside these walls rather than the organ beating in his chest.

"I don't know what happens," he whispers, shaking his head. "I haven't even thought about that yet. I thought we had more time."

It's on the tip of my tongue to tell him that we could. If he'd just stay, we could. But I don't say it. If that isn't an obvious option to him, then do I really want him to stay?

My teeth sink into my cheek for a moment before I mutter, "Well, the clock's just run out. The bubble's burst, and it's time to head back to reality."

"Don't say it like that."

"Why? It's true." I motion toward him, despair taking hold. "You're leaving, right?"

He gnaws on his lower lip, the way his eyes fall to the floor making it clear he is, even if he doesn't want to admit it. And as I stare at the guy who I've spent weeks with, laughing and smiling and fucking and healing, I don't recognize him.

Maybe Cole was right after all.

Sleeping with him didn't mean I knew who he really was, it only made me blind to the parts I didn't want to see. It let me fall for an illusion; the fantasy of the man I thought him to be.

Right now, he's showing me who he really is.

A fraud, a coward, a liar.

He's proving he hasn't changed.

If I can fall in love with someone like that, then what the hell does that say about me?

The thought takes me off guard, knocking the wind out of me like a gut-punch. I thought I was fighting against the emotions he was pulling out of me; pushing back and shoving them away to save myself from the possibility of feeling like this. Yet it seems he snuck past my defenses anyway.

I don't have long to linger on the revelation, because Avery takes a slow step toward me, snapping my focus back to the present. My immediate reaction is to move away again, to put distance between myself and the thing causing me pain.

And I fucking hate that his tortured whisper only makes me feel it more.

"I don't know what you want me to do."

To stay, to fight, to scream.

To do fucking anything other than lie down in submission, yet again.

On some level, I always knew it would come to this. He'd be placed in a situation where he'd finally have to show himself—his *real* self—to his father. And while I'd hoped he'd be up to the task, it's obvious now that he isn't.

Maybe he never will be.

And here I am, in love with him anyway.

My teeth grind together so hard, I'm liable to crack a molar. At least it'll pair well with the broken heart struggling to beat in my chest.

"Go," I whisper.

"What?"

"I said go, okay? That's what I want you to do." The lie is bitter on my tongue, but I swallow it down anyway. "Go and don't fucking look back."

"Kaleb—"

"Go!" I snarl, the word cracking and shattering as it leaves my lips.

I'm barely hanging on now, and if he doesn't get out of here, there's no telling what might happen. Will I drop to the floor and beg? Scream at him some more? Say something I shouldn't…or maybe something I should?

Tears well in his eyes, threatening to spill over, but he quickly blinks them away before crossing the room. With every step he takes toward the door, a piece of what we've built here dies, only to become dust beneath his feet.

My stomach rolls when the sound of the door hinge creaking greets my ears, but just when I think I'm in the clear, he stops and clutches the door frame.

Baby, please. Go. Don't make this harder.

He doesn't turn around, though, just stands there, shoulders slumped in defeat before whispering out into the darkness.

"I'm a different person than I was when I got here. You're a big reason for that."

My jaw clenches as I try to rein in my emotions threatening to spill to the floor, joining the remains of my mutilated heart.

"From where I'm standing, you're exactly the same."

My vision blurs as I slam the door closed, flick the lock in place, and press my back to the wood for support, only for my knees to give out and I drop to the floor. The throbbing ache in my chest has its own pulse, like a blade stabbing the stupid organ that resides there with every beat it takes. Reaching up, I rub the spot, as if it'll be enough to ease the pain.

As if it can erase the facts.

The bubble burst, and just as I feared, devastation is left in its wake.

But it doesn't feel real. Not until the next morning when Elijah comes up to me at the breakfast table and asks, "Where's Avery?"

I don't have it in me to meet his gaze when I answer with a single, heart-wrenching word.

"Gone."

TWENTY-NINE

Avery

Two Weeks Later — August

It's been fourteen goddamn days, and every attempt to reach Kaleb since leaving Alpine Ridge has gone unanswered. I can't blame him for it, what with the way I up and left, no fucks given about the responsibilities I was sloughing off. Logic isn't enough to stop me from being disappointed, though.

Okay, maybe heartbroken is more accurate.

And not just about Kaleb either. I miss the camp itself.

I miss the days spent under the sun, the campfires when evening took hold. I miss catching Kaleb's eyes on me when I least expected them, the places he'd take me to be alone. I even miss the kids—Elijah most of all.

So I've spent the past couple weeks craving a place I never thought I'd belong to begin with.

The fucking irony.

Needless to say, if there is such a thing as hell on Earth, I've been living in it since the moment my car crossed the border into Washington and entered the Vancouver city limits.

To make matters worse, whenever my damn phone makes a noise, I'm instantly checking the screen like a lovesick fool, hoping and praying to find Kaleb's name on the screen. It never is, of course; it's almost always my father, seeing as he's the only person I have after abandoning or alienating every other person in my life.

It's not my father's name on my screen right now, though. It's not Kaleb's either. But the name I find instead does send a similar jolt of electricity through my core.

Alpine Ridge Office.

While I know it could very well be Colin—and it would make the most sense for it to be him—even just the slightest chance that the guy who stole my stupid, withering heart will be on the other end of the line has me scrambling to accept the call.

"Hello?" I say on an exhale.

"Avery?"

It takes me a moment to place the voice, but the second I do, I'm hit with a wave of guilt.

"Elijah. Hey, kid. What's up?" There's a beat of silence on his end, and it has my back stiffening with worry. "Elijah, is everything okay? Is something wrong? Why are you still at camp?"

Glancing down at my watch, I note it's the last day of camp, and well after the time the kids should've been picked up.

"You just left."

Shit.

"You and I both know I wasn't supposed to be there at all."

There's a rustling on the other end of the phone, and I can almost see Elijah vehemently shaking his head in response. What's worse, though, is the way I can hear the tears cracking his voice when he speaks.

"You told me we both were. You said we fake it 'til we make it, to believe in ourselves, and all this other crap that all turned out to be a lie."

"Elijah, none of that is a lie."

"Then why did you leave?"

Swallowing harshly, I utter a gruff, "It was just time for me to go."

"You keep lying!" he shouts, his voice breaking some more. "Stop lying. Dayton and Colton already told me everything."

Dread has my blood freezing like ice in my veins. "What did they say?"

I hear his shaky breath on the other end of the line before he word-vomits everything he's been holding back.

"They said you only talked to me and were nice so I'd tell my dad how great you are and you'd get back into college. And when you got what you wanted, you left like it was nothing." He stops, a garbled cough coming through the phone speaker that's enough to break my heart in two. "And that's…really fucked-up."

I don't have it in me to remind him not to cuss. Not when everything he's said is the truth. The whole plan was fucked-up. I thought the same thing going into the summer, but I still went along with it anyway. Executed it to perfection and then got the hell out of Dodge.

And Elijah was the collateral, just like Kaleb said he'd be.

I'm slammed in the gut by another wave of guilt, and this time, I don't try to fight it. Instead, I let it drag me under and force myself to feel it.

"It was fucked-up," I agree softly. "I hurt you, and I'm sorry for that. But I'm not sorry for being someone you could confide in. And I promise you, everything I said to you this summer was the truth."

"I forgive you," he whispers after a moment. "But I'm still mad at you for leaving."

The coil wrapped around my chest eases up ever so slightly. "Oh, c'mon. Things couldn't have been that bad without me there."

"They sucked."

I scoff. "You're telling me that once I left, everything went right back to how it was on the first day? Colton and Dayton stopped hanging out with you? You stopped having fun? Because I have a very hard time believing that."

"No, but it wasn't the same without you there," he replies immediately.

His honesty stings, but it's the soft sniffle on the other end of the line that's my undoing.

"I know." My lungs ache from the pain I know I've caused him. Pain I wish, more than anything, I could take back. "If it makes any difference, I would've much rather been there for the rest of the summer instead of here."

"Then why did you leave?"

My teeth sink into my cheek before I murmur, "It's…complicated."

"It was your dad, wasn't it?" his disembodied voice asks. "I saw him by the lake the same day you left. Well, I didn't know it was him. I had to ask Kaleb who it was."

Just hearing Kaleb's name is a shot to the heart. One I'm not prepared for in the slightest, nor for the way it steals all the air from my lungs. My eyes sink closed, and I drop my head to my chest, attempting to breathe through the pain of my own making.

And God, it hurts.

Love fucking hurts.

Clearing my throat, I somehow manage to find my voice, but it comes out only as a sullen whisper. "Yeah, it was my dad. The whole plan was his idea." I pause and swallow, the truth tasting like bile as it leaves my lips. "But it's still my fault. I'm the one who went along with it."

"Why?"

Because I'm a coward, lying down and submitting.

The funny thing is, it's not Shame screaming this in my head; it's my own thoughts. The same ones that have been playing on repeat since Kaleb told me to go and not look back.

And it's a choice I've regretted ever since.

Knowing the whole truth is far too heavy for a kid Elijah's age; I offer him a sugar-coated version of it instead, framing it in a way he's sure to understand.

"Pretty much the same reason you keep going to camp. I did it to make him happy."

Even if it cost me my own, apparently.

Happiness doesn't seem to exist without Kaleb. Not anymore. Not when I know what it feels like to be so obscenely, disgustingly filled with joy because of him. All the things that used to give me some sort of serotonin boost just feel bland in comparison. Dulled to a shade of gray.

There's nothing like him.

Elijah's voice calls on the other end, breaking through my thoughts.

"Avery? Are you still there?"

Shit.

Clearing my throat, I mutter, "Yeah, sorry. I'm here. Uh, what'd you say?"

"I told you that I understood why you left," he relays. "And then I asked you if we're still friends even though I kinda yelled at you."

I roll my lips in to contain my chuckle. "Of course, kid. You're one of the best friends I've got."

It's not until the words are spoken that I realize how true they are. It might not make much sense, but somehow, Elijah and I are cut from the same cloth. A little bit insecure, a lotta bit weighed down by parental expectations.

My only hope is that he pushes back and fights for what he wants. He could end up like me if he doesn't, and that's the last thing I want for him.

Elijah lets out a long sigh. "I thought you'd be mad at me for yelling at you. I'm glad you're not."

"I couldn't be mad at you for telling me how you were feeling."

"Yeah, I guess. I don't like saying the hard things, though."

My brows furrow. "The hard things?"

"Yeah, you know," he insists softly on the other line. "The things that people won't like to hear. Or the things that kinda scare me to say."

Believe me, kid. I know the feeling better than I care to admit.

"You can always tell me the hard things, kid. Promise."

I listen to Elijah ramble on for a bit after that, not quite zoning out, but not being as attentive as I should either. It's hard when my mind is racing, reeling and circling around all the things I should've done differently.

All the things I'd change if I could finally break free of the chains binding me.

"Avery, can I tell you something else?"

I smirk and murmur, "Yeah, sure."

Feeling like he's about to tell me something ridiculous that happened after I left camp, I settle back into the couch and wait for the tale.

There's a pause on the other end of the line before his soft voice drives rusty nails into my heart.

"I'm not the only person whose feelings you hurt. Kaleb…he wasn't the same without you here. He was crabby a lot, and the rest of the time he seemed really sad."

If I didn't know any better, I'd say the kid is trying to hurt me for leaving. But he isn't that kind of person. He's just…saying the hard things.

It's not his fault if it rips me to shreds by hearing it.

Releasing a mangled cough, I try to breathe around the emotion clogging my throat when I mutter, "Now I really know you're stretching the truth. I'm sure he threw a party the second my car left the parking lot."

"If the party were a funeral, sure."

I choke on a laugh, still feeling the sting of his admission despite his quick wit. Which, come to think of it, sounds a lot like someone else I know.

"Maybe I shouldn't have left after all. You've clearly spent too much time around the twins."

"Dayton," Elijah corrects, and that has us both laughing a little. It quickly fades, though, leaving a sobering silence between us before he whispers, "Avery?"

"Yeah, kid?"

"I just want you to know…I really like you and Kaleb together."

A knot catches in my throat, and this time, I have no choice but to let my voice crack around it.

"Yeah, kid. Me too."

My conversation with Elijah has been on my mind a lot the last few days, and if I thought I was down in the dumps before his call, it's nothing compared to now. Now, I'm downright miserable. Sulking in self-pity and regret.

And because misery loves company, it seems my father wants to get in on the action.

He's been overly present the past few days, using some vacation time for us to take the boat out or grab lunch at his favorite restaurant downtown. And while some father-son bonding would be fine and dandy, he spends most of the time talking about me going back to Foltyn in the coming weeks.

The problem is, the more I think about setting foot on that campus as a student again, the more apprehensive I get. Not because of Kaleb or missing baseball or anything else, but rather because I don't want it anymore. After what I did to Aspen and Keene, I don't deserve it. And after going along with this plan of Dad's, I only feel more unworthy of a second chance. It's eating away at me like a parasite, and I know if I don't do something about it soon, I may lose my mind.

Which is why I find myself walking downstairs this morning like I'm walking into my own execution, a pit of dread sitting in my stomach when I turn the corner to find my father in the kitchen.

"Avery," he notes, barely glancing up from his coffee and paper sitting on the island. "I'm surprised you're still here. I'd have thought you'd be heading out to see some friends before classes start."

Acid burns the back of my throat at yet another reminder of what I'm about to do, and it has me swallowing a few times to rid myself of the taste.

Say the hard thing.

Say the hard thing, and let the chips fall.

"Actually, I'm not going." I mutter, steeling myself for his reaction.

He's not fazed. "To see your friends? That's fine. There's always—"

"No, Dad. I'm not going back to Foltyn."

To his credit, my father does meet my gaze this time, his eyes narrowing. "What do you mean you're not going?"

"Exactly that," I utter calmly, despite feeling anything but. "I'm not sure what there is to not understand."

There's a beat of silence where he studies me before setting down his coffee.

"What in the world has gotten into you?" Pressing his palms to the counter, he rises to stand. "After all the work we've put in over the summer—"

Oh, no.

"Let's get one thing straight: *I'm* the one who put in the work, not you," I snap, despite my better judgment. "I busted my ass at that camp, I earned my way back into Foltyn, and now, I get to decide if that's even what I want."

"What you want?" he echoes through a bark of laughter. "You're barely an adult. Do you really think you have any clue about what you want?"

"Maybe not, but I sure as fuck know what I *don't* want. And being like you takes the number one spot."

He blinks a few times before shaking off my blow. "I don't know what's gotten into you since going to that camp, but—"

"What's gotten into me is that I'm so sick of living a lie. Because all it's done is make me fucking miserable."

Jesus Christ, he can't really be this dense?

But apparently, he can. I shouldn't be surprised, since he never listens to a word I say.

"Living a lie?" His brows furrow, and he takes a step back to lean against the counter behind him. "Son, if you don't think Foltyn is the right fit, then we can transfer you."

"For fuck's sake, this doesn't have anything to do with school and everything to do with the fact that I'm gay!" I shout, tossing my arms out in front of me. "That's the lie, Dad. I'm. Gay."

Shame claws at my mind, but I don't back down or cower from it.

The gloves are off now. The hardest thing to say in my life is out in the open…and the weight of is slowly starting to dissipate.

My father, on the other hand, looks equally dazed and confused as he crosses his arms over his chest. "Look, if something unseemly happened at that camp, you can tell me. Colin might be a friend and a client, but you're my son. If you were put in some sort of position—"

"The only position I've been put in was thanks to you, Dad." I can feel my face contort with some mixture of a grimace and snarl. "You're the one who orchestrated this entire thing, after all. And I'm not just talking about me spending half the summer at Alpine Ridge either. Every hateful word or malicious action that's ever come from me is all in direct connection to you."

"How dare you put your decisions on me?" The words come out with a harsh bite but still in his low, even tone. Always keeping his composure. "You have this thing called free will. Use it. Don't blame me for your mistakes."

"How dare *I*?" A maniacal laugh leaves me, and I rake my fingers through my hair. "How dare *you*, Dad? I've been your disaster in the making for *years*. I've turned my back on myself, on the things I want, on what is gonna make me happy, and for what? So I can be like you? So I can be filled with hate and ignorance?" I shake my head, my sardonic laughter slowly fading. "No, Dad. I'm done living that way."

He scoffs, his hands dropping to grip the counter behind him. "I never—"

A violent, feral snarl leaves my mouth, and I slam my fist down on the counter. "Just stop talking and fucking listen to me for once!"

He opens his mouth to say something, but the look on my face must make him think better of it. I can feel the blood pumping through my veins with every beat my heart takes, and I focus my mind on it. Using it as a cadence to follow as I speak in a low, even tone. The same one he's taught me over the years.

"When I look in the mirror, I hate myself. I hate the person I've become; the one you've had a hand in creating. You wanna talk about owning mistakes? Well, this is yours. Raising me to see myself as less than, and all over something I can't control. I have voices in my head screaming at me about how vile and disgusting I am, and it's been slowly turning me into someone I can't stand." My voice cracks slightly, but I clear my throat and push through. "You've made me despise myself for far too long, and I'm not gonna do it anymore. I've worked too fucking hard to put those demons to rest for you to break them back out of their cage."

"Avery. Son, look…" He looks almost pained as he looks at me, eyes a mess of confusion. "If this is some sort of cry for help, we can find you a—a shrink or someone. We can fix—"

"I'm not a problem for you to fix! This is who I *am*, Dad. It's who I've always been. I've just been terrified to show it." I slowly link my fingers behind my head and look up at the ceiling, doing my best to calm my racing heart. Tears threaten to spill over and I blink them back, doing my best to keep my shit together.

"I found someone who saw me—the real fucking me—Dad. Someone who showed me what it was like to be free. To not hide in the shadows from who I am. To release some of this shame that I should've never had to live with in the first place. And he gave me the confidence to look at myself in the mirror and make the changes I need to in order to be happy with the person I see staring back at me." I can't keep the emotions from thickening my voice anymore, each word cracking and breaking as I speak. "And then you showed up at camp and…I tossed him aside. I walked away from someone I love because I was afraid of what you'd think of me. But I'm not gonna do that anymore. I never should have in the first place."

A few stray tears manage to escape, despite my best efforts, but they're tears of healing as much as they are tears of pain. I feel lighter and lighter with every word and each salty drop. Like the weight of the world is slowly starting to recede.

"And, yeah, I probably do need to see a therapist—a fucking good one at that—if I'm gonna keep working through all the self-loathing and resentment that's built up inside me over the years."

"Then we can do that," my dad insists, his tone softer than I expected.

"I don't think you understand," I say with a watery laugh. "It's not going to change who I am. I'm still gonna be gay. So you can either get on board with it or—or…"

I trail off, the alternative not clear in my mind. Him cutting me off feels like the most obvious, and if that's reality, I'll live with it. But I wouldn't put it past him to weave in some darker scheme into the mix.

Clearing my throat, I drop my hands and lower my gaze. "I don't expect this to change overnight. In fact, I…I don't expect anything at all from you. Other than maybe a trip to the best conversion therapy center money can buy. I'm sure those still exist, if you look hard enough."

My father's knuckles are stark white as he grips the counter behind him, shoulders slumped forward slightly as he stares at his abandoned coffee on the island.

"Is that really how little you think of me?" he asks, voice barely louder than a whisper.

Just like that, I shatter entirely, tears spilling down my face. "You've never given me a reason to believe otherwise."

His shoulders cave inward, hands leaving the counter to cross in front of him. He's silent as I stare at him, looking anywhere but at me. At the pain he's caused. It's only when he lifts one hand to cover his mouth and raises his gaze that I find his eyes rimmed with red.

And for what might be the first time in my entire life, I watch my father cry.

"I'm so sorry, son," he says, voice barely distinguishable from behind his hand. " I'm so, so sorry."

He loses it after that, arms wrapping around himself and chin dropping to his chest while he leans back against the counter. Like he's doing everything he can to hold himself together as his shoulders shake with every sob racking his body.

Tears continue streaming down my face too, a physical release of anguish and shame that's been a long time coming. And while I know this doesn't change the past, it's proof that maybe—just fucking maybe—some things can be fixed.

That perspectives can shift.

With time.

THIRTY

Kaleb

Two Months Later — October

School has been back in swing for a little over two months, and I can firmly state that senior year isn't nearly what it's cracked up to be. Granted, those feelings may be due to a certain blond-haired idiot being noticeably absent from campus, but I do my best not to think about that.

He texted and called me a few times since leaving camp, asking to talk, to give him a chance to explain. As much as my heart wanted to cave and hear him out, what's the point? It's only gonna cut the wounds open more.

He's never far from my mind, though.

The place is tainted with him. All I see now are the good memories from freshman and sophomore year, before things got all fucked-up. The ones where we'd grab a quick bite after morning lifting or go for a few extra rounds in the cages after everyone else decided to head out for the night.

Where I'd catch his easy smile or hear his laughter; two things I became intimately familiar with over our weeks at Alpine Ridge. And despite every fiber of my being telling me to shove it away, to come back to reality… I fucking miss him.

Sometimes I can ignore it. Shove it down and keep on keeping on. But moments like right now, where I'm dressed in uniform and sitting in the outfield in the hours before a game, make it damn near impossible.

Because he should be here. Long-tossing with one of the other guys or warming up on the mound or—

"Earth to Kaleb?"

I glance up to where Keene is stretching a few feet away from me. His brows draw down beneath his catcher's helmet, and I realize I must've missed something he said.

"Shit, sorry. Can you repeat that?"

My teammate chuckles. "I asked how you're feeling about the game, but from the way you were just lost in space, I have a feeling that's the furthest thing from your mind."

Shaking my head, I meet his dark gaze head on. "Yeah, that's my bad, man. I'll lock it in before the game starts."

"I don't give a fuck about that. It's just a fall scrim." Releasing his legs from the butterfly stretch he'd been holding, he moves into a 90/90 stretch. "Where's your head at?"

I debate for a solid ten seconds on if it's stupid for me to be feeling this way, let alone to admit it aloud. And to *Keene* of all people.

In the end, I play it off with a severely watered-down version of the truth.

"It's just...weird that Avery isn't here."

Keene's brows crash together at the center. "Uh, yeah. I guess I hadn't really thought about it in that way. But it's really no different than when the seniors don't come back."

"Yeah, sure," I agree absently. "It just crossed my mind, that's all."

He studies me, still frowning. "Look, I get this is awkward. I know you guys were friends—"

"We really weren't," I cut in with a shake of the head, though it's not lost on me that, not very long ago, we were so much more than friends. "I mean, at one point, yeah. Freshman and sophomore year. But not when he outed you and Aspen."

"I know," he says with a nod.

He seems content to just leave it at that, but I find more words spilling from my lips like word vomit.

"He's just so frustrating, you know? I thought I knew who he was, only to be shown a side of him last year that I had no desire to be associated with. When he was saying all that awful shit to you guys, there was no part of me that wanted someone like that in my life. How the fuck could I, you know? How could any decent human?"

He's silent for a moment, appearing to mull over my words before asking, "But?"

I cock my head. "What do you mean, *but?*"

"You were speaking in past tense." When I frown, he adds, "When talking about all the shit he said and what he did, you said there was no part of you that *wanted* him in your life."

I hadn't realized I'd even done it, to be honest. But now that it's staring me dead in the face, the reason is obvious: The person I knew Avery to be last year and the guy I spent the entire summer with are two entirely different people.

Now I'm struggling like hell to determine which one of them is real.

Ah, shit. So much for playing it off.

Letting out a long exhale, I meet his gaze and level him with as much earnestness as I can muster. "I hope you know I'm on your side when it comes to what happened last spring at Family Night."

If possible, the indent between his brows deepens. "I'm aware. Why would I think any differently?"

"Because I spent the entire summer with Avery at Alpine Ridge?"

I'm not sure what kind of reaction I was expecting from him, but it certainly isn't him throwing his head back in laughter.

"You're telling me the same Avery Reynolds who was our teammate the past three years spent the entire summer wrangling rugrats with you in the wilderness?"

Only half of the summer, actually, thanks to his dad.

But I just answer with a soft "yep" instead.

"Well, that had to be interesting," Keene muses, still laughing. "I can't imagine him anywhere outside of a country club or marina with a bunch of fancy yachts."

"He wore boat shoes the first day we went hiking," I say automatically, the memory swirling in the forefront of my mind. Of course, it's quickly paired with the moment on the dock when I helped him care for the wounds he stubbornly self-inflicted, and soon enough, I'm replaying every moment of the six weeks I spent out there with him.

The bad ones hurt to think about, yeah. But it's the good ones that sting the most, like antiseptic on a fresh, gaping wound.

"Talk about a fish out of water," Keene jokes, a little smirk on his lips.

With my mind still lingering in the memories from the mountains, I don't have it in me to offer him more than a half-hearted *hmph*.

That's when Keene's laser-like focus feels more like a scalpel carving into me when he murmurs, "There's something else you're not saying."

Perceptive, this one.

All thoughts of stretching or pre-game prep are gone, both for me and for my teammate, who is silently waiting for me to drop the truth-bomb capable of ending our friendship. I rub the back of my neck and send up a silent prayer to whoever may listen that it won't happen.

"We…slept together."

Steeling myself for the worst, I glance up to find my teammate gawking at me like I'd just told him flying monkeys exist outside the fictional land of Oz.

"You're joking."

My teeth sink into the side of my cheek as I shake my head.

There's a beat of silence while he continues staring at me before he lets out a little laugh. "I'm sorry, but you're gonna have to spell this out. You slept with him, or you *slept* with him?"

"Both, technically," I mutter, the words coming out with as much misery as I'm feeling. The problem is, I'm not sure which part of it hurts more: still wanting Avery, knowing I shouldn't, or the thought of losing one of my friends because of it. A friend who has every right to hate my guts for the admission I just made.

A friend who is…fucking *laughing* at me like a goddamn lunatic.

"Sorry, I just…" He pauses, clearly still processing, before another laugh slips out. "I don't mean to laugh. I think I might be in shock."

"That I could betray your friendship so spectacularly?" I ask dryly.

"No, that I didn't realize you were into guys."

An ironic statement, coming from him, but it's enough to pull the smallest smirk out of me. I wasn't expecting that to be the thing he'd focus on.

"It wasn't a secret. My family knows, so do all my friends back home. It just wasn't something that I've been super loud about since coming to college."

He nods a couple times, and it only makes me feel like even more of a dick that he didn't know, considering all that's happened. At least he doesn't seem perturbed by it, though, snapping his fingers and pointing at me like he just solved an advanced algebra equation.

"You know, now that you mention it, I think I remember seeing you acting all chummy with a guy a few times on campus last year. I just assumed he was a good friend."

"Chummy?" I echo with a sharp laugh. "And you know what they say about assuming."

"Yeah, yeah, you're right. Makes an ass outta both of us," he says through his chuckles, waving me off. His expression sobers a bit, and he gives me a contemplative nod. "Well, now it makes so much more sense why you turned him in after Family Night."

"Apart from it being the right thing to do, you mean?"

"Well, sure. Though it's a little more nuanced than that now, don't you think?"

I glance up to find his lips twitch into something of a smile, but not quite reaching it. A massive wave of guilt hits me like a linedrive to the chest, and I damn near rub my sternum from the ache it causes.

"I'm really sorry, man. I know it was a shitty thing for me to do, especially knowing what he put you and Aspen through." More guilt eats at my thoughts, and I drop my eyes to the grass beneath me. "He showed up at camp to follow through on this asinine plan his father thought up, and I was pissed. I wanted nothing to do with him.

"For the first few weeks, both of us were drowning in tension, barely hanging on to our sanity, and it was screwing up our ability to work together. So we did what we had to do and…buried the hatchet." My throat constricts from the memory of a lamp-lit dock and secret notes swimming to the surface, and I whisper, "The last thing I planned on happening was us falling into bed together."

Keene's silent for a brief moment, and I don't have the balls to look up at him. To witness whatever betrayal or fury is sure to be present in his features.

"Yeah, well, if I've learned anything recently, it's that you don't get to plan who you fall in love with."

My blood freezes in my veins, and my eyes snap up to find him watching me with meticulous scrutiny.

"Why do you—"

"Oh, no. We're not playing this shit off," he cuts in with a shake of his head. "You've been cagey and depressed since the semester started, and I've been trying to figure out why. But the answer was written all over your face the second you said his name."

Well, shit.

"That doesn't mean I'm in love with him," I immediately negate.

A sharp, disbelieving laugh fills the air. "Oh, really? Because I was wearing the same exact face all summer while Aspen was gone, leaving me here alone to miss him like a fucking limb. And last time I checked, I only felt that miserable because I'm head over heels for the idiot." His brow arches, and he doesn't hide his self-satisfied smirk. "Do I need to keep going, or are you done lying to yourself?"

So this is what it feels like to be on the other end of "I told you so."

I let out a disgruntled, irritated sound in concession.

"I don't want to feel this way about him," I mumble in defeat. "But while we were out there, I saw a side of him I doubt anyone else knows exists. And to say it's fucked with my head might be the understatement of my entire life."

"Okay," he says slowly. "So what are you gonna do about it?"

I blink at my teammate—my friend—who has every right to shun me like a leper for what I've done. Yet, instead, he seems to be showing me…compassion?

"Wait. You don't hate me?"

He lets out a soft scoff before shaking his head. "If I hated you for who you fell in love with, I wouldn't be any better than all those right-winged Bible-thumpers who wanna send us to hell for being gay. Or bi, in my case."

He makes a fair point, but it's still not an equal comparison.

"Those people aren't your friends, though. They didn't…sleep with the enemy, or whatever," I mutter, tossing my hand out.

"Even with the shit he did, Avery's never been the enemy." He pauses, his head bobbing back and forth before he continues. "Well, maybe a bit of one in Aspen's eyes, but never in mine."

I gawk at him, not sure if I heard him wrong or if he's the most highly evolved human I've ever met. "You're serious?"

His brown gaze collides with mine, and he nods. "I don't know how much he told you about what happened between us last year. On Toppr, I mean. But even if I didn't know it was him on the other end of those messages at the time, I got a deeper look at him. Same as you. I saw his fear and shame and confusion written in black and white, and while those things may have stemmed from different places, they were ones I'd felt too." He lifts one shoulder in a shrug. "So, no, he's not the enemy. The enemy is the person who makes someone feel like they're less than by being different. By being who they really are."

Avery's father instantly comes to mind, and my thoughts shift to a darker place.

He's the one person who Avery seeks approval from the most, and he's sure to be the one reason Avery continues sinking into old patterns. Even with all the progress he seemed to make over the weeks at camp.

"I'm assuming it was a secret?" Keene asks, breaking into my thoughts.

I nod. "Apparently, we weren't careful enough, though, because Colton figured it out and it became a whole to-do." Tilting my head back, I stare at the blue sky overhead and let out a sardonic laugh. "You haven't been to hell 'til you've been lectured by an eleven-year-old about your choice of bedmates."

"Been there, done that. Got the t-shirt and trauma to prove it," he muses wryly. "And man, Lexi was a hardass about it too."

Still starting at the sky, I think about Cole and the cold shoulder I'd received the rest of camp. Even with Avery gone, he still pulled back. Probably because he could see how much Avery's absence affected me, which only proved just how far off the pedestal I'd fallen.

Things really haven't been the same since.

"Yeah, well, I'm assuming she's still speaking to you."

Keene lets out a low whistle. "That bad, huh?"

I finally shift my attention back to Keene and give a helpless shrug. "Let's just say…he was very clear about his feelings toward Avery, and they're a lot more in line with what I expected from you instead."

My teammate—my *friend*—cocks his head and stares at me, a pensive look crossing his features. And if I see any emotion in his eyes, it's not anger or betrayal or resentment.

It's…empathy.

"Am I surprised? Yeah, of course. But that's all." He offers a little shrug, a small grin forming. "As cliché as it'll sound, I just want you to be happy, man."

I scoff, knowing right now, I'm anything but. If anything, I've been wallowing in misery for weeks, and I don't know how to change it.

"Yeah. Me too."

"Then what's stopping you? Colton? Me?" He shakes his head and waves his arm out to the side. "If you love him, go get him. Don't throw it all away."

If only it were that simple.

Our fight the night Avery left snakes its way into my thoughts, causing them to reel with all the emotions I'd been feeling in that moment. The fear, the resentment, the despair.

The agony of watching the person I love fall back into a pattern I wanted nothing more than to break him free of.

"You've seen some of his shame, man. It runs fucking deep. Maybe even deeper than I've seen. And I just…I don't know how to be with someone who won't take control of their own happiness. Who is too afraid to say *fuck what everyone else thinks* and chase what he wants, consequences be damned. And as much as I want to help him get there, I can't hide us forever. It would feel like going backward. Like I'd have to go back in the closet and wait for him to finally come out of it. And…" I trail off and pick at the grass, frustration welling up inside me. "I don't know if he'll ever be ready for that."

"Sounds like he's on his way, though, from the little you've shared." Keene leans back, resting his palms on the ground behind him, more relaxed than I thought possible given the topic at hand.

I shake my head, still staring at the ground. "Two steps forward, three steps back."

"Sometimes the people we love need a little bit more time to reach the point we've already made it to. Doesn't mean they won't. And it also doesn't mean they can't use a hand to guide them along the way."

The last thing I was expecting was Keene urging me to be with Avery, let alone pull some philosophical bullshit out of his ass to push me in that direction. But, then again, the situation he wound up in with Aspen must've granted him a lot of insight on what it's like to love someone who is too afraid to love him back.

Or, at least, *was* too afraid.

With how much I've been seeing Aspen around, I'm under the impression that fear may have finally subsided. That's what I'm hoping for anyway.

"How are you two?" I ask, shifting the topic away from my abysmal love life.

"I'm making him work for it, but…" A little grin pulls at his lips and he lifts a shoulder. "We're mending."

Thank fuck.

From the few times I'd checked in with Keene this summer—mostly out of my own guilt for sleeping with Avery—things sounded pretty grim. But if things have taken a turn for the better, maybe that's the real reason he's choosing not to hold any grudges toward the guy who almost destroyed his relationship.

"Glad to hear he finally got his head outta his ass."

"Yeah, now we just gotta yank yours out, and we'll be golden," Keene jokes while he rises to his feet and dusts himself off before offering me a hand.

I take it and let out a dry laugh while he pulls me to my feet. "What the hell is that supposed to mean?"

He aims a wary look my way as he releases me, only to hold up both hands in surrender.

"Look, don't shoot the messenger, but from where I'm standing, Avery hasn't been the only one letting other people's opinions stand in the way of his happiness."

The truth in his statement stings like an angry hornet, and it's all I can focus on. How hypocritical I've been without even realizing it.

From Keene's curious expression as his gaze travels my face, he's aware of it too.

"Just something to think about."

THIRTY-ONE

Kaleb

I'm stiff and sore after a weekend of scrims, and the only thing I want is my bed and about thirty ice packs covering every inch of my body. Seeing as that's the closest I'll get to happiness, I'm eager to shower, get my shit together, and get the hell outta Dodge.

I'm just about there, too, quickly tidying up my space when I notice my glove is missing. I swear I grabbed it when I left the field, but from its lack of presence in my cubby, bag, or anywhere else I look, I obviously didn't.

Hoping one of my teammates might've grabbed it by mistake, I start asking around. There's still quite a few of them lingering in the locker room, Keene included, but none of them have seen it either.

Well, shit.

With one last person in mind, I head down the hall to Coach's office and rap my knuckles against his open door.

"Hey, Coach. You didn't happen to see my glove lying around, did you?"

His eyes lift briefly before falling back to his desk. "There may have been one in the dugout when I left, but I can't be sure. The field's still unlocked if you wanna double check, though."

Damnit.

"Okay, thanks," I reply, and with a long sigh, I grab my bag and set out on a scavenger hunt. Luck seems to be on my side, at the very least, because the second I'm through the tunnel that leads into our dugout, there it is, sitting on the bench against the back wall.

Annoyed with myself, I grab it and start back the way I came, only for movement on the field to catch my eye. Specifically, someone in street clothes standing out on the pitcher's mound.

What the hell?

I'm about to call out to whoever it is—threaten to call security or something if they don't get lost—but as he turns enough for me to catch his profile, recognition slams into me like a freight train.

Avery.

My stomach clenches at the sight of him standing alone on the mound; a place I've seen him many times before but somehow is so unfamiliar now.

Instinct calls for me to go, slip out the way I came unnoticed and forget I saw him. My brain agrees, logically knowing that nothing good can come from an interaction.

But, damn, my heart won't fucking listen.

The stupid thing is shouting at me to remember what Keene said a few days ago, pleading for me to get my head outta my ass and go to him.

Clearing my throat, I force myself to speak.

"Hard to believe they'd let you within a hundred yards of this place."

His body stiffens at the sound of my voice, and he slowly turns to face me.

He looks good. Better than anyone should dare when they're in the presence of the person whose heart they pulverized beyond recognition. His blond hair is swept back off his forehead, looking as if it were recently cut, and he's wearing the same gray Foltyn Baseball hoodie he'd spent most of the summer in. Pairing it with some dark-wash jeans that cling to his muscular thighs, and he's the most beautiful, heartbreaking thing I've ever laid eyes on.

"Kaleb. Hi."

Jaw locked, I offer him a small nod in greeting.

We stare at each other, the ten feet separating us feeling more like a thousand miles, and it has my heart aching in my chest. Squeezing painfully behind my ribs. Pleading for me to close the distance and finally have him in my arms again.

But I don't move.

I don't speak either, despite wanting to ask him what the hell he's doing here, standing on the field, with no one around. After the weeks I've endured without him, I suspect that's not the question that would come out. Or maybe it's the worry that my emotions will betray me, cracking and breaking every word as it leaves my lips.

Wariness paints Avery's expression as he looks at me before he glances away and offers the most ridiculous opening line I've ever heard.

"How are you?"

A disbelieving laugh leaves me, and I shake my head.

How the hell do I even answer that?

Part of me wants to stick it to him by saying I've been great. Yet the majority of me wants him to know just how fucking miserable I've been because of him. *Without* him.

"I really…" My voice sounds grated and raw, just like I feared, and I clear my throat again. "I'm not interested in doing small-talk with you, Avery."

"Kaleb—"

I shake my head, cutting him off with a sharp, "No."

There's no part of me that wants to do this; wants to stand here and pretend that I'm okay or happy or anything other than heartbroken by his betrayal. Because that's what it was—a betrayal of himself, and of me—when he decided to walk away.

He made the choice then, and it's the same one I make now.

Tears of longing and heartache threaten to spill over, but I blink them back as I turn toward the dugout. My feet carry me away from him, my heart screaming at me to go back and hear him out, but I don't listen to it. The last time I did, it ended up shattered on the floor beneath his feet.

I can't do that again. I fucking won't—

"I came out to my dad."

The admission has me grinding to a halt, my back going ram-rod straight before I slowly turn in place. His throat bobs when he swallows, and those blue eyes gleam as he watches me, waiting for my next move.

"You came out to your dad," I echo, blinking a couple times as the statement really registers in my brain.

"A couple months ago."

If he wanted my attention, he has it now. That was the one, sure-fire way to get it.

In spite of myself, I take a couple steps back toward him, my approach slow and measured while I force out a question I'm not sure I want the answer to.

"How did that go?"

He lets out a little huff before a sardonic smile appears. "At first, about how I expected. Told me he'd get me into therapy to sort out my confusion, asked if something *unseemly* happened at camp."

A sinking feeling tugs at my stomach, because this is what I feared. Or something worse, like him kicking Avery out, disowning him, God knows what else. I wouldn't put anything past the asshole at this point.

My teeth scrape over my lower lip, a hollow feeling taking hold.

"I'm sorry."

"Don't be. It had to happen." A wry sort of scoff slips out, and he shakes his head. "Believe it or not, he actually…apologized."

Now that, I wasn't expecting. My face must show it too, because a soft laugh leaves Avery.

"Yeah, that's pretty much the look I had when it happened. But he did, and… I don't know. It feels like he means it. I think it took me breaking down and screaming at him for him to really understand just how deeply his words sank into me, you know?"

The hollowness in my chest starts to dissipate, however slightly, at the hope tinting his tone. Despite the evidence his father's given previously, I find myself having hope too. Maybe he really has seen the light, even if it's only a pinprick right now. There's a chance it'll grow.

For Avery's sake, I hope it does.

"Good. You deserve it," I tell him earnestly. "Hearing you out is the least he can do after all the pain he's caused."

His gaze holds mine for a few heartbeats, so many unspoken things swirling in his eyes, before his attention drops to the ground.

"Yeah, well, it wasn't just him. I'm just as responsible for my own suffering." He shoves his hands in his pockets and kicks the rubber beneath his feet. "Guess you can add that to the ever-growing list of things you've been right about."

Emotion catches in my throat, but I clear it away. "I didn't want to be right about it."

"Doesn't mean you weren't."

Stifling silence surrounds us, his admission hanging in the air like a dark cloud.

I should go, I know that. But now that I'm right here, so close to him, I can't move.

So instead, I speak.

"So, uh." I swallow hard, "I assume you being here means they really did let you back in?"

I know it's why he left camp early—his father wouldn't have yanked him if there was even the slightest chance he was unsuccessful in his mission—but I haven't seen him on campus since the fall term started. And believe me, I've been looking.

In spite of myself. At every turn.

"Yeah, they did." A wry smile pulls at his lips and he drops his gaze to the ground. "But I didn't accept their offer."

"What?"

"The dean offered me a spot back at Foltyn, and after thanking him for his consideration, I turned him down."

I can't control my eyes from bugging out of their socket at the statement. "*Why?*"

Getting back into school was exactly what he wanted. Hell, it was the entire reason he ended up at Alpine Ridge in the first place, and now he's just *turning it down?* If I didn't know any better, I'd think he fell ill with some sort of disease that made him lose all common sense.

Yet, from the look on his face, this decision was made with a sound mind.

"I know you're probably thinking I'm crazy, but…I couldn't take another easy way out."

"What are you gonna do, then?"

"Haven't quite figured that out yet, but I've got a few options. Not that it really matters anymore."

I blink a few times, still a little in shock. "Of course it does, Avery. It's your future we're talking about. That should matter more than anything else."

How is he being so cavalier about this?

But when I truly study his face, I realize it's because he's at peace.

"You know, I believed that at one point too," he starts, slicing through my thoughts. "I believed graduating on time and making my dad proud of me and all the other noise should be my top priority. I was miserable as hell living like that, but it was all I knew. Then I ended up at summer camp, of all places, with the one person who took those things away from me."

My skin heats, both from his words and the way he's staring straight into my soul, as he takes a few slow steps toward me, closing the distance between us to nothing more than a foot.

"The funny thing is, somewhere in the midst of all the blisters and sunburns and outdoor activities with our group of chaotic gremlin children, I realized there are far more important things than what brought me to camp in the first place. Like allowing myself to be free of the shame and fear that have been controlling me. You're the one who gave me that."

"You did the work—"

"But you gave me the strength to try. The means to succeed. You silenced the deafening screams, taught me how to lock up the darkness and finally let in the light." He pauses and wets his lips before glancing around the stadium. "So while trying to get back into Foltyn might've been the goal when all this started, it's not worth it anymore. It's not important, and I sure as fuck don't want it."

My disbelief can't be contained, leaving my body in the form of incredulous laughter. "Then why are you here? If this doesn't matter, why come back? Why tell me all this—"

"Because I love you."

The words are a hundred volts straight to my heart, reviving the organ instantly; filling it with new life and pumping warmth to the rest of my body.

My head, on the other hand, isn't convinced.

"Avery…"

"No, just let me get this out," he murmurs, his eyes pleading.

One hand reaches up, slipping around my neck to cradle the back of my skull, and I shiver with the feel of his skin against mine for the first time in what feels like a lifetime.

"I've fucked up a lot, I know that. And, honestly, I know I will again. I can't promise you perfection; I'm a work in progress at best. There will be moments when I revert back to those old habits or when shame creeps in, and it'll be hard to witness. But never will I ever turn my back on the person you helped me become; the person you saw all along."

A somber smile pulls at his lips while his gaze maps my face. "I'm so fucking in love with you, Kaleb. So I'll give you my all—every shameful, imperfect part of me—and I can only hope it's worth a fraction of you."

If I thought I was shot up with warmth before, it has nothing on how I'm feeling right now. Hearing him bare his heart and soul to me, handing me every piece of who he is—every flaw he has and misstep he's yet to make—has my entire being consumed in heat. In hope.

In love.

And God, I love him.

I'm stupidly head over heels for the guy, having fallen in spite of myself. So while I know loving him won't be easy, I do know there's no one I'd rather guide through the hardest parts.

My eyes rake over his features, mapping every line and freckle on his tanned face while he waits, ever so patiently, for an answer. The one I knew all along, despite fighting it at every turn.

But I'm done fighting for anything but us.

"Don't make me regret this."

It's a plea, dragged over the broken shards of our past, and barely recognizable to my own ears. But Avery hears it perfectly, his blue eyes shimmering when a promise falls from his lips.

"Never will I ever."

And then his mouth is on mine, stealing my breath, my thoughts, my heart. Taking everything I am and offering himself in return, knowing neither of us are willing to stand in the way of what this has become. What *we* can be.

That's the difference in this kiss from all the others.

It's a hello and goodbye all in one.

It's us leaving the past in the past, ready to start on an entirely new chapter. One that doesn't erase the pain and shame and hurt but uses those things to shape what comes next. Shaping our story into something even better. And as I lose myself in the feel of his fingers sliding through my hair and my tongue teasing the seam of his lips, I can't wait to find out what that is.

We break apart far too soon, chests heaving and hearts racing as I drop my forehead to his. My emotions are still in the clouds, lingering among the stars as his soft breaths coast over my lips, and it's a high I've never experienced.

Because what I feel for him doesn't happen every day.

"I love you, baby," I whisper, the words I'd been terrified of before now leaving with ease. "And I'll never ask you for perfection. All I want is to be the hand you reach for when things get difficult."

"You already are. You have been since the beginning."

Unable to stop myself, I pull him back in for another scorching kiss. My hands sink into the soft, golden strands of hair at the back of his head while I mold my mouth to his, wanting to live in this moment for the rest of my life.

Unfortunately, that doesn't happen, because there's a loud cough from nearby before a booming voice calls out across the field.

"Not to interrupt, but I've gotta lock up and get going."

Coach.

I freeze instantly. He knew I was heading here to look for my glove, and probably came to see if I was successful. And my dumb ass completely forgot about that tidbit the second I laid eyes on Avery.

God, how could I be so stupid?

My stomach rolls, worrying how Avery's going to react to being caught like this. But rather than recoiling or freezing like I did, Avery presses one more gentle kiss to my lips and slowly pulls away.

His attention shifts to a spot over my shoulder, and he clears his throat softly before calling out, "Yep, no problem. We're just about to head out."

Gnawing at my lower lip, I turn and find Coach staring at the two of us, his expression completely void of emotion. Either he's got one helluva poker face, or I'm just delusional enough to think we might be in the clear.

Until he goes and ruins it.

"I'll take care of this, since it seems you got a bit distracted," he says, holding up my glove. "Have a good one, guys."

I cough and give him a faint nod. "Yeah. Thanks, Coach."

With that awkward encounter under our belt, Avery and I make ourselves scarce, heading out so Coach can lock up. My mind spins faster than an Olympic figure skater, whirling out of control by the time we reach the parking lot. Even when Avery takes my hand and leads me to where my car is parked, I'm weighed down with worry and guilt for being caught like that.

It's definitely not the way I envisioned starting over with him, and I know that's the thought written on my face when Avery turns in front of me, leaning against my passenger door.

"I'm sorry. I should've been more careful," I say in a rush.

"It's fine, I don't care." He shakes his head, a little smile on his face. "And besides, I already told Coach."

Told him?

"Coach knows I'm gay," Avery says calmly, elaborating before I can ask him to.

Of course, the revelation leaves me momentarily speechless before a sputtered, "S-since when?" leaves my mouth.

"Well, I've been making my rounds on this apology tour to…" He blows out a breath and laughs. "Well, pretty much everyone? Coach was the stop before yours, and it just kinda came out."

"No pun intended, I'm assuming."

"I had to give him a reason to help me talk to you." The hair on my neck prickles as suspicion creeps in, and my eyes narrow, which only pulls another carefree laugh from him. "What? Did you think I just snuck in there of my own volition?"

Uh, yes?

"Don't act like you don't have a habit of breaking into places you shouldn't," I reason. "We both know better than that."

"For once, I went by the rule book, Mr. Goody Two-Shoes. Coach gave me the go-ahead and let me in. And more importantly, gave *you* a reason to come back to the field after everyone else was gone."

I'll be fucking damned.

"This whole thing was a setup."

He nods. "One Coach was all too happy to assist in if it meant you got your head outta your ass and started playing ball the way he knows you can."

"They were scrims," I protest.

"Yeah, well, you take it up with him."

I'm in the middle of rolling my eyes when Avery's hand snakes out, snatching the front of my shirt before pulling me toward him. His lips are on mine again, this kiss more consuming than the last as the entire world blurs into the background.

All that's left is the two of us at the center of it.

"You wanna come back to my apartment with me?" I whisper, tugging at his hoodie. "There's a bit of lost time we have to make up for."

He hums, a slow grin spreading over his face. "I love the sound of that. Trust me. But there's actually one more thing I need to take care of first."

His attention flicks over my shoulder then, and I frown in confusion before turning to follow his gaze, only for it to land on Keene heading toward Aspen's Impala.

A sense of pride has my chest swelling with emotion when I turn back to him.

"Do you want me to go with you?"

"Nah. This is something I've gotta do on my own." He grins before stealing another quick kiss. "Text me your address. I'll be over right after I'm done."

THIRTY-TWO

Avery

Running out in front of a moving car is far from the dumbest thing I've ever done, and considering the person behind the wheel hates me with the burning passion of a thousand suns, it's definitely not the brightest move either. Yet, here I am, jumping in front of Aspen's '67 Impala like I'm a cat with eight lives to spare.

"Wait, wait, wait!" I shout before the car can leave the parking lot.

Aspen slams on the brakes before the front bumper takes me out at the knees, and my hands collide with the hood to steady myself. His shock quickly turns to fury when he registers *who* he almost turned into road-kill, and his palm lands on the horn.

I wince, but when I don't back down, he rolls down the window to shout at me over the noise.

"Move!"

I still don't move.

Instead, I stare at them through the windshield until he finally lays off the horn. It's only then, despite his clear frustration and the ringing in my ears, that I manage to calmly state my intention.

"I need to talk to you."

"You—" Aspen cuts himself off, a scoff leaving him before he tosses his hand out. "The only thing you need to do is get the fuck out of my way before I hit you."

"Pen, just relax," Keene says from the passenger seat, speaking for the first time.

Aspen looks like he'd rather jump off a bridge when he glances over at Keene, but I use his momentary distraction to press a little further.

"I know I'm the last person you want to see, and I have no right to ask anything of you, but I'd really appreciate you giving me five minutes. Ten tops."

"The only thing you're gonna be getting from us is ran over if you—"

"Would you just let him talk?" Keene asks, clearly exasperated.

"Baby, there's no way you're actually considering this. After what he's done?"

Keene's attention moves between me and Aspen before he calmly says, "Park the car."

Aspen's brows draw down. "Kee—"

Keene doesn't allow him to finish, clicking his seat belt off and shoving open the car door instead. He lets it fall closed behind him before motioning to where Aspen's still sitting in the vehicle.

"You can either park the car and join us or go home and I'll do this without you."

Fury doesn't begin to describe Aspen's expression before he concedes, shifting the car into reverse.

Keene leads me toward the stadium and drops down on one of the benches near the entrance, watching me with a wary expression when I take a seat at the other end. Nervous energy radiates off me in waves, but if he can feel it, he doesn't let on. He just keeps quietly looking at me while we wait for Aspen.

Who, as soon as he's within shouting distance of me and Keene, starts laying into me.

"How the hell are you even here?"

I shift my attention to find him storming across the pavement, not stopping until he's standing beside Keene. His eyes are overflowing with animosity as he glares down at me, venom falling from his tongue with ease. "Last time I checked, you aren't a student here anymore. You know, on the account of you being expelled for your shining display of assholery."

Keene winces. "I think what he's trying to say is that we're surprised to see you."

"No, I'm pretty sure I said what I meant," he snaps, eyes still locked on me.

Fuck, this isn't off to a good start.

Knowing that my time is limited, I try to find the best place to start. I've been winging it with pretty much everyone on this apology tour, figuring it made more sense to just speak from the heart, or whatever. Even with Kaleb, I had no idea what I was gonna say, and that was the one I was most nervous about, by far.

But now that I have these two in front of me, I'm realizing *this* is the biggest conversation of all. Not because I worry Kaleb will change his mind if it doesn't go well, but because I truly don't want Aspen or Keene to think my actions had anything to do with them.

It was all me.

Gnawing on the inside of my cheek, I shift my attention to Keene and say one of the dumbest things I probably could.

"I texted you. Back in July."

His eyes flick to Aspen for a brief moment. "Yeah, I got it."

Damn.

In those first few days back from camp, still very much in my feelings, I sat on my bed and typed out the longest text imaginable to Keene; both an apology and explanation. Don't get me wrong, I didn't expect his forgiveness from a stupid text alone, but I certainly didn't anticipate him purposely ignoring it either.

Then again, wasn't that exactly what I deserved?

"Okay, great. Um, well, what I really wanna reiterate is how sorry I am about what happened last spring. What I did—outing the both of you—was wrong. Fucked-up. There's no doubt about that, and I want you both to know I see that." My gaze flicks from Keene to Aspen and back again, unable to read either of their expressions. "There's no excuse, so I'm not going to downplay it or try to give you a reason for how I acted. But I do want you to know I'm not that person anymore."

The two of them remain silent long after I finish speaking, or at least, that's how it feels until Aspen finally responds.

"So what I'm hearing is," he starts in a slow, even tone with his sapphire eyes trained on me, "you expect us to believe you've just suddenly turned over a new leaf from being a complete and utter dick for the better part of a year?"

"Pen—"

"No, Kee," Aspen cuts in, glancing at Keene before pointing at me. "He's the fucking reason everything went to shit, all right? The reason we just went through hell all summer. The reason I almost lost you."

"He might've been a catalyst—"

"That's such bullshit," Aspen mutters with a scoff, but Keene quickly pins him with a glare.

"Really? Correct me if I'm wrong, but I don't think Avery held you at gunpoint until you left the state for weeks on end. Without a word." Despite Keene's even tone, Aspen winces, and it's clear I'm missing a chapter about the effects of my actions. But it's also obvious there's more to it than *just* my involvement; a fact that Keene proves when he tacks on, "You and I are just as at fault for us falling apart last spring as he is."

I feel slightly better by having this information—only slightly—and it's short lived when Keene's attention returns to me.

"But you're right about one thing: What you did was fucked-up."

My teeth sink into my cheek, and as I hold Keene's mahogany gaze, a deeper sense of regret floods my chest. To the point where it might as well be an anvil pressing down on my ribs.

Because, as much as I will take the blame for the mistakes I've made, I'm getting tired of hearing that phrase from people. From myself too.

"There aren't enough words to express how sorry I am," I manage past the knot that's lodged itself in my throat. "I might've laid out my reasoning behind my actions earlier this summer when I texted you, but in the end, I know they're all excuses for the shittiest, most cowardly thing I've ever done."

They both remain silent, their gazes locked on me. Aspen's is still very much a scrutinizing glare, filled with heat and outrage, but Keene's has shifted, regarding me with more curious contemplation than wariness now.

"What brought this on?" the latter finally asks.

Spending weeks in the forest falling in love with a person I want to be worthy of.

"I've done a lot of work on myself this summer," I go with instead, mostly because explaining every clandestine detail of my summer with

Kaleb will take way too long. "Like I said, I'm not the same person who outed you or said all those vile things to you last year. At least, I really don't want to be. The first way I could think of to prove it was by taking responsibility for my actions and apologizing. Face-to-face."

There's another unbearable silence, covering us like a weighted blanket, but I restrain myself from breaking it and sit in the discomfort of the moment instead.

God knows I forced them into one far worse.

"You are different," my ex-teammate confirms eventually.

I drag my gaze up to find him staring at me with intrigue, but it's quickly yanked away by Aspen's scoff.

"Kee, you can't actually believe—"

"I can, actually," Keene snaps, his voice sharpening for the first time. "You think you're the only person who can do a little soul searching and come out the other side with a new perspective?"

"No, but—"

Keene glares up at him, halting his thought mid-sentence. "If you deserve forgiveness, don't you think he might too?"

"I don't deserve it," I break in, my gaze flicking from one to the other. "After treating you both the way I did, forgiveness is the last thing I deserve. That's why I'm not asking for it. But if you're willing to offer it, then I'm going to prove myself worthy of it."

In reality, I know this is only the first step of many to make amends for what I've done to them. No amount of apologizing can reverse what I did that day, and it definitely can't give them back the time they lost because of it.

That's a feeling I know better than anything.

"I'm just glad I didn't ruin what the two of you have," I find myself uttering, guilt weighing down my chest. "It's rare to find someone who you can be yourself with. Who you can trust with anything, your heart included. And that's what haunts me most of all; knowing I could've cost you that."

Keene's head cants to the side while he stares at me, a slow smile creeping onto his face.

"He did a number on you, didn't he?"

Aspen glances at his boyfriend, dark brows drawing down in confusion. "What the fuck are—"

"Babe, not right now," Keene cuts in, motioning with his hand for Aspen to stop talking. Which makes Aspen's icy eyes flare, though I can't tell if it's still with fury or something a little more…sensual.

Keene doesn't notice, though. He's still staring at me, waiting for a response.

If I was questioning whether or not Kaleb had spoken to him about us, all of that is gone now. And, truthfully, I don't mind one bit if he—or anyone else for that matter—knows.

Having Kaleb is the only thing I care about; the rest is just noise.

Smiling like a fool, I drop my gaze to the ground between my feet and nod. "Yeah, he fucked me up pretty good. In the best way possible."

"Then what the hell are you doing here talking to us?"

My head snaps up, finding Keene's gaze still locked on me.

His question takes a moment to truly sink in, the hidden meaning within it becoming more and more clear when a small smirk lifts his mouth at the corner. Pair it with the gleam in his eyes, and the unspoken intention may as well be a neon billboard with flashing lights.

Go get your man.

An easy smile of my own forms, and I rise from the bench, ready to do just that. But before I walk away, I stop myself, having one more thing to say.

"Thank you."

He gives me a faint nod, brow arched in challenge. "Don't screw it up."

Never again. Not in a million years.

"Did I miss something?" Aspen mutters under his breath just as I start toward my car.

I hear Keene's low chuckle before he says, "Yeah, but it's not my story to tell."

Warmth floods me instantly, despite the statement not being meant for my ears. Because it's still for my benefit, even when he doesn't owe me a damn thing.

I was cruel, hateful, and the worst kind of human to them both, and most people wouldn't hesitate to return the favor. They'd take their knowledge and fight fire with fire, letting the power it holds destroy anything in its path.

Instead, he tucks it in his back pocket for safekeeping.

If that isn't forgiveness, I don't know what is.

THIRTY-THREE

Kaleb

A knock on my apartment door has me bolting up from my couch, ending my hour-long session of surfing through Netflix titles while waiting for Avery. I flick open the lock and yank the door open with far more force than necessary, and if it were anyone else on the other side, I'd probably be embarrassed by my eagerness.

But the second I find Avery's devastating smile waiting for me, my heart melts.

"Hi," I say on a soft exhale.

If possible, his grin grows wider as he takes a step over the threshold and slips a hand around the back of my neck.

"Hi, yourself," he murmurs.

I'm not sure who moves first, but it doesn't matter when our lips collide in a brutal crash that nearly knocks me off my feet. My hands instantly wrap around his lower back, steadying myself before pulling him against my body to deepen the kiss. That's all it takes for the worry and tension and heartache from the past few months to disappear.

Completely erased by the feel of his lips on mine.

"How did it go?" I ask between kisses. "You took longer than I was expecting."

"Aspen almost hit me with his car, to start."

"*What?*"

Pulling away, my gaze quickly takes stock of him, assessing for any possible injuries. But Avery's quick to drag my lips back to his.

"I said *almost*," he murmurs against my mouth.

"But—"

"Is this really what you wanna talk about right now?" He shifts, pressing one kiss after another to my jaw in quick succession while mumbling between them. "Because, as I recall, you mentioned something about making up for lost time."

Yeah, he makes a good point. Which is why I concede without batting an eye.

"Fine, tell me after."

And then it's my turn to reel him back in for more.

Lips still molded together, I grab Avery by the front of his shirt and blindly lead us deeper into my apartment. We leave a trail of clothing along the way, stripping each other down to nothing as we head straight for my bedroom down the hall.

After fumbling with the handle, I haul him inside, then break the kiss by pushing him down on my bed. He lands on his back, bouncing against the mattress with an amused chuckle, but it quickly dies when I kneel between his thighs and cover his body with my own.

Slipping my hand between us, I palm his cock and rub the heel against the sensitive spot below the head; a place I've learned is his favorite to be touched.

"Christ, Kaleb," he hisses against my mouth before kissing me again.

My fingers wrap around his length, and I give him a firm stroke while my tongue teases the seam of his lips. He opens for me instantly, and I dive in for more, kissing him with a furious need. Taking no prisoners as I devour him.

He's already arching into my touch, seeking more friction as I jack his length slowly, only to tease the head while I roll my palm over it. It's enough to pull a tortured moan from his lips, and he shakes his head.

"Inside me, Kaleb. Please, don't make me beg."

Besides those three little words from earlier, that may well be the best thing I've heard all day. As much as I love tormenting him, I don't have the patience for it right now. In fact, if I'm not inside him in the next twenty seconds, I may lose my damn mind.

"I'll save it for round two," I promise with a low chuckle.

Pressing a kiss to his jaw, I push back and grab the lube from my nightstand and make quick work of coating myself with the liquid. My heart hammers wildly against my ribs as I position myself between his thighs again, swiping the head of my cock against his rim.

I press my hips forward until the tight ring of muscle gives way, allowing me to slide inside. His ass pulses and clamps tightly around me while he adjusts, and I swear, nothing has ever felt this good. I doubt anything ever could.

"God, I missed you," I rasp against his lips before stealing another kiss. "I missed you so fucking much, baby."

He moans into my mouth when I start moving faster, pistoning my hips against his ass. Our bodies rock together in a steady rhythm like that, chasing a high only the other can provide, until it's not enough. Never will it ever be enough.

I want to own and be owned by him in every way possible.

Shifting my weight back to my heels, I grip Avery's hips and take him with me until he's straddling my lap, my cock still buried deep inside his ass. Impossibly deep, from the way he's clamping around me.

"Fuck," he groans, his forehead falling to mine as he adjusts.

I give him a second, pressing a soft kiss to his lips before whispering, "Feet on the mattress, baby. On either side of me."

He leans back, eyes tinting with confusion, but he obeys the order, planting them on either side of my legs.

"Mmm. Looks like I just need my cock inside you to make you listen," I tease, equally playful and seductive. "Put one hand behind you and lean some weight on it."

Once again, he doesn't look sure, but he follows my instructions anyway by shifting his weight back until he can place one hand on the bed.

"Perfect, baby. That's exactly it," I praise, already loving this new position.

I hold his hips, keeping most of his weight on my thighs. With him right where I want him now, I rock my pelvis back and give him a sharp, measured thrust. His eyes widen, a long groan falling from his lips.

"Oh my God," he pants when I pump onto him again. "Keep going just like that."

I have no intention of stopping. Not until both of us are breathless, boneless, and covered in cum. Fuck, even then, I might try to find a way to tease my cock back to life after I've filled his ass to the brim.

Sharp twinges in my lower abdomen alert me that I won't last much longer, and from the soft groans and pants leaving him, neither will he.

I wanted to take it slow, really savor the moment. I wanted to make this feel different than all the times before. I wanted him to feel how much I love him in the way I worship his body.

Painstakingly slow. Unrushed adoration.

But that's all gone right out the window.

It's not long before Avery's using the hand resting on the mattress for leverage to meet my hips, placing the other on my neck to steady himself while our bodies collide. He finds a rhythm quickly, riding me with every drop of his hips over my length as much as I'm fucking him with relentless, upward thrusts.

That's when I realize this *is* different than all the times before.

It's never been a fusion of souls, melding together and becoming one.

"You're so perfect, Aves. So mine."

I continue praising him like that, enraptured with awe as he bounces up and down on my dick. His own is trapped between us, leaking all over our stomachs as we continue moving together, rocking and grinding and chasing. Using each other, taking what we can. Seeking what only the other can give.

I realize now, that's not just pleasure but love too.

"Fucking hell," he groans, his head falling backward. "I'm so close already."

"Good. Come," I pant. Leaning forward, I take the opportunity to lick a path from his collarbone to his throat. "I come undone when your ass clenches around me, baby. Let me feel it. Take me with you."

Just the thought has me ready to burst at the seams.

Avery's gaze darkens, blue irises taking on an indigo shade as his hand leaves my neck. Reaching between us, he palms his cock and strokes it with quick, furious movements, hand moving over his length in a blur.

That's it, baby.

Spurred on by his frenzied movement, I match his pace, driving my hips forward as fast as I can. It feels like heaven every time I impale him impossibly deep on my cock.

Like coming home, like finding that one missing puzzle piece.

Everything about it is so fucking perfect, I'm not even sure it's real.

But when his eyes find mine again, I realize it doesn't matter. If it's a dream, then let me stay asleep forever.

"Kaleb, I—"

He doesn't have the chance to finish, his orgasm hitting him like a ton of bricks and stealing his ability to speak. Cum spurts from his cock, landing on both our stomachs.

"God, I love watching you fall apart for me," I rasp, still pistoning into him with quick movements. "Love feeling you grip me like a fucking vise."

My hold on his hips tightens, and I lose all sense of control, fucking up into him with the frenzied need to find release. Instinct alone has taken over, my body driving itself closer and closer to the edge until there's no place left to go but over.

And then I'm weightless, barreling toward the earth while slamming my hips upward one final time. My body shakes as I come deep inside Avery, burying myself to the hilt while his ass constricts and pulses around me from his own climax.

"Holy shit."

Sated and gasping for air, I wrap my arms around his back and pull him tight against my chest, supporting his whole weight again. His hands slide up and down my spine, fingers dancing lightly over each vertebrae as we both try to catch our breath.

Finding the crook of his neck, I rest my forehead over his thrumming pulse and come down from my high, completely immersed in this man in my arms.

Nothing matters but him.

We have to move eventually, though, because my knees are starting to ache, and I can feel my softening dick slowly slipping from his ass. But I'm still greedy for his touch, so I do the best thing I can think of by pulling out and dropping us down to the mattress in a heap.

Avery chuckles when I land half on top of him, his body vibrating against me. "We're still covered in cum. You know that, right?"

I do, I just don't give a shit.

"Is that supposed to deter me from post-sex cuddling?" I ask, glancing up at him.

He laughs. "Apparently not."

Regardless, I do shift off of him, but only to grab my underwear from the floor to wipe us clean, shooting him a look that says *happy now?* Then I'm back in the bed, tucked into his side with my head resting on his shoulder, and enjoying the feel of his skin pressed to mine

My fingers trace over his stomach, dipping into the valleys between his abs when he suddenly breaks the easy silence that settled over us.

"What position was that?"

"Some variation of lotus, I think?" When he lets out a low hum, I frown. "Why, was it not okay?"

"Oh, quite the opposite. I think that may be my new favorite."

I laugh, propping myself on an elbow so I can look at him easier. "I'll make a note of it."

"Good. I like being able to ride you while you can still fuck me."

His eyes take on a shy glimmer, despite the filthy things we just did to each other, and I think there will never be a day when this amazing man doesn't find a way to surprise me.

"Mmm. So what I'm hearing is you're starting to get greedy," I tease.

"Only for you."

I'm about to pull him into my arms and kiss the daylights out of him when he shifts away, moving to get off the mattress entirely.

Uh, I think the fuck not.

"Where the hell do you think you're going?" I chide, frowning like a petulant child.

Then, because I'm just as greedy as he is, my fingers wrap around his wrist, and I drag him back onto the mattress. He lands with a laugh, which quickly turns into a gasp when my other hand slides up his chest to grip his throat.

His teeth sink into his lower lip, biting back a sinful smirk. "I was just gonna get a glass of water. Is that okay?"

"Nope," I say, popping the P. "You're not going anywhere."

"Oh, really? You planning to tie me up so I can't escape?"

I let out a low hum of approval. "That could be arranged, if you'd be into it."

His nostrils flare, eyes smoldering with lust and intrigue, surprising me once again. But not as much as his raspy, "I think I would."

A grin spreads over my face. I'd meant it as a joke, but with that tidbit of information, a whole slew of new, dirty fantasies unlock in an instant. It's a damn good thing we have all the time in the world to explore them, now that he's back in my arms for good.

My hand leaves his throat then, moving to brush back the sweat-dampened strands that have fallen over his forehead. His eyes lock with mine as he leans into the touch, almost nuzzling my hand, and it's such an innocent and vulnerable act, I can't help my heart from swelling at the sight.

"I love you."

From the smile that overtakes his face, I may as well have hung the moon and all the stars in the sky just for him.

"Never have I ever been happier to hear three words leave your lips."

I chuckle and press my lips against his jaw, because I know exactly what he means. It was the same thought I had when he said it the first time—and every time since.

"Well, Aves, I think we both have to put a finger down for that one."

EPILOGUE

Avery

Eight Months Later — June

"**Y**ou're gonna make us late if you keep this up."

I glance up from where I've been swirling my tongue around the tip of Kaleb's cock for the past ten minutes—seizing the opportunity to make use of his morning erection—and shoot him a wicked smirk.

"So you're gonna be a stickler for the rules this summer, too, hmm?" I ask, giving him another lick to the spot below his crown.

"Only during working hours."

I hum softly before taking the head between my lips with a gentle suck. "Good thing those don't start for another fifteen minutes."

His fingers tighten in my hair, and he lets out a soft moan. "You only have five to make me come."

With the way I've been teasing him this morning? Piece of cake.

"Set an alarm, then," I mutter between licks. "But I don't think I'll need more than two."

He chuckles softly, but then the asshole reaches over and actually grabs his phone.

"Five minutes," he utters, a flare of heat in his gaze when he drops it back to the mattress. "And…go."

I can't stop myself from laughing softly as I take him back between my lips, diving deeper this time but still only taking a few inches of his length. He slides over my tongue with ease as I torment him with my mouth, flicking and swirling some more before scraping my teeth along the underside of his shaft.

"You look so fucking perfect with my cock between your lips, baby." My gaze lifts, meeting his while his dick slides farther between my lips, and he lets out a soft curse. "God, the things you do to me."

I smirk as best I can with him still between my lips before finally giving him what he wants—my mouth wrapped around him all the way to the hilt. My hands grip the outside of his thighs, holding him in place as he starts arching into me, and his hands tighten in my hair.

There's nothing I love more than making him lose control; coming undone from my touch. And that's exactly what I'm going for right now.

He twitches between my lips, pulsing as he slides over my tongue all the way to my throat, and I know he's close. From the soft pants leaving his lips, he's gonna be at the peak of ecstasy any second, ready to jump. All he needs is the slightest push.

"Shit, baby. I'm right there. I'm—"

His words are cut off by the blaring sound of the alarm going off, scaring the shit out of me and breaking my concentration. My movements falter, and he notices because he's trying to force me back onto his length.

"Don't stop, don't stop," he begs, arching for more, but I'm already pulling off him to silence the godawful sound coming from his phone.

"Sorry, babe," I pant, tapping his screen. "I'm just following your lead with the whole *working hours* thing."

He sits up, leaning against his elbows to glare at me. If looks could kill, I'd be six feet under. Or tossed in the middle of the lake. Or thrown off the ledge of Lovers Leap.

Of course, it only makes me smile.

A sharp scoff leaves him. "You're evil, you know that?"

"Ah, but you love it." I lean in and press a kiss to his jaw before tacking on, "And me."

"God only knows why some days," he grumbles before pushing me off him. Unfortunately for me, he pushes a little too hard, sending me tumbling off the bed to land on the floor with a thud.

His face appears over the edge above me a second later. "Shit, are you okay?"

I shift to stand up and wince. Apart from the bruise I'm sure to have on my hip and elbow, I'm fine, so I nod. That's when Kaleb bursts into laughter.

At least he waited until after he knew I was okay, I guess.

"Dickhead."

That only makes him laugh harder as he grabs his boxers. "I think that's instant karma for edging your boyfriend before work, Aves."

I roll my eyes. "As if I won't receive the full wrath of your retaliation tonight."

In reality, I'm looking forward to it, as well as picking up where we left off last summer. Minus the whole mental gymnastics of fighting our feelings for each other, obviously.

But I'll admit, the sneaking around part will definitely be fun.

We both dress quickly, donning our green camp counselor shirts, khaki shorts, and sneakers before setting out for the parking lot. Despite him being still slightly irritated with me about leaving him hard up, we're all laughs and stupid smiles when we finally reach Colin waiting near the activity board, clipboards in hand.

He spots us immediately, waving us over to where he was talking to a few of the new counselors-in-training starting this summer. "There you both are. I was starting to get worried."

Kaleb and I share a sheepish look, barely managing to rein in our smirks as Colin hands Kaleb the clipboard with our list of campers this summer. He dismisses the CITs before returning his attention to us.

"Am I gonna have problems with the two of you this year?" the director asks while my gaze travels over the list, looking for one name in particular.

"I can't make any promises for Avery, but I'm always on my best behavior," Kaleb chimes in beside me.

I scoff and shoot a glare at him. "If I remember correctly, you were the one causing most of the problems last summer."

His hand rests on his sternum, a look of mock horror on his face. "Me? I'm offended by that insinuation."

Colin lets out a long sigh, not amused in the slightest. "Don't make me regret pairing you together again, you hear me?" He turns to walk up the steps to the lodge, then pauses to pin us with a disapproving look. "And do me a favor: Keep your escapades out of the kitchen this summer. We still have to pass inspections by the Health Department, you know."

Kaleb and I gape at each other, dumbfounded, as Colin ventures back into the lodge and leaves us reeling from this revelation.

"I didn't tell him," I say the second he's out of earshot, raising my hands in surrender.

"Well, obviously, I didn't either." He frowns, worry in his eyes when our gazes collide. "You know I'm letting you do that on your own time. I don't wanna—"

"Oh, no," I cut in, shaking my head. "He knows we're together. I meant I didn't tell him about the pantry."

Kaleb's jaw drops a little, gaping a little as he stares at me.

"What? Why are you looking at me like that?"

Reaching toward me, he slides his palm into mine and links our fingers. "You just never fucking cease to amaze me. You know that?"

This again?

I roll my eyes and pull from his grip to head off to the parking lot. If I stick around, he's sure to turn into a pile of sappy, mushy goo.

Of course, that doesn't stop him from calling out, "I'm proud of you, baby!" after me.

The reality is, I'm out in the capacity that I wanna be; the people who need to know, know, and the rest… Well, it's not really any of their damn business anyway. At least, that's what my therapist has instilled in me over the past eight months I've been seeing him, so that's what I'm going with.

Oh, yeah. It turns out, my dad could throw money at this problem after all.

By some act of God, he found a therapist who specializes in working with the queer community, and more specifically, clients overcoming repressed sexuality and internalized homophobia.

More often than not, I leave those sessions feeling more raw than I'd like, but I know it's just because it's working. No one said this kind of healing would be easy. But having Kaleb as a support system really does make it a little more bearable.

And my dad? Well, he does his best. I dread the days I have to go home after a session and talk to him about something specific, per my therapist's request. The conversations are almost always strained or awkward and sometimes painful as hell. But he listens. He hears me, and it's more than I expected from him.

That has to count for something.

The kids start arriving shortly after, and it's when Kaleb's hauling bags for two new campers over toward the cabins that a familiar truck pulls into the parking lot. The back doors swing open instantly before the LaMothe twins come barreling out like bats outta hell.

"Colton. Dayton," I greet my boyfriend's brothers with a smile. "Good to see you guys."

"Hey, Avery! I didn't know you'd be here this summer," Dayton says brightly, a big grin on his face in return.

He's been a lot easier to convince of my intentions, both with Kaleb and in general, so I'm not surprised by his warm response to my presence.

"You really came back," Colton notes, studying my face.

I cock my head to the side, narrowing my eyes inquisitively. "Of course I did. I can't think of anywhere else I'd rather spend the summer."

Okay, maybe that's not entirely true. The location itself wasn't what brought me back—that was all Kaleb. I'm happiest wherever he is.

"Did you leave your boat shoes at home this time?" Colton asks almost immediately.

Even if it's meant to be a dig more than a joke, I don't let myself get perturbed by it. After all, I knew I'd have to put in some work with him, and that's one of my main goals this summer. So I just smirk and reply, "I left the boat shoes at home. Figured they'd be better use to me after camp."

"After camp?" Dayton asks, slipping back into the conversation.

I glance between the twins, weighing my options for a moment before dropping my voice. "Well, as long as you can keep a secret…I'm planning to take Kaleb sailing once we head back to the city."

Dayton's eyes bug out, but it's Colton's head that cocks to the side, studying me skeptically. "You have a sailboat?"

"What do you think the boat shoes are for?"

Colton shrugs. "Being a douchey prep boy?"

"Colton Thomas!" Kaleb's father calls, drawing all our attention over to the truck. "That's uncalled for."

When I glance back at the twin in question, I find his gaze cast down at the ground, and he mutters a disgruntled "I'm sorry" under his breath.

Dayton, on the other hand, is completely enamored by this new information, eyes lighting up when he asks, "Can we go sailing when you take Kaleb?"

"You'd want to?"

"Uh, duh. Cole's more into boats than me; I prefer planes." He pauses, eyes becoming two hazel saucers before he asks, "Wait, do you have a plane too?"

I let out a sharp laugh. "Uh, no. Sorry to disappoint."

He simply shrugs. "Boats are still cool."

"Well, I'll tell you what." My attention shifts between the two of them, a smile pulling at my lips. "I'll take you guys out in August. But you're not allowed to say anything to Kaleb about me taking him. Deal?"

Dayton's all for it before he's hustling off to find Kaleb, meanwhile Colton doesn't do more than nod slightly before joining his twin.

Into boats, my ass.

I don't have more than a second to linger on the thought, though, because their father is rounding the truck and handing off one of the duffles.

"Avery. Sorry about Cole," Mr. LaMothe greets, offering me his hand. I slide my palm into his, but I'm not prepared for the quick half-hug he pulls me into. "It's good to see you."

Mr. LaMothe has been nothing but kind to me since Kaleb brought me to Bend over spring break. Both of his parents were welcoming, actually—despite their knowledge of my and Kaleb's rocky past—and I couldn't be more grateful for it.

"Nice to see you too, Mr. LaMothe."

"Eric," he corrects with a knowing grin as he hands me the other bag. "Give Cole some time; he'll come around."

Both Kaleb's parents, as well as Kaleb, keep saying the same thing, and while I'm going to give it my all, I'll admit, things aren't exactly off to the best start. But rather than being a Debbie Downer, I nod and give him a tight smile.

"I'll keep that in mind."

From the way his grin spreads, he must read the apprehension all over my face. Thankfully, he doesn't comment on it, and just offers me a friendly nod.

"Well, hey, I'll let you get back to working. Don't be a stranger, all right? Teresa and I are hoping you'll be back over at some point once camp is over."

My chest swells a little, knowing, at the very least, I have their approval. "Yeah, I'd like that."

"Perfect. Tell Kaleb to keep those two in line for me, all right?"

I laugh, shaking my head. "I think I can do that."

He's gone after a few more parting words, hopping into the truck and pulling out of the parking lot before I have the chance to drop the twins' bags off with one of the CITs.

I'm in the middle of telling them what cabin the twins are in when my name is called from somewhere behind me.

"Avery!"

Turning on my heel, I find Elijah barrelling toward me at full speed, no signs of stopping. I brace myself for impact, and it's a good thing too, because he slams into my chest with a bear hug moments later.

"You came back."

"I only told you I was about eighty times," I remind him with a laugh.

With permission from Dean Marshall, Elijah and I have remained in touch over the past few months. I was worried he may not let it happen, all things considered, but I think his perspective of me changed when I turned down my place at Foltyn. He even mentioned something about being a good example for Elijah, which blew me out of the water to hear.

But the kid's become something of a little brother to me, and I know there's so much more I can learn from him.

Elijah finally releases me and shrugs. "I know you said you'd be here, but you could've changed your mind."

"From where I'm standing, it seems like you're the one who changed yours," I return, giving him a dubious look.

One of the last times we spoke, he said he wanted to tell his father that he didn't want to come back to camp this summer; he'd rather go to some nerdy tech camp instead. Yet, from his obvious presence here, it seems that didn't go very well.

Or he chickened out on telling him; it's a toss up at this point.

He lets out a soft sigh. "He said I can do it once I'm a little older. Something about 'being a kid and spending time outside' or whatever," he mutters, imitating his father's voice as he quotes him.

Laughing, I shake my head. "Hey, that's a decent compromise, right?"

"I guess." His brown eyes flash from me to something behind me, and I turn to find the LaMothe twins and Kaleb talking to each other. He lets his gaze linger there for a moment, as do I, before he asks, "How are things with Kaleb?"

My stomach fills with those stupid butterflies that never quite seem to settle these days. Especially when I'm looking at him. "They've been pretty great, honestly."

"Good. Glad you got your head out of your ass."

"Language!" I say, chuckling some more. Mostly because I can't fault him for that particular opinion. I'm pretty happy with the decision myself.

Elijah completely ignores my reprimand and tries to glance at the list in my hand. "Who am I bunking with this year?"

I glance down, reading it over until I find his name.

"Liam and Max," I reply. There's a brief hint of disappointment that crosses his features before he shakes it free, but it doesn't stop me from calling him out on it. "Is that not okay?"

"No, it's fine. I just thought I'd be with Cole and Dayton again."

Arching a brow, I ask, "You want me to see if we can swap it?"

That gets his expression to light up a bit, and he nods. "Can you do that?"

"I'll see what I can do," I murmur, chuckling. "But, hey, why don't you head over to them and catch up while I see about getting your bunking arrangements changed."

He nods, grinning like a fool before racing over to where Kaleb and the twins are. The three twelve-year-olds start talking excitedly between themselves, and my boyfriend quickly takes that as an opportunity to sneak away.

A huge grin pulls at my lips as I watch him approach, matching the one he's giving me. My hands find his waist as soon as he's within arm's reach, dragging him as close as I dare with kids and coworkers milling around.

After all, Kaleb wants to remain *professional,* or whatever.

He doesn't seem all that strict on it, though, because he reaches up and links his arms around the back of my neck.

"So I just heard something interesting," he muses, both his brows hitched up in a teasing fashion.

"And what might that be?"

"You're taking my brothers sailing in August."

"That secret lasted all of five minutes," I gripe, rolling my eyes. "Remind me to tell Dayton that he's not allowed to steer if he can't keep his trap shut."

"Actually, Cole was the one who said something."

Curiosity piqued, I murmur, "Really?"

He nods, his thumb scraping lightly through my hair. "Seemed pretty excited about it too."

I damn near let out a sigh of relief. It's not much, but it's progress, so I'll take it. Of course, the second Kaleb sees my anxiety start to disappear, one of his stupid fucking smirks appears. One I know all too well.

Just like I know what almost always comes after it.

I pin him with a warning look. "Don't fucking say it."

"What?" he asks, blinking at me innocently. "I wasn't gonna say anything."

"Uh, huh. Sure you weren't."

His grin grows as he leans in like he's going to kiss me, only to whisper his favorite saying softly against them.

"I told you so."

THE END

ACKNOWLEDGMENTS

Well, y'all…we finally have a book that was more of a pain in the ass to write than Don't You Dare, and I honestly shouldn't be surprised it was Avery who gave me those issues. I never had any intention of writing Avery a book at all because I don't love writing a redemption arc, and let's be real, did Avery really deserve it anyway? But in the end, I fell in love with him and Kaleb, and I hope you—my readers—did too.

This book was two years in the making, and honestly, I'm surprised it's even here at all, but to everyone who had the utmost patience with me while I worked on making this book into a product I could be proud of releasing: thank you.

To Madi, for sitting on FaceTime with me for hours and hours and even more hours. You're the best babysitter around, even when we visit Yap City too much.

To Sarah and Cassie, both the standard and alternate covers of this book are amazing. They're everything I wanted, and I am in awe of both of your talents. Thank you for bringing my visions to life.

To Hydrus, thank you for creating a custom poem to showcase Avery's struggles. Your poetry is some of my favorite, with such deep emotional prose that always put me in my feels, and to have you work on something so personal means the absolute world to me.

To my alphas/betas, Emily, Holly, Jackie, Amy, and Abby, and anyone else I might be missing: Thank you for making sure Avery was indeed redeemable, and for pushing me to finish this when I was desperate to throw in the towel.

To my editing team, Shauna and Amanda. I don't have the words to describe how grateful I am for you turning this around so quickly, and for making this book as clean as possible. I'm a chaotic little gremlin when it comes to my deadlines, but I couldn't do this without you.

To my Enclave and my Legacies. Thank you for supporting me, promoting me, and being my core readership—some of you since the early days of my career. You don't go unnoticed.

And to anyone I may have missed (because there's always someone), and to my readers. Thank you for continuing to come back for more, and for trusting me on whatever journey I may take you on.

I love you, I love you, I love you.

—CE Ricci

ABOUT THE AUTHOR

CE Ricci is an international best-selling author who enjoys plenty of things in her free time, but writing about herself in the third person isn't one of them. She believes home isn't a place, but a feeling, and it's one she gets when she's chilling lakeside or on hiking trails with her dogs, camera in hand. She's addicted to all things photography, plants, peaks, puppies, and paperbacks, though not necessarily in that order. Music is her love language, and traveling the country (and world) is the way she chooses to find most of her inspiration for whatever epic love story she will tell next!

CE Ricci is represented by Two Daisy Media.
For all subsidiary rights, please contact:
Savannah Greenwell — info@twodaisy.com